WIND RIVER WRANGLER

LINDSAY McKENNA

ZEBRA BOOKS
KENSINGTON PUBLISHING CORP.
http://www.kensingtonbooks.com

ZEBRA BOOKS are published by

Kensington Publishing Corp.
119 West 40th Street
New York, NY 10018

All Kensington titles, imprints, and distributed lines are available at special quantity discounts for bulk purchases for sales promotion, premiums, fund-raising, educational, or institutional use.

Special book excerpts or customized printings can also be created to fit specific needs. For details, write or phone the office of the Kensington Sales Manager: Attn.: Sales Department. Kensington Publishing Corp., 119 West 40th Street, New York, NY 10018. Phone: 1-800-221-2647.

Zebra and the Z logo Reg. U.S. Pat. & TM Off.

First Printing: November 2016
ISBN-13: 978-1-4201-4174-0
ISBN-10: 1-4201-4174-0

eISBN-13: 978-1-4201-4175-7
eISBN-10: 1-4201-4175-9

10 9 8 7 6 5 4 3 2 1

Printed in the United States of America

Chapter One

The doorknob slowly, soundlessly, turned.

Shiloh Gallagher stood, her hands clasped against her chest, her whole focus on the slow movement. Oh, God, it was her stalker! *Again*. Painfully, she swallowed against a tightening throat. She stood in her New York City apartment, feeling almost faint with fear. The police didn't believe her. They said it was all in her head. Some even suggested that because she was a *New York Times* best-selling author, she was making such a big deal to get publicity. Oh, God . . . Her entire body was so tense she felt like she might snap and fall into a million terrified pieces.

The doorknob slowly turned in the other direction.

Her heart was pounding so hard in her ears she couldn't hear anything else. Her hands were damp and clammy, fingers white as she gripped them together. She wanted to cry out for help. But no one would come. No one cared.

The doorknob stilled.

Would her stalker try to break in? Instantly, her gaze flew to the four locks she had on the thick mahogany door. It was a solid door. She lived in a tenth-floor apartment in an old building from the 1930s. Things were made to withstand the test of time. She licked her lips, praying her stalker would leave.

This had happened nearly every day of the week for the past two weeks.

The police were tired of her calls. They had come out to investigate. Dusted her doorknob for fingerprints and found nothing. No one else in the building had seen anyone, either, as the officers canvassed her floor.

Her knees were quivering so badly Shiloh thought she would fall. Who was doing this to her? First, faxes had come over her machine with the words: "I'm going to get you." And then, her landline had a message with a man breathing heavily. The police said because she was a romance writer, one of her crazed fans, a man, was behind the notes and calls. *Harmless.*

For six months, she'd been tortured daily. Shiloh couldn't write. She lived from one mysterious noise, sound, fax, or phone message to another.

A crazed fan?

Was that her stalker's identity? A man who read her best-selling romance novels? A sick, perverted bastard?

The doorknob slowly started moving counterclockwise.

Shiloh gasped, her hand against her mouth. Her eyes widened enormously. What if he had a way to get past her deadbolt locks? She lived like a terrified animal in her small apartment. Afraid to go out. Afraid to walk the hall any longer, fearing someone was waiting for her. She'd stopped having lunch with her editor, Molly Williams. Every time Shiloh tried to sneak out to go get groceries or see her editor, the hair on the back of her neck rose in warning. As if someone were watching her.

The knob stopped turning.

Her heart thundered. She tried to hear over the pounding of it in her ears.

Desperately, Shiloh wanted to call the police. They were

so tired of her calls after the first two months, they'd say yeah, they'd send over a cruiser, but no cop ever showed up. Lip service. No one believed her.

Had she ever seen this guy? the police always asked. No. She never saw him. God knew, she was looking for him, but on a crowded New York City street, he could be anyone. What did a crazed romance fan look like?

The knob turned again.

Her breath jammed in her throat. She was shaking physically now. Her knees felt so weak, Shiloh thought she might fall onto the carpeted floor.

The knob stopped turning.

A sizzling bit of relief tore through her. How many times was it going to happen? Who was standing on the other side of that door? What did he want? She instinctively knew this man wanted to kill her. She *felt* it. The policemen just nodded, as if bored, when they came to her door on other occasions, and she could see they didn't believe her.

Her whole world was on a slow-motion reel of destruction and she felt as if life was one long, unending nightmare. Tears squeezed out of her eyes as she pressed her hand hard against her mouth. Her gaze was riveted on the doorknob, breath jammed in her aching throat. She waited.

How many times would he twist the doorknob? Why was he doing this to her? Shiloh had never hurt anyone in her life. She tried to be kind and generous to everyone she met. She had seen the world's ugliness at ten years old when her stepfather, Anton Leath, had stabbed her mother, Isabella, with a skinning knife in a fit of rage. She had stood in the entrance to the kitchen, frozen.

Just like she was frozen right now.

Oh, God, why wouldn't this harassment stop? What had she done to deserve this? And no one believed her! Except for Molly, who was clearly worried because she had a book due in six months. Shiloh could see the look on her forty-year-old editor's face, wondering if she was going to meet the contract deadline or not.

The doorknob remained still.

Releasing a hesitant breath as her hand left her lips, Shiloh couldn't tear her gaze from it. Was he standing outside her door? Waiting? Did she dare peek out the peephole? Every time she got up the gumption to do it, the hall was empty. The police had demanded an identification. A face.

Pushing herself, her motion wooden and jerky, knees nearly failing her, Shiloh forced herself to the door. She held her breath, slid the brass circle off the peephole. Looking out, she saw the carpeted hall that led to the elevators at the other end of it. The hall was empty.

With a little cry, she slumped against the door, eyes tightly shut, her knees giving way. As she slid down to the floor, her back against the door, her heart continued to pound in her chest.

She couldn't go on like this.

Every cell in her body was on high alert. Her brain screamed at her to run away. To leave the city. Disappear. Get rid of the stalker no one could find.

Swallowing against a dry mouth, her throat tight, a huge lump aching in it, Shiloh sat, feeling vulnerable and unable to defend herself.

It was just like that afternoon when Anton Leath and her mother got into a heated argument. She'd stood there, paralyzed, terrified of her stepfather who was angry and abusive to her mother and to herself. Only this time, her mother had rounded on him, screaming at him. He'd picked up the knife he had laying at the end of the counter. Her mother was preparing roast beef for dinner that night.

Tightly shutting her eyes, Shiloh would never get that afternoon out of her head. On bad days, she'd remember it all too clearly. It was as if it happened in slow motion, the knife rising in Leath's large, thick hand, her mother's eyes widening in disbelief as he pushed her into the corner so she couldn't escape. The blade slicing down savagely. Her mother's terrified screams, arms flailing. Blood spurting out of her chest. Blood all over the wall and the kitchen counter. And then, blood across the floor as she sagged downward, Anton breathing heavily, watching her slip to the floor, knife gripped hard in his hand.

It was then Shiloh had turned, racing out of the kitchen, as if on fire. She'd run out the front door, out onto the sidewalk, screaming for help. Fortunately, there was a cop on the beat half a block away. He heard her shrieks and came running. All Shiloh could do was sob and point toward the open door. Screaming "Mommy! Mommy! Mommy's hurt! Hurt! Help her! Help!"

The words rolled around in her brain and Shiloh sobbed softly, burying her face in her hands. That was nineteen years ago and it was still as fresh, vivid, and stark as it was the day her mother was ripped out of her life. Her father had died two years earlier from a massive heart attack. So young . . . so alive. Shiloh had been so fiercely loved by both of them. And when she was just ten years old, her parents were both gone. Tragically gone.

Sniffing, the hot tears rolling down her taut cheeks, Shiloh looked around her parents' apartment. She'd lived there since birth. An apartment filled with memories, photos of her mother and father. Daily reminders. Good memories. Antiques they'd collected over the years were here and there. She loved the nineteenth century and her mother had painstakingly created a beautiful retreat. A place for her mother to paint and for her to write. A place to dream and create. She'd been so happy here. It was her sanctuary against the world. She loved New York City. Loved it's throbbing vibrancy, jogging daily in Central Park, walking the streets, buying food from a street vendor, watching someone play a guitar and putting money in his open instrument case. She'd been born in this city. It was in her blood.

But now her family's quaint, quiet apartment felt like it was closing in on her. She wanted to run away so badly she could scarcely control herself. She was shaking, crashing from all the adrenaline that had surged through her bloodstream. Shiloh couldn't stand up if she tried. So she sat on the floor, back against the thick, heavy mahogany door, staring toward the two windows that brought such bright, wonderful light into her home.

She had been at her tiger maple desk, working on a chapter on her Mac, when she'd heard the squeak of the brass doorknob being turned. She'd frozen, her gaze flying to it, the adrenaline slamming through her. It always reminded her of the same feeling she'd experienced when her mother had been murdered. And Shiloh hated it.

Rubbing her face, scrubbing away the tears, she tugged a strand of her red hair across her shoulder. Twisting it nervously around her finger, she tried to think through the fog of her dread. Her mind flip-flopped over so many ideas, but they kept coming back to one: calling Maud Whitcomb. She had been a dear friend of her mother's. Maud had bought several of her mother's very expensive paintings. And always, Maud, who was like a maternal grandmother to her, pleaded with Shiloh to come out to her Wyoming ranch for a visit.

Shiloh never did. She always kept in touch with Maud because she was an important person in her life. Especially since the murder of her mother. It was Maud who had flown back after Isabella's death, and been there for Shiloh while Child Protective Services sorted out whom she was legally to be given to.

In the end, her mother's younger sister, Lynn, and her husband, Robert Capland, had agreed to take her in because she was family. They too were shattered by her mother's death. The good news was that they lived in New York City, just a few blocks away from where Shiloh had grown up. Maud had hung around, a lynchpin emotionally for Shiloh for nearly two weeks, making sure she was settling in at Aunt Lynn and Uncle Robert's apartment, before she reluctantly had to leave to go back and help run the Wind River Ranch.

Shiloh never forgot Maud Whitcomb's grit, her responsibility toward her, or the ongoing attention and care for her over the years afterward. Maud never forgot her birthday. She'd send her JPEGs from time to time of the ranch, horses, buffalo, or cattle, saying she should come out West. It would do her good. In the last six months, that's all Shiloh had thought about: leaving New York and visiting Maud. Running away.

Chewing on her lower lip, brows dipping, Shiloh stared down at the beautiful nineteenth-century tapestry on the floor. It was from Persia, pale cream colors in the background with brilliant patches of woven flowers all across it. She loved that rug. It always lifted her spirit. Always made her yearn for the beauty of real wildflowers. What would it be like to walk through a field of them? That wouldn't happen here in New York City, she knew. But the rug fulfilled a yearning in her for nature.

The last six months, she'd been jogging less and less on her route through Central Park. Now, June first, she knew the grass would be a vibrant green, all the trees in full leafy green wardrobe. She ached to get out of the apartment, stretch her legs, feel the wind in her face, feel the throbbing life of the outdoors surrounding her. Shiloh wrote every day, but she made a point to jog every day, too. It was balancing mental activity with physical activity. It suited her. It had worked for years. Until her stalker silently, like a deadly, toxic fog, entered her life, unknown and unseen.

Now, Shiloh felt the adrenaline leaving her body. She was exhausted. She had to do something to break this cycle.

Slowly getting to her feet, she shuffled stiffly to her desk where she wrote. The window was curtained, a transparent white chiffon that made the other skyscrapers of New York look like archetypal symbols in a fog. Every book she'd written had been written at this desk.

Looking at the phone, she wondered if she could write anywhere else but here. Shiloh had never traveled outside the city. She lived in a fishbowl, but she was happy in it, with no need to go elsewhere. Everything she needed or wanted was right here. What should she tell Maud? The truth? That she was a coward? Running away from a fight? Couldn't take it anymore? That's how Shiloh felt: tired, beaten, and maneuvered into a corner where there was no escape. Just as Anton had shoved her mother into the corner of the kitchen, trapping her so he could stab her to death. She had no way to escape, either.

But Shiloh did.

Suddenly, she didn't care what Maud or her editor thought of her. She'd tried to dismiss the stalker. Tried to work with the police. But still, the stranger tormented her. Maybe if she was gone for two months, her nemesis would leave. No more faxes. No more heavy breathing over the phone. No more doorknobs twisting one way and then the other, the stalker wanting in to get to her.

With new determination, Shiloh picked up the phone, praying that Maud would allow her to travel to Wyoming for a visit to see her. It was the only hope she had left.

"Roan?" Maud Whitcomb called from the steps of the Wind River Ranch office porch. She waved toward a cowboy mounted on a blood bay quarter horse. He rode like he was born to the saddle, his gray Stetson low over his eyes, shading them from the welcome overhead sunlight. She saw him turn his gelding her way instead of heading down to where he and other wranglers were going to push about twenty head of cattle from one pasture to another.

She held on to her bright red baseball cap as the breeze picked up. When Roan drew near, she called, "I need to talk with you for a moment." She saw the man's hard, lined, and weathered face remain unchanged. It was his gray eyes that narrowed slightly. Maud pulled the screen door open and walked back to her office. Her husband, Steve Whitcomb, was behind the counter. This was where all the tourists coming in for a weeklong vacation would check in.

"I want to talk with Roan in back for a moment," she told Steve. Usually, Maud manned the desk midweek, fussing over paperwork, and her sixty-year-old husband was off with the wranglers doing ranch work to keep the place up and running.

"Got it," he told her, giving her a wink.

Roan opened the door, brushed his dusty boots off before entering. Taking off his Stetson, he nodded toward Steve, who nodded back.

"Come to the other office," Maud called, waving Roan to follow her.

Frowning, Roan wondered what was up. He was part of the wranglers behind the scenes who kept the largest ranch in the valley operational. He wanted nothing to do with the dude ranch families who came here on vacation.

He hit his hat against his thigh and dust flew off it. In long, casual strides, he headed down the highly waxed oak floor to the other office Maud had disappeared into. His curiosity was piqued because for the two years he'd worked at the ranch, Maud had never asked him to come into the office to speak privately with her. Other than giving him raises that he'd earned through a lot of hard, consistent work, she rarely called him aside.

Entering the office, he saw Maud sitting behind her messy desk. She'd taken off her baseball cap, her silver and black hair short and just below her ears. She was frowning, her expression worried.

"Shut the door, Roan. Thanks."

His straight, dark brown brows rose a little over the request. "What is this, Maud? A stealthy new procedure now in practice around the ranch?" Roan asked, giving her a teasing grin as he came over and settled in the chair. It was a normal chair but he wasn't normal size. He was six foot two and two hundred pounds of brute muscle. Good thing it didn't have arms on it or he'd never have fit into it. The metal chair squeaked as he sat down, hat resting on his long, hard thigh.

Maud chuckled a little and leaned back in the chair, rocking it slightly. "Some things need to be said behind closed doors."

"Sounds serious." Roan saw the sparkle in her eyes. Maud was fifty-five years old and a force to be reckoned with. The ranch had been in Steve Whitcomb's family for a hundred years. He'd asked Maud to run the Wind River Ranch because he was a world famous architect. She'd put the ranch on the map decades earlier with the help of her husband, Steve. Both were damned hard workers, regardless of their age, and that had Roan's respect. Steve liked escaping his always busy architectural practice and throwing a leg over a good horse and working with the wranglers whenever he could. It was one of the few ranches in Wyoming to be flourishing, thanks to his wife's vision and passion for this valley.

"Well, it's serious enough." Maud pulled out a color photo from her pocket and slid it across the desk to Roan. "And the reason I'm roping you into this is because you used to be Army Special Forces. You have skills and talents most of my other wranglers don't, with some exceptions like Cord McCall who is an ex-Delta Force operator."

Nodding, Roan said, "McCall is a good man."

"And he's doing wonders with our new River Walk Hiking Trail," Maud agreed. The mighty Snake River ran parallel to Highway 89. Both ran through the ranch. Maud figured to take advantage of the situation. Her idea for a River Walk had met with enthusiasm from tourists driving through the area, on their way to Jackson Hole, fifty miles north of where they were at. Now, families would stop, take a break from the driving, sit and have an impromptu picnic at one of the many wooden tables, and hike along the lush, beautiful Snake River. It was money in the ranch coffers to keep their business vibrant and healthy.

She looked up at Roan. "This conversation is between you and me. Of course, my husband, Steve, already knows about it."

"You got it," Roan murmured, picking up the photo. Looking at it, he felt his chest expand. It was a helluva unexpected reaction. One he'd never had before. The red-haired vixen staring at him with huge evergreen-colored eyes, her face oval, with a perfect nose and stubborn chin, made his heart beat harder. That was a strange reaction to have to a picture, and Roan unconsciously rubbed his chest beneath the chambray shirt he wore. It was damp and clung to him. "Who is this?"

"She's a dear friend of ours," Maud began worriedly. "Her name is Shiloh Gallagher. Years ago, I bought some paintings from Isabella Gallagher, her mother. She was a very famous oil painting artist whose work with landscape is well known. I met her daughter, Shiloh, who was five years old at that time when I first met her." She touched her brow. "It's a really sad story," she admitted. "I made a lasting friendship with Isabella and her husband over those years because I liked them. Never mind the money I spent acquiring her paintings," Maud said, and smiled fondly. "But they are worth every penny. Anyway, I fell in love with her daughter. Her husband, Jeffrey Gallagher, was a best-selling thriller writer. He'd been in the Air Force, a jet fighter pilot, got out and married Isabella, and started writing for a living. Jeff was a wonderful man," Maud said wistfully. "Handsome devil, loved his wife and daughter like they were sacred beings."

"Sounds like a pretty happy, creative family," Roan said.

"All creative to their bones. Yes. Anyway, six months after I'd first met them, Jeffrey died of a massive heart attack. God, he was only thirty-five years old, Roan. Such a loss. It was completely unexpected. He and Isabella had a love that was so rare and beautiful," Maud said, her voice going soft. She shook her head. "Like the love I have with my husband. We married when I was twenty and we're the best of friends and we love each other. You just don't see that kind of love very often, Roan. And when you do, if it happens to you, you savor it, you keep the flame of it alive and strong because real love IS rare."

He shook his head. "I don't think the love bug is going to bite me, Maud, so I don't have to worry about it."

She snorted and gave him a one-eyebrow-raised look. "Roan Taggart, you're a damn fine-lookin' man. I see the way women look at you in Wind River."

Shrugging, he said, "I'm not cut out for settling down, Maud. Let's just leave it at that." He held up the photo. "So, she's the daughter of your friend Isabella?"

"Yes, but I need to tell you more sad stories," and she went on to fill Roan in on the fact that Isabella had been murdered by Shiloh's stepfather, Anton Leath, when the girl was only ten years old.

She saw the line of the wrangler's mouth tighten, his eyes turning that icy gray when he was upset about something.

Maud didn't see it often because Taggart was what she called an interior person. One never knew what he was thinking or feeling unless he wanted to let you know about it. *Stoic* was a word Maud would use to label the tall, powerful wrangler. She was sure it was because of his black ops background. Cord McCall, was similar, but not as hard to read as Roan. They were different, she supposed, due to their military experiences. One look at Roan's deeply tanned face, the harsh lines at the corners of his eyes, and Maud knew he spent his military years out in the harsh elements. He was no desk jockey, that was for sure.

"Now, Shiloh called me an hour ago. The poor girl is at her wit's end," Maud began, and then dove into the reason why, that currently, she had an unknown stalker after her for the last six months. She told him the entire situation. "She can't write. She's a best-selling author like her daddy was, but this never-ending situation has her so shaken and terrorized that she's mentally paralyzed by it all."

Frowning, Roan growled, "That's a helluva note, Maud, that the police are telling her it's all in her head. Where do they get off saying that?"

Maud gave him a frustrated look. "Darned if I know, Roan. It isn't right. Anyway, Shiloh asked if she could come out for a visit for two months. Stay with us. The only place I can put her is where you're staying: It's the only employee house that isn't filled. It has three bedrooms and currently, you're the only one in the house. I wanted to find out if you'd be all right with that arrangement. There's a kitchen, living room, and office for anyone staying there. But you'd be sharing living quarters with her and I needed to feel you out before I tell her it's okay to come West for a while."

Roan studied the photo in his hand. Shiloh Gallagher had to be twenty-nine years old according to what Maud had told him. Damned if she didn't look twenty-five or so, her features unlined. She wasn't model pretty, but she had an arresting face, with huge intelligent-looking green eyes. His gaze dropped to her mouth and he felt himself stir. Her mouth would make any man go crazy. Her upper lip was full, but thinner than her lower one. The shape of her mouth made him feel heat in his lower body. "Is she married?"

"No. Single. Never did marry. I don't know why. Shiloh's a beautiful girl."

She was hardly a girl, but Roan said nothing because he was fully reacting to her as a woman. He wondered if she was curvy or rail thin. He was disgruntled over his avid curiosity. "I have no problem with it. You know I get up early and come in late. She's going to have to fend for herself. I'm not cooking for her."

"Right," Maud agreed. "She's pretty shaken up, Roan. You might find that stressful until, hopefully, Shiloh will start to relax."

Shrugging, he slid the photo onto the desk. "Maud, I just hope I don't stress her out with my award-winning personality," he said, and he cracked a small, sour grin.

Maud cackled. "I think you'll like her, Roan. She's a very kind person. An introvert like you. Just remember, she's trying to write. Because of the stalking, she's suffering from writer's block and she's got a book due to her editor in six months. So, she's under a lot of other pressure."

"I'll handle it, Maud. No problem."

"Good," Maud said, relieved. She sat up in the chair. "I'll call Shiloh back, let her know she can come, and I'll find out what time she's arriving tomorrow. I'd like you to pick her up at the Jackson Hole Airport. So take that photo with you."

He stood, settling the cowboy hat on his head. "Don't need the photo." Because her face was already stamped across his heart. Whatever that meant. "I'll find her after she deplanes, don't worry. Just get back to me on the time."

Roan thought Maud looked more than relieved. He knew from being around the matriarch for two years that she cared deeply not only for her family and friends, but for those who worked here at the ranch. Maud treated everyone as her children, loved them to death, nurtured them, held them when they were hurting, and celebrated when happy things happened in their lives. She was a well-loved icon in the long, oval valley. She'd even rubbed off on him, which was a miracle in itself. He smiled occasionally now, thanks to her mother-henning him. She was tall, five foot nine inches, but she'd hugged the hell out of him sometimes, just to let him know he was loved by her.

"Will do," Maud murmured. She gave him a warm look. "Thanks for doing this, Roan."

"Anything to be of service, Maud." He lifted his hand, turned, and opened the door. Maud had allowed him to choose five acres on the ranch to build his own cabin, which he was in the process of doing. She wanted her employees to be happy. She paid them well and Roan felt damned lucky to have driven in one day and asked if they needed another wrangler. Thank God they did. Maud and Steve had given him respect and liked hiring military vets because they were such hard, consistent workers. Roan had thought getting a job after leaving Special Forces would be tough. But it hadn't been. He owed the Whitcombs a lot.

Chapter Two

Shiloh wearily stepped beyond the security area of the Jackson Hole Airport, a knapsack on her back, her computer in a nylon carrying case across her shoulder. Maud had said she was sending one of her wranglers, a Roan Taggart, to meet her at the airport.

Midafternoon sunlight lanced through the windows of the small but busy airport. She thought it would be easy to pick out the wrangler, but every man here, just about, wore a cowboy hat, boots, or a baseball cap. The writer in her, the observer, took note of the clothes they wore, listened to their dialect, the words they used. She halted near the wall and looked around.

"Ms. Gallagher?"

Shiloh jumped. She almost screamed at the man's low, deep voice coming from behind her. Heart leaping like a wild thing in her chest, she whirled around, her eyes huge with fear. Her gaze shot upward to look into the man's craggy, weather-lined face. Mouth going dry, she felt mesmerized by his pale gray eyes, the pupils large and black, glittering with intelligence. He wore a set of jeans, a white cowboy shirt, the sleeves rolled up to just below his elbows, a gray Stetson hanging loosely between his long fingers.

His hands were large and work worn. There was nothing soft about this man. The word *tough* came to mind. Not only that, he was tall like a New York City skyscraper, his shoulders incredibly broad. She looked at his forearms dusted with hair, the muscles taut from a lot of work. Gulping, she said, "Yes, I'm Shiloh. A-are you Mr. Roan Taggart?" Her heart nearly melted when he gave her a slight smile, warmth replacing his icy gray gaze.

"Yes, ma'am, I am. Sorry, didn't mean to startle you. May I get your luggage over at the carousel? If you'll point out the bags to me?"

Now her heart was swelling in her chest and it wasn't from fear. Sexuality oozed off this man like rain being soaked into thirsty, dry ground. Her lower body felt suddenly hot and needy. When he swept his gaze across her face, lingering on her breasts beneath the pale green tee she wore, to her chagrin, her nipples began to harden. Oh! Embarrassment! She saw a flicker of some emotion in his narrowing gray eyes for a split second, and then it disappeared. Her pulse leaped.

The man was not pretty-boy handsome. Rather, he was stoic-looking and simmering with closeted power she felt tightly wrapped around him. The elements had sculpted his flesh and as he had lifted his hand to place the cowboy hat over his short brown hair, she saw the calluses across his palm and fingers. An unexpected warmth sizzled through her, easing her nervousness. Did she see concern in his eyes? Shiloh wasn't sure as she wove in and out of the crowd toward the carousel where luggage was arriving.

"I'm afraid I have a lot of bags," she apologized.

Roan deliberately cut his long stride in half for her. Damned if Shiloh Gallagher wasn't twice as good-looking in person as in that photo of her. She had long red hair and when they crossed a slat of sunlight, Roan saw the gold and ginger highlights among the strands. Tall and willowy, she was small-breasted. He liked the natural sway of her rounded hips, thinking her butt was one fine piece of real estate. Roan wasn't immune to an attractive woman. He always appreciated them. Shiloh, however, for being a best-selling author, looked more like a young woman who was a hiker and outdoors person, not some stuffy, famous person. She wore comfortable jeans and had on a pair of tennis shoes. No one would ever look at her and think she was a writer, used to sitting at a computer. Roan smiled to himself. Looks were always deceiving. Or? What was the saying? Don't judge a book by its cover?

As a Special Forces operator, his life depended upon being observant. He was ruthless in his observation of Shiloh Gallagher. Some of her red hair was in a long, thick braid, falling between her shoulder blades. He could tell she was working out by just her graceful walk. Her hands were supple, fingers long, nails blunt cut. The only scent around her was her own, unique feminine scent that stirred up lust in him. Glad she didn't wear perfume; in the house it would be hell on his sensitive nose. He did pick up a subtle honeysuckle fragrance, figuring it was probably the soap she used either on her hair or her skin.

More than anything, he liked the freckles sprinkled across her nose and cheeks. It made him feel good that she didn't try to cover them up with makeup. She wore pink lipstick, but he could discern no other cosmetics. It seemed that Shiloh, despite being a bona fide city slicker, liked to be au natural.

Roan wondered if her mother, Isabella, had been the same way. Maybe he'd find out later because Shiloh seemed shy. He sensed a lot of vulnerability about her and wondered if she was able to protect herself. Could she defend herself if needed?

Shiloh had walked ahead of him and Roan watched as she halted and helped a gray-haired lady among the travelers who had accidentally dropped her purse. Roan stopped, assessing the interaction. Shiloh was the only one who seemed concerned. She quickly picked up the purse, smiling at the woman, chatting with her, helping her place the strap back upon her rounded shoulder. She asked if she needed more help. The woman said she did, so Roan walked over and cocked his head toward Shiloh.

"Can I be of help here?" he asked her.

Nodding, Shiloh kept her hand on the elder's arm. "Yes. This is Mrs. Ellie Sanders. She has a bag, Mr. Taggart. Could you possibly get it and carry it out for her? She's meeting her brother who hasn't shown up yet."

Tipping his hat to the elder, Roan said, "Ma'am? Why not show me which bag is yours? I'll be happy to carry it out for you."

Ellie gave him a look of relief. "Oh, thank you, son. My brother will be here shortly. If you can just carry it outside to the benches, I'll wait for him there."

"Yes, ma'am," he murmured.

Shiloh kept her arm on the woman because she limped badly and didn't seem all that sturdy.

Grateful that Roan would do this for her, Shiloh wondered if the hardness of his facial features was only skin-deep. She'd watched his eyes turn kind, his deep voice grow gentle as he chatted respectfully with unsteady Ellie. As a writer, she gleaned information from small things, such as voice, body language, and watching a person's eyes. Humorously, Shiloh thought Taggart would make a great romance hero. He wasn't pretty and he wasn't exactly charming, rather rough-hewn. But he had courtly manners and he was kind to the flustered Ellie, so he got a gold star from her because of that.

As Shiloh stood at the carousel waiting for her luggage to appear, she watched Roan with the elder who was half his size. He didn't try to hurry her or force her to walk faster than she could. She watched Ellie fall under his spell. Who wouldn't? Shiloh almost swore she saw the woman become more plucky, more active, smiling all the time with rugged Roan Taggart at her side. Yeah, this cowboy could make a woman feel really good about herself.

Frowning, she turned and saw her first bag arrive, so she hauled it off the carousel and set it nearby. She had six bags in total since she was going to stay with Maud for two months. She knew Roan would be back in a few minutes after settling Ellie outside to wait for her brother.

It was utter pleasure watching Roan walk casually back into the airport and head in her direction. The man moved with a masculine grace Shiloh had rarely seen. And on him, it was a perfect fit with his rugged quality, his work-worn jeans, those ropy lower arms and large hands. There was such a blatant sensuality about him. His masculinity was squarely in her face. She noticed how many women's heads swiveled as he strode by them. Tucking away her smile, Shiloh picked up her last suitcase and set it down next to the others.

"Got them all?" Roan asked, halting.

"Every last one of them."

"It'll take me two trips. Why don't you come with me and I'll take you to the truck?"

She snorted. "If you take three, I can get the other three."

Roan gave her a steady look. "Code of the West, Ms. Gallagher. Men do the heavy hauling."

She was about to protest but he wrapped his hand around her upper arm. The instant his fingers brushed her skin, wild, fiery tingles radiated in every direction. With a quick breath, Shiloh opened her mouth to protest.

"No excuses," Roan growled, marching her in front of him.

She had the good grace not to put up a fight with the cowboy. Twisting a look across her shoulder, she said, "You wouldn't last a day in New York City. Women are on their own there, believe me." He probably opened doors for women too.

"I made the mistake of going there only once," he said, taking the first three suitcases in hand. He saw the amusement deep in her green eyes, that wide, lush mouth of hers pulling tentatively into a smile. There was nothing to dislike about Shiloh. He especially liked her name. It rolled off his tongue like melted honey. And he'd like to taste that mouth of hers but, he darkly reminded himself, she was Maud's guest.

After leading her to the white Chevy pickup truck with WIND RIVER RANCH painted on the door, he opened it for her. "Climb in," Roan said, putting the suitcases in the rear bed. The sun was warm and bright in a cloudy blue sky. Roan walked back and retrieved the rest of her luggage. As he slid into the truck, he asked, "Did Maud tell you that you'll be staying over at one of the employee houses? That there's a room waiting for you?"

"Yes." Roan filled the cab of the truck. Somehow, and she didn't know how, Shiloh felt a very protective feeling extending invisibly from him to her. She felt embraced by it and it was wonderful, de-stressing her. Maybe it was the warm look he gave her as their eyes briefly met? As if he was trying to reassure her?

"Then you know you'll be doing your own cooking?" Roan saw her nod. "Do you feel like going over to the local grocery store to buy your food? Things you like to eat?"

"Sure. It will feel good to be able to walk around for a while. My legs are cramped up from that darned economy seat in the plane."

Driving slowly out to the asphalt road that would take them into Jackson Hole, Roan said, "I thought you were a best-selling author."

"I am. Why?"

Shrugging, Roan murmured, "Just thought all you authors were rich."

"I wish it were true," she said. "I make a decent living, but I'm not rich. Maybe later, if my books continue to be popular, that might happen."

"So that's why you flew the cattle car instead of business or first class?"

Shiloh nodded, already in love with the sharp, jagged peaks rising in the west near the airport. "Right. What are these beautiful mountains called?"

"The Grand Tetons, but we'll be driving for about an hour south of here. In the Wind River Valley, where we're going, you'll see two mountain ranges on either side of it: the Salt River and Wilson ranges. They aren't as exciting as the Tetons, but they'll do."

She sighed. "The Tetons are stunning." And then she glanced at his rugged profile. "You're lucky."

"Well, you have canyons in New York City," he said. "Skyscrapers are mountains of another type."

"You're a writer."

Roan shook his head. "No way."

"The way you see things. That's creative. And you're right: All the tall buildings do create canyons. And our skyscrapers do look like mountains."

Roan shouldn't feel good about her enthusiastic compliment, but he did. There was such an ease between them he could neither explain, stop, nor change. "Well," he drawled, "I'm no writer."

"I think everyone can write. Even if it's into their personal diary. I have a wonderful software called Alembic. I put my daily journal entries in there." She saw him give her a cool look. "Okay, maybe you don't think you're a writer. But you DO have a way with words." She enjoyed going down the long hill. Far below she could see a town and assumed it was Jackson Hole. To her left was the Elk Refuge, a ten-foot fence for as far as she could see to keep the elk off the main highway.

"Let's not talk about me," Roan said gruffly, uncomfortable. "What kind of books do you write?"

Inwardly, Shiloh squirmed and then hesitated. Finally, she said, "I'm a romance writer." She saw his brows shoot up. Then, she saw that catlike grin cross his beautifully shaped mouth. Heat pummeled her face and she knew she was blushing! Tucking her hands tensely into her lap, she waited for what she knew was coming. Telling a man she was a romance writer was like green-lighting the guy to either make some snide remark about the genre or to believe it was a come-on, which usually led to him making a pass at her.

Giving her a sidelong glance, Roan saw she was blushing to her roots. He saw anxiety in her eyes, felt her defensiveness. It was even in her voice. "I don't imagine you tell too many people what you write."

Anger stirred in her. "I'm PROUD of what I write, Mr. Taggart. I'm not ashamed of it. I tend NOT to tell men precisely because of the way you've just reacted."

So, the filly had some spunk in her after all. Roan wasn't going to argue the point because she was right. "Maud said you were a best-seller. That means someone likes your books." Roan really didn't want to get into an adversarial position with Shiloh and upset her. Maud would be pissed off for starters. He thought he'd smoothed it over with that casual kind of comment.

It felt like steam was coming out of her ears as Shiloh sat there tensely, her hands knotted in her lap. It was a huge disappointment to her that Taggart was like any other male finding out about her occupation. Upon first meeting him, he seemed different. But in all fairness to him, Shiloh knew she was absolutely stressed out and she wasn't seeing much of anything realistically right now because of the stalker.

She rubbed her scrunched-up brow. "Look," she whispered, "I'm really out of sorts, Mr. Taggart. Just the long flight. I don't mean to come off as snarky."

His heart winced. There was a wobble in her voice, as if she were going to cry. Giving Shiloh a glance, he saw her face hidden by a curtain of her red hair. "I'm the one who is at fault here, Ms. Gallagher. I apologize. You're obviously a good writer and you have an audience who loves your books." Roan wasn't sure he should let her know he was aware of her stalker problems. She'd come out here to get away from them. He pulled into the grocery parking lot, glad for the diversion.

"Let's go in and get you some grub," he said, trying not to sound so gruff. Instantly, he saw her respond positively. How sensitive was this woman? He walked around and opened the door for her. Shiloh hesitantly took his hand and he helped her out. She looked at him as if he was going to bite her. He felt worse about the way he'd handled the conversation with her.

Shopping wasn't really his thing. When Roan came to the store, he got what he wanted and was out as fast as possible, not liking crowds of people.

"Thank you," she murmured as she laid her hand into his. There was regret in Taggart's eyes. Her fingers tingled, encased by his rougher ones. In fact, it looked like her hand had been swallowed up by his.

To Roan's surprise, she was quick and efficient. She knew what she wanted. There was enough food for a week in her cart and Roan carried the bags out to the truck for her. Shiloh was inquisitive, always looking around. Like him. Only she was very sensitive. She was a writer. Maybe there was some common ground he could plow with her. On the way back to the ranch, he decided to try again and, hopefully, not stir her up into defensiveness or anger.

"I noticed you observe a lot," he said, sliding her a glance.

"Part of being a writer, I guess. My dad always did it. I probably picked it up unconsciously."

"What are you looking for?" Roan wondered, driving down Highway 89 south, which would eventually allow them to leave the town behind. Fifty miles south lay the Wind River Valley.

Shrugging, Shiloh said, "Just the way people act or behave. Body language. Voice inflections. Facial expression. If I see something I haven't got in my repertoire, I catalog up here," and she tapped her head. "It helps me create believable and sympathetic characters my readers can fall in love with, root for, and put an emotional investment into."

"Why do you say 'sympathetic'?" Roan found himself wanting to talk to Shiloh. It wasn't one of his finer points: carrying on a social conversation. He was usually abrupt and if one or two words would suffice, that was the end of his sentence. Maybe because he'd never been around a writer, she was like a bug under a microscope to him. His body begged to differ with him. There was something deep driving him to get to know her better. Maybe two months with a woman underfoot wasn't going to be as bad as he thought it might be. He liked women. In bed. Outside of it? No. Of course, Maud Whitcomb was his employer, and he always enjoyed being around her.

Opening her hands, Shiloh said, "Readers of romances need to connect on a compassionate level with the hero and heroine. If one is unsympathetic, it turns them off and they'll never buy another book from you. They want to emotionally connect with the characters."

"Then," Roan struggled, frowning, "these men are perfect?"

Shiloh laughed and felt heat moving into her face again. Every time Taggart looked at her, she felt as if he were looking through her and knew every secret she carried. "No. They have weaknesses and strengths, but not a fatal flaw."

"Fatal flaw?"

"Yes. Some of the not-so-nice traits humans have like being a robber, a liar, or a murderer are some examples," she said, her hand going to her neck as the gruesome spectacle rose in her once again. Shaking off memories of her mother's murder, Shiloh said in a strained voice, "Developing a character is a lot of work. The hero and heroine have to be believable to the readers."

"You'll find plenty of characters here at the Wind River Ranch," he said wryly, turning down the half-mile drive that would take them to the ranch.

Shiloh was thinking he was one himself, but said nothing. He'd probably take it the wrong way. "Have you always been a wrangler, Mr. Taggart?"

"Call me Roan. No, just the last two years."

"Roan? That's different. Where did you get that name?"

Now he was the bug under her microscope. He could feel Shiloh zeroing in on him. If it had been anyone but her, Roan would have shut them down in a helluva hurry. The look in her green eyes became sharpened and curious. "My parents."

"But," she stumbled, "was it a name of a favorite grandfather or uncle? That's a very odd name and it's very old. In fact, it goes back to Germany, I believe. It's a derivation of the German word for raven."

He slid her a glance. "You're a walking encyclopedia. My father's side came from Germany in the nineteen hundreds and settled in Montana. And yes, my grandfather's name was Raven, so Dad decided to give me a variation of it."

"I'm good," she teased, giving him a smile. Her heart flipped when he smiled back at her. That mouth of Roan's was dessert of the finest kind. It was a wide, chiseled mouth, his upper lip thinner than his lower lip. It was a mouth that shouted of masculinity and confidence. What would it be like to kiss this man? Shiloh winced inwardly. He was probably married with a pack of kids. Where was *her* head? Her body?

"You are good," Roan murmured. He slowed down as they rolled into a populated area. The ranch sat in a flat area, mostly buildings and corrals. "Sometime you'll have to tell me the story of how you got your name."

"It's interesting," Shiloh promised, craning her neck, excited about seeing a real Western ranch. "How far is it to Wind River Ranch where I'll be staying? Maud had said it was a long way from Jackson Hole."

"It's fifty miles as the crow flies," Roan said. "But it goes through some pretty valley areas along the way."

Shiloh saw the lush, green valley below the four-lane highway of 89A. "It looks like one of my mom's paintings. She never did landscapes in this area, but over in Colorado and the Rocky Mountain area. Those were favorites of mine."

"Wind River Valley got its name from the Snake River flowing north to south through it. The valley is nearly a hundred miles long and anywhere between twenty to fifty miles wide. It's bracketed by two different mountain ranges. You'll be able to see the Salt River Range from the kitchen window of the employee house where you'll be staying."

"This is so different from New York City," she sighed, relaxing for the first time in so long. She heard him chuckle but he said nothing further. Through half-closed eyes, tiredness lapping at her, Shiloh wanted to stay awake to absorb the beauty around her, but at some point, her eyes drooped closed.

* * *

The jolt of the truck leaving the asphalt highway and crossing a metal cattle guard that made a lot of racket jolted Shiloh out of her sleep. Momentarily disoriented, she looked around, realizing she was in a large, grassy valley. There were few homes around, and fenced pastures everywhere. Wiping her eyes, she sat up.

"Get a little shut-eye?"

"Yes," she said, her voice still thick with sleep. "Where are we?"

"Home," he murmured, gesturing with his hand toward the windshield. "Up ahead you'll see the main ranch house. The two-story log home was created in nineteen hundred by the first Whitcombs traveling through this area. They fell in love with it, staked a claim, and started building that ranch house you see. Over the generations, everyone added to it. Now, it's about five thousand square feet in total."

"Wow, that's big," Shiloh said, staring at the huge home. Nearby she saw two red barns, both three stories tall. There were a lot of pipe rail fences. In some of them, she saw Herefords. In others, pretty-colored horses. There were a lot of smaller log cabins down on the other side of the main house. "What are those?"

"They're the tourist cabins. Maud and Steve rent them out every year. Some people come to fish out of the Snake River, others like to hike, or they want to backpack into the Salt River Range," he replied, and motioned to the snow-capped blue-gray mountains. "They handle about twenty people per week from May through September."

"I imagine it helps them financially," she said, excitement thrumming through her. Her heart leaped as she saw two cowboys on horses galloping down a path between two of the huge, oval corrals. "This is so magical," she whispered, thrilled.

Roan pointed to his left. "See that single-story house

coming up on your right? The yellow one with white shutters?"

"Yes."

"That's where you'll be living. It's one of the employee houses."

"It's beautiful," she whispered, feeling excitement building in her. "I've always dreamed of coming out West."

The vibrancy, the thrill in her low, husky voice, riffled across Roan's flesh. He glanced over and saw her cheeks were flushed. Her eyes were shining with joy. She was incredibly alluring. And his lower body heated up some more. Damn. What the hell was going on here? Roan tried to remain immune to Shiloh's enthusiasm but it was impossible. One moment she could be a mature adult; the next, childlike and unafraid to show how she felt. Shiloh rolled down the truck window, sticking her head out as they passed a couple of wranglers riding sleek horses.

"Are you looking at the wranglers or their horses?" Roan asked drily, pulling in and parking in front of the main office.

Laughing airily, Shiloh said, "I'm single, but I'm not desperate." She thought she saw some jealousy in his eyes. No, that couldn't be true. It was her inability to read a person accurately. The stress. The relief that she was free of her stalker made her giddy. Roan probably thought she wasn't acting her age. She'd always been like this, but he didn't know that. "And to answer your other question, I was looking at those incredibly gorgeous horses they were riding."

Roan gave her a quirked mouth response as he put the truck in park and turned it off. "Ever ride? Maybe in Central Park?"

"No. The closest I got to a horse was when my parents took me to a fair. I was seven and I got to ride a pinto Shetland around in a circle. I was in heaven," she sighed, giving him a smile. Shiloh could see he wasn't used to spontaneity.

"Good to know," Roan said gruffly. "Stay put. I'll open the door for you."

He was really old-fashioned! Shiloh sat impatiently, wanting to get out, smell the air, look around, and simply absorb everything about the ranch into her five senses. As Roan opened the door for her, she looked up at him. "Has anyone ever accused you of being a throwback to a bygone era?"

One eyebrow lifted. "As in a Neanderthal? Oh, wait . . . Cro-Magnon?"

She burst out laughing, loving his dry sense of humor. No smile; just a glint in his eyes that told her he was teasing her. "I was being nice."

"I'm a realist." Roan held out his hand to her.

This time, Shiloh took it without hesitating, finding his manners touching in a world that had lost some of its social veneer. Roan had it in spades. "Thank you," she said a little breathlessly as he released her fingers. She could literally feel the heat of his body; they were inches apart. She inhaled deeply, his masculine scent mixed with dust and sweat. Heat tore down through her and she gazed up into those gray eyes that studied her in the building silence. He wanted her. The thought was shocking. What was more shocking and disconcerting to Shiloh was she wanted him! Flustered, she quickly moved away.

Roan shut the door and motioned to the wooden steps. "Thatta way." He stood back, watching the way her hips moved and he could feel himself thickening. The woman should have a license for the way she moved in such a natural, graceful sway.

Swallowing hard, Roan scowled and headed up the stairs to open the screen door for Shiloh. What a helluva fix. Now he was going to be teased by her twenty-four hours a day. Not that he thought Shiloh was a tease. She wasn't. Their bedrooms were separated by a hall. Dragging in a deep breath, Roan opened the screen door for her, gesturing for her to walk into the office.

Roan introduced her to Steve Whitcomb, the owner, who gave her a warm smile of welcome and a hearty handshake. He stood back when he saw Maud come rushing out of the second office, her arms open wide, a huge smile of welcome for Shiloh on her face. He glanced over at Steve, nodded good-bye, turned, and left. As he took the stairs down to the gravel driveway, he was damned glad he had to work the rest of the day. First, he'd take her bags of groceries over to the house and put the items in the cupboards. That way, he wouldn't be tempted to stare at Shiloh like the slavering wolf that he really was. Mouth tightening, Roan climbed into the pickup and drove it over to the main barn. What the hell was he going to do with a beautiful, available woman under his roof?

Chapter Three

"Welcome to the ranch," Maud said, her voice emotional as she threw her arms open to Shiloh and hugged her gently and then released her.

"Thanks so much for having me, Maud."

"Oh, honey, I've been wanting you to come out for a visit for a long time. You look exhausted," she said, patting her arm. "Let's get you over to the employee house. I think you might want to rest for a while?"

"Sounds wonderful," Shiloh murmured, squeezing Maud's strong, darkly tanned hand. "It's just the stress of travel."

Maud led her out of the office, plopped her ever-present red baseball cap on her head as they walked down the stairs. "I think it's six months of awful, accumulated stress on you, Shiloh, that has you so tired."

"You're right," she admitted, giving her a smile. They walked across the asphalt road and down a red-tiled path that led to the three yellow employee houses sitting in a row. Gazing upward, Shiloh loved the fluffy white clouds over the valley, the magnificent Salt River Range still clothed in white snow off to her left. "I already feel better just being out here, Maud. Your ranch is incredibly beautiful. It's so green, so alive."

Maud smiled. "Did Roan find you at the airport in time?"

"He sure did. About scared the crap out of me."

"Oh?"

"He came up behind me and called my name. I about jumped out of my skin."

Maud smiled. "Did he tell you he was in black ops? U.S. Army? A Special Forces weapons sergeant?"

Rolling her eyes, Shiloh said, "No, but it sure explains why he came up behind me so silently. I never heard or felt him coming. He's pretty close-mouthed." And then she laughed a little. "Well, if he was black ops, why wouldn't he be that way? Right?" She grinned over at Maud, who chuckled.

"He's a good man. Smart. Loyal. And he's a darned hard worker. Roan's been with us for two years." As they took the left fork where the path split into a Y, Maud glanced up at Shiloh. "You remember I told you that you'd be sharing the employee house with one of our wranglers?"

"Yes."

"Roan is the one. Are you okay with that?"

Her heart beat a little quicker. He was so sinfully male. His masculinity was making her lower body ache and reminding her how long it had been since she'd made love. Shiloh saw Maud give her a concerned look. "Oh, it's fine. He was very nice." And her lips lifted. "I told him he was very old-fashioned."

"Cowboys are made that way. Knights from a bygone age," Maud agreed. "But you're comfortable with him being there?"

Shrugging, Shiloh said, "Fine. Not a problem." There was no way she was going to tell anyone how drawn she was to Roan. Heck, she couldn't even explain it herself!

Placing her hand momentarily on Maud's shoulder, she said, "I'm just appreciative you'd let me come out here and roost for a while." Shiloh could see the concern in Maud's eyes dissolve. She didn't want to worry her mother's old friend. Roan was an adult and so was she. Of course, she didn't know what Roan thought of her, but she knew how her body was sure reacting to him. Shiloh wasn't going to tell Roan a thing. Whatever was going on, was obviously one-sided.

Roan was rough around the edges. Untamable. Look, but don't touch. Because Shiloh felt that if she ever kissed him, he would take her and there would be no stopping his sweet assault upon her. She would melt like a marshmallow over an open fire. Roan had masculine power around him to burn, and although she wasn't afraid of it or him, it made Shiloh circumspect. He was a man who played for keeps, her instincts told her. At least, that's what her life experience told her. She didn't own an encyclopedia on the male of the species, or even how to find, keep, and grow a relationship. For a writer who wrote happily ever after, her love life was a sad story of continuous train wrecks and loss.

As Shiloh walked into the employee house, she fell in love with its size, high ceilings, and open-concept kitchen–living room. "Wow," she murmured, looking around. "This is great, Maud. It's so open! So light."

"Typical Western style of living," Maud assured her. "I'm sure Roan told you that he wasn't the chief cook and bottle washer around here? That you two split all the kitchen duties and keeping the house cleaned up?"

Grinning, Shiloh followed her into the living room. It was laid with gold and red cedar flooring, a few colorful Western motif rugs here and there, lending more color. "That he did. I'm fine with it."

"I'm sure you'll work out something with him. He's pretty flexible."

"I didn't get that impression at all."

Maud grinned. "He's a tough, closed-up hombre, but he has a good heart. Roan's kind to animals, so I'm sure it crosses over to being kind to humans, as well. All the tourists who come here seem to like him a lot."

"Okay," Shiloh teased, "I'll take your word for it."

"Here's your bedroom," Maud said, gesturing into it. "It's right across the hall from where Roan sleeps."

Inwardly grimacing, Shiloh stepped into the room. "Ohhhh, this is gorgeous, Maud. It looks like vintage nineteen-thirties decor! I love it!" She turned. "You do know I love that era, don't you?"

"I didn't, but I do now. Go on in."

Shiloh stepped into the room. It had a colorful water lily–designed Tiffany lamp up on a walnut dresser. The bed had a crescent-shaped walnut headboard and was covered with what looked like a Depression-era quilt, a real patchwork quilt that had been hand sewn. There was a light green velvet settee made of walnut, the legs curved and elegant. What caught Shiloh's eye the most was a gorgeous vanity. It had a sun ray beveled mirror held in place by walnut on either side of it. She loved the fact there was a large rolltop desk in one corner with good light above it. "This is perfect for me to sit and write," she said, gesturing toward it.

"We have a large office here you can use if you want," Maud said. "I'll show it to you, but if you want to sit in here and create, that's fine with me."

"I love this room," Shiloh murmured, moving her hand along the old quilt. "There's just something about the Depression era, having so little, yet the gorgeous handmade furniture that came out of that period still stands the test of time to this day."

"You'll love the bathroom more," Maud promised with a grin.

Following the older woman, Shiloh smiled. "This is like a hotel, Maud. A shower, bath, and a Jacuzzi. What more could a girl want?" Indeed, cedar wood glowed warm and golden beneath her feet. There was a huge glass-enclosed shower big enough for two people along with two huge, circular rain-shower nozzles. The bathtub was from the 1930s and sat up on brass claw feet. On the other side of the vanity was a hot tub big enough for four people.

"Oh, I thought you being a writer and all, a good hot soak in a Jacuzzi would get you to relax and put your brain in neutral for a while," Maud teased. "Be sure to pour yourself a glass of wine, set it on the side over there, and life's good."

Running her hand along the gold-and-black-swirled granite counter, Shiloh appreciated all the thoughtful additions to this bathroom. "Really, this is heaven, Maud." She gave her a warm look. "I should have come out here a long time ago."

Maud slipped her hand around her waist and gave her a gentle squeeze. "You always have a place to come home to, Shiloh. That's what I really wanted you to know." Maud gave her a softened look. "I know your aunt and uncle are still nearby in New York City, but I'd like to think that you're ours by proxy."

Touched, Shiloh slid her arm around Maud's shoulders and whispered in a trembling voice, "Thank you, Maud. You have *no* idea how badly I wanted you to say yes to me coming out here. I was at my wit's end."

"I know you were. Maybe things will slow down out here for you and you can get back to writing. We're a busy ranch but the tourists who visit us weekly are on the other side of the road. They won't be coming over to these homes to bother you, so no worries. We've got a nice white picket fence around each of them to give you privacy and there's a lovely alcove out back, away from prying eyes, that you might want to take advantage of. It faces toward the Snake River in the distance."

Emotion swept through Shiloh as she gave the woman a grateful look. "You've given me so much, Maud. I hope I can repay you someday. Do let me know if I can help out. Do some work? You aren't letting me pay for staying here, so I feel I have to do something to carry my weight."

Maud gave her a sly smile. "You said in your phone call you wanted to see what it was like to be a cowboy. Right?"

"Yes."

"On days that you feel up to it, go with Roan for part of a day. Ride with him."

Gulping, Shiloh said, "Oh, I don't really think he'd be open to that."

Shrugging, Maud said, "He rubs off on you after a while."

"Does he know this? That I can tag along with him?"

"Sure he does. All you have to do is speak up. It's his job to take care of you while you're here with us."

Grimacing, Shiloh muttered, "I bet he sees me as a babysitting job."

Chuckling, Maud said, "Ask him."

Sure. Roan just invited an open dialogue. *Not.* "I'll think about it, Maud. I don't want to be a pain in the ass around here. I know I'm a city slicker."

"Honey, you could never be a pain in the tush to anyone even if you tried real hard," Maud murmured, giving her a sympathetic smile. "Now, if you're out riding around, you might feel a pain there, but that's because you haven't rode before. And the more often you ride, your body will stretch and just naturally accommodate and you won't be stiff and sore anymore."

"Right now," Shiloh said longingly, "I just want to crash and sleep on that beautiful bed."

"You go right ahead," Maud encouraged. "Roan usually gets in around six P.M."

Glancing at her watch, Shiloh saw she had two hours. "Great. I'll catch a nap." She hugged Maud. She was deeply tanned, wiry, and tightly muscled. Maud wore a cowboy shirt of blue and white plaid, the sleeves rolled up to just below her elbows. In her back jeans pocket, Shiloh spotted a pair of well-worn leather work gloves. She knew Maud was fifty-five years old, but she looked forty, young and vibrant. Her black hair was threaded with streaks of silver, but on her, it looked stylish with her square face and those pale green eyes of hers that missed nothing. When Maud settled her cap on her head and waved good-bye to her at the door and left, Shiloh sighed, smiling tiredly as she looked appreciatively around the quiet home.

It felt like a heavy blanket was descending upon Shiloh as she decided to put her clothes and other items away after she took a nap. Sliding her shoes off, she lay down on the bed. The thought as she closed her eyes was that she was safe. Finally. And within moments, Shiloh spiraled into a deep, healing sleep.

Roan walked into the employee house at six-thirty P.M. The day had gotten cloudy and it looked like it might spit rain sometime tonight. He looked around after entering, thinking he'd see Shiloh. The house was utterly quiet. Roan wasn't sure he was looking forward to seeing the woman or not. His body sure as hell wanted to, but he didn't. There was no place in his life for a woman right now. He had too many other irons in the fire. Still, her red hair, that glint in her forest-green eyes, beckoned to him whether Roan wanted to admit it or not.

Walking in, he quietly shut the door and dropped his gray Stetson on a nearby wooden peg. First, he had to get a shower. Filthy with dust because he'd helped some wranglers herd cattle into another pasture, Roan wanted to get the grit off his skin.

As he ambled down the wooden hall, he lightened his walk, seeing the door to Shiloh's room open. Frowning, he slowed to a stop. She was asleep on the bed, curled up into almost a fetal position, on her right side. Seeing how deeply she slept, as if she hadn't rested easily for quite some time, Roan began to understand the stress created by the stalker, and how it had deeply affected Shiloh. Flexing his hand into a fist and releasing it, Roan thought he would like to get his hands on the bastard who had tortured her nonstop for six months. Even in sleep, as his gaze moved from her long legs up across her curvy hip to her breasts and then to her face, Roan could see subtle lines of tension throughout her body.

She had an attractive oval face, a stubborn-looking chin, some strands of her red hair dropping across her smooth brow. Her lashes were long, curved against her high cheekbones. She slept with her hands beneath one cheek and it stirred his heart. *Childlike* was a word that came to mind when Roan gazed at her freckled cheeks and nose. It was her mouth, the perfect, sensual shape of it, that his body reacted to.

Roan felt himself stir. Cursing silently, he stepped in and pulled the door closed. The less he saw of Shiloh, the better off he was going to be. Running his fingers in an aggravated motion through his short hair, he stepped across the hall into his bedroom. Worse, he had inhaled her sweet, feminine scent. He'd spent too many years in danger and his senses were finely honed. He could pick up an odor and know if it was Taliban or not a hundred feet away from where they were hiding. Her scent reminded him of a wildflower meadow that sat near the cabin he was building and it was playing havoc on his body. *Damn.*

Emerging from a hot shower, Roan changed into a pair of clean Levi's and a black T-shirt. He traded his cowboy boots for a pair of hiking boots. As he walked past Shiloh's door, he listened, but heard nothing. All her luggage that he'd put in her room was exactly where he left it. She was exhausted. That realization twinged at his heart.

Scowling, he rubbed his chest and wandered into the kitchen. Grabbing a cold beer out of the refrigerator brought back strong memories of his A-team. Usually they were living at an Afghan village and alcohol was off-limits. It was one of the few good memories Roan had about getting to Kandahar, to the Special Forces compound, and being able to get a cold beer. The fine sand and grit got in every crack and crevice of a man's body. He was always chafed raw around his collar and other places. A cold beer washed that crud out of his throat and gave his mouth a clean taste. Tipping it back, he drank deeply, the one concession he gave himself at the end of a tough day of wrangling.

Roan wanted to forget Shiloh was in the house as he rustled up some food from the refrigerator. He wasn't heartless. Choosing two T-bone steaks, he put them on the wooden cutting board. He was big on salads, bringing out an armful of veggies and placing them on the counter. Wondering if Shiloh enjoyed them, he made more than usual. Grabbing flour and other ingredients, he whipped up some biscuits. Unsure of when she might wake up, if at all, Roan went ahead and made dinner for himself. He would cook up her steak later, if she wanted it.

Going to the living room, he turned on the television and selected a news station. That's all he wanted was the news. He'd gotten a newspaper earlier and would read it as he ate. This was his normal nightly schedule. Nothing fancy. Just rest.

Roan half turned, sensing movement before he saw her. It was Shiloh coming out of her room, rubbing her drowsy eyes, her hair tangled around her shoulders. She was barefoot. Smiling to himself, Roan thought she looked like a child, not the woman she was. Yawning, she suddenly halted when she became aware Roan was watching her.

"Oh . . ."

"Feel better?" he asked, turning back and heading for the kitchen.

Shiloh felt drugged. The shock of seeing how large and broad-shouldered Roan was with that tight-fitting black T-shirt yanked her awake. She saw his gray eyes narrow upon her like a predator stalking his quarry. Unsure of whether to feel alarmed or not, her lower body sizzled instantly beneath his sweeping gaze. "I don't know yet," she admitted thickly, walking into the living room. The wood felt warm beneath her bare feet. Late western sunlight slanted in a set of windows on that side of the house, glinting and showing the gold and red in the wood. Her heart was beating a little quicker.

"Feel up to eating something?" Roan asked, glancing her way as she came and stood at the edge of the kitchen, looking unsure.

"I could eat." Shiloh sniffed the air. "Something sure smells good. What are you baking, Roan?"

"Biscuits."

"A man who cooks. I like that. Do all cowboys know their way around a kitchen?"

The corner of his mouth curved faintly. "It was a learn-or-starve situation."

She chuckled, pushing the hair away from her face and across her shoulders. Roan Taggart didn't look like a cowboy right now. Her imagination ran wild. Perhaps a dark, sexy biker on his black Harley hog. Or a mixed martial arts fighter. Or . . . in her bed. Wow . . . her drowsy brain was really stuck on sex, wasn't it? "You said I had to cook for myself."

Hitching one shoulder, Roan replied, "I'll let you off the hook tonight. You've had a long flight and you looked like you were going to keel over from exhaustion at the airport. We're having T-bone steaks, corn, biscuits, and a salad. Sound edible to you?"

Her heart warmed. His voice was low and husky, but she saw a glint in his gray eyes, maybe amusement. Maybe he felt sorry for her? Shiloh wasn't sure. "It sounds wonderful. Thank you. Is there anything I can do to help?"

"You could set the table." He pointed up to the cabinets nearby. "Dishes in there and silverware down here." It felt strange to have a woman underfoot. Roan liked a woman in his bed. But in his house? When Shiloh came close, he could smell her feminine scent. His body stirred. *Again*. Dragging in a deep breath, Roan was unhappy with himself. Whatever door that was open between them remained that way. He'd always been able to shut out emotions when necessary because his survival was at stake. The only danger here was his damned body beginning to ache for hers. Shiloh wasn't doing anything to cultivate that kind of a reaction from him. Roan tried to ignore her puttering around the kitchen barefoot. Worse, the sway of her hips got him. Big-time. She could wear sackcloth and he'd still see those hips of hers moving. She was shapely in all the right places and his hands practically itched to curve around her.

"What time did you come home?" Shiloh asked, putting the two white ceramic plates on the square cedar table.

Roan looked up at the stove clock. "About an hour ago."

"I didn't hear you come in."

"You won't."

She hesitated at the drawer next to the stove where he

was cooking the T-bone steaks. "Because you were in black ops?"

Frowning, Roan cut her a quick glance. "Did Maud tell you I was in Special Forces?"

"Yes." Shiloh carried the flatware over to the table, placing it. "In my mind's eye I could see you as an operator. Or"—she smiled a little—"maybe a biker on a big Harley motorcycle, or a mixed martial arts fighter."

His flesh riffled listening to her smoky voice. "You've got quite an imagination." He could envision several scenarios with her in bed with him, too. But he didn't think she'd appreciate him being verbal about his fantasies that involved her.

"Yep, that's me. When I see a person, I fantasize who they might be beneath the clothes they're presently wearing. Faces tell me so much."

Roan checked on the biscuits. They'd be crispy about the time the medium-rare steaks would be ready. "Have you always done that?" His curiosity about her was new to him. Maybe if he knew Shiloh better, she wouldn't be such a damned magnetic draw for him. Maybe she had a dark side, was a bitch in disguise . . . anything to make her less appealing to him. However, looking at her face, Roan couldn't see anything but honesty in her drowsy expression. He knew body language as well as breathing. Body language interpretation had saved his life too many times to count. Shiloh was open toward him. She wasn't putting her arms across her chest, her eyes weren't moving rapidly, as if looking for someone to jump them. Her stride was relaxed, not tense or shorter than normal. All those things served to tell Roan about a person's state. She also candidly met his gaze and held it.

"What? Read faces?" She smiled sleepily and discovered the salt and pepper shakers in a nearby spice rack.

"Yes."

"My Dad did it. I remember him teaching me about people, their expressions, and their body movement from the time I was six until he died. He used to take me to Central Park and we'd sit on a bench and he'd ask me what I saw in a face as someone jogged by or walked their dog past us." Shiloh halted at the edge of the kitchen, thinking how much Roan filled it with his powerful, muscular presence. The man was big. His hands were big. So were his feet. Shoulders so broad. And a chest that reminded her of someone who swam a great deal; maybe a diver, her imagination whispered.

"Your father was teaching you body language?"

"Yes. He was a jet fighter pilot in the Air Force, but I think he always had a love of people and what made them tick the way they did. A curiosity. You'd see it in the characters he wrote so richly about in his books."

"What did he write?" Roan put on an oven mitt and drew out the tray of biscuits. He set it on a trivet next to the stove and pulled down a straw basket. Without a word, Shiloh came over and quickly took a spatula and transferred the golden-brown biscuits to the basket. Roan smiled a little to himself. She was a team person. That was another box ticked off in his world of people. He'd always been a team player in the A-team. Everyone relied on everyone else. They all had specialties and, as a group, they were powerful. Shiloh took the biscuits over to the table and then went to the fridge and found the butter.

"My dad wrote military thrillers. His first book went number one on the *New York Times* Best Seller list."

"And how many did he write before he passed?" Roan pointed toward the plates on the table. Shiloh must have read his mind and understood what he wanted without even saying it. Which shook him. She brought the plates over so he could put a sizzling steak on each one of them. It wasn't lost on Roan that she'd accurately pieced together what he wanted. That was pretty amazing to him.

Taking the two plates, Shiloh set them on the table. "He wrote four books. Every one a best-seller."

He could hear the pride and the sadness in her voice. And when he looked into her eyes, Roan saw how much Shiloh still missed her father.

Turning off the stove, he removed the skillet from the burner. "When did you start writing?"

Shiloh was shocked when Roan came over and pulled out the chair for her to sit on. That was right: He was old-fashioned. But her heart skittered with pleasure over his thoughtfulness. Now, he looked like a gallant knight to her, scarred, hardened by many battles, seeing too much and yet surviving.

"I started writing when I was six, believe it or not. My Dad used to have me read what I wrote to him. He always praised me and that's probably why I kept at it." She unfolded the white linen napkin and spread it across her lap. Everything looked so good on the table and she was salivating, hungry for the first time in a long time.

"Did you get published because of your father's work?" Roan wondered, spooning heaps of corn onto his plate.

"No. That doesn't happen in publishing," she said, taking the bowl from him. Their fingers met, warmth skating up into her hand. Shiloh watched as he lobbed tablespoons of butter onto the steaming corn. Did the man worry about cholesterol? Apparently not. Roan was in fit, athletic condition. It was usually those who were overweight, not getting exercise, and had a genetic predisposition, who had to worry, instead. "I published at eighteen, which is very young, really."

"Your father's publisher?"

"No, they weren't interested in women's romance. I went to another publisher who was."

"And did you mimic your father's success?" He saw pink come to her cheeks.

"Yes, I did. My first book was a runaway best-seller. Sure surprised me. Surprised the publisher, but believe me, we were both happy about it."

"And how many books have you got in print?" Roan watched the way her mouth moved as she chewed a small piece of the steak. It sent a pang of need through his lower body.

"I'm twenty-nine now, and I've been writing two books a year." Until the last six months. Shiloh's stomach tightened. She'd hit a dry spell. A writer's block. And she was too ashamed to confide it to Roan, even though he seemed sincerely interested in her career. Just having him sitting next to her, the breadth of his shoulders, that craggy profile, those glittering, intelligent gray eyes, excited her as no man ever had. A couple of recently dried strands of Roan's dark brown hair dipped over his furrowed brow. He ate heartily, the expression on his face one of a man enjoying everything he put into his mouth. Shiloh tried not to stare at his mouth.

Everything about him shouted to her that he was a man in charge. A leader. Not a follower.

"That's impressive. I couldn't write one book, much less two a year." Roan wasn't going to denigrate her writing romances. He could see she loved what she did. Following in her father's footsteps, but still being original and an individual. He finished off his steak in no time. The basket of biscuits went pretty quickly too. The type of hard, physical work he did daily, he tucked away a good five to ten thousand calories a day to make it happen.

"I think," Shiloh said, "it's in your genes. I hear the argument that writers are made or they're born with the skill. And I really feel at this point, it's an inner thing, a genetic ability. I know my father passed it on to me."

"But there are people who have no writers in a family and they get published."

"Right," Shiloh agreed, opening the warm biscuit, inhaling the odor of it and slathering it with butter. "I call it the storytelling gene. People who love to tell stories are frequently writers. And if they don't publish, then you often find them in many different careers, but they still like to tell a story." She looked over at him, her eyes warm. "Your face has a story to tell."

Mouth quirking, Roan growled, "It's a top-secret face, Darlin'."

Heat collected in her lower body as he rasped out the endearment between his lips, although Shiloh thought it was probably done with tongue in cheek. She found herself wishing the endearment had been said with affection. "We all carry secrets," Shiloh said. "There isn't a person on this earth who doesn't."

Nodding, Roan wiped his mouth with the napkin. "On that, we can agree." He rose and picked up the plates. "You going to eat your salad?"

"No. I'm stuffed. Thanks. Would you like me to wash the dishes? Help out in some way?"

"You can start carrying your share of the load around here tomorrow," he said, taking them to the sink.

He had a nice butt. Everything about Roan Taggart was sexy, Shiloh decided, defeated by her hungry body. His walk was so damned confident. The word *indomitable* came to mind. Shiloh couldn't imagine anyone standing in his way.

"Dessert?" he asked, turning toward her after he washed off the dishes and put them into the dishwasher.

"What do you have?"

He grinned sourly. Shiloh had perked up at the question and Roan bet she was probably a sweet eater. "I bought a coconut cream pie from the grocery store the other day. Interested?"

"Not right now. Maybe later?"

Shrugging, Roan brought the pie out of the fridge. "Do what you want."

Shiloh got up and made them coffee. "Would you like a cup, Roan?" She liked calling him by his first name. She saw a silver glint in his eyes when his name had rolled off her tongue. It sent her heart skittering. The look he gave her made her burn. Swallowing against a dry throat, Shiloh lowered her lashes. Roan Taggart wanted her. It was a raw, hungry look. Clasping her hands, she didn't feel threatened by him. Just . . . desired. How long had it been since she was honestly attracted to a man? *Years*. Too many of them.

"Pour me some, thanks." He took his plate of pie to the table. Whether Roan wanted to admit it or not, Shiloh was easy to be around. She wasn't a pest. She didn't get underfoot. She wasn't a nonstop talker, which drove him absolutely nuts. She listened. Asked intelligent questions. And she was a team player. Where she saw an opportunity to help out, she went for it. He thanked her as she set the steaming mug in front of him. Roan wasn't about to tell her she was dessert to him. It was a good thing Shiloh couldn't read minds.

Chapter Four

Roan snapped awake. It took a millisecond for him to key his hearing. Moonlight filtered weakly through the semi-opaque curtains pulled across both windows. His six senses were online and he quietly moved out of bed. He wore only a pair of dark blue cotton pajama bottoms, his upper body naked. Twisting the doorknob, he quietly opened the door. Slipping like a shadow into the darkened hall, he sensed someone moving around out in the kitchen. Shiloh? He glanced at the watch on his wrist. Three A.M.

Halting in the living room, he saw Shiloh in the kitchen, putting a copper teakettle on the stove. Her hair was unruly and she was wearing pale pink silky pajama bottoms and a pink cotton tee that outlined her breasts to perfection. *Hell.* She looked sleepy, hair tangled, and wasn't exactly graceful with her movements.

The realization that she could not really take care of herself came across strongly to Roan. It wasn't that Shiloh was weak or stupid. And maybe because of his black ops training, he was at the other end of the spectrum; too alert and having that situational awareness that could help save his life. She was obviously sleepy, rubbing her eyes, yawning. There wasn't anything to dislike about her and Roan's mouth flexed downward and thinned. Shiloh wasn't helpless, just not alert to her surroundings. Maybe he could help her open up her awareness a little more since she was being stalked. It could save her life someday.

"Shiloh?"

Shiloh gasped, whirling around. The cup she had in her hand dropped. It shattered on the floor around her feet. Her eyes widened enormously as she saw the darkened shadow of a man in the living room. A scream nearly lurched out of her mouth. Heart thudding like a freight train in her breast, she saw him emerge from the shadows. And then her lower body got in the mix. Roan Taggart was so damned male.

"Oh . . ." she whispered, "you scared me . . ." and she crouched down to begin picking up the bits of the broken ceramic cup.

Roan scowled and halted at the edge of the kitchen. He saw her hands shaking as she tried to pick up the pieces. One shard had already sliced her finger, red blood oozing out and dripping on the floor. "Stop," he ordered her.

Lifting her head, Shiloh felt the full impact of his protectiveness in that moment. Her finger smarted because she'd accidentally cut it. "What?"

"Don't move. And stop trying to pick up the pieces. Let me get a dustpan and broom. You're barefoot and if you move at all, you're going to cut the soles of your feet." Roan turned and walked to the closet on the other side of the door.

Gulping, her sleep torn from her, Shiloh watched the play of muscles in his long, broad back. The man was in incredible condition. When Roan turned around, her gaze absorbed his darkly haired chest, its powerful expanse. Mouth going dry, she followed that thin, dark line of hair down through his rock-hard abs until it disappeared into the waistline of his pajamas. Shiloh remained where she was, sticking her bleeding finger into her mouth. The metallic, salty taste made her wrinkle her nose. She watched as Roan quickly swept around her, placed the shards into the dustpan, and then transferred them to a large wastebasket at the end of the kitchen counter.

"Okay," he growled, "why don't you walk out of the kitchen? I need to look at your hand." Roan dumped the dustpan contents into a nearby trash can and put the items away. Turning, he saw Shiloh had gone over to the sink, running cold water and then soaping down the cut on her finger. She had a mind of her own. Not surprising. Smiling a little to himself, he ambled into the kitchen and moved close enough to where she was washing her hand to inspect the cut.

"Let me take a look at it," he said, and he held out his sun-darkened hand toward hers.

Shiloh felt the heat of Roan's powerful body. He was so close her nostrils automatically flared and she inhaled his male scent. Her heart was still tumbling wildly in her chest, adrenaline still surging through her. She turned off the faucet and placed her hand in his wide, callused palm. Roan had beautiful hands. His fingers were long and strong-looking. His nails were blunt cut and clean. Dark hair smattered across the back of it. The moment she made contact with his palm, shocking heat soared through her fingers. Her heart turned mushy as he gently held her hand and then, with his other one, took her index finger and looked at the deep cut across it.

"This is going to need a couple of stitches," he muttered, looking up, her face six inches from his. Roan wasn't prepared for the gold dappling in the forest green depths of her eyes. Her pupils, large and black, widened as he gently cradled her hand. Her skin was soft, telling him she didn't do hard work for a living. Her nails were short and she had a clear polish on them. Artistic, long fingers. As he tried to stop the vision of her fingers trailing down across his chest, Roan's mouth tightened. "What were you doing up?"

Shiloh saw the intense concentration in his gray eyes as he assessed the cut. It was deep and long. And it stung, still bleeding heavily. "I . . . ummm . . . had a nightmare," she said, and quickly glanced up expecting to see censure in his eyes. But there was none. Instead, his eyes became dove gray and she saw sympathy . . . maybe tenderness in them. Roan's hand closed a little more around her hand. It felt so good, so stabilizing. Shiloh felt safe for the first time in a long time. He was so massive against her, all sleek, powerful muscles, a male animal at its finest, her wild imagination told her. She felt his strength, wanting to reach out and slide her fingers through that dusting of black hair across his chest. Her body ached. The man was sensual as hell. She pulled her hand out of his, afraid of herself, not him.

Roan took a step back. He pulled some tissues from a nearby box and wrapped her bleeding finger with them. "And I scared the hell out of you by not announcing myself. That's why you dropped the cup."

He missed nothing. Shiloh wasn't sure she was relieved or alarmed by his intelligence and swiftly cobbling the situation together. Maybe because Roan had been black ops he was used to sizing up a situation and then distilling it into a neat little nutshell. His life probably had depended upon this skill. "Yes, you scared the living bejesus out of me." She saw a faint curve at one corner of his mouth, his eyes now a darker gray, like a storm was coming, maybe.

"It won't happen again," Roan promised her in a low tone. "Keep pressure on that finger and go sit on the couch. I'll fetch the first aid box."

Shiloh nodded and followed him out of the kitchen. She took one corner of the couch, resting her injured hand in her lap. In moments, Roan was back. Silent. Like a shadowy ghost. He turned on the overhead light, and she winced, covering her eyes for a moment.

Roan had to sit close. He had gone to his bedroom and found a black T-shirt and pulled it over his head. He was unsure of the look Shiloh was giving him; she seemed afraid of his bulk and size. But maybe it was just the fact she was still high on that adrenaline charge that had shot into her bloodstream when he scared her. Feeling bad, Roan pulled out everything he'd need from the medical kit and put on a pair of latex gloves.

"You ever been stitched up before?" he asked. His knee was against her knee and he gently guided her hand to his hard, curved thigh.

"No."

"Not many places for a kid to get scraped or injured in New York City, huh?" he teased, threading the needle. Roan looked up and saw her watching him with wide green eyes. Her hair was lusciously mussed and he found he wanted to tunnel his fingers through that mass and feel how strong and silky he knew it would be.

She heard a bit of amusement in his voice. "No . . . not many. Is this going to hurt?" she asked, and tucked her lower lip between her teeth, her brows lowering. She saw his chiseled mouth quirk.

"Yeah, it will. But I'll put a pain deadener around where I have to stitch and that will help you a lot."

"Well, at least you didn't lie to me."

Roan chuckled a little, taking off the bloody tissue and setting it aside. "Honesty puts everyone on a level playing field." He looked up and drowned in her worried expression. "Do you faint from the sight of blood?"

"I . . . don't know."

"From pain?"

"I don't think so . . ." He held her hand in his, cradling it, and Shiloh could feel his latent strength as his fingers curved comfortingly around hers. He gave her several shots of lidocaine around the cut to numb the area it so it wouldn't cause her ongoing pain and stress.

"Why don't you sit back, close your eyes, and not watch?" he suggested drily.

"That's a good idea," Shiloh admitted, a little breathless. The heat of his hand was incredible! She felt little electric shocks moving up her hand and into her wrist. Leaning against the couch, she tried to take a deep breath and relax. But how could she relax with Roan this close? Literally, she could smell the warmth of his flesh, the sage scent of the soap he'd used to shower with.

Roan carefully put the first of the needed three stitches into the deep cut. Every time he had to put the needle into her flesh, Shiloh flinched.

"Hurt?"

"No. I just feel the pressure of the needle, is all."

She didn't move her hand. She had given him her trust. Roan found himself respecting her courage. Shiloh had tucked her lower lip between her teeth, worrying it. Wanting to distract her, he asked, "What are you doing this morning? Going to write on your latest book?"

"Uhh, no . . . I have writer's block. I talked to Maud about it and she said I should follow you around and learn to be a cowgirl, instead. She said my block would disappear if I got my mind off it for a while."

"Maud is a wise woman," Roan agreed quietly, going for the second stitch. "You're doing fine, Shiloh."

His rumbling praise went through her like hot sunlight, warming her core, making her ache even more for him.

Roan's head was bent, dark brows drawn downward in concentration, his hand steady and obviously having stitched someone up before. "Thanks . . . you probably think I'm a big weenie." She saw his mouth hook into a faint grin. His entire demeanor changed in that moment. Gone was the hardness. Instead, she saw the man beneath that mask he wore like a good friend. And he was breathtaking to her.

"Never a weenie. You're doing fine."

"Thanks . . ."

"You said you had writer's block?"

Cringing, Shiloh groaned. "Yes. Not that I like admitting it. It's embarrassing."

"Caused by the fact you've been stalked for six months straight?" he asked, and he looked up for a moment, holding her humiliated stare. Her eyes went wide with surprise, probably because he got the crux of the reason for the block.

"Why . . . yes . . . how did you know?"

Shrugging, Roan saw he could easily distract her. She didn't wince or take in a ragged breath as he closed the cut with the third stitch. "Maud had told me about the situation before you arrived," he told her, quickly tying a knot. Placing the needle and thread aside, he drenched the stitches with antiseptic and then carefully placed a waterproof bandage around his handiwork.

"Somehow," Shiloh murmured, "I don't think you guess about much at all." She saw his eyes glimmer for a moment before he finished up with her finger. She saw amusement come to his gaze. He was a man of few words.

"There. How does it feel now?" he asked, releasing her hand. Roan didn't want to. Instead, he had a vision of tugging her hand gently toward him and then levering her breasts against his chest, angling her chin and dropping a hot, searching kiss on those mobile lips of hers.

Turning her hand that still vibrated with heat from his touch, she said softly, "Much better. Thank you," and she looked up at him as he soundlessly rose, the medical kit in his hand. "How did you—"

"Special Forces operators are trained for all kinds of things," he told her. Turning, he walked out of the living room and disappeared down the hall.

Sitting there, Shiloh felt as if the sun had left the room. Did Roan Taggart realize how larger than life he was? The man filled the room with his quiet, intense presence. Was that because of his black ops background, too? She'd run into a lot of people in New York City, but never anyone like him. His presence soothed her, calmed her, and made her feel protected when she hadn't felt safe in six months. Moving her hand, Shiloh had no pain from the injury. She felt him appear and looked up. He was heading to the kitchen.

"Were you making yourself something to eat?" he asked over his shoulder. Reaching up into the cupboard, Roan brought down two cups.

"Yes," she admitted, standing up. "When I get this nightmare, I need to drink a cup of milk so I make myself some hot chocolate. That way, I'll go back to sleep."

"Take a seat at the table," he directed. "I'll make us some."

"But you said I needed to take care of myself while I'm here. I could make—"

Roan gave her a dark look. "It wasn't written in stone, Shiloh. Relax and have a seat."

Frowning, she took the chair at the other end of the table where she could watch him. Did Roan know how delicious he was to watch? The sleek, graceful movements of his body? She watched the ropy play of muscles in his forearms as he brought the chocolate out of the cupboard, lined up the sugar bowl, a salt shaker and located marshmallows. Going to the fridge, he pulled out a carton of milk. Even after he pulled on that T-shirt, she could see every detail of his magnificent chest and abs. He was in such great shape.

"Do you work out in a gym?" she wondered.

"Yes, it's called being a wrangler," he answered, and Roan hitched up one eyebrow and glanced with amusement at Shiloh. Her face was partly shadowed because the only light on in the kitchen was over the stove. She looked so earnest. Serious. And when she moved her fingers through her hair, trying to tame those stubborn strands, Roan felt his heart stir. God knew, he had put a steel clamp over his desire for her as he stitched up her finger. The shadows caressed and emphasized her breasts and he saw the nipples standing out, pushing against the fabric, as if begging to be touched. Roan didn't see any arousal in Shiloh's eyes. Just tiredness and a type of lingering exhaustion that came from long-term stress. The stalker was making her pay in so many ways and he found himself getting angry, wishing he could find the son of a bitch.

"You'd put the guys in Manhattan to shame," she told him.

"Oh, the gym routine?" Roan asked, and chuckled a little, pouring the milk into a pan and turning on the gas stove.

"Yes."

"Do you work out, Shiloh?"

"Sort of . . . I jog in Central Park every day that I can. Just . . . well . . . lately, the last few months, I haven't. I can't just sit and create all day long. I'm restless by nature. Usually, I get up about every twenty minutes from what I'm writing and go do something else."

"Because you were worried about the stalker? Is that why you haven't jogged?"

Grimly, Shiloh nodded. "Yes. And believe me, it was killing me in another way. I have to get up and move around."

Roan put the chocolate, sugar, and a bit of salt into the saucepan, and stirred the contents. "I couldn't sit more than ten minutes if you asked me to. Not in my DNA."

"Is that a good thing if you're black ops?" Shiloh wondered. Roan was a tall man, his shoulders pulled back with unconscious pride, confidence radiating from around him like a galaxy. There simply was no hint of weakness anywhere in Roan. She liked his droll sense of humor, too. And she waited, almost breathless, to see him smile. Oh, he never really smiled, just that one corner of his mouth hooking upward sometimes. Shiloh felt like she was some kind of amusing little toy barging into his masculine world. He didn't laugh at her, however. She just felt like she was so different from him. Like two aliens from two different planets getting together for the first time to learn about each other.

"I don't know many operators who aren't wanting to be on the move. We're a restless lot by nature."

Rubbing her face, Shiloh began to feel less tense. Just talking to Roan, listening to his low, husky voice, was a balm to her frayed nervous system. "Would you mind if I accompanied you tomorrow? Maud said I could. I don't want to stay here in this house alone. At least . . . not yet . . ."

Shrugging, Roan said, "Sure, no problem." He poured the heated mixture into the two cups, added marshmallows, and brought them over to the table. He slid one cup toward her awaiting hand. He sat down at her left elbow. His legs were so long that he accidentally brushed her left knee. Moving the chair back a little because he saw the reaction in her face, Roan knew that his hoping she'd be a little drawn to him was wishful thinking. And he purposely kept his gaze above her breasts because those nipples were standing strong, begging to be touched, suckled. Shiloh had given him no hint that what he felt toward her was about to be reciprocated. "Drink up," he told her.

"Mmmm, this is good," Shiloh murmured, giving him a warm look of thanks. "You really are handy in the kitchen." She saw Roan's eyes change, a glint in them. She wasn't sure what it meant, but the feeling radiating from him was like a velvet embrace around her shoulders. What would it be like to slide her fingers down that hard-muscled fore-arm, sun darkened, dusted with dark hair? Something cautioned Shiloh not to try to find out. There was intense sexuality oozing out of his pores. She could practically feel it. And worst of all, her nipples were puckered. Groaning inwardly, Shiloh didn't want to try to move the material be-cause it would only draw his attention to them. *Geez Louise.* What was wrong with her body? It suddenly had a mind of its own! At least around Roan, it did.

There was nothing she could do. If she tried to put her arms across her chest to hide them, then she couldn't drink the hot chocolate. Her breasts tightened with just the thought of Roan's callused fingers grazing her nipples. What must it feel like? Her mind had gone off the deep end for sure. Shiloh never looked at men in sexual terms. And that's *all* she could see in Roan when he was near her. Shiloh was convinced the stress of the last six months had finally caught up with her and she was having some kind of lusting meltdown.

"I'm going to be riding out to the Pine Grove area to-morrow," he told her. Roan could see the sudden realiza-tion and awareness in her face about her nipples pressing proudly against the material she wore. A pink flush had crept up her throat and into her face. The sudden skittering of her eyes said it all. She had a momentary panicked look in them and then quickly looked away from him.

Roan made sure he didn't look down at her breasts, having no wish to make Shiloh any more stressed or uncomfortable than she already was. He laughed at himself because in the past, in Special Forces, he could have any woman he wanted when stateside. Didn't take much to get one, either. They always hung around well-known Team clubs off base. For some, it was a notch in their gun belt when they bedded down a vaunted sergeant out of the A-teams.

"I don't know how to ride a horse," Shiloh confessed, giving Roan a concerned look.

"No worries. We'll find you a nice, quiet mount and I'll walk you through everything." He saw instant relief on her face. Roan decided Shiloh was incapable of hiding her feelings. "How often do you get these nightmares?"

Squirming, Shiloh admitted haltingly, "A couple of times a week. Sometimes more, if I get faxes from him."

Nodding, Roan saw the terror banked deeply in her green eyes, wishing he could remove it. "What are the nightmares about?"

Rubbing her brow, Shiloh felt fear snaking through her. "Just . . . a shadowy man's form moving from one building to another, coming after me."

"Do you see a face?" No wonder she screamed and dropped the mug when she saw him in the shadows of the living room. *Damn.* Roan felt bad now.

Shaking her head, she muttered, "No, but I wish I did. I wish I knew who this bastard was. He's taken my life away from me, Roan. I can't explain it, but I'm so fearful now." Giving him a misery-laden look she admitted, "Like right now? I happened to catch your shadowy figure in the living room and it just punched every fear button I own. I'm really sorry. It wasn't you. It's my damned imagination, I guess."

"I'm glad you can separate me out from your stalker," he teased, trying to make her feel better. Roan would have liked to put his fist through the man's face. "Look," he said, "this guy is gutless. He can't face you."

"I would never associate you with a stalker, Roan," she said, giving him a frown. "I'd give ANYTHING to know who he is. No one in law enforcement will believe me. They think I'm making this up to get newspaper and Net publicity." She snorted. "That is so crass! I would NEVER do anything like that! Any publicity I've ever received, I've earned the hard way by writing a darned good book."

Hearing the fierce passion in her words, seeing it in the defiant look in her eyes, Roan nodded. "So the FBI or local law enforcement aren't trying to follow down the phone used for those faxes?"

"Correct." She rested her chin in the palm of her hand, feeling the frustration. "I mean, the only way they're going to believe me is when they find me dead in my apartment someday. Then it will be too late."

Just the thought of Shiloh dead made his heart feel as if a fist had suddenly squeezed it. "Do you have any idea who it might be? A pissed-off male fan?"

Shrugging, Shiloh sighed. "I don't know. I've gone through my e-mail correspondence with my readers and I can't find anything to suggest something like this."

"You do have male readers, don't you?"

"I do. Not many, though, mostly women."

"If it were a man, Shiloh, why would he want to do this to you?"

Rolling her eyes, she muttered, "I don't know. Maybe my love scenes? In a romance there's always love scenes. I'm known for hot scenes. Not erotic, but hot."

Roan tried to keep focused on the discussion, and not forming fantasies of love scenes and erotic images of her in his bed. His senses told him she'd be damned sensitive, hot, and a little wild in bed. He'd bet money on it. But this wasn't the time to go there. He saw the hurt in her eyes, the worry. Her lips were thinned. "So, do all authors get some men who are like that? They get turned on by the love scenes and then start stalking you? Unable to separate reality from fiction?"

"I don't think it happens often. But it's happening to me," she mumbled, shaking her head. "That's sick, Roan. I'm writing a novel. I'm not the heroine in that novel."

"There's some people who can't separate out reality from fantasy," he told her quietly. "They're mentally ill."

"That's also what I think is going on but I can't prove it."

"He's a sexual predator." The thought turned Roan's stomach. Shiloh was a beautiful, sensitive soul, completely unable to defend herself against someone like that. He felt every protective cell in his body stand at attention. There was no way in hell anyone was going to touch or hurt her. No one.

"I hope I'm wrong," Shiloh admitted quietly. "I hope he's gone by the time I get back to New York. Forgotten me."

Grimly, Roan didn't think that was the way it worked with a sick son of a bitch like that. "Look, maybe there's room to investigate this in other ways. You need to first get caught up on a lot of lost sleep. Then, some fresh air, sunshine, and working yourself physically will help too." He saw a grin come to her lips, her eyes starting to sparkle.

"Now you sound just like Maud. Get on a horse! Roll up your shirtsleeves! Wear a pair of leather gloves and cowboy boots! Go to work." She laughed a little. "Did you two conspire?"

Her laughter was like a creek singing to him. It was low and smoky. His flesh riffled with possibilities. Roan tamped down his reaction. She was running scared from a sexual predator. And what was he? One in disguise? Wanting her?

But he would never stalk Shiloh. If there was some kind of connection, Roan would know it. And he had no problem in asking Shiloh to her face if she'd like to go to bed with him. Roan had rarely been turned down, but he was more than willing to risk it because, whether he wanted to admit it or not, Shiloh made him run hot and he wanted to capture that smile of hers for himself.

Chapter Five

Roan watched Shiloh's reaction to the black-and-white paint horse named Charley, a fifteen-year-old gelding. She approached his box stall in the large barn the next morning. Charley was generally used at the dude ranch portion of the Wind River Ranch and was a children's horse. Maud decided Charley was a good fit for Shiloh.

The air was chilly at nine A.M.; most of the dude families who were in for the week were over at the chow hall. Roan had dropped in to see Maud, who was out in her machine shop. She was an ace at welding, fixing small engines and making spare parts to fit some of their aging farm equipment. He'd best let her know that Shiloh was going to be with him for the day. Otherwise, he'd be missing in action. Maud had glowed and smiled, giving her nod of approval.

Roan wasn't sure he liked the twinkle in her large green eyes. The rancher was wise and crafty, to say the least. She had broadly hinted from time to time that he should think about settling down, having a family. *Right*. And those weren't just idle words coming from his boss. No, Maud Whitcomb was a master chess player on the board of life. She'd even provocatively dangled the one thing he'd wanted the most since leaving the Army: to build a cabin he could call is own. After the first year, she'd gifted him with five acres of land on the other side of Pine Grove, on Wind River Ranch property.

Maud provided the logging package that would help make his home, a cedar log cabin, a reality. Roan spent every waking minute out at his small spread when he wasn't wrangling for the Wind River Ranch. The cabin was coming along after a year of his hard work and he was pleased with the progress he'd made. Roan wasn't one to stand idle for too long, anyway. The need to be outside in the elements, to battle them and win, was overriding. He'd gotten the shell of the cabin up, roofed with cedar shake shingles, and now, this coming season, he could start building the inner guts of the house, the plumbing and electricity; all of which he had knowledge of. Being a Special Forces A-team member, he'd become skilled at many other areas of life.

Shiloh twisted a look over her shoulder as she stood at the bars over the stall door, staring in at Charley, who was finishing his hay for the morning. "He looks awful big," she said, worrying her lower lip. Charley's big brown eyes studied her as he calmly munched his hay, his small, fine ears flicking back and forth. Roan came to a halt at her side. He towered over her, but it made her feel safe.

"Actually," Roan drawled, pulling on his leather gloves, "Charley is pretty small. He's only fourteen hands high. Taller than a pony but nowhere near the height of the other working horses here at the ranch. Most of them are fifteen and sixteen hands tall."

"Oh." Shiloh studied the horse. He had a long black-and-white mane, his forelock fuzzy and thick between his ears and draping down across his broad forehead. "Is he . . . friendly?"

"You mean, is he ornery?" Roan placed his hand beneath her elbow, wanting to touch Shiloh. Any excuse would do.

He pulled her gently to one side and then released her. Picking up a red nylon halter with a lead rope attached to it, he said, "Charley's an old man. He's been around and he knows the drill. He has one speed: slow," and Roan grinned, sliding open the box stall door. "Now, watch what I do, Shiloh, because from now on, you'll be doing it instead."

Standing to the side, she watched as Roan murmured hello to Charley, patted him in a friendly manner on the neck, and then slid the halter over his nose, buckling it on top of his head. Roan turned.

"Got that?"

Nodding, Shiloh said, "I think so."

Roan saw the trepidation in her eyes. "Okay," he murmured, and after unbuckling the halter and sliding it off Charley, he handed it to her and said, "Your turn."

Gulping, Shiloh watched Roan step aside. She stepped into the thick cedar shavings on the floor of the stall. The sweet smell of alfalfa made her inhale more deeply.

"Always slide the door shut before you do anything," Roan advised, angling his chin in that direction. "A horse will escape. And then, you'll have to hunt him down and find him. Not what you want to do."

"Right," Shiloh said, gripping the halter in her hand. Turning, she slid the door shut. Anxiety shot through her as she approached the munching horse. Roan reached out, hand on her elbow, guiding her to one side of Charley.

"You never approach a horse head-on, Shiloh. See how their eyes are set? On the sides of their head? They can't see you if you walk up directly in front of them. You want your horse to see you coming so you don't spook him. Always quietly approach them at an angle." His mouth twisted in a slight grin. "If a horse is spooked, he usually leaps straight ahead. And you can get hit and run over. Another reason to always approach from an angle. Okay?" He forced himself to release her elbow as she stood close to him. Shiloh had tamed her red hair into a ponytail. Roan had suggested she wear Levi's, her cowboy boots, a tee, and a blue chambray long-sleeved shirt over it. Later on in the morning, it would turn warm. And in the afternoon, it would get hot. Layers were always a good thing.

"Okay," Shiloh said, hesitantly reaching out to pet Charley's sleek, gleaming neck. He was a beautiful horse, really. Just—big.

Charley snorted. She jumped. Scared.

"It's okay," Roan reassured her, touching her shoulder, seeing the fear come to her eyes. "Horses are always clearing their noses. That's normal."

"I thought—I thought he was going to bite me," she said, and she cast a look up into Roan's features. The man's face was iconic. Someone who had weathered many things in his life other than just the storms and challenges he must have endured as an operator. His mouth teased her. It was a wide mouth, well shaped and strong. Gulping again, nervous, Shiloh fingered the halter and rope.

"Nah, Charley isn't a biter." He kept his hand on her shoulder and gently gave her a nudge forward. "Go put the halter on him. He isn't going to do anything but eat."

Shiloh gave the horse a look. "Just stand there, Charley. Don't run over me," she said, and she leaned down, pulling the halter over the horse's nose. With trembling fingers, she finally got the halter buckled. Feeling relief, she stepped back with the nylon lead rope in her hand.

"Well done," Roan praised. He saw instant relief in her eyes. Roan wanted her to learn her way around the horse, but didn't want to stress her out so much that she'd never want to go near one again.

His low, deep voice vibrated through Shiloh, making her feel an intimacy with Roan that hadn't been there before. Warmth moved through her heart. A building heat bloomed in her lower body. The man was so damned sensual, it constantly rocked and engaged all her senses. And equally, she lapped up his sparse praise, desperately needing to feel all right and that she wasn't being a pain in the ass to him. Roan looked pleased, one corner of his mouth hooking upward, a warm gleam in his eyes as he met hers. Automatically, her breasts tightened beneath her tee and even though she wore a bra, she could feel her nipples tightening. Shiloh had no experience with what was happening between them. The sweet scent of alfalfa hay mixed with the fragrance of the cedar shavings in the stall. Charley snorted again. This time, she didn't jump. Roan's half smile deepened, silent praise that made her feel halfway confident about her learning to ride a horse.

"Okay, in the future, we feed our horses early so that by nine A.M., they're ready to be taken out of the stall, put in the cross ties, brushed, and cleaned up. Then, we saddle up and start the day's work." Roan pointed to the alfalfa hay that was nearly gone. Charley was eating it with relish. "He'll be done in about ten minutes. Come with me and I'll show you where the tack room is located."

Shiloh slid Charley's stall door shut, locked it as Roan instructed, and then followed him down the wide, airy concrete walkway. She loved seeing the way he walked; boneless, confident, and yet, she could feel a fine tension running through him. She wondered why, following him as he opened the tack door and walked in.

Roan showed her where the switch was.

Shiloh looked around the huge tack room. It smelled of leather, Neatsfoot oil, leather soap, and she inhaled it deeply. Roan was watching her obliquely. "It smells so good in here!" she whispered, her eyes widening as she drank in the saddles, bridles, martingales, cinches, brushes, and other tools that hung on hooks on the dark umber wooden walls.

"One of the best smells in the world," Roan agreed

quietly, resting his hands on his hips. He didn't want to be affected by Shiloh's almost childlike reaction to the tack room. This was a place he always enjoyed being in, cleaning up the saddles and bridles with a soft cloth and leather soap. He could see the awe and the pleasure shining in her eyes as she walked to the saddle wall, touching some of them lightly, almost reverently. The tension she normally carried in her face melted away. Maybe Maud was right after all: Shiloh needed to immerse herself into being a Westerner, get involved in riding, caring for her horse, being responsible, and she would let the stalker and New York City dissolve away. It was a good distraction for her but Roan worried about when she left and returned to her home. The stalker would still be there. He didn't have the heart to tell her that. At least, not yet.

"Every saddle is used by a specific horse," he told her, motioning to the plastic nameplates above each one. "Charley's is there on your left, in the center. See it?"

Shiloh quickly spotted it because his name was carved in wood just above the gear. She saw the saddle and it was padded on the seat, sewn in a diamond-like pattern. "This looks comfortable," she said, smiling over at him. She saw him nod and push the brim of his Stetson up a bit on his brow. Roan was so pulverizingly male, it kept her feeling like her lower body was constantly on simmer. Wanting him, Shiloh had no idea if he had a girlfriend or was in a serious relationship with another woman. He was just too drop-dead gorgeous to be available.

"It's a comfortable saddle to ride." Walking over, Roan showed her the bridle above the saddle. "This is Charley's bridle," he said, and he pulled it off the hook, settling it into her open hand. "Every horse has a bit in its mouth and that's the way we control the animal." He tapped the clean silver bit. "Charley has what we call a soft mouth and this is called a snaffle bit. His mouth is sensitive and he responds quickly if you pull on his reins." He took the bridle, slid it up her arm, and settled it across her shoulder. "This is how we carry the bridle. Slide your arms through either end of the saddle and lift it off its resting place. It weighs about twenty pounds."

Shiloh was surprised at the weight as she did as he instructed.

"Good," Roan murmured. "Now, follow me."

Walking out into the barn once more, Roan showed her where to put the saddle and bridle near the cross ties. She felt good, being able to heft the heavy leather saddle around by herself. Maybe she wasn't as much of a weakling as she first thought. Her confidence began to blossom. She followed Roan to Charley's stall. He stepped aside.

"Okay, so go in and get Charley. He's cleaned up his hay," he said, and the floor was clean.

Feeling proud of herself, she led Charley out of the stall on the nylon lead. Roan came up to her, settling his hands on her shoulders.

"Never walk in front of a horse, Shiloh." He eased her off to one side of Charley. "Remember? He can't see you because his eyes are on the sides of his head?"

"Darn," she murmured, apologetic. "You're right."

"If he got spooked, he'd lunge forward to run away from whatever scared him. You'd get run over in the process." Roan forced himself to release her shoulders. Even though he wore leather gloves, he could feel the softness of her skin beneath the blouse she wore. "By being on either the right or left side of him, he can see you. If something scares him, he'll leap away from you. A horse will never run over a human if they can help it."

"That's good to know," Shiloh said wryly, grinning.

Roan took her hand, placing it just below the snap on the halter and lead rope. "Always walk your horse like this. That way, you have a grip and control on his head. The horse can't move away from you as long as you manage where you want his head. Take Charley down to the ties," he said, and he pointed down the walkway.

Nodding, Shiloh tugged on the lead rope. Charley came, walking quietly at her side. She smiled proudly, feeling happy and pleased with herself. Roan walked on the other side of Charley, his unforgiving profile making her once more want to explore and kiss that strong mouth of his.

Roan showed her how to place the panic snaps on each side of Charley's halter as he stood quietly between them in the middle of the breezeway. "Panic snaps are just that," Roan told her, showing her how to open it at an instant's notice. "Sometimes a horse will get spooked while in ties and they can twist turn and end up choking themselves to death on one of these cross ties." He ran his gloved hand down the length of sturdy nylon rope. "All you need to do is pull this lever down and it immediately opens the snaps and stops the horse from killing itself while in panic mode."

She grinned. "I should have a set of these for my life."

Roan's mouth stretched. "I think everyone should have a set." She was a feisty filly and he felt his heart opening more toward her. Yes, she was a city slicker, no doubt, but she had moxie and she wasn't afraid to try new things. Two things he liked to see in a woman he was interested in. Roan tried to push away his desire for Shiloh. Tendrils of red hair softly caressed her flushed cheeks and he wanted to fall helplessly into her shining forest-green eyes. When his gaze dropped to her curved lips, everything in his lower body went on red alert. Groaning inwardly, he felt his erection stir. *Not good.* It would be hell to ride with later, so he placed steel control over his body. Their laughter echoed around the area. It felt damn good to laugh. Roan didn't do it often, but the warm fuzzies in his chest just kept opening up and making him feel a sharpened, edgy hunger for Shiloh.

Snapping it closed, he said, "Let's mosey back to the tack room." This time, Shiloh walked in front of him and that was a mistake. The sweet sway of her hips, those long legs of hers, made him groan internally. Already, visions of having her naked, lying in his bed on her back, and him running his fingers down her rib cage, enclosing those hips, opening her thighs, hit him broadside. Giving a shake of his head, Roan felt like he'd been poleaxed. What was it about sweet, shy Shiloh that called to him like a mermaid siren? Roan grimly reminded himself those mermaids sang sailors to their deaths, too.

In the tack room, Roan guided her over to several wooden toolboxes sitting on the shelf on another wall. "This is your horse-grooming kit," he told her, lifting one and placing it into her hand. "We groom our horses before we saddle them. We need to get the dirt, dust, and sweat off their skin where we're putting the saddle blanket and saddle. If a horse isn't cleaned up, sores can result."

Shiloh nodded and Roan showed her where to put the toolbox out of the way so the horse wouldn't get tripped up into it. When he chose a currycomb, he set it into her hand, showing her how to hold it. His fingers were strong and her flesh leaped as he gently curved her fingers around the wooden handle.

"Now, a curry is used only for the meaty parts of the horse," he told her. "You'd never run these sharp teeth down a horse's legs. It would hurt him." He positioned Shiloh on one side of Charley, putting her left hand on his rump, and then wrapped his hand around hers to show her how to use the currycomb.

Shiloh's mouth went dry. Roan was standing right behind her, maybe an inch or two between them. She could feel his male heat, his scent in her nostrils, her hand tingling wildly as he showed her the way to curve the curry in order to clean the horse, but not hurting his thin skin. Next came a lesson with a stiff brush that would take all the dead skin, mud, or dust loosened by the curry off the horse. Lastly, he showed her how to use the soft dandy brush as a final cleansing of the horse and his legs.

Her heart was pounding in her chest and it wasn't from fear. She felt herself going achy as she worked in tandem with Roan as he showed her the ropes of grooming the horse. By the time they were done, she felt dampness between her thighs. A quiver moved through her and Shiloh was never more aware than in this heated moment how sexually starved she really was. Roan just turned on every sexual button she had. And yet, he didn't seem to be attracted to her, his words and movements brisk and to the point. There was no teasing in his eyes, no suggestive movement of his body toward hers. It was all business from Roan's end and she swallowed hard, wishing it was otherwise.

Next came learning how to saddle a horse. That was more complex. Roan showed her and then she emulated him. Only, she didn't sit the saddle on Charley's withers where it should have gone the first time. More than once, she felt Roan's patience with her. She was worried he'd be in a rush, frustrated with her mistakes, but he didn't seem to be.

"Okay," Roan said, congratulating her, "you're now ready to throw a leg over your horse once you get him out of the cross ties and into the barnyard." He pointed in that direction. Settling his hat on his head, he watched as she removed the panic snaps from the horse's halter and sedately led him down the concrete passageway and outside. Shiloh didn't have a cowboy hat; she wore a dark green baseball cap instead. Roan untied his big quarter horse gelding and walked over to where she stood with Charley.

He dropped the horse's reins, being ground-tied trained. "Here's how you mount your horse," Roan said, and slid the toe of his boot into the left-hand stirrup and straightened, throwing his long, powerful leg up and across Charley's back. Roan found Shiloh was very good at show-and-tell. She picked it up immediately. And Roan wasn't disappointed as she copied him, sliding that nice-looking rear of hers into that saddle.

Roan positioned each of her feet into the stirrups, showed her how to clamp her thighs against the saddle, keep her toes up, heels down. And then he showed her how to guide Charley with the reins. Touching Shiloh was the best part of this educational process with her. He noticed that when he did touch her, her cheeks would flush. There was something living and organic happening between them and as much as he tried not to respond to it, certainly not let Shiloh know about his reactions, Roan damn well wanted this woman in his bed. Where she belonged.

"Okay, we're good to go for a ride," he told her, quickly mounting Diamond, his blood bay quarter horse gelding. Gesturing toward the pine grove that stood two miles away and to the east of the ranch, he said, "Cluck with your tongue and Charley will move forward."

To her surprise, the old paint did just that. The movement felt good. Shiloh laughed a little. "It feels like I'm in a rocking chair!"

His body responded to her infectious, low laugh, the sparkle that came to her eyes that held surprise over her discovery. The expression on her face was of an excited child off on some fantastic adventure. It warmed Roan's heart to see that kind of reaction in a grown woman. Shiloh might be a hard-working writer, responsible, meeting deadlines, organized and disciplined, but she could drop that demeanor when given the opportunity and revert to being a kid. That made him smile, but he covered it by grazing his jaw with his leather glove.

"For now it will feel good," he agreed. "But an hour in

the saddle is going to test you in all kinds of ways." She wouldn't be able to walk straight, after her thighs had stretched wide across Charley's broad back. Shiloh would be stiff and sore for days to come but if she rode every day, her muscles would adapt, stretch, and no longer bother her. She'd have a pair of riding legs then. Roan would like to get his hands on her legs. With a muffled curse she couldn't hear, Roan grimly thinned his lips, unhappy with his libido that had a brain of its own.

The warmth of the sunlight embraced Shiloh and she rode close to where Roan rode, their feet occasionally brushing up against each other. He rode tall and proud, his broad shoulders thrown back with confidence. Every inch a tough, rugged cowboy, it inspired Shiloh's active imagination. Maybe she should write about cowboys next? They were iconic. The Wild West. Hardy. Independent. Unsmiling. She looked around at the activity now going on. A string of families on horseback were going in another direction, riding between several large pastures. She saw a herd of brown and white Herefords on the other side. The breeze was soft, grazing her cheeks, and she inhaled deeply, smelling the lush grass and the clumps of pine trees here and there. The gentle sway of Charley between her legs seemed perfect. She was warm, lulled almost into a semi-meditative state, and she had one of the most handsome men in the world right next to her!

Soon, they left the busy center of the Wind River Ranch behind and were on a wide, well-beaten trail leading toward a thick grove of pine trees that looked as if it stretched about half a mile in length and width out in the middle of flat, grassy floor. Everywhere she looked green pastures covered the land. It looked to her like combed strands of hair, only it was thick grass instead. Shiloh appreciated the grove as they drew near. The pine trees reminded her of pincushions, sticking up from the slight knoll where they grew. She couldn't see the screeching blue jays hidden among the pines. There were two trails ahead. One led down toward the middle of the grove, the other went around to the end of it and disappeared.

"See that red-tailed hawk sailing above us?" Roan asked, pointing upward.

Looking up, glad she had sunglasses on, Shiloh saw a hawk flying about a thousand feet above them in lazy circles. "He has a red tail?"

"Yes. He and his mate live on the edge of the grove. When we ride around it, I'll point it out. They have a big nest made of wooden sticks up in the tallest, oldest pine."

"So beautiful," Shiloh sighed, turning and giving him a wispy look. "The sky is so wide and large out here. It's nothing like New York City."

"You can't see the sky for all the skyscrapers," he snorted.

Laughing, she nodded. "I just love how big and bold this country is," she said, and she turned in the saddle, looking around, appreciating the greenness of the pastures, the content animals eating and the powder-blue sky surrounding them from above.

Roan was beginning to see Shiloh honestly relax. Maybe for the first time in a long time. The sun glinted in her red hair, burgundy and gold threads among the strands. He found himself wanting to pull that thick, slightly curly hair out of the clip she wore to keep it gathered up. What would the strands feel like running through his exploring fingers? How would Shiloh respond as he kissed her lips? Her mouth was driving him to distraction. His erection stirred. *Not now.* Not in a saddle. He'd be in constant agony, firmly willing himself not to respond.

"This is . . ." she sighed, tipping her head toward him, meeting his dark eyes, ". . . wonderful, Roan. Thank you so much for putting up with me this morning. I'm sure you don't want to be teaching a city slicker how to ride a horse."

"Don't worry about it, Shiloh." Her name slid off his tongue like hot honey. He was in so much damned trouble. Roan could see the transfixed look in her green eyes; she was overwhelmed and mesmerized by all the ongoing beauty surrounding her. He understood Shiloh's awe and appreciation. "There isn't a day that goes by that I don't feel like you do. It's beautiful country."

You are beautiful. The words almost escaped his mouth. Fuming with himself, Roan wondered why in the hell he couldn't remain immune to Shiloh. The way the breeze picked up strands at her temples, the glint of gold and red in them, emphasizing her large, intelligent eyes, all conspired to make him harder, not softer. *Dammit.*

"I just never realized how *big* the West was," she admitted. "I feel like I've missed something really important." She rested her hand holding the reins on the saddle horn, loving the soft sway of Charley. It was like getting rocked by her mother when she was a child; a wonderful, maternal, and nurturing feeling that always had made Shiloh feel not only loved, but safe.

"Do you think you'll write about your experiences out here?"

She smiled a little. "I was thinking about it. I mean"— she gestured her hand toward the sky—"this place is *so* inspiring! It's untamed, beautiful and wild nature. I just feel like I'm bubbling over inside with joy," she said. "It does something good to me. . . ." and her voice trailed off. Shiloh held his interested gaze, felt that masculine heat surround her once more like invisible arms. It was palpable. Every time he studied her with that intensity of his, she felt . . . well . . . like his woman. Like he was claiming her. Branding her as his own, maybe?

Her flights of imagination were taking off and truly

crazy. Shiloh tried to tell herself that because Roan was an operator in the military, that look he gave her was due to past training. Still, her breasts automatically tightened, her nipples hard and rubbing erotically against her cotton bra. The sensations were new. Exciting. Driving her to distraction. She didn't see desire in Roan's eyes. No, if anything, she felt like he was a scientist. She'd rather be his lover than looked upon as an interesting petri-dish experiment.

Chapter Six

Roan tried to remain immune to Shiloh as they rode around the far end of Pine Grove. About halfway around it, he pulled his horse to a halt. Raising his arm toward a huge pine tree, the top of it containing the red-tail nest, he pointed it out to her. She got busy and pulled out her cell phone and took photos of it. He felt himself go hungry as she became excited and awed as one of the hawks flew back to the nest. The hawk had a four-foot wingspan and when it came in for a landing, Roan had to admit, it was impressive-looking.

There was a stand of cottonwood trees a little farther around the edge of the grove, a small stream nearby. He decided to pull up there, get her off the horse, and give her legs a stretch. Roan dismounted and walked over to Charley's head, his hand on the reins.

"Go ahead and dismount," he told Shiloh. He watched as she gripped the horn with her left hand, placing the reins on the horse's neck, and swung her leg across Charley's rump.

"Oh, geez," she muttered, grimacing as she slowly lowered herself to the ground. "My legs are killing me." She looked up to see him grin a little. The gleam in Roan's eyes made her very aware she was a woman and he was a man. Leaning down, she rubbed the insides of her legs near her knees. They felt tender.

Roan pulled the reins over Charley's head and let them drop to the green grass. The horse was ground-tied trained and wouldn't move from the spot. "What you don't want to happen is that the skin inside of your knees has been rubbed raw. Is any skin broken? You should check."

Hotly aware of Roan's closeness, she tenderly touched her Levi's inside her knees. "No . . . they feel okay. No broken skin. Yet . . ." Straightening, she grinned up at him. "But my thighs . . . I feel like a chicken that got its drumsticks ripped apart," she said, laughing.

His mouth twitched. He opened one of the saddlebags on his horse and pulled out a bottle of water, handing it to her. "Yeah, that pretty much says it all, Tenderfoot. Drink all of this. Need to keep you hydrated. City people don't realize even when they ride a horse, they're sweating a lot more than normal. You lose water and that's not good." His gloved fingers met hers. Damned if Roan didn't feel momentary sparks of heat in his fingertips. There was such joy shining in Shiloh's eyes, the change in her was startling. Mesmerizing. Roan felt like he was meeting another woman, not the one he'd met earlier at the airport.

"Come on," he said gruffly, lifting his hand. "Follow me." Roan led her over to beneath the sprawling limbs of a very old cottonwood tree. He gestured for her to sit down on the lush grass beneath it. He sat down, back resting against the rugged-looking grayish trunk. Shiloh plopped down, removed the green baseball cap, her ponytail loosened between her shoulder blades. The crimson tendrils only enhanced the natural pinkness in her cheeks. Roan purposely pulled his gaze away from her mouth. The woman was calling to him on every level—intellectually, physically, and emotionally—and yet, she'd made no obvious sign or signal to him. She was probably caught up in the wild, natural beauty of the West.

Sipping from the canteen of water, Shiloh sighed, gazing around. "Will the horses be okay out there? You haven't tied them up."

"They're ground-tied trained," Roan murmured, tipping his head back, slugging down half the bottle of water he'd pulled from one of his horse's saddlebags. His Adam's apple bobbed.

Shiloh couldn't help but stare at him. His flesh was deeply tanned and the red bandanna around his thick, strong neck only emphasized the maleness of him. He tipped his Stetson back on his head, one knee drawn up, his elbow resting on it. With the leather chaps on, he reminded her of a long-ago knight dressed in a coat of armor. But more to the truth, Shiloh felt walls around Roan. Why? Compressing her lips, she decided to ask.

"Are all black ops guys walled up?" she asked, sliding him a glance. There were small fanlike lines at the corners of his eyes, telling her he was outside a lot, squinting against a harsh sun.

Tipping his head in her direction, Roan caught and held her curious gaze. "Now, where did that question come from?" he teased. "What do you mean?" He saw the seriousness in her gaze and he hadn't been expecting such a surprising observation from her. He saw her cheeks grow pink with blush.

"It's just a feeling I get from you," she murmured, a little defensive. "I was thinking because you were in black ops, that you had to hide in different ways, and that was the reason for feeling you were guarded?" She boldly searched his amused gray gaze.

He drank the rest of the water and capped the bottle,

considering her explanation. "When you're an operator, Shiloh, you can't allow your emotions to get in the way of what you're doing. You put them away. Out of the way."

Her brows fell. Shiloh felt sorry for him. "Really? I mean, men are human. So are operators. Doesn't it bother you to always hide your feelings?" She watched his mouth curve into a slight, sour smile.

"Let me put it another way. If you had the barrels of AK-47s staring back at you, and the guys at the other ends of those weapons wanted to kill you, what would you do? Would you go hysterical? Let your emotions get the better of you?" He took off his hat, wiping his sweaty brow with the back of his arm, and settled the hat on his head once more. "Or"—he pinned her with a hard look—"would you ignore how you felt and focus on what you had to do to defend yourself, shoot back and kill them instead of them killing you?" He saw her face go blank for a moment, saw some emotion he couldn't interpret deep in her green eyes as she mulled over his questions.

"I guess," she said, and shrugged a little, staring down at the bottle between her hands, "I don't know how to put my feelings aside." She lifted her chin, holding his calm gray gaze. "Is there such a thing? Can you really do that?"

"Sure you can. It's training, Shiloh. That's all it is. You find out real quick that if you let your emotions run you, you aren't going to be thinking clearly enough to survive."

"Wow," she muttered, thinking about that. "I've never not run on my emotions."

"But you haven't, until lately, ever been threatened with a life-and-death situation. Right?"

She scowled. "Well," she began hesitantly, "that's not quite true. . . ."

Roan's brows dipped as he felt a shift in her thoughts. Nothing obvious, but as a long-time operator who was used to picking up on a person's real feelings, this snagged his full interest. Studying her, he saw she was avoiding looking at him, that her full lower lip was being chewed on between her teeth. There was a lot more to Shiloh's story than he'd originally realized. He had to tread lightly, feeling as if an IED was sitting between them. Invisible, but there just the same. He saw her worrying the water bottle, slowly turning it around between her fingers, staring hard at it.

"Can you talk about it?" he wondered, holding her unsure gaze. She looked so scared for a millisecond and then hid her reaction from him. It took everything not to lift his arm and place it around her suddenly tense shoulders.

Shrugging, she whispered, "It's not something I tell many people about."

"Does Maud know?"

Shaking her head, feeling bereft, Shiloh uttered weakly, "No . . ."

Roan's mouth thinned and he waited. He knew there was trust building between them, felt it and saw it back at the barn when they worked with Charley. Whatever Shiloh was holding on to, it was big. He could feel her emotionally wrestling with it. Had he accidentally stepped on an IED with her? Sure as hell felt like it. And here, he thought her simple question about his walls was a tempest in a teapot. Yet, there was a side to him that was ultra-protective toward any woman or child who couldn't adequately defend themselves. Roan supposed it came from his upbringing, his dad who said it was the place of man to protect those who were vulnerable, no matter what. But there was more to it than just wanting to protect Shiloh. His reaction to her was almost visceral.

"That's all right," he said, "You don't have to talk about it" he said quietly, meeting and searching her eyes fraught with anguish. What had he stirred up?

Shiloh knew in her heart she could trust Roan with her life. Literally. Don't ask her how she knew it. She just did. And the way he gruffly asked her, his eyes clearly concerned, something very old and painful broke deep within her. "I trust you," she said, a little breathless. For a moment, she watched the horses contentedly eat the thick green grass around where they stood.

Pulling her legs up against her body, Shiloh wrapped her arms around them, staring out across the grassy valley. "When my dad died of a heart attack, I was eight years old, and I saw my mother fall apart. For a year after that, she was lost . . . she loved my father so much. It was hard on both of us in different ways." Shiloh pushed some strands of hair away from her cheek, feeling the anguish return, pushing up through her, making her want to cry. "And then, my mother was at a Manhattan gallery opening for her paintings, the rich and famous attended it. She met a multi-millionaire construction owner, Anton Leath." Her mouth curved downward, corners in. So many feelings came to life within her. Feelings she didn't ever want to feel again. But here they were just as bright and intense as the day she'd felt them. Would they EVER go away?

"You didn't like him?" Roan asked, seeing her expression grow pained. He sensed such anxiety and anguish around her and yet, it wasn't showing up on her face. His arms literally itched to enfold her, hold her against him, hold her safe from something tragic that had happened to her. He found himself holding his breath and, at the same time, starting to automatically shove his own feelings down in that box. It was an instinctive, trained reaction whenever he felt danger. But the danger was around Shiloh. Because he cared a helluva lot more than he should, Roan knew he was being deeply and intensely affected by her reaction.

As she shook her head, the words stuck like peanut butter in her throat. She felt it closing up on her, felt the

terror stalking her once more. "My mother didn't know,"
she began hoarsely, refusing to look at Roan. "She didn't
know. . . ." Rubbing her face, trying to will away that time
in her life, she could feel the powerful protection of Roan
invisibly surrounding her. He hadn't made a move to touch
her, and yet, she felt that blanket surround her like unseen
arms and it gave her the courage to go on. "Leath was a
sexual predator." Her words came out quietly. Filled with
angst. "I was nine when she married him. I never liked him.
I was afraid of him. He seemed so nice on the surface.
Always smiling. But he kept touching me. Always touching me. I hated his touching my hair, my shoulder, or my
clothes. I didn't want his contact, but my mom thought it
was sweet of him to pay so much attention to me."

Roan closed his eyes for a moment, his mouth harden-
ing into a thin line. He had no idea. None. But hearing
Shiloh's low, pain-filled voice, it was starting to rip him
apart internally because he couldn't not care for her. His
gloved hands slowly flexed into fists and he had to force-
fully remind himself to relax. "Then," he rasped, "it wasn't
a stepfather's-caring-for-his-child kind of contact?" Roan
knew it wasn't, but he could see Shiloh struggling. His
heart crashed when she looked up at him, like that child of
nine, utterly unprotected, being hunted by the bastard, her
eyes filled with anguish.

"N-no, it wasn't. The first time he came into my room it
was at night when I was ten. My mother had gone to sleep,
and he sneaked in. He began touching my chest, my hips,
and I screamed. I tried to get away from him, Roan. I think
my scream scared him and he quickly got up and left."

Closing his eyes for a moment, Roan pinched the bridge
of his nose. He wanted to kill this son of a bitch. No child
should ever be harmed. *Ever.* Something inside him whispered that Shiloh needed to talk it out. And by talking it
out, she could maybe start healing. But Roan sensed it was

her deepest, darkest secret. And it was so damned toxic to her. Now he was beginning to understand why she was so rattled by a stalker. "What happened next?"

His voice was fraught with barely held emotions. Shiloh didn't have the courage to look over at him, but she felt his raw care. "He left me alone for a while after that. I wanted to go to my mother and tell her, but I was afraid. She was so happy with Anton. I couldn't understand why she didn't see what he really was. And I wanted her happy. I didn't want to ever see her like she was that year after my dad died. I thought . . . well, I thought, maybe it was me. Maybe I did something to make Anton treat me like that."

Roan laid a gloved hand on her arm. He met and held her glistening eyes. "Shiloh, you were a child. You couldn't understand what was going on, but you were caught up in a lot of emotions that children simply can't figure out or walk through. Don't blame yourself." His fingers curved more firmly around her arm and he saw some of the darkness lift from her narrowed eyes. Her mouth, once soft and full, was compressed, as if to hold back a tidal wave of tortured feelings, grief, and guilt.

Shiloh nodded jerkily, starving for Roan's steadying touch. Did he realize by touching her, he gave her strength? It calmed her inwardly. When he released her, she wanted to turn and crawl into his arms, feel them wrap around her because he made her feel safe. "You're right, of course." She sniffed, giving him an embarrassed look, and quickly wiped the tears out of her eyes. "Anton stalked me. I could always feel his eyes on me, on my chest, between my legs. I felt stripped and naked even though I was wearing clothes. I could feel the heat of his gaze on certain parts of my body.

"A week later, he came into my bedroom. He woke me up. His hands were all over me, touching my chest . . .

trying to open my legs. I started to scream, but this time, he clamped his large hand over my mouth." She trembled, closing her eyes, reliving that night. "He tried to touch me with his fingers and I kicked, hit at him and I finally got away. I ran out of my room, screaming. My mother woke up. He met her and said I was having a nightmare." Her voice turned bitter. "I came so close to telling my mother that night when she walked me back to my room. I was so torn, Roan. I was so afraid of Leath. I knew he was going to hurt me. I knew it. . . ."

It took every bit of control on Roan's part to sit still, to simply listen. Not move. Not haul Shiloh into his arms where she needed to be. "Did you ever tell her?"

Sniffing, Shiloh whispered brokenly, "Yes, I did. I told her about three days later. I was so torn. She was so happy. And here I was telling her that her husband was a sexual predator." Rubbing her face, she uttered, "I was so scared. I wasn't sure if she'd believe me or not. And if she did, I was afraid of Leath and what he might do to us. I-I just didn't know what to do."

Roan reached out, gently sliding his hand across her tense, gathered shoulders. "You did the right thing, Shiloh. Parents are supposed to protect their children." He saw her give a jerky nod, her hands covering her face. "What did she do after you told her?"

His physical presence buoyed her wildly fluctuating emotions. Lifting her hands away, Shiloh gave him a miserable look. "She confronted Leath about it that night when he got home. They had a horrible argument. My mother was wild with outrage and anger. It escalated in the kitchen. H-he had a skinning knife on the counter, sharpening it while my mother prepared a beef roast at the other end of the counter. He had a huge collection of knives. I hated that we'd sharpen them in the kitchen, hated the sound it made," she said, and shivered. Choking, she managed to whisper, "Their argument escalated. He stabbed my mother four or five times moments later. I ran screaming out of the apartment. I ran down the exit stairs and screamed for help. Thankfully, a policeman who was on his beat was just passing by our building and came to my rescue."

Roan's arm tightened around her shoulders. He saw the utter loss in Shiloh's wan features, the loss in her damp, dark eyes. "Did they get him?"

Nodding, swallowing against a lump in her throat, Shiloh whispered unsteadily, "I led the two policemen up to our apartment. Leath was gone, but my mother . . . oh, my poor mother . . . she was dead. She'd bled out. Dead at twenty-nine years old. I-I just screamed and cried. One of the policemen picked me up, carried me out of the apartment, called Child Protective Services, and stayed with me. He didn't want me to see it. But I already had."

And it was with her to this day. Roan knew that one. He'd seen and done things in Afghanistan that would never leave him, either. He understood what she meant. "My mother's younger sister, who lived a few blocks away, came and got me later. My aunt Lynn and uncle Robert raised me until I was eighteen. Then, I moved back into my parents' original apartment, where I've stayed ever since."

"What happened to your stepfather? Did they find him?"

"Yes. They caught up with him and charged him with first-degree murder." Wearily, she added, "There was a trial when I was eleven years old, and I testified against him. It sent him to prison for only twenty-five years because his lawyer fought for and got second-degree murder charges leveled against him, instead of first-degree, which would have put the bastard on death row where he belonged."

"And the judge and jury knew that he was a sexual predator, too?"

"Yes, it all came out at the trial." Shaking her head, Shiloh said, "I don't know how I got through it all. If I hadn't had my aunt Lynn . . ."

Roan could not imagine any child that age having to do what was asked of her. A new respect flowed through him for Shiloh. She might look young and beautiful, her face unmarred by life, but the tragic wounds she carried were still inside her. The loads she carried . . . The guilt . . . The grief . . .

Unconsciously, he moved his hand across her tight shoulders, trying to assuage some of the tension he felt beneath his gloved fingers. "You did the right thing for the right reasons, Shiloh. You know that now, don't you?" he asked, pinning her with a searching look, holding her marred green eyes. Tears were leaking down her cheeks, falling into the corners of her beautiful mouth. A mouth he wanted to cover, to kiss. Roan knew he could give back to this woman who had so much taken away from her. He also realized that her trust with men in general was more than likely broken. And he was a man. He monitored his touch across her shoulders. She hadn't pulled away or made any movement to suggest she didn't want him touching her.

"Y-yes, I know I did the right thing." And then her face scrunched up and she buried it in her hands. "But it got my mother killed," she said, and she sobbed, broken over what she'd done.

Oh, hell!

Roan couldn't stop himself and he rasped, "Come here, Shiloh . . ." and gathered her up in his arms, pulling her against him. She came without fighting him, huddled, face in her hands as she turned her cheek against his chest. He couldn't stand a woman's or child's tears. It was the one thing that he had no defense against. Never had. Shiloh was quivering like an animal caught in an invisible trap that held her in place and she couldn't escape it. He smoothed her hair with his hand, holding her tight against himself, wanting to will away her pain because she sure as hell didn't deserve to be carrying it.

Roan knew how impressionable children were. They were wide open, innocent, without anything written on their hearts and minds. His father and mother had been good parents. Roan knew from experience what parents were supposed to do to protect their children, teach them to be confident and strong, allow them to make mistakes, grow and learn from them.

Shiloh's young life wasn't anything like his had been. As Roan held her, she sobbed softly into her hands, her whole body shaking. He closed his eyes, resting his jaw against her head, the strands of her hair tickling his chin. Gently, he smoothed his glove up and down her strong, supple spine. She might look soft but Roan had a whole new perspective on her: She was steel strong inwardly. She had to be in order to survive. He simply couldn't imagine a trial of that magnitude with a scared little girl at the center of it. Her testimony put Leath away. The strength that took shook Roan as little else would. Shiloh was strong because life had tested her long and early. Amazed, he began to see her in a completely new light. No longer was he going to think of her as a city slicker. As an Easterner. Those labels carried certain assumptions that really didn't apply to Shiloh.

He unconsciously pressed a kiss to her hair, murmuring low, gruff words meant to heal her, help her. As his gloved hand came to rest on her wet cheek, he gently removed her hands from where she was hiding her face. She made a little sound of desperation, as if ashamed, turning her face more deeply into his chest. His blue chambray shirt was splotched with her tears and he could feel the warmth of them against his flesh beneath the material. Mouth tightening, he cupped her cheek, allowing her to hide beneath his large hand, trying to give her solace. Or maybe, give her some of his strength to get through this storm of agony.

Roan didn't know how long he held Shiloh in his arms. She finally quit weeping. And gradually, that fine quiver within her dissolved too. As the birds sang and flew around them, the scent of her hair and skin tantalizing him, he looked out over the verdant valley.

The horses were calm, resting, one rear leg cocked. The sky was a darker blue as the sun rose higher. The breeze no longer held a cold edge to it as it lifted strands of Shiloh's red hair here and there. He felt her breasts pressed to the wall of his chest, noticed how soft and rounded they were. He could feel himself responding, growing hard with yearning. And he forced himself to stop responding to her.

Just how broken was Shiloh's trust in men? Did she see some or all men in her stepfather? How much damage had he done to her? And did she view Roan through that toxic, stained lens of her life? Lumping him with all men? This was a minefield Roan had never anticipated. He thought she was just a romance writer. Writing frilly stuff that had no value, really. And her real life was a friggin' ongoing nightmare. He wondered how she could create anything under that kind of pressure. It once more served to tell Roan just how resilient Shiloh really was. He had to stop seeing her as a helpless, ignorant Easterner.

His mind ranged over her nightmare the other night in the house. Was it about that time in her young life? Roan wasn't sure. But he'd find out and he didn't look too closely at why he wanted to know.

Gradually, her breathing went from ragged to slow and deep. Shiloh had innocently placed the palm of her hand over his heart. Her touch felt good. And he wanted to make love to her even more than before. There was depth to Shiloh. Roan knew bad experiences honed and shaped people's emotions and lives. And as soft as she felt in his arms, all curves in the right places, her femininity, she was a survivor. That appealed to Roan more than anything else. He'd lived as an operator and knew life-and-death up front and close. Knew how it had shaped him, changed him, made him strong in ways most people would never be. And he knew internal strength was the most important power to have because it kept a person moving forward in the worst of times.

Shiloh had done that very thing at age eleven when she became the prosecution's star witness in the murder of her own mother. The resilience and strength she possessed blew him away. He hadn't seen it in her. And usually, he was very adept at assessing a person. But he hadn't with her. Why? Roan's mouth twitched and he stared sightlessly across the valley as he realized his whole reaction to her had been purely sexual. Shiloh was beautiful. Willful. Her feelings on the surface. Like a ripe fruit to be plucked and eaten. And he did want her in every possible way.

His brows flattened out as he considered her in this new, realistic light. Whether Shiloh was aware of it or not, she was a warrior. That what she'd survived, most eleven-year-olds would not have survived without wounds scarring their souls forever. She, on the other hand, had not only survived, but she had thrived. She had a career and she was highly successful. The only reason she was here was to get a respite from her stalker in New York City.

And that concerned him deeply. Roan tightened his arms around her for a moment, trying to feed her some of his strength. She was relaxed in his arms. Trusting. Not stiff. Not tense. But . . . at ease. For whatever reason, Shiloh trusted him. Roan closed his eyes. He wanted her to trust

him and to come to him, to want him as much as he desired
her. Then, and only then, would they be on equal, respectful footing with each other. Roan wouldn't chase Shiloh.
He'd let whatever was between them, if anything, unfold
naturally. He refused to push her, get her in a corner, or
manipulate her.

More than anything, Roan wanted Shiloh to be drawn to
him just as much as he was to her. Could it happen? And
why the hell did he WANT it to happen?

Chapter Seven

The feeling of being protected was so overwhelming to Shiloh as she lay in Roan's arms that it made her want to cry all over again. Only this time, tears of relief. She had always felt this sense of safety around him, but now, she was getting a taste of it firsthand and it was incredible. As he gently moved his gloved hand across her shoulders and then slowly down her back, she thought of him doing this to a fractious, wild-eyed horse. Well, she was one, in a sense.

Licking her lower lip, Shiloh didn't want to move out of his embrace. She could feel the slow, solid beat of his heart beneath her ear, the rise and fall of his chest as he breathed. Most of all, her eyes closed, she absorbed each of his ministrations. The roughness of the leather across the thin fabric of her shirt made her tense and skitter with fire of the most pleasurable kind. And those tiny, heated shocks tightened her breasts, hardened her nipples, and then dove straight down to remind her how long she'd gone without sex. She knew she wanted Roan in bed. But she'd been so scared. Commitment was something she'd never been able to muster and manage. And she knew without a doubt that Roan Taggart was not the kind of man who played around.

He played for keeps. She wasn't sure at all if she could. At least, not yet.

But to feel his quiet power, the strength of his arms around her, the sensitivity he possessed, as if knowing she needed to be tenderly held, made her stop and look at herself. What did she really want? She wanted a marriage like her mother and father had. Yet look what had happened to them. It scared her to death. Shiloh was afraid to fall in love because she could never take the loss of the man she fell in love with. It would destroy her. Utterly. Forever. Unlike her mother, she didn't possess that backbone to survive the loss and move on.

"Better?" Roan inquired, his lips against her hair. He could smell the scent of her and it was the most incredible fragrance in the world to him. Her hair was a mix of pine, a sweetness, the scent to her skin and the fragrance of the honeysuckle shampoo. He felt her nod, felt her hand move from the center of his chest to her cheek. If he didn't release her, he was going to do something really stupid: kiss her. Take her mouth, ravish her, taste her, feel her woman's burning heat. His heart counseled otherwise, knowing she had trust issues with men.

Yet, she'd willingly collapsed into his arms, huddled against him, scared and grief-stricken by revisiting her traumatic past. Roan had not felt any resistance on Shiloh's part toward him. He wanted to kiss her so badly, to heal her, and he knew he could. Not fooling himself, yes, he wanted her sexually as well, but he was content to wait on that part. His senses told him she would allow him to kiss her. But what if he was wrong? It would destroy whatever trust had just been quietly built between them. Shiloh was shattered in another way. He knew if he kissed her, it could cut two ways. Either it would be healing and supportive to her, or it could trigger darker issues she had and their trust would be dissolved, nothing left between them to build on. Roan decided not to kiss her. The chances of being wrong would make him pay too great a price and he wasn't willing to risk it.

"Yes, I'm okay now," Shiloh whispered, her voice hoarse from crying so long and so much. She felt his arms relax and she found herself sitting up, near him, already missing his embrace. Wiping her eyes, removing the beaded tears still on her lashes, she gave him an apologetic look. "I'm sorry, I didn't mean to spoil your day." She saw his gray eyes lose their hardness, saw a warmth in them that curled around her heart and made her breath hitch. Something told her she was seeing the real Roan without his game face on for the first time. And it stunned her; it called to her heart and fractured soul. There was such a sense of care, of protection radiating toward her that her eyes widened. Her heart started a slow pound and urgency thrummed through Shiloh as never before. When the hard line of his mouth softened, she shook inside with a need so urgent that she felt starved for more of his attention, his touch. It felt as if the earth had literally moved beneath where she sat.

"Darlin', you have NOTHING to apologize for. All right?" And Roan drilled a look into her eyes, asking her to hold his gaze and not skitter away as she had done so many times before. Frightened animals and humans could never hold another's gaze. Her eyes were red-rimmed, the softness of them tearing heavily at his guarded heart.

Shiloh sniffed and gave a brusque nod, her lower lip trembling. She was tearing him apart. Trying to be so brave in front of him. Roan wondered if this was how she looked when having to live with Anton Leath in her home with her mother; putting on that brave front even though she felt like a defenseless rabbit living with a rabid wolf underfoot.

To hell with it. He reached out and gently wiped away a last tear clinging to her pale cheek. Even through his thin leather glove, he could feel the pliancy of her soft skin. Shiloh blinked once as he grazed her flesh, taking that tear away. Roan didn't see fear, disgust, or terror in her eyes when he touched her. It told him a lot. She didn't fear him and their trust was still solid between them. Roan wanted to do so much more; frame her face, take that soft mouth of hers and capture it beneath his own, give and take with her, taste her fire, hear those sounds of pleasure catch in her slender throat. He was such a goner for this woman; knowing her tragic past made him just that much more protective of her than before.

"In my eyes," he told her gruffly, veiled emotions behind his words, "you're not only a survivor, Shiloh, but you're courageous. You're a warrior of another kind." *My kind*. He didn't dare say that, seeing her eyes suddenly lighten with hope and with another emotion he couldn't translate. Pinkness seeped back into her wan cheeks and Roan felt good being able to say something that made Shiloh feel a little bit better. She'd gone through a special hell. One that made him want to shake his head because he couldn't conceive of any eleven-year-old in that kind of circumstance. And she still turned out to be the beautiful, kind, and shy woman who was sitting right in front of him.

Dropping his hand to his thigh, he saw how his roughly spoken words fortified Shiloh. Her back straightened more, the tension bled off her shoulders, and he could see some of her normal confidence returning. It struck him that Shiloh might not have a support network back in New York City. And he wanted to find out.

"Are you close with your aunt and uncle?" he wondered. He watched her sit and clasp her hands in her lap.

"It's a long story, Roan. My aunt and uncle were childless by choice. When my mother was murdered, I was sort of forced on them. I knew I was an imposition to their lives, but they did their best to accommodate me. Both of them were career people."

"So, no mother at home?"

Shaking her head, she offered quietly, "Aunt Lynn hired a full-time nanny to be with me, to take me to school, pick me up, and make all my meals."

Wincing internally, Roan remembered his family. To this day, they ate together. No matter what the ranch demanded, they all sat down together at night for dinner. It was a time to talk, exchange ideas, get support, and laugh. They laughed a lot around the dinner table. Cutting her a glance, he could see her cheeks had gone wan again. Damn, she was so easily touched by her emotions. Like a barometer. "But you got to see them on weekends?"

"Mostly, yes. They have a beautiful cabin in the Adirondack Mountains and we usually went there on weekends, which I just loved. It fed my soul."

Rubbing his jaw, Roan watched the horses eating grass, his mind and heart on Shiloh. She really didn't get the nurturing she needed after her mother was killed in front of her eyes. God, that had to be a terrible sentence for Shiloh, considering how shy and sensitive she was. Roan swallowed hard, feeling his throat tighten, feeling anger toward her aunt and uncle. Were they so narcissistic, so self-centered that they couldn't see what a little girl needed after having her mother ripped savagely from her life? Hire a nanny? Let the nanny be the stand-in for the dead mother? He wanted to curse, but tightened his lips instead.

"Wasn't that hard on you? Having a nanny?" He turned, watching her telling expression.

Opening her hands, Shiloh whispered, "No one could replace my mom, Roan. The nanny was wonderful. She was made aware of my loss and she tried her best to step in."

"Why didn't your aunt?" he growled.

"Auntie Lynn was focused on her career. She's a very

competitive person, Roan. She had goals she needed to meet."

His mouth turned grimmer. His eyes hardened as he glared out at the horses. Roan did not want her to see his rage. Life was never fair, but in this kind of situation, Shiloh was like a piece of raw meat and her aunt might as well have poured salt in her wounds. She wasn't there for Shiloh. A shadow. Doing her duty, but emotionally bankrupt with the child. Roan knew there were women who were childless, who made that choice, but none of them fit Lynn's prototype. They were nurturing and maternal. And they could give back and were unselfish. Lynn was a piece of work, in Roan's estimation.

Nervously moving her hands, Shiloh added, "My family has always been goal-oriented, Roan. Even I am."

Roan understood what she was doing and let it slide. It would do no good to denigrate Auntie Lynn. At least the woman put a roof over her head, fed her, hired a nanny, and paid for her needs. That was better than nothing, but not by much, in his opinion. He pushed to his feet, turned, and offered her his hand. "Come on, there's a special place I want to share with you."

Looking up at his tall, shadowed figure, Shiloh saw his eyes were warm. And it fed her heart and soul. Reaching out, she slid her hand into his gloved one. She could feel him monitoring the strength of his holding her fingers, careful not to hurt her. "Where are we going?" she asked, coming to her feet.

Roan released her hand. Didn't want to, but there you go. He had to or else. "There's a flower meadow not far from here," he said, gesturing with his finger. "I thought it might cheer you up. This time of year, the early flowers are blooming." Instantly, he saw happiness flood her green eyes, those gold flecks set deep within them. His heart raced momentarily. Damn, but it made him feel good to know how easily he affected Shiloh in a positive way. And then Roan wondered what her eyes would look like if he kissed her. He knew how to love a woman. Knew how to give her pleasure that would float her off into that treasured space where lovers went.

"I'd like that," she said, her voice strengthening. "Are you sure it's okay? I know you said you had to ride fence line today."

Always thinking of others first. It was a good way to be and it only made Roan like her that much more. He placed his hand lightly in the small of her back, guiding her toward Charley. "It will be all right," he reassured her. Roan saw the instant worry replaced with excitement. "Better keep your cell phone ready when we get there. You'll probably be taking more than one photograph."

Grateful that Roan helped her mount up, she took the reins from his hand, looking down at him. "I love flowers. How did you know? Did Maud tell you that?" He stood with his large hand on Charley's rump, the other resting against the swell of her saddle. He was larger than life, a quiet, intense cowboy with those warm gray eyes that continued to thaw her frozen soul. Shiloh was amazed that he was allowing her to see the real Roan Taggart. It left her breathless.

"No, Maud didn't tell me." He smiled a little and patted Charley's neck. "Just a feeling."

She watched him walk over to his large black gelding, gathering up the reins. Both rider and horse were lean, tight, and in top athletic condition. Her lower body was simmering with need. Her skin still skittered in memory of his touch. For a man who was so rugged, he had a gentle touch. When looking at Roan's hard, weathered face, Shiloh would never have dreamed he had tenderness within him. Taking a ragged breath, she clucked to Charley as he led the way around the hill.

* * *

The wildflower meadow was a special place. Roan always liked it because it was on the property where the cabin was being built. Before, he wasn't going to tell Shiloh about his cabin or even let her know it was on the Wind River ranch property. Now something in him moved him to show it to her. Roan didn't know why, only that he sensed it would make her happy. The tragedy she carried within her ran her life; now she was targeted again, only this time by a stalker. He wanted to ask her more but he'd upset her enough for one day. Roan would choose another time, a better one, to try to get her thoughts.

They rounded the hill and the meadow was on a slight slope downward onto a basin area of the valley floor. To the left, less than a quarter of a mile away, stood his half-finished log cabin. In the morning light, the slats of sun made the cedar logs on the eastern side of his cabin glow like newly minted gold coins. He had drawn back a bit, riding half a horse length behind Shiloh, watching her. The gently sloping meadow was filled with many kinds of newly blooming wildflowers. The dew was still thick on the lush grass that the horses walked through, sparkling like rounded bits of tiny rainbows as a breeze rippled across the area.

Roan heard a soft gasp escape Shiloh as he watched her slowly pan and take in the color across the meadow. He pulled up, absorbed in her discovery of the flowers peeking out among the long and short strands of grass. Only able to see her profile, he went hot as her mouth curved upward. She pulled Charley to a stop and twisted around in the saddle, catching his studied gaze.

"This is incredible, Roan!" she gasped. Shiloh saw him nod, the corners of his mouth tipping upward as he dismounted and dropped the reins to his horse. The warm sunlight felt good, the light strong. His face was shadowed as he walked up beside her horse, putting his hand on his rump.

"This is one of Maud's favorite places," he said, and gestured out toward the slope of the hill. "Want to get down? Walk through them? Smell them?"

This was just what she needed after such a hard, deep cry. Shiloh still felt fragile and tentative. "I'd love to," she admitted, a catch in her tone. She saw a gleam in Roan's eyes, but was unable to interpret the look. His face was more relaxed. Dismounting awkwardly, she felt his gloved hand slip beneath her elbow and steady her as she put her feet in the dew-laden grass. Her skin tingled and she ached to step those few inches and turn into him to be held again. Shame made her step away and pull Charley's reins over his head as he eagerly began to eat the lush grass. What must Roan think of her? There was no recrimination in his eyes that she could see. If anything, she felt a powerful mantle of protection around her emanating from him.

"Go ahead," he urged her quietly, taking the reins from her hand. "Go explore," he added, and he smiled a little, seeing the sparkle in her eyes. Roan's heart expanded as she responded to his low, gruff tone. She pulled the cell phone from her pocket, turned, and moved slowly into the flowers. There was yellow balsamroot, red gilia, white Richardson's geraniums, pink shooting stars, purple monkshood, and blue lupine throughout the area.

Roan was content to remain with the horses and watch her bend down, cup a bloom, and inhale its fragrance. The sunlight picked up the burgundy, gold, and copper strands of her ponytail, which moved across her shoulder every time she bent down. She was like a kid in a candy store, enthusiasm evident in her face as she took photos of her favorites.

Around him, mid-morning was waking up in earnest.

Hearing the red-tail behind him, he turned, looking across his shoulder toward Pine Hills, seeing one of the hawks leaving their nest. The chirping of birds was a tranquil song to him; one he'd never get tired of hearing. Roan kept his gaze on Shiloh as she slowly worked her way down the hill, looking for new flowers so she could photograph them. He knew there was nothing like this meadow in New York City. It must look like a kaleidoscope to Shiloh. Or maybe something else because she was a writer and saw things differently than most others.

Wrapping his arms against his chest while contented horses eagerly munched the grass, Roan found himself feeling happy for no discernible reason. Shiloh was graceful. He watched her put her arms out to balance herself here and there. There were a lot of gopher holes in the hillside and she couldn't see where she was stepping, the grass covering up the many mounds where the pesky creatures lived in town-like burrows. If a horse ever accidentally stepped into one, it could break a leg and send the rider flying. He didn't like gophers.

Once Shiloh made her way to the end of the slope, she turned and looked up at him, waving and smiling.

Roan felt his skin riffle. He lifted his hand and smiled in return. Her ponytail had pretty much worked its way loose and now her hair lay about her shoulders like a gleaming red and gold cape. Almost the colors of aged cedar. Like his cabin. Frowning, he lifted his chin, staring in the distance toward his home. On weekends, he would drive out here and work from dawn to dusk, returning back to the ranch center because there was no furniture in there yet. He'd set the major posts for a porch he wanted to build around half the cabin. The idea of having a rocking chair there that he could mosey out on with a cup of hot coffee in the morning appealed to Roan. He laughed to himself because at an earlier age, he'd never contemplate a rocking chair.

But life had moved on and he'd changed. Things that had been important to him as an operator in the Army were now in the past.

Gazing toward Shiloh, he watched her walking around the edge of the meadow. As she started a long climb up toward him and the horses he could see her pant legs from her knees downward were soaked with dew. Smiling to himself as Shiloh drew nearer, he saw her cheeks had bloomed with pink once more. Even better, there was life in her green eyes again, no longer dull or rife with pain and memories. Her hair had a slight curl to it, the crimson waves lovingly outlining her oval face. Trying not to stare at her breasts too long or the gentle sway to her hips, he kept trying to control his hungry body.

Roan couldn't help but grin as she came up the hill, breathing hard, cheeks flushed, her green eyes shining. It had been a good decision to bring her here, help her orient to the present. Let the past ebb out like a tide and give her some downtime from the brutality of it all.

"I just got lost in the beauty of all those flowers, Roan." Shiloh pulled some of her strands away from her face, smiling up into his hard, serious-looking features.

"You looked like you were having fun." Roan found himself wanting to sweep Shiloh into his arms. She was so alive. So . . . tempting. Gesturing down to her wet, darkened Levi's, he drawled, "The only downside is wet pant legs."

Laughing, she nodded and smoothed her hand against her knee. "That grass is heavy with dew!"

"It's like that every morning until about eleven A.M.," he said. The breeze moved her hair and, without thinking, he reached out, capturing some of those wayward strands and then tucking them behind her ear. Roan saw her stand very still, her pupils growing large and black beneath his touch. Cursing to himself, he dropped his hand, realizing how intimate the gesture had been. Shiloh suddenly looked shy and she lowered her lashes, moving over to where Charley stood, and picked up his reins. Roan wanted to touch her again. Everywhere, starting with that ripe mouth of hers.

"Thank you for showing me this meadow. It's so perfect. So beautiful," she said, holding his gaze as she pulled the reins over Charley's head.

"I thought it might be a positive change for you," he said, holding her stare. Roan saw desire in Shiloh's eyes. When her pupils grew dark and large, he knew how to interpret that telltale sign. She had liked his touch. Right now, Shiloh was fragile. He shouldn't have done it because it was like taking advantage of her when she was vulnerable. Kicking himself inwardly, he was finding by being around her, touching Shiloh was coming way too naturally for him. He tried to blame it on the fact that her red hair was loose and a glorious, shining crown around her shoulders. He tried to convince himself that her green eyes were only temporarily warm and soft with longing because she was raw from her earlier weeping in his arms.

As much as Roan wanted to tell himself that holding Shiloh was the humane thing to do, it went a lot deeper than that for him. He was protective toward her from the beginning and now he understood, in part, why. His operator's senses had told him she was under genuine threat. And it had been proven to him. Whether he wanted to or not, Roan was emotionally invested in Shiloh because she'd turned into his embrace and wanted his arms around her. It made him feel good as a man to do that for her as a woman. And his heart felt like it was going to burst out of his chest. Rubbing the area, Roan scowled and mounted his horse. Shiloh followed suit. Each time she was a little less gawky and unsure of herself, gaining confidence in herself and her horse.

"See that cabin?" she said, pointing in that direction. "Who lives there?"

Roan pulled his black gelding up alongside her paint. "I do." He saw her eyes widen enormously as she looked at him, then at the cabin, and then back at him.

"But," she stammered, "you live at the employee house."

Smiling a little, he saw the confusion in her eyes. "It's a shell of a cabin," he explained. "Taken me a year of working on my days off to get it this far. Would you like to ride over and see it?"

"I'd love to," Shiloh admitted. "It looks like it's glowing gold in the morning sunlight. So pretty," she sighed, giving him a warm look. "You're a man of many surprises," she added in a teasing tone as their horses walked beside each other through the grass.

"What? That I'm building a cabin?"

"Yes. This looks a lot more like you. Raw, natural. Beautiful."

He snorted. "Men are not beautiful."

She grinned broadly. "Sure, they can be beautiful." He was to her. What he'd done for her earlier was an incredible act of kindness. Love. *Love?* Well, maybe she was going overboard. Roan certainly felt sorry for her and probably felt like he had to do something to help her. She saw him grimace and then shake his head. "Men are beautiful in their own way," she proclaimed archly, enjoying his sudden chagrin.

"You're a writer. Can't you come up with a better adjective than that for us?" he griped, giving her a teasing look in return. Shiloh had settled the baseball cap on her hair and it gleamed in the sunlight. Roan found himself wishing she'd wear it down all the time, understanding that long hair got in the way at times for a woman. Still, he itched to take off his gloves and tunnel his fingers through that thick, soft mass of red strands.

Chuckling, Shiloh shrugged. "In my books, I sometimes refer to the hero as beautiful. Seen through the eyes of the heroine, who loves him, of course."

"Call me anything, even late for dinner, but do not ever call me beautiful."

Her lilting laughter surrounded him and God help him, Roan felt his heart blossom with such fierce feelings for Shiloh, it left him stunned.

Chapter Eight

Shiloh noticed how the large, two-story cedar cabin logs had mortar between them and she saw thick posts standing around half of it. There was a gravel driveway leading up to the cabin and a hitching post nearby. Tall cottonwoods, their leaves a spring green color and still growing out for the coming summer, surrounded the cabin on three sides. The only side that wasn't hidden was the eastern side, the main entrance. She saw a large wooden door with a brass door knocker on it, gleaming in the sun's rays. Everything about the cabin had a warmly old-fashioned, nineteenth-century kind of feeling except for the steeply sloped dark green tin roof. There was a two-car garage off to one side that had already been built on a concrete slab, both dark green aluminum bay doors closed. Keeping in mind that Roan had said he was building this by hand, she couldn't help but be impressed with his workmanship.

Halting at the hitching post, they dismounted. Roan showed her the type of knot to put through the iron ring so that she could easily pull the reins out of a knot. He didn't think she'd want to know much about his house building. Most women couldn't care less about something likc this.

And yet, Roan saw interest in her eyes as she walked at his side toward the front of the cabin.

"Why is the roof so steep?" she asked him, gesturing upward.

Roan stood close to her, his hands on his hips. He could smell her feminine scent and it went straight down to his lower body. Damn. "It had to be steep to force snow buildup to slide off the roof, preventing the weight of it from caving into the cabin itself. We get two or three, sometimes five feet of snow in a blizzard piling up on a roof. If it's steep like this, the snow will slide harmlessly off, maintaining the integrity of the cabin." Roan glanced over at her. "I don't suppose New Yorkers get that kind of snow dumped on them?" he teased, and he couldn't help but grin. Shiloh's cheeks colored and her eyes sparkled as she met and held his gaze.

"We get snow, but not like Wyoming." She felt her heart open as he smiled. Roan didn't do that often and it sent her heart spinning wildly with yearning. Her lips tingled just thinking about kissing this cowboy. Tearing her mind from her lower body's wants and needs, she pointed to the large posts in concrete on the front and sides of the cabin. "What are these huge posts for?"

"You really want to know?" Roan was having a tough time taking her seriously about the construction phase.

She snorted. "Why wouldn't I?" Giving him a challenging look, Shiloh added, "What? Women don't build houses? So we shouldn't be interested in them? Is that it, Roan?" Shiloh was half teasing and half not. She saw his cheeks grow ruddy and damn if he wasn't blushing! Her lips twitched as she tried not to smile. "That's it, isn't it? I'm a woman. And because I live in New York City, I betcha think I don't even know one end of a hammer from the other. Right?"

Taking off his hat, Roan ran his fingers through his short hair. He wasn't going to lie to her. "That about sums it up. Yes." He settled the hat back on his head, enjoying the vitality in her expression. Getting Shiloh out on a horse, in the great outdoors, was working a minor miracle from Roan's perspective.

"At least you're honest," she muttered, turning away from his apologetic-looking gaze. She walked forward and placed her hand on one of the twelve-foot tall posts. Turning, she said, "This is known as a four-by-four. These types of posts are used to anchor in something pretty heavy or something you want to stand the test of time. You'd put them at the corners of walls, or in areas where you need extra load-bearing strength." She patted the post. "And I will guess that all these posts are in prep for a wraparound porch you're going to eventually build. Am I right?" she asked, and gave him a narrow-eyed look.

"I'll be damned," Roan murmured, a slow smile hooking one corner of his mouth. "What do you know? I'll bet you watch the DIY channel on TV. Or maybe you've taken some courses over at your local Home Depot store?" He saw the blaze of challenge in her green eyes, liking this feisty side to Shiloh. Who knew? With an internal groan, he forced himself to put a steel clamp on his desires for this red-headed hellion. Every time Roan discovered another facet of Shiloh, he wanted her even more. It was driving him crazy.

Shiloh made an unhappy growling sound in her throat. She leaned against the sturdy post, her arms crossing her breasts. "Like a woman can't know something about construction? Give me a break, Roan. You really ARE a Neanderthal throwback. I've handled my fair share of building things. And yes, I know which end of the hammer to use. Further, I know how to test a hammer to see if it's made correctly. Do you?"

Chuckling, Roan walked over to her. "I do. You stand it on its head and if the handle remains upright, it's balanced and built properly. Well, now that I know you're a regular contractor type, do you want to see more?"

She smiled up at his shadowed face. "You bet I do. Building is exciting to me. It's like writing a book: You're building from the foundation upward and by the end of the book, your house or novel is built. Or"—she shrugged, pushing off from the post—"the story is told, lock, stock, and barrel for my readers."

Roan slid his glove beneath her elbow, guiding her around to the south side of the house. "Nice analogy," he congratulated her. He didn't want to drop his hand, but he forced himself to do so. "I've got the blueprints for the cabin inside, but you're right, I'm going to build a wraparound porch on the north, south, and east sides of the cabin."

"Are you using cedar planking?" she wondered.

He gave her a praiseworthy look. "Normally, I would. But because we get eight months of winter and the weather is very hard on wood, I'm going with Trex. It's a composite material made of plastic and wood fibers from reclaimed and recycled resources. It helps the environment, it weathers much better than wood, and it's cost-efficient."

"I've seen Trex," Shiloh said, nodding. She saw the confusion in his expression. Thinking a city slicker wouldn't know a thing about building a house. "Okay, I'm going to stop making you suffer, Roan." She held up her hand. "I'm a yearly volunteer for Habitat for Humanity. I've helped build five houses over the years, working with other volunteers. That's where I learned about construction." She saw his gray eyes flare with an unknown emotion. His mouth softened a little.

"You just keep surprising me, Shiloh. And here I thought as a writer you just sat eight hours a day creating."

She chuckled. "I do that, too, but my life isn't one-dimensional, Roan. Never was until of late," she said, and she grew sad. "The last six months . . . well, with this stalker, I haven't felt safe leaving my apartment or driving out to where the next house needs to be built." Giving him a painful shrug, Shiloh quietly admitted, "With my vivid imagination, Roan, I think this guy is going to jump out of the shadows, capture and kill me. It's really stopped me from doing a lot of things I love to do." She gave a flourish of her hand toward his cabin. "Like this. It's so inspiring. I love working with raw wood. I love the smell of cedar. I love to see things come together and look beautiful after a lot of hard work."

Rubbing his jaw, he eyed her. Shiloh's sadness dissolved the moment she started talking about building a house. "Well, out here, you don't have to worry about your stalker. Not while I'm around. And maybe"—he pointed with his chin toward the cabin—"you might want to come out on my days off and help me a little. Get a hammer back in your hand?" He saw her expression blossom with joy. The woman moved and touched him in ways no woman ever had. And Roan couldn't explain why. His body sure as hell lusted after her. But more, he liked the quality of her heart. She was a good person in a dangerous situation with that stalker.

"I'd LOVE to do that!" she whispered, clapping her hands. "I'm REALLY good, Roan. My specialty is drywall. I love spackling and I'm VERY good at it. I know how to work with plumbing and stringing electrical wire, too.

Another specialty is painting. I just love to paint. It's so creative."

Scratching his jaw, Roan shook his head. "Maybe I should sit down with you here and ask you what *else* you do besides write best-selling books'?"

Giving him a coy look, Shiloh shook her finger at him. "Shame on you for trying to pigeonhole me as a one-note person, Roan Taggart. Everyone has many sides to them and everyone is multifaceted." Her grin increased and she tapped his massive chest with her index finger. "Even you," she said, and she turned around and walked up to the door and waited for him to open it for her.

Little hellcat. But he meant it affectionately. As Roan strolled up to her and opened the door, pushing it open for her, he asked, "Are you hiding any more fiery parts to yourself that I should know about so I don't step into it with you?"

Laughing a little, Shiloh stepped up into the cabin. "I guess you'll just have to wait and see."

Roan followed her in. He'd gotten in all the windows and light poured into the wide-open area. Watching Shiloh, he saw her walk over to the wall, run her hand down the length of electric cable between two joists. She was testing to see how taut it was—or not. Smiling to himself, he enjoyed watching her as she saw the cabin through experienced construction eyes. Shiloh was clearly a toucher. She caressed the wood, the electric cord, the lip of the windowsill, ran knowing fingers down the caulking around the window and then knelt down, looking at the floor he'd recently installed.

"Wow, this is gorgeous cedar," she murmured, running her palm across the highly polished gold and reddish floor. "Beautiful job." Roan had not laid a common floor. It was a diagonal-herringbone parquet floor. There was a diamond pattern in darker wood and cedar around the edges of it. And the wood had to be cut to just the right length and then carefully fitted. As her gaze slid across the floor, she saw it had been perfectly laid, a testament to Roan's patience, care, and eye for detail. A perfectionist. "This parquet design is awesome," she murmured, her voice filled with pleasure.

Roan felt his skin tingle. He felt good being praised by Shiloh; she understood the hundreds of hours it had taken him to create the intricate diagonal herringbone design with the cedar. "Thanks."

She looked up, her hand flat on the warm wood floor. "Why did you pick something so intricate and demanding? You could have just laid them straight across and been done with it."

Roan pointed to one of the two large windows facing east. "I wanted the sunlight to come in here every morning and show the design and different grains and colors of the cedar. Artistry, I suppose," he said, and shrugged, giving her an amused look.

Her respect for Roan rose a thousand percent. This cabin was a testament to him. Who he really was. The side of him unseen by others. The discovery thrilled her. Shiloh knew if a house was poorly made, it meant the person was lazy and taking shortcuts. But a cabin like this, a floor like this, told her about the depth of man who was a wrangler, but so much more. "Well, it certainly is artistry," she murmured, sliding her hand slowly across the sunlit wood. "It's gorgeous. I'd wake up every morning, come out here with coffee, and watch the sunlight steal silently across this floor, highlighting all the wonderful colors, the wood grain."

Roan almost said, *I want you to wake up at my side every morning, too*. Where the hell had that thought, that driving need, suddenly come from? Chagrined, Roan had no idea what to say. The woman left him tongue-tied sometimes. He continued to marvel at the awe in her expression, down on her hands and knees now, moving her fingers gently across the pattern, almost reverently following it with her fingertips.

"You know," Shiloh murmured, sliding her fingers to the dark diamond wood design around the edges of the herringbone pattern, "you love wood. Only a person who truly felt the wood, let it speak to them, could design a floor like this." She shook her head and twisted a look up at him. Shiloh saw warmth and pride in his gray eyes and it made her feel good. "There's so much more to you, Roan . . ." she whispered more to herself than to him.

He came over and crouched down in front of her, his hands hanging loosely over his knees. "Maybe we've both been guilty of putting each other in a labeled box?" he teased, catching her gaze, seeing her flush.

"Touché," Shiloh murmured. She sat up, leaning back on her booted heels, hands resting on her long, curved thighs. "Would you mind a second pair of hands here helping you on your days off? I take direction well. If I don't know something, I'll ask."

"You're a team player," Roan praised, feeling suddenly happy. His whole chest felt like it was expanding with an unfamiliar joy as he drowned in her dark green gaze. Her eyes reminded Roan of being deep in an evergreen forest with tiny bits of sunlight falling through the foliage like gold and diamonds.

"I've always been a team person," Shiloh murmured. When she started to get up, Roan stood, offering his hand to her. He'd taken off his gloves and they stuck out in the rear pocket of his Levi's. She wanted to touch this man and slipped her fingers into his large, worn hand. Warmth curled up through her as his sun-darkened fingers wound around hers, gently pulling her to her feet. She saw heat flash through his narrowing gray gaze, saw his eyes go stormy. His fingers tightened briefly around hers. He should let her go. But he wasn't. And she wasn't trying to pull her fingers from his. Drowning in the desire she saw in his eyes, Shiloh realized Roan wanted to kiss her. Going hot from head to toes, her body gnawed with need, Shiloh knew all she had to do was take one step forward. Roan had held her as she cried earlier. She wanted those long, strong arms around her again. The feeling of safety within his embrace tore all the darkness away from her.

Throat growing dry, her gaze settled on his mouth. A wide, strong mouth, well defined, and she felt beyond needy for Roan. Somehow, Shiloh knew he would be a skilled lover and he would put her first, not last. And all of this transpired in a heated second strung between them. Reluctantly, he opened his fingers, allowing her to reclaim her hand. She should have stepped forward, should have taken the unspoken invitation burning in his eyes. Inwardly, Shiloh called herself an emotional coward. Why couldn't she kiss Roan? He wanted to kiss her. She wanted to kiss him!

Shiloh didn't move, her hand dropping to her side. Her heart was beating so hard in her chest, he must have heard it, he was that close to her. Roan hadn't moved, his eyes tracking her every expression, reading her, wanting her. Trying to swallow, she helplessly opened her hands and whispered, "I'm afraid, Roan. . . ." There, it was out. The truth.

"I can see that," he drawled.

There was no judgment in his tone. His voice was low, mellow, and her skin reacted, desperately wanting his touch, his callused fingers gliding and discovering her.

Frowning, Shiloh forced herself to look up at him. Roan deserved her courage, not her cowardice. "You wanted to kiss me."

"I still do."

Her mouth went dry. Her heart amped up, thundering in her breast. "I—I'm afraid."

"Because?"

His patience embraced her. She sensed him monitoring her, that kindness in the recesses of his gray gaze made her feel safe. It gave her the courage to go on. "Because I know you're not the type of man who wants a one-night stand, Roan."

"And you are?" he asked, one brow raised questionably.

Her mouth quirked. "No . . . no, I'm not built like that, either."

"It's just a kiss, Shiloh."

She stared hard at him. "A kiss is never just a kiss and you know it." She watched his mouth twitch, warmth drenching his gray eyes. "It . . . well, it's always meant more to me than that. I can't help it. It's who I am."

"You're saying there has to be more important reasons to kiss than just to kiss?"

Roan was maddening. She glared at him, frustrated. Jamming her hands on her hips, she muttered, "Yes."

"You play for keeps, Darlin'."

Wincing, Shiloh tore her gaze from his. "I don't take liking someone lightly, Roan. I—just never had it in me to just have a fling and walk away from it the next morning."

Nodding, he murmured, "I didn't take you for a woman who played around much."

"Thanks. That's a compliment."

"Are you presently with another man?" Roan wanted to know, damn his soul. There was such powerful yearning tautly strung between them; like a living, heated connection that was screaming to be satiated.

"No . . ."

"Not the last six months, I would guess?" Because that's when the stalker entered her life, imprisoning her. He saw angst in her face and she chewed momentarily on her lower lip. He knew that meant Shiloh was experiencing stress, and he felt bad, but they had to broach this topic. Roan had no idea what the fallout would be, one way or another. But at least he'd know if Shiloh was interested in him or not.

"Yes . . . that . . . of course." Shiloh shook her head and walked away from him and took a few steps, turning around. "I guess you could call me commitment-phobic, Roan. I don't enjoy saying it about myself, but that's my track record." Pushing her damp palms down her thighs, she added, "Maybe I've never fallen in love. I mean, really in love. I meet a guy, and it seems good and positive . . . And then, when things start to get serious, I get scared. I mean, I panic." She looked at him through her lashes, feeling shame. She felt she wasn't whole. It was a feeling; one that she'd never been able to get rid of.

"Panic over what?" Roan wondered, taking off his hat. He placed the Stetson on a wooden peg next to the door and came back, standing a few feet away from Shiloh. Whatever was going on with her was tangled. And complicated. Why would he ever think otherwise?

"I-I don't really know."

"You lost your father when you were young?" he probed gently, seeing her bow her head, staring down at her feet.

"Yes." Shiloh lifted her chin, holding his kind gaze. Despite Roan's size, his muscle, his height, she felt nothing but care emanating from him toward her. The expression in his eyes was full of caring. This was no longer about the kiss. This was about her. Them. *Maybe.* "Why?"

Shrugging, Roan said, "You said earlier that your mother

and father had a very deep love for each other. That after he suddenly died, your mother was lost. For a year?"

Painfully remembering that time, Shiloh gave a jerky nod. "It was the worst year in my life," she admitted softly.

"I'm no shrink," Roan said in a deep tone, "but is it possible you were at such a young, impressionable age when you lost your dad, that when you grew up, a relationship scared you?"

"What do you mean?" Shiloh wanted to cringe and hide within herself because the eagle-like look in Roan's eyes scored her to her soul; as if he suddenly understood everything about her flawed personality. Shiloh wanted him to think good thoughts about her, not see her as distorted, less than, or perhaps not a whole woman.

"Maybe you're hesitant to commit to someone you love because you're afraid you'll lose them? Like your mother lost your father?" he asked, searching her eyes. Roan saw the impact of his observation in her expression, especially her wide, intelligent eyes. His words struck her like an RPG going off beneath her feet. Roan told himself it was always easy for a stranger to see another person's wounds. It was never easy to see one's own scars, however.

Rubbing her wrinkled brow, Shiloh slowly turned away, walking around the shell of the cabin, absorbing his words, what he saw in her. "God," she muttered, halting and staring across the cabin at him, "I never saw this. I never did. . . ."

"Don't be hard on yourself, Shiloh. It wasn't yours to see. When we're in the middle of a firefight, you never have the overview." Roan could see her mind working at the speed of light, saw sudden awareness dawn within her as she sponged in his observation. He saw anguish in her eyes, sadness, and finally a spark of awareness he read as hope.

Roan hoped that she could break this unconscious

pattern of being afraid to get into a serious relationship with someone and riding it out to its natural conclusion. Not afraid to even take the first step to find out what it might be like. Shiloh wasn't a risk taker because she felt if she fell in love, that love would be torn away from her, just as her mother's husband was torn away from her. Even as an eight-year-old, she saw the heart-wrenching destruction of her mother's soul over the loss of her loved one. Roan felt deeply for her, but there was little he could do to help her out of that deadly mind construct she'd erected when so young. To change that pattern, Shiloh would have to consciously face her fears and overcome it.

And then, he asked himself, why was he pursuing this at all with her? To what end? Yes, he wanted this woman in his bed. He wanted to be inside her. He wanted to hear her sweet cries of pleasure. He wanted to please her. Why? Damned if Roan knew. But there was something sweetly innocent about Shiloh that wasn't a put-on; it was simply her. It was who she was. The idealist who wrote about love and romance. Her books always had happy endings that she probably had searched for, and had not found for herself. The books fulfilled a part of her life that had fallen through the cracks of hard knocks and traumatizing experiences at eight years old. But books were no substitute for the real thing. Roan even wondered if she was a virgin. How commitment-phobic was Shiloh? Did a kiss send her into panic? A man wanting her in bed? Or after being in bed, did the relationship get too close to her fear of loss, so she ran? Grimacing, Roan thought he shouldn't use that word. Maybe she left the relationship out of fear. The distorted pattern ran her personal life.

Shiloh stood quietly, feeling such a deep, internal shift within herself, she couldn't describe it. But she sure felt it. That shift was palpable, deep in her unconscious. It scared her. It liberated her. Shiloh felt . . . vulnerable. Really feeling

ALL her emotions, not just some of them. It was as if she were falling, but it wasn't frightening. It was just . . . well . . . different. And uncomfortable. But no panic, thank God. She hated when she panicked. It only happened when a man got too close to her heart.

Lifting her lashes, she held Roan's steady gray gaze as he studied her from across the room. It was as if he realized that she'd shattered inwardly. As if . . . as if he could feel what she had just encountered. And that first rush of vulnerability sweeping through her right now, for whatever reason, was awakening her on levels she'd never before experienced. And Roan Taggart knew it.

Chapter Nine

Roan entered the employee house at nearly seven P.M. Tiredness moved through him, but it was taken away as he saw Shiloh in the kitchen, making them dinner. The house smelled good, like he was home, not just at an employee residence. Roan automatically inhaled the aromas as he shut the door and put his hat on a nearby peg.

"I'm late," he apologized, fighting the desire to walk into the kitchen and talk with her. Since their intense discussion at his cabin a week ago, Roan had decided to back off from Shiloh. Given her past, pressuring her about moving forward in a relationship with him was put on hold. Shiloh was wearing her Levi's and a red tank top that lovingly outlined her breasts, her red hair in a sloppy knot on top of her head. She was busy frying something in a large iron black skillet. When she turned, her smile made him go hot, made him ache so damn much for her. *Hands off*, he warned himself. If Shiloh wanted him, she had to come to him. Not the other way around.

"Good thing," Shiloh teased, smiling as she placed the fried chicken into an awaiting bowl. "I got so immersed in the chapter I was writing, I lost track of time. I thought dinner was going to be late, but you're right on time." Shiloh felt her heart open to Roan. Since their talk, he'd been different. Maybe less available. She couldn't pinpoint what had happened between them. He seemed to be respectful of her understanding of why she always ran from a relationship, never toward it. Grateful for Roan's thoughtfulness, Shiloh still missed the warm intimacy they'd originally established when she first came to the ranch. "Why don't you grab a quick shower? I still have to make us a salad."

Nodding, Roan fought the need to walk up to her, touch her cheek, look deep into her green eyes. He now lived in a new hell of having Shiloh in the house, just a hall's width between their bedroom doors. But he was old enough to know what not to do. Shiloh had to have time to digest their last, serious conversation. And already, he could see evidence of subtle changes in her behavior because of it. Nothing overt, nothing in-your-face. Just a sense that something deep within her had shifted. And, he hoped, for the better. Roan hoped it would lead to her allowing him into her life. "It won't take long," he promised, sauntering through the living room, heading down the hall toward the bathroom.

Yearning moved through her lower body as she watched Roan, dressed in a dusty pair of Levi's and a dark green cowboy shirt, the sleeves rolled up to his elbows, walk away. How she wanted him to touch her. Hold her. The past week had been the best and worst of her life in some ways.

She put the last of the fried chicken in the bowl and set it in the oven to keep warm. Moving to the sink, she washed her hands and then pulled out all the salad ingredients. The look in Roan's eyes told her he still wanted her. Nothing had changed. Shiloh swallowed hard because a part of her wanted him. Wanted to kiss this man who gloried in being outdoors challenging the elements and winning. There was nothing soft about Roan. Nothing. Yet, he'd been tender with her when she'd cried and he'd held her in his arms. Shiloh could not forget those moments, forever stamped on her frightened, wary heart. Could she overcome her past pattern of running when things got serious in a relationship? She didn't know.

Later, as they sat at each other's elbows, eating dinner, Roan detected a subtle happiness about Shiloh. Again, nothing obvious, but his operator's senses told him that. "You said you were writing a chapter? On your latest book? The one that's due to your editor's desk?"

"Yes." She shrugged. "I woke up this morning WANTING to write." She met his gray gaze, seeing his interest. Roan, she was discovering, was a very good listener. And he listened to her without ever interrupting her flow of thought. "First time."

"Is this a good thing?" he wondered, adding more spoonfuls of whipped potatoes onto his plate.

"Sure is," she sighed. She spooned some green beans onto her plate. "Ever since the stalker came into my life, my writing has turned off."

"Kind of expected?"

"I suppose," Shiloh muttered. "It's hurt me in so many ways, seen and unseen."

"It's what we in the military call 'psy ops' or 'psychological warfare.'" He wanted to reach out and squeeze her hand, make her feel safe because so often, Roan saw Shiloh was frightened. Always looking over her shoulder. When he took her into Jackson Hole the other day, she was tense and on guard; as if still expecting the unknown stalker to leap out of the shadows. It hurt him to see her in this mode, but since then, she made some kind of internal breakthrough and she settled down. There was more peace in her face, less tension. The flightiness that was always there seemed to be gone the last three days. Shiloh was struggling and Roan knew all humans went through times like this. He wished he could be of more help to her.

"Good way to put it," she griped, giving him a tight smile.

"Food's top-drawer," he praised, wanting to get her mind off the stalker. "You're really blooming as a cook around here." Roan saw her cheeks turn pink, her shyness returning. He wondered if her aunt and uncle had ever taken serious parental interest in Shiloh as she grew up beneath their roof. Her lack of confidence in herself was stunning. And yet, she'd gone on to become a world-renowned writer, so there was some confidence expressing itself through her. He had a hunch her father's loving care and interest in her at such a young age had forged that creative link with Shiloh. It was a healthy, vibrant part of her that was alive and well.

"Thanks," she said, feeling good about it. "When you said you and the other wranglers were going to be out building fence, I figured you'd be starving by the time you got home tonight." He'd already eaten two chicken breasts, a thigh, and a drumstick. The man knew how to tuck it away. And yet, Roan was made of nothing but hard, sculpted muscle, powerfully built, but not muscle-bound. His dark brown hair was still damp from his recent shower. She could smell his male scent along with the sage soap he'd used.

"Yeah, we got a lot done. It's a good crew I work with." He studied her profile. "So, tell me about writing today? What inspired you to do it?"

Shiloh hesitated. "I don't know. I just woke up with this driving need to put words to paper."

"Does it always happen that way?"

"Yes. I love waking up every morning, feeling that inner

drive and excitement to find out what my characters are going to do next."

He smiled a little, polishing off the potatoes and gravy with a piece of bread. "I've never been good at writing, so you're sort of an anomaly in my life."

"What? Something to be studied under a microscope?" Shiloh teased, grinning. When Roan smiled, that well-shaped mouth of his sent raw, hungry heat flowing throughout her. Shiloh couldn't keep her gaze off his long, spare hands, the calluses she saw on his palm and fingers. A hand she wanted to touch her, explore her and . . . She had to stop going there.

"No," Roan murmured, getting up and taking his plate to the sink. "Interest in how a creative person thinks. How you create. This is all new territory for me."

"I can't explain the process. I once had an editor ask me if I thought writers could be made or were just born the way they were."

Roan poured them coffee, brought the mugs over to the table, and sat back down. "What was your answer?"

"I told her I felt they were born. I mean, you can teach someone the basics of writing, the structure. But you can't teach them how to create. That's where it separates the girls from the women." She stood and took her plate to the sink. Turning, she saw Roan was watching her as he sipped his coffee. Her skin tingled with pleasure. The man's look aroused her body to a level of urgent need. Sitting down, she put cream and sugar in the cup of coffee. "It's a driving, inner passion, Roan. It's not something you can develop by thinking about it. You either have it, or you don't."

"Sort of like falling in love? It just happens?" Roan wondered why the hell he'd picked such an example.

Giving him a grimace, Shiloh muttered, "I've never

been in love, so I wouldn't know what those feelings were, Roan. Sorry."

"Bad example," he agreed. Roan saw the regret in her eyes. "But what you experience is an inner passion or drive to put those words down on your computer?"

"Yes." Shiloh touched the center of her forehead. "This may sound weird, but I see, like a color movie screen moving across my brow, the characters and the scene. I can move inside each character and know what they are thinking and feeling. I hear them talking. I feel their emotions. It's very real to me. And then I write down what I'm seeing, hearing, and feeling from them. It's exciting because I don't know what they're going to say or do."

"Kind of an amazing process," Roan admitted, enjoying getting to know how she wrote a book. "Has it always been like this for you?"

"Yes."

"Did your dad teach you this method?"

"No. But he had the same movie-like process. I definitely think he passed that writing gene on to me," she said, and smiled fondly, still missing her father. Even now, after all these years. Her dad was someone she could confide her dreams to, who encouraged her, and he got just as excited about them as she did. And then Shiloh realized Roan was showing her that same level of interest, even excitement. She could feel his genuine interest and it made her feel good.

"I've never heard of such a thing, but it sounds like what we called the 'imaginal world.' Part of what we did as operators was to imagine our bullet hitting the target when we're practicing out at the range. Much like an athlete visualizes himself or herself being successful at what they're trying to do."

"Yes, it's sort of like that, but it comes from within me,

Roan. It's like it's a living entity, a part of me, that just bubbles up, grabs my attention, engages all my senses, and off I go to write another book."

"Well," he said drily, sipping his coffee, "whatever you have, genetic or otherwise, it's a highly sophisticated ability and skill."

"I've always been grateful to have it." Shiloh felt good beneath his praise. Roan might not be a writer, but he was trying to understand the process and in the end, understand her. It made her feel desired. Respected. The men in her life had all wanted to let their friends and world know they were going with a famous writer. They had used her. And maybe part of why she took herself off the market was because her fame was an impediment. It drew the wrong kind of man. Looking over at Roan, she knew this cowboy wasn't the least bit interested in her because of her fame. The questions he asked, the insights he'd garnered, all showed her he was interested in her as a human being. And that was giddily refreshing as well as scary to her. But now, at least, she knew where her fear had originated. Shiloh would be forever grateful to Roan for his startling insight into why she could not make a relationship work.

"Are you pleased with what you wrote today?"

"I am. It's a rough draft and what I do is put it away for about three months after I've written the manuscript. Then, I return to it to edit and polish it."

"Have you ever had writer's block before?"

Shaking her head, Shiloh said, "Never. My dad never did, either." Painfully, she offered, "I think it's the stalker, my mind is on him. He's stolen my focus."

"Did you think that writer's block meant you'd lost this skill?"

"I didn't really know." She gave Roan a worried look. "I was scared I'd lost it."

"But if it's a genetic gift, you can't lose it," Roan pointed out mildly, giving her a slight smile.

"You're right . . . of course. But you're more pragmatic and logical than I am."

Roan leaned back in his chair, enjoying their conversation. "If you can build houses," he said wryly, "that makes you logical, too. Don't shortchange yourself, Shiloh."

She felt her heart swell with a quiet happiness. Roan was such a refreshing change from the men she knew in New York City. "I think you're right."

"And speaking of building houses," he said, "how would you like to come out tomorrow and work with me? I need to get that porch started. Interested?" and he pinned her with his gaze. Her cheeks flushed and he saw eagerness dancing in her eyes.

"I'd love to!"

"Will it interfere with your writing schedule, though?"

"No. It will be all right."

"I bought you a good pair of leather work gloves. They're in my toolbox at the cabin."

Touched with his consideration, she said, "That's even better than roses and chocolate." Her heart rolled in her chest over his thoughtful gift.

"Well," Roan drawled, "I wouldn't go that far. But you are certainly worth buying roses and chocolate for, too."

Her heart swooned over his dark, low words. Shiloh knew if Roan did something like that, he meant it. It wasn't about trading them off to get her into bed, which is what her other men usually tried to do. Without success. "Thanks," she murmured, giving him a shy glance, "that means a lot." And it did. More than she could say.

"We'll leave at eight tomorrow morning," Roan told her. "I spend dawn to dusk out there. You up for it?"

Was she ever!

* * *

There was a decided chill in the air when they arrived at Roan's cabin. The eastern sunlight bathed the front of the two-story cabin, making it look like molten gold. Shiloh wore loose Levi's, knowing she'd be down on her knees off and on all day. Laying porch was kneeling work. She wore a dark red tee with sleeves and a heavy, dark blue chambray shirt over it, plus her Levi's jacket to ward off the chill. To be able to work closely with Roan all day long brought another kind of excitement to Shiloh. She liked being close to him. He always made her feel happy. Lighter.

Roan pulled his black Chevy pickup to the garage and climbed out. He unlocked one of the doors and retrieved two toolboxes filled with carpenter tools. He gave her the smaller, lighter wooden toolbox.

"Your gloves are in this one," he said, handing it off to her.

"Thanks." Today, Roan wore a black baseball cap, not his cowboy hat. Shiloh took the toolbox and followed him to the south side of the house. He had on Levi's and a black T-shirt that sinfully outlined his upper body; she was salivating to slide her fingers across the fabric to feel his muscles beneath it. Such fantasy!

Her imagination always went wild around Roan. He inspired her on so many levels. He looked more like a black ops soldier today, not a cowboy. She wondered how many times he'd had a brush with death. He always seemed so calm and centered. Nothing seemed to rock his world, unlike her own. And it was that quiet steadiness that appealed so strongly to Shiloh.

Roan put her to work right away. He uncovered the Trex that was six feet long and told her to measure it to a certain length, then go over to the garage where he had his radial saw set up and cut them to those lengths. Shiloh liked that he trusted her. He got to work building the wooden frame.

Shiloh became lost in the process of measuring, carrying over the Trex, and then cutting it. She heard Roan hammering almost constantly and sometimes would look out the garage to see him laying down the four-by-four cedar posts that would be the template for the porch. Just watching his darkly tanned arms, the muscles in them, the gleam of sweat on them as he worked, made her feel needy and hungry for him. He worked slow but sure and the pounding of the hammer was like music of a different sort to her.

Within the first hour, Shiloh had the south side of the porch cut to lengths and had carried them over to the wooden frame. Roan was on his knees and sat up, resting back against his heels, wiping the sweat off his face. He caught and held her gaze as she straightened, brushing off her shirtsleeves.

"Time for a break," he told her, motioning to the large ten-gallon dispenser of water he carried in the back of his truck. "Let's hydrate." He pushed to his feet, laid his hammer down, and took off the leather construction belt from around his narrow hips.

The sun had risen higher, feeling warm on Shiloh. She had tamed her hair into a long, single braid down her back to keep it out of the way. Pulling off her damp leather gloves, she stuffed them in her back pocket. Roan pulled the container to the end of the tailgate, filling two plastic glasses with water. He handed her one.

Their fingers met and Shiloh selfishly absorbed his momentary contact. "Thanks," she said, thirsty.

Roan pushed the container back into the bed of the truck. The day was going to be a bright blue sky, no clouds, and the land was warming up. It was perfect. He sat down on the tailgate and patted a spot next to him. "Come sit. It's good to take a rest."

Shiloh tried to still her heart as Roan gave her a long, heated look. The man wanted her. She wanted him. Why was she still standing in the way? Frustrated with herself, she hopped up on the tailgate, swinging her legs beneath it as she sipped the last of the water. When Roan took off his baseball cap and wiped his sweaty brow, she thought he was incredibly rugged-looking, and so damned sexy. Trying to quell her body, she sat and gazed around at Pine Grove, not far from the cabin. The wildflowers in the nearby meadow were now blooming in wild profusion and looking like a rainbow swath to Shiloh. The air was sweetly scented with all their fragrances and she inhaled it deeply, thinking that this place was so much better than Central Park in New York City.

"Looks like you've got enough Trex cut to lay," Roan said, gesturing to the Trex she'd stacked near the wooden frame.

"I think so."

"You're a hard, consistent worker," Roan murmured, catching her gaze. Red tendrils curled and stuck to her temple and cheek. She was perspiring from working too. "Any problems handling that stuff?"

"No. I've worked with Trex before." Shiloh had to wear a protective face mask to prevent herself from inhaling small particles as she cut it. "Do you want me to start laying it down?"

Roan smiled a little. "You're a regular workhorse, Shiloh."

She grinned a little. "I love feeling taxed, physically. The last six months, it's killed me not to go for my daily jog through Central Park." She had already taken off her jacket, but while carrying wood, she'd kept her protective chambray shirt on her arms. Splinters and cuts were always a possibility.

"You've jogged every day here," Roan said. The gleam of perspiration was across Shiloh's face. She looked healthy, flushed, her eyes radiant with happiness. This was a woman who worked as hard as he did, and loved doing it. Just one more thing to like about her, Roan thought. The way her mouth moved, her lips, made him burn with longing. She seemed at ease in his company. Not wary. Not threatened. He wondered what she would do if he tried to kiss her. It was a thought, but that was all it was. Roan knew if Shiloh came to him, it would be the only way.

"And I love it." Shiloh gave him a silly grin and tapped her head. "I have the most well-honed muscled brain in the world. I need to give my physical body the same kind of workout to stay in balance."

Nodding, Roan finished off his cup of water. He slid off the tailgate, pulled the water container forward, and filled his cup again. Shiloh held hers out to him for a refill. "You're a smart woman, balancing off mental with physical activity," he praised. "A lot of people wouldn't realize that."

She thanked him for the water, drinking all of it quickly, slaking her thirst. Handing the cup back to him, she asked, "Were you in danger when you were in Special Forces?" The need to know Roan was driving her to ask more personal questions of him. She saw his mouth purse slightly as he considered it.

Allowing the water container to sit on the tailgate, he leaned against the truck frame. "Sometimes. Depended upon where my A-team was placed."

"Like, Afghanistan? Iraq?"

"Yes. Sometimes South America."

She smiled and shook her head. "You really have been around."

"It was interesting," Roan said.

"I'll bet you could write great books about your adventures."

"All of mine are top secret," he said drolly, setting the cup next to the container. "Can't breathe a word about them."

"My dad always wrote from his military experience."

"Yes, but probably a lot of what he did wasn't black ops–related. Right?"

"Right."

"Tell me about your growing-up years, Roan," she said, and tilted her head, holding his amused gaze. She felt as if he were humoring her like a petulant, inquisitive child.

"My father was in the Army for thirty years, so I was a military brat."

"Was he in Special Forces like you?"

"Yes, he was. That's why I went into the teams."

"So did you and your mom move around a lot?"

"No, because he was black ops and always being sent overseas to some country. We stayed at the Army base where his unit was based here in the States. My mother, Grace, was born and raised in Montana. And usually, we lived on her parents' ranch when he was ordered overseas. I didn't kick around the globe like a lot of military brats because he was an operator."

"So you grew up on your grandparents' ranch?"

"Yes. Liked it a lot."

"I don't remember much, but my dad was always getting moved from one Air Force base overseas to another, every two years. I was five years old when he left the Air Force and started his writing career, which took off like a rocket."

"We were lucky kids, then."

"Why lucky?" she wondered, watching how relaxed his face became when he reminisced.

"We had an anchor. A place to stay and plant roots. I think that's important. We could make friends. Get to know the community around us."

"You're right," she murmured. "I didn't like moving very much."

"I was restless when I was younger," Roan admitted. "In the teams, we moved around every two to three years, depending upon what our assignment was." He gave her a wry smile. "Now that I'm older, I like sitting in one place with no desire to be a tumbleweed anymore."

Shiloh gestured to his cabin. "Did you buy the land from Maud to live here?"

"Actually," Roan said, pushing away from the truck and pulling on his gloves, "Maud gave me this land as part of my employee package. She likes to help military vets and she's given each of the wranglers who were in the military five acres to build a home on. It's rent-free and it's ours. She's a very generous woman. She also bought the cabin package for me."

"Wow," Shiloh murmured. "That's incredible!"

"Knocked my socks off, too," Roan admitted with a grin. "She's a good person, a great people manager, and she really does support vets. The woman rocks in my world."

Sliding off the tailgate, Shiloh pulled on her gloves. "What a wonderful, priceless gift she's given to you," she murmured, gesturing around the area. "It's so beautiful here. Quiet. Healing."

"All those things," Roan agreed. "Come on, let's get you busy laying that Trex you cut. By the end of the day, if all goes well, we should have the first step in the porch laid."

"And next will come the railing?"

"Yeah," he chuckled. "The work is never done when you build a house. Always something else." As he walked with her to the cabin porch area, Roan appreciated the sway of her hips. He could see Shiloh truly enjoyed what she was doing, as if this country were breathing new life into her. Maybe it was helping to dissolve all the built-up fear she'd experienced over the last six months. Frowning, Roan settled the baseball cap on his head, wishing he had more info on her stalker.

Chapter Ten

Where the hell was Shiloh Gallagher?

Anton Leath sat in his Manhattan apartment. He'd made morning coffee earlier and scoured the *New York Times* intently as he smoked his second cigarette of the morning. It was his only bad habit, not even one he could give up while spending years in federal prison for murdering Isabella Gallagher.

His thick blond brows drew downward as he scanned the arts section, looking for Shiloh's name.

Nothing.

His thick lips flattened. Opening up his laptop on the round table, he decided to go to her Facebook page. He'd gotten onto it with a false name. She had twenty thousand followers and all were avid readers of her books. Smiling as he went to her page, he knew that she had probably never even given his name a second glance. She was too busy gathering a reader base to maintain the popularity of her books. *The little bitch.*

Hatred welled up in Anton. Why the hell hadn't he realized Shiloh, at ten, was standing in the kitchen doorway, watching him stab stupid Isabella? In the bloodlust of killing the woman, he'd allowed Shiloh to escape. Because he was going to stab her next. But the kid had run out of the apartment before he could get his own shit together to go after her.

With a shake of his shaggy head, his blond hair barely touching his thick, heavily muscular shoulders, he stubbed out his cigarette in a nearby ashtray. Scanning Shiloh's Facebook page, he saw her daily entry. All it referred to was what she was writing.

So where was she? Anton had staked out her apartment with binoculars. He could easily stand in the shade between two ten-story apartment buildings, six feet of alleyway between them. It was the perfect hiding place where he couldn't be seen, but he could see her. Unsure if the parole board had contacted Shiloh after he was given five years off for good behavior and released from prison, Anton had come back to the city to finish what he started.

But all of the last week, there were no lights on in her apartment. She had chiffon curtains across all her windows so he couldn't see well, but he could always see her at her desk. Where did she go? Did she run away? On vacation? What? Anton didn't know.

After being released from prison, he'd located her apartment, watched her, got her daily schedule, and then began a slow but sure campaign to unhinge the woman. Anton wanted her so distracted that when he went in for the kill, Shiloh Gallagher would never see it coming. And he'd do it in such a way that the cops would never pin it on him.

For the last six months, Anton had watched his stalking techniques work like magic on Shiloh. Last month, she rarely left her apartment, now a virtual prisoner in it. She'd become too afraid to jog daily in Central Park. Now, instead of going out to get her groceries, she had them delivered. His lips twitched. There was a soaring feeling of triumph flowing through him as he finished his coffee. He shut the lid on his laptop and stood to his six feet, stretching languidly, feeling his muscles flex.

Today, he'd go to the gym and do a two-hour workout with heavy weights. He'd picked up weight lifting in prison and found it not only made him fit and healthy, but it also took off the angry edge that was always with him. If Shiloh, at eleven years old, hadn't been the star witness for the prosecution, he'd never have gone to prison. Too many years of his life had been lost and as he walked down the hall to the bathroom, Anton swore he would find Shiloh. And he would kill her.

By the end of the day, the sun close to setting, Shiloh sat on the newly constructed porch, her hands draped between her open thighs. The sun spread silently through the wide valley. In the west rose the jagged Wilson Range. To the east were the Salt River Mountains. North lay the narrow valley where Yellowstone National Park sat as well as the Grand Tetons National Park.

She tugged off her work gloves, which were damp from her perspiration. Watching Roan get them two cups of water from the big dispenser in the bed of his truck, Shiloh smiled to herself. Looking to her left, she felt satisfaction. She'd cut Trex to the correct lengths for all three sides of the porch. Between them, they'd screwed it into place.

Shiloh held out her hand as Roan stopped in front of her and gave her the plastic cup. "Thanks," she murmured.

Roan sat down next to her, about a foot between them. "I would never have guessed a writer could lay a porch," he told her wryly, turning, meeting her eyes. Shiloh's hair was mussed, her ponytail coming somewhat loosened over the afternoon's hard work. Tendrils stuck damply to her temples and cheeks. He could see she was happy, her green eyes radiant, her mouth curving into that soft smile of hers. His body wanted her, no question. Roan had worked to ignore her feminine side, the woman in her. When Shiloh had shed her chambray shirt, stripping down to a sleeveless tee that outlined her breasts beneath it, Roan had groaned inwardly. The sweat had gleamed off her shoulders and arms as she used fasteners to screw the Trex into place. She was a woman who wasn't afraid to get her hands or herself dirty. Another plus in his book.

"And who would have guessed an Army Special Forces guy would build his own home?" she teased in return. She watched his Adam's apple bob as he tilted his head back, slugging down the water, thirsty. His flesh glistened and his masculine scent filled her nostrils. Her heart squeezed with a combination of need and happiness. Working with Roan today made her feel so different. So . . . fulfilled. And yes, working as a team member on something important made her happy.

Shiloh had always known she was a team person. And Roan had been a patient instructor when necessary, quietly directing her or showing her how to use the air-powered nail gun. She remembered how impatient and angry Anton Leath had become with her as a child; Roan was the complete opposite. This allowed Shiloh to not only enjoy working beside him, but also the pleasure of simply being in his company. He was a hard worker, just like herself.

Roan grinned as he lifted the cup away from his lips. He slanted her an amused glance. "So, what is a Special Forces soldier in your opinion, I wonder?" He didn't want to admit it, but he was interested in how Shiloh saw him. Roan knew being identified as a black ops person led others to prejudge him. And with Shiloh, he wanted her to see *him*, not the label or the operator. Why? His heart tugged in his chest as he watched her expression become serious and contemplative. She didn't take anything he said lightly. Instead, he could see her thinking over the question fully. Shiloh cared. But did she care about him, specifically? Or did she care in general about any human being whom she was interacting with? Roan wanted her to care about *him*. He didn't look too closely at why.

Settling her elbows on her knees and cupping her hand beneath her chin, Shiloh tilted her head, holding Roan's gray gaze. "My dad, even though he was an Air Force combat pilot, knew plenty about the world of black ops. Did I tell you that he worked as a CCT over in the Middle East? That he was on the ground, as a pilot, calling in jets or other aircraft to protect black ops groups?"

Roan's brow rose a little. "No, you didn't. You're just full of surprises, aren't you?" He saw her give him a wolfish grin. A CCT was a communications specialist on the ground directing air, weapons, and bombs onto hot targets. These men were sometimes enlisted and sometimes actual Air Force jet pilots, who remained deep behind enemy lines, with a black ops group, and worked the air portion to keep soldiers safe. It was a very dangerous job and Roan had worked primarily with enlisted Air Force CCTs, never any pilot officers. It gave him a new appreciation of Shiloh's father, and his respect for the man rose even higher.

"I didn't know if you'd be interested." Shiloh saw him nod, as if understanding what she meant. "My dad used to tell me stories about the black ops groups he worked with. Nothing that was top secret, of course, but he could tell me incredible stories and I hung on every word. Later, he would go on to write about this type of thing, but never about actual events."

"With his background, I imagine he could pen a really good suspense and adventure tale," Roan said.

"He did. They were so alive, Roan." She smiled fondly. "I was young, but my aunt and uncle allowed me to start reading his books when I was fourteen. They felt I was old enough to understand them. I just fell in love with my dad's storytelling. I hung on every word he wrote. I loved it because it brought back wonderful memories of me sitting at his feet when he'd tell me one of his black ops stories."

Roan could hear the grief and longing in Shiloh's quiet voice as she reminisced about her father. "I need to go to the library in Jackson Hole and pick up a copy of one of his books." Because by knowing her father, he would know Shiloh better. Roan decided to stop denying to himself why he wanted to do it. Shiloh interested him as no other woman ever had. He saw grief deep in her eyes and couldn't go there with her. His father, Al, was alive, healthy and living on his Montana ranch. He wished for Shiloh's sake that her father hadn't died in his prime. She missed him terribly.

"Oh, if you want, I have all of Dad's books on my iPad. I can lend it to you and you can read the e-book version."

Nodding, Roan said, "I'd like that. Thanks."

"So," Shiloh murmured, "you asked me what I thought of Army Special Forces soldiers?"

Roan more or less internally steeled himself. "Yes. Fire away." He knew she would.

Laughing a little, Shiloh said, "I can only surmise from what my dad told me. He said of all the black ops groups, the most well-rounded one was U.S. Army Special Forces. That only sergeants with six or seven years could try for an A-team. The guys he worked with not only knew the language of the area they were in, but they had certain skill sets, like weapons, combat medicine, mechanics, communication, and things like that. They were well read and they respected and knew the customs of the people they were living among. They were sharp, intelligent men, who missed little and were well aware of the political situation of that country. He said what impressed him the most was the amount of intel that you guys could wring out of the local populace."

"That was because we earned their trust."

"Right," Shiloh agreed, nodding. Her lips curved. "So, I know you're a very astute person, Roan. You watch a lot and say little. You're a good observer of the human condition. I've seen how you've worked with me today. You were patient, easygoing, explained things, and never once lost your temper or became impatient."

"People don't learn when you're yelling at them or cutting into the confidence they're trying to build," he said. Roan wasn't sure if he felt comfortable with all of Shiloh's accurate assessment of him. He rarely allowed anyone inside himself, to really know who he was, warts and all. But Shiloh's keen insights were unsettling. At the same time, Roan didn't feel like she'd use that knowledge against him. He prided himself on knowing human potential. She wasn't a cream puff or a pushover. She was like her father in that she respected others, never judged them, but was interested in what made them tick the way they did.

"You're a good teacher, Roan. You made today so much fun for me." Shiloh searched his gray eyes, sensing a shift between them. She felt an overpowering need to kiss this man. Never had she wanted anything more. And she saw desire in his eyes—for her. It was there. In plain sight.

Tension swirled around them and Shiloh's throat grew dry, an ache in her heart for enigmatic Roan. Her pulse sped up as she saw a slight narrowing of his gray eyes as he studied her in the throbbing, heated silence between them. Without thinking, Shiloh fractionally leaned toward him, tipping her chin upward. Her eyes met his. A lush heat flowed down through her, settling hotly in her lower body. Her fingers itched to touch Roan's hard jaw, to feel the stubble that darkened his face rasping beneath her fingertips.

And then, he lifted his hand, sliding his roughened fingers across her slender jaw, eliciting wild, sparking heat through her skin, making her breath hitch. Shiloh felt her heart swell with a wealth of unexpected emotions and needs for Roan. It surprised her. And she allowed herself to be angled toward his descending mouth, his eyes narrowed like a hunter upon hers as he drew her closer. Shiloh could feel the moistness of Roan's breath as he lowered his head toward hers. Automatically, her lips parted. His fingers tightened just a bit against her jaw, holding her in place. Right where he wanted her. Lashes sweeping downward, Shiloh strained forward, lifting her mouth toward his. She could smell the sweat, the dust of the day and his unique male fragrance. It made her thighs clench with desperate need of Roan.

His mouth barely brushed hers. Butterfly light, as if gently introducing himself to her. A keening sensation shot hotly through her as she felt his mouth skim hers, latent power held in check, a promise of things to come.

Lifting her hand, Shiloh placed it against the hard wall of his chest, his T-shirt damp with sweat, clinging to his flesh. Wanting more, Shiloh sought and found his mouth hovering a bare inch above hers. She understood what Roan was doing. He was making sure this was what she wanted. It was. As her lips moved slowly, tasting him, tasting that power she felt leashed tautly within him, a soft moan caught in her throat. Roan tasted of male and sunlight. His mouth met hers more firmly, gliding, tasting and memorizing her. There was no hurry. It was slow and delicious, like tasting the most exquisite dessert Shiloh had ever encountered. Just the way he eased his mouth more surely against her parted lips, she knew he was skilled at making love with a woman.

Somewhere in Shiloh's mind, it occurred to her that, like a black ops soldier, he moved in carefully, all senses alert, wanting to understand the situation fully before committing. In his line of work if he didn't slowly approach an area, it could get him killed in an ambush. Shiloh knew Roan didn't see her as an enemy or threat, but his approach to her told him he cared enough about his potential partner to see if she wanted to engage with him or not. Or just a little. Or a lot.

Her fingers instinctively curved slightly into the damp fabric as he took her lips more surely, connected with her, silently inviting her to meet and meld fully with his mouth. Her heart was thundering and she couldn't hear anything except his ragged breath, the moistness flowing across her cheek and nose as he deepened their exploration of each other. He sipped at her lips, his mouth curving more strongly against hers as she responded in kind, letting him know she wanted more. Shiloh had scooted closer to him, sliding her other hand around the thick column of his neck, feeling him tense, a low growl issuing from deep within his massive chest. The sound spurred her on and she parted her lips more, allowing her hunger to drive her forward.

As his fingers dragged through her hair, her scalp erupted with tiny, pleasurable tingles, making her moan, the sound vibrating through her, telling Roan how much she wanted his continued touch. His hand cupped the back of her head and he pulled her closer, angling her so that he had full access to her wet lips. Shiloh's whole world focused on Roan, his maleness, his holding her captive while he tasted her with a maddening leisure that made her drown in wavelike ripples of heightening pleasure.

There was such caged animal power around him; as if he

were holding himself in tight check. Shiloh sensed Roan wanted much more than just a kiss. Her mind was full of swirling light and she could feel the primal hunger within herself leaping forward, committed to this man. In every possible way. She lifted her hand from his chest, sliding it along his rugged jawline, the stubble covering it like wildfire spreading through her fingers, moving straight to her tightening breasts, puckering her nipples.

Roan moved his tongue slowly across her lower lip. Shiloh tensed with hunger, a cry lodged in her chest, her hand tightening against his jaw and neck. The man knew exactly what he was doing: a slow, sweet assault upon her senses, teasing her, pulling her toward him, discovering her one delicious inch at a time. As Roan moved to the corner of her mouth, she trembled violently, opening her mouth more, asking him to enter her. Every cell in her body was suspended for a moment as she boldly touched his tongue with her own. Instantly, she felt him freeze, as if to stop himself from grabbing her and throwing her down on the porch and taking her right then and there. The reactive sensation swept intense yearning through Shiloh and she felt for the first time what Roan really wanted from her. It was raw. Primitive. Starving. As he met her tongue, she quivered, pressing herself wantonly against his chest, trying to somehow get a little closer to Roan, to dissolve into his masculine power that twisted and eddied like feverish heat between and around them.

Shiloh's breath grew ragged. Her heart was pulsing heavily in her breast. She was not afraid of Roan and ran toward what he was offering her. An ache began to throb between her thighs and Shiloh felt dampness between them. All the man had done was kiss her! That was how much power he held over her and for once, Shiloh embraced it. She felt his fingers caress her scalp, the sensations swift, heated shocks rocking through her body. His breath was punctuated against her cheek and nose. The tension mounted in him until Shiloh felt as if he would snap and break, unleashing that throbbing sexual power she sensed so intensely around him.

Roan reluctantly broke their kiss, pulling back just enough to hold her barely opening eyes. They were breathing hard. Both were tense. Needy. Wanting. She gulped and fearlessly met his stormy gray gaze. Shiloh had never seen a man who was a hunter. But she saw one now. There was an intense feeling around Roan, raw and untamed, as he studied her, his nostrils flaring to catch her scent. He ruthlessly dug into her opening eyes, reading her, trying to understand where she was at within herself and what she wanted from him.

"This is your call," he said, his voice low and guttural.

Shiloh felt him remove his fingers from her hair. She wanted to groan over the loss until he began to sift them through her strands, sending new and wonderful heat through her ripening body. Roan ruthlessly searched her eyes. It was so hard to speak, her body online, her brain offline. Licking her lower lip, tasting Roan on it, she managed a trembling, "I don't want you to stop. I don't want to stop," and she fearlessly met and held his intent gaze. There was a bare movement of the corner of his well-shaped mouth curving upward. She felt as if she were quivering from the inside out with excitement coupled with a desperate yearning for Roan in every possible way.

Large hands, long, callused fingers curled around her shoulders. Her flesh was wild with throbbing need as he gently smoothed the rumpled fabric against her shoulders and upper back. "Sure?"

Shiloh gulped. It felt to her as if she were stepping off into space. Instinctively, she knew committing to Roan was going to change her life. This man played for keeps. He made no attempt to disguise his need for her. She saw it in his gray, silver-flecked eyes. Felt it like a fiery blanket surrounding her. "Very sure." She saw his straight, dark brown brows fall. For a moment, she panicked. Was Roan backing off? Worried in some way? Doubting her? Himself?

Roan moved her hair across her shoulder. "You're a brave little thing. You know that?" he said, and his mouth curved carelessly.

Shiloh wanted to melt in his hands. They moved through the silk of her hair. She saw appreciation in his expression, pleasure burning in his eyes as he continued to tangle his fingers, as if exploring. It was such a sensual experience for her. "I know what I want," she admitted, breathless. His smile grew male and he released her hair, sliding his hands down the length of her arms, capturing her fingers within his.

"This changes everything, Shiloh. You know that, don't you?"

Giving a jerky nod, she whispered, "Yes. You play for keeps, Roan. You're not a one-night-stand kind of man." She watched him lose his smile as he studied her with hunger. Finally, he was allowing her to see how he really felt toward her. To be desired by this taciturn, intense warrior made every inch of her body spring to thrilling life. She wanted his hands all over her, exploring her, teasing her, giving her pleasure. Roan was skilled. That much was obvious, but this man had such depth that he engaged her on deeper levels. Roan was a one-woman kind of man. He wasn't the type to walk away. She'd walked away from three relationships in her life precisely because they were getting too close. She was so afraid of loss. Loss of the man she'd give her heart to. Her mother was utterly smitten with her father. She'd given her soul to him. Only to have her soul ripped apart, her heart utterly crushed, when he'd died so young. So suddenly.

"You're afraid."

Roan's low, deep voice flowed through her wall of fear. She saw questions in his eyes. What was she afraid of? "Not of you."

Nodding, Roan cupped her hands within his spare ones, studying them. "The fear you have is deep, Shiloh."

"It has nothing to do with you." She saw that hooked, one-cornered smile tug at his mouth. His eyes never left hers; as if he were memorizing her, burning her into his mind, his heart. His soul? She didn't want to go there. Didn't even want to think beyond tonight.

"I think it does."

Her lips thinned and she looked away, feeling the roughness of his fingers upon hers. Her flesh was starving for his touch, tiny jolts of heat flying continuously up her hand and into her wrist as he gently moved them within his fingers. He handled her as if she were a priceless, fragile being who might shatter if touched wrongly. Forcing herself to look up at Roan, she saw his eyes had grown gentle with questions once more. The man inspired trust. Now she was getting a taste of what he'd said earlier about villagers trusting the A-team members. Roan cultivated it like breathing.

"I—" she stumbled, frowning. Shiloh felt ashamed in even admitting it to Roan, but she pushed herself because he was a man of honor. He presented himself exactly as he was. No games. No mask. No charade. Roan deserved her honesty. "I don't have a good track record with men," she began in a halting voice. "At a certain point, I break it off. . . ." Shame swallowed her whole and she couldn't hold the sympathetic look that she saw come to Roan's gray eyes.

"Is that a promise? Or is it a warning, Darlin'?"

Hearing the roughened words, she shrugged. "I just can't seem to commit, Roan. You're right: I get scared. I break it off. I haven't had that many relationships. Three." Shiloh felt as if she were severely lacking. A wound so large in her that it controlled her life. That wasn't something to be proud of and she felt humiliated by admitting it to Roan.

"And you're afraid you'll break it off with me the same way you did with the other men?"

The man went straight to the heart of everything! No messing around. No diplomacy. Just straight to her heart. Swallowing hard, Shiloh held his gaze. "Yes." Her heart squeezed in pain, as if she had already lost Roan before she ever got to know him. To be loved by this man. Grief spread through her chest and she pulled one hand free of his, pressing it against her heart. Her voice held unshed tears in it. "You don't deserve that, Roan. You're a good, hardworking man. You're honest. I've never met anyone like you before. I-I don't want to hurt you because of myself." Shiloh shut her eyes, feeling the heat of tears fill them. She didn't want to cry in front of Roan. He would probably think her weak.

She felt Roan gently pry her hand away from her chest and she opened her eyes. He was watching her with those dark gray eyes of his, and she felt an invisible embrace from him. He seemed stoic and unmoved by her emotional words. His mouth was relaxed. There was no tension in his face. Just calm. Like a starving thief, she absorbed the warmth of his hands around hers. He had such strength, yet his touch was gentle. Shiloh somehow knew he'd be a tender lover if that was what she needed. Roan read people just as well as she did. And he knew that she was presently emotionally fragile. She trusted him with her life, no question.

"Then," he said in a deep tone, "let's just take it a day at a time?"

Compressing her lips, Shiloh forced the tears away and opened her eyes. Roan looked like an unruffled Buddha, as if her admission wasn't really that terrible. And if it was, he'd weighed and evaluated her fear and was not scared of it or of her fleeing from him. She wondered if anything ever frightened Roan. Just looking at his hard, elemental features, she knew he'd suffered greatly. And yet, he sat quietly, holding her hands, fully accepting her just as she was. Unafraid. Wanting her. Wanting to share something of value to both of them with each other. "Okay," she said in a strained voice, "one day at a time . . ."

Chapter Eleven

Roan rummaged around in the kitchen. Shiloh was taking a shower while he prepared dinner. She'd grown very quiet on the trip back to the employee house from his cabin. There was a sense she desired him coupled with a deeply ingrained fear. He panfried some fresh trout that Maud had placed in his fridge earlier. Roan tried to sense his way through Shiloh's present state. Maybe he'd said too much too soon to her? Maybe he shouldn't have kissed her at all? His mouth still burned hotly in memory of her soft, opening lips blossoming sweetly beneath his mouth. He could still taste her on his lips. Never mind he'd gotten an instant erection over her fearless, bold kiss with him. The woman was a complete turn-on. His body reacted long before his mind became engaged in the process.

He'd taken his shower first at Shiloh's insistence. Maybe she needed some alone time in her bedroom to collect herself from that world-tilting kiss they'd shared. He'd never look at the porch again without remembering that torrid, slow, deep kiss with Shiloh. Damn, but the woman was certifiably a turn-on. Roan wasn't sure she was fully aware of her impact on him. Her head was in the clouds, literally, because she was a writer. And she seemed somewhat detached from the effect her face, body, and the way those sweet hips of hers moved had on men. From his perspective, she really was the total package. Even more, Roan liked her fearlessness. She'd made the move to kiss him first. She'd wanted him as much as he wanted her. That had surprised him, but it didn't take a nanosecond to celebrate the discovery and then kiss her senseless in return.

Roan heard the bathroom door open and Shiloh pad down the hall to her bedroom. He forced himself to focus on cooking. He was the one who told her they'd take it slow. His body was more than ready and so was he. But right now, their kiss had brought up a huge red-flag warning. Giving Shiloh credit for being honest with him about her pattern in relationships, Roan knew she cared enough for him to admit it. And he'd seen the shame in her eyes when she'd divulged the truth.

Roan ruthlessly looked at himself, his part in all of this. He needed alone time to sift through the deeper meaning and his reaction toward Shiloh.

The door to her bedroom opened and he cast a glance over his shoulder as he placed the fried trout onto a platter. She came into the kitchen, and he saw that she'd dried her hair and it was captured into a loose knot on top of her head. The clean pale-green tee made his lower body clench. And even though she wore a pair of white capris, her slender legs made him want to run his hand down them. In the capris Shiloh looked like a young girl with bare feet. Smiling to himself, Roan focused on the food. One moment, a woman. The next, a young girl. He liked discovering Shiloh's quicksilver facets.

"How can I help?" she asked.

"Set the table?" Roan glanced over to see the dark green of her eyes, understanding she was still processing what had happened between them too. "Maud left us some fresh trout in the fridge. Thought we'd have that, some peas, and a salad?"

"Sounds great. I'm starved."

So was he. For her. Roan didn't say anything. He wanted to kiss her again. Take her all the way. Placing his considerable patience online, he told himself their relationship, or whatever he wanted to call it, was complicated. Shiloh was complex.

The pleasant clink of plates and flatware made Roan realize just how lonely he'd become before Shiloh had stepped unexpectedly into his life. She moved quietly, saying nothing, but he could feel her warm, feminine presence just the same. This made Roan realize what he was missing in life: a relationship.

Shaking his head, he brought the veggies from the fridge to make them into a salad. Since when had he ever wanted a long-term relationship with a woman? He wasn't thinking a week or even a month with Shiloh Gallagher. He was thinking a lifetime. His heart clearly was not in sync with his head. Neither was his body. Her bold kiss vividly told him what he'd never really found. Until now. *Until Shiloh.*

Taking a deep breath, Roan ordered himself to stand down. Her soft mouth had dismantled him on every conceivable level. He hadn't been thinking about kissing her. His mind was focused on that porch. Did he like having her company while they installed it? Yes. It was new. It was . . . well . . . amazing. She had a way of getting inside walls he kept well in place around him. Shiloh was like silent fog stealing over the landscape of himself, subtly infiltrating him as a man before he ever realized it. And once he did, it was too late.

Roan didn't put the blame for the kiss on Shiloh. It had just HAPPENED. As if the chemistry had built and built, and the explosion that occurred as a result had taken them both by surprise. He wondered if Shiloh felt the same.

Roan honestly didn't know. Her green eyes were always alive with intelligence, but he couldn't read her penetrating mind. Or her heart. Now, he wished he could.

Within minutes, Roan had everything assembled for their dinner. Shiloh had taken the bowls of salad over to the table and he brought the fish and a dish of steaming peas slathered with fresh basil leaves in melted butter. She had thoughtfully brought out a half dozen of his biscuits left over, warmed them in the microwave, and placed the butter and honey next to them. Shiloh knew how much he liked his homemade biscuits and he smiled to himself.

As Roan pulled her chair out for her to sit down, he said, "How are your hands?"

Shiloh shrugged. "A few blisters is all." She opened them as he sat down, showing her palms to him. "No big deal."

Roan settled into the chair and gently held one of her hands, looking at two small blisters caused by the nail gun she'd used all day. Her skin was soft. Fragrant. His nostrils flared, catching the scent of her lilac soap combined with the shampoo Shiloh had used. "You should have let me do most of the work," he said, reluctantly releasing her hand. He opened his palm, showing her the thick calluses created by constant hard work around the ranch. "I've already built the calluses up to protect my skin."

"I'll just put Band-Aids on them and they'll be fine." Shiloh placed one trout on her plate.

"Did you get blisters when you worked on those other homes?" he wondered. It was a special hell watching her graceful movements as she added a hefty amount of peas to her dish.

"Always." Shiloh smiled a little. "I've got a sedentary career, sitting in a chair for hours at a time. When I volunteer to work on a house, the first couple of weeks my palms are a mess, but after that, I get calluses and I'm fine for the duration."

Roan put two trout on his plate, leaving the last one for Shiloh. She needed to eat more, but he said nothing. "I'm going out tomorrow morning to work on the cabin." He wanted to ask her to come along, but thought better of it, not wanting Shiloh to feel as if he expected anything of her. She'd warned him off and he respected that.

"What are you going to do tomorrow?"

"Start putting up the railing." Every cell in him wanted her to come along. Roan liked her quiet, feminine company. He had no fantasy about kissing Shiloh again. He'd promised to give her the room she needed. And frankly, she was stressed enough.

"What kind of wood will you use for the railing?"

"I'm using cedar. It's insect-proof. I've got it stacked in the garage to keep it out of the elements and dry. The boards have to be straight." And water always bent boards if they weren't protected from the harsh elements. He watched her lashes lower as she consumed the trout. Damn, gazing at those lips of hers move as she ate was sending a twisting, needy ache straight down to his lower body. The woman was a certifiable riot to his body. She wrote romances. She had to know her effect on him. Didn't she? Roan decided unhappily that Shiloh didn't realize how she affected him at all. Reminding himself that if she'd only had three relationships in her life, her experience with men was limited. The same with sex. Or lust. Or . . . damn, his mind just wouldn't get out of that life-changing kiss Shiloh had shared with him.

"Whenever I worked on a house crew, I built porches, railing, and then went inside and we started the interior work. I did insulation, drywall, and painting."

"You're multiskilled," he teased, one corner of his mouth lifting as he met and held her gaze. Wanting to drown in those forest green eyes, Roan forced himself to break off contact. If he didn't, he was going to give his soul to her. Could one kiss REALLY make him feel like this? He'd kissed plenty of women in his time, but no kiss had ever packed the punch, the depth, and the feverish heat that came with it when Shiloh shyly touched his lips in return.

Shrugging, Shiloh hungrily finished off the first trout. "I'm not any good at plumbing or electrical." She offered him a small smile. "I'm always worried I'll get electrocuted. You know, put the two wrong wires together and get zapped?"

He nodded. "Plumbing and electric are my specialties."

"Good thing," Shiloh said with a quiet laugh. "Because I have a healthy respect for electric. I stay away from it."

"Did you get zapped once? Is that why you're gun-shy?"

"No. It just scares me. No logical reason," she said, shrugging.

"Take the second trout," Roan urged, pointing his fork toward the platter. "You need to put some meat on your bones, Shiloh." Her name rolled off his lips like an endearment.

"Thanks."

Roan watched her lift the platter and slide the trout onto her plate. No matter what Shiloh did, it was done with grace. He wondered if she'd ever taken ballet lessons, but tamped down the question that almost flew out of his mouth. "Think you'll work on your book tomorrow?"

"I'm not sure," Shiloh admitted. "I've been ruminating on this great scene in my head, but I'm not sure it's ready for birth yet."

"Do you see your books as children?"

She lifted her chin, regarding him in the gathering silence. "Yes . . . I guess I do. I never thought of it like that." Giving him a silly grin and tapping her head, she said, "Brain children."

When Shiloh smiled, Roan's heart widened like windows being thrown open to allow sunlight into his dark soul. She didn't realize her effect on him, and a lot HAD happened between them, Roan acknowledged. Even more reason to keep their conversation light and keep things status quo like before the kiss. Roan realized he was now going to be looking at Shiloh, at their situation as "before the kiss" and "after the kiss." Unhappy with his heart that truly had an emotional mind of its own, he put his emptied plate aside and dug into the large salad.

Shiloh awoke slowly, the sun stealing around the edges of the curtains. Rubbing her eyes, she turned over, looking at the small round clock on the bed stand. It was nine A.M.! The house was quiet and she realized as she pulled off the covers, her feet touching the cool cedar flooring, that Roan had left many hours earlier. Probably at dawn. He was used to getting up as darkness was giving way to the coming day.

Pushing hair out of her eyes, Shiloh sat in her lavender cotton nightgown, struggling to wake up. She didn't wake up fast in the morning, anyway, needing that cup of coffee to jolt her back to reality.

Yawning, she stood and stretched her hands over her head, feeling her body, feeling how her heart automatically centered around Roan. Shiloh touched her lips, remembering that life-affirming kiss she'd shared with him. Her heart wanted to be out with Roan at his cabin, working alongside him like the good team they were. She loved the cabin, loved the layout inside it. Roan had been creative in how he'd designed the rooms, leaving the kitchen and living room open-concept and airy. He was a man who clearly thought things out before starting a project.

Was she a project to him? Shiloh gathered up a clean set of jeans, an orange tank top, and socks, and walked down the hall to the bathroom to get a hot shower. Why had she kissed Roan? It had been a blinding, spontaneous action on her part. *She* had kissed *him*. Not the other way around. Groaning, Shiloh stepped into the bathroom and set her clothes on the small vanity. She gathered up her tangled mass of hair and plopped it into a knot on top of her head. Turning on the faucets, she looked forward to the water and the scent of the lilac soap she loved so much.

Even beneath the spray of water sluicing across her face and body, Shiloh couldn't stop thinking, couldn't stop feeling Roan's mouth moving against her lips. The man knew how to kiss! Just thinking about it made her clench inwardly and her body go into an instant ache of yearning.

Her imagination took flight as she covered herself with the bubbles of the lilac soap across her arms. What would his long, roughened fingers feel like sliding across her flesh? How would she react? Shiloh could feel the fever of wanting him already making her breasts tighten. She felt restive, unsettled, needy and pining for his touch upon her.

By the time Shiloh emerged from the bathroom, she decided her wild imagination had full control over her physical body. Padding out to the kitchen, she saw a hand-scrawled note left on the counter. Picking it up, she read, "Shiloh, pancake batter in the fridge. Left some for you. R."

Her fingertips tingled as she held the note. Her heart swelled. She sighed audibly and set the note aside. The man wasn't selfish, that was for sure. Roan knew how much she loved pancakes. A soft smile played at the corners of her mouth as she opened the fridge and drew out the pitcher that held the batter. As Shiloh made herself a big stack of pancakes, her mind kept returning to the same question. Why was she afraid to step into a relationship with Roan?

As she slathered butter between the stack and then poured warm maple syrup over it, she frowned. Roan played for keeps. Was that what scared hell out of her?

Feeling she wasn't capable of commitment but knowing Roan was built that way was the dilemma. As Shiloh hungrily dug into the pancakes, savoring the nutty flavor, the hint of cinnamon combined with the sweet maple syrup, she knew the problem was with her. She didn't want to hurt Roan. He'd demonstrated consistently that he was a gentleman, that he was sincere and he cared about her. He was sensitive to her needs, too. Knew how to share. Was a team player.

She was in so such trouble.

Shiloh was surprised she finished off the pancakes, feeling as if she'd eaten too much, but thinking about or being around Roan always spurred her appetite. Both stomach-wise and sexually. He'd been right: She was terribly underweight. Six months of being stalked had made her feel like a trapped, frightened animal, confined to her apartment. Just surviving. She'd lost her appetite long ago.

Roan made her want to live again. To dream.

The realization hit Shiloh and shook her to her core as she sat at the table finishing off her third cup of coffee. Roan was vital. A man of the earth. He relished hard, demanding work. His body was ripped and she ached to explore every inch of him in her bed. Her mind kept going there with him. Shiloh knew from just that kiss, Roan would be an exquisite lover. He would take her to places she'd never known existed except in his arms, him inside her, him loving her until she melted like hot syrup all around him. Geez. She had it bad!

Standing, Shiloh was frustrated sexually and emotionally. She rinsed her dishes and put them in the dishwasher. Finishing off her coffee, she decided that keeping busy would get her mind off Roan and her lusting body. The house needed a good weekly cleaning. And it was her turn to do it, anyway. Right now, Shiloh wouldn't be able to sit and create a thing. Putting some Band-Aids on her blisters, she got to work.

Sweat dripped off Roan's brow as he sat up, resting against his boot heels and wiping his brow with the back of his arm. His stomach growled. It was noon. The sunlight was strong, lancing through the newly created railing he'd put up earlier. He liked the play of shadow and light, liked the dark bars sliding silently across the Trex porch.

His mind and body automatically went to Shiloh, remembering her down on her hands and knees yesterday, placing nails into the Trex like a pro. She sure as hell caught on quickly. The nails were long and designed to solidly hold the wood in place. He'd seen the play of muscles in her forearms and biceps as she handled that nail gun with ease and familiarity. His mouth flexed. Let's face it, he thought, he'd been in a male world without females around for the last twelve years of his life. In Special Forces, he was in the company of men only. He knew that would change now that women were allowed into combat. The point was, he was never around women.

Women were forgotten in the combat of their black ops missions. While it was true half the team was married, the other half wasn't. Roan had wanted it that way; not to be distracted by a woman or family left at home. He enjoyed the hell out of women in bed, and even having a meaningful relationship with one woman when he was stateside. Roan had never led that woman on as to their relationship and how it was going to end when he was redeployed.

Now, it was different. Shiloh was different. Damn, the woman was under his skin, worse than an itch that couldn't be scratched. Laughing to himself as he slowly rose to his full height, hammer gun dangling in his gloved hand,

Roan knew the shoe was now on the other foot. Instead of walking away from the woman, he was walking *toward* Shiloh. And he didn't want to walk away from her. How the hell had THAT happened? When? Roan prided himself on knowing himself pretty well. He was a hard-core realist. Not a romantic. Not an idealist. In his line of work, pragmatism helped him survive.

He picked up the sound of a truck coming his way. Lifting his chin, he looked toward Pine Hills. There was a dirt and gravel road between the hills and he saw one of the white ranch trucks appear. Who? Walking along the southern part of the porch that still needed the railing built, Roan placed the hammer gun on the deck and dropped his sweat-darkened leather gloves next to it. Taking off his black baseball cap, he ran his fingers through his damp hair and settled the cap back on his head, his focus on the truck coming his way.

Maud? Sometimes, especially on a Sunday afternoon, she'd be out and about in her truck, checking the massive ranch. The weekly tourist families left at ten A.M. And the rest of the day was spent getting ready for another six families to come in for a week beginning at four P.M. the same day. She always stole time about now to drive around the ranch, checking on the fencing, the pastures, and the animals. It was just part of being a rancher.

Roan held on to his surprise when he saw it wasn't Maud, but Shiloh. As she parked in front of the garage, he stood at the stairs of the porch, hands resting on his narrow hips. His eyes slitted as he watched Shiloh open the door. His body automatically tightened. She'd arranged her hair into a topknot that seemed to be coming undone. Her tank top was a pale green, lovingly outlining her upper body and he wanted to curve his hands around her torso, move them upward to feel the firmness of her breasts, feel them tighten. The Levi's she wore were loose but still hinted strongly of her long legs. Unhappy with himself, Roan took the steps down to the sidewalk to meet her.

"This is a surprise," he told her.

Shiloh turned, smiling, holding out a plastic box in his direction. "I felt bad knowing you were out here all alone, without any help putting up that railing. I just made us dessert for tonight and thought you might like a warm piece of apple pie right now for lunch."

His hand met hers. Roan savored the brief contact as he took the plastic box, a huge slice of pie enclosed in it. "You didn't have to do this," he murmured, affected by her thoughtfulness. Her topknot was sliding off to one side, giving her a girlish look, tendrils soft around her temples and flushed cheeks.

Shiloh laughed and shut the door, walking with him up the steps to the cabin porch. "Sure I did. You left me pancake batter this morning in the fridge. Remember?"

He couldn't tear his gaze from her radiant green eyes. Shiloh looked so happy. Happy to see him? Roan didn't know and he gave her a sour smile. "What? You're the kind of woman who, if I leave pancake batter for her, will make me a real, honest-to-God apple pie?" he teased. Roan sat down on the top stair of the porch. There was plenty of room for two people to sit there and not be crowded up against each other. He hoped Shiloh would sit with him. She did.

Pushing tendrils of runaway hair away from her cheek as she sat down, her back against the railing, Shiloh said, "I am. That was so sweet of you, Roan. Thank you. I mean, how many men would think of that? You deserved something for your kindness."

The breeze was playful and as Roan opened the container, the wafting scent of cinnamon and nutmeg filled his nostrils. "I knew you liked pancakes" was all he said, digging into the warm pie with a plastic fork that she provided for him. Hell, she'd be surprised if she'd known he'd slowed at her door at five thirty this morning, wanting so badly to push the door open and go in and find her in bed. Wake her up with a kiss. Watch her melt into his arms as she'd melted into him yesterday . . . Tucking all those torrid thoughts away, he focused on the delicious, warm apple pie. It dissolved in his mouth.

"Good?" Shiloh asked, tucking her legs against her body, arms wrapped around them.

"Better than good," he mumbled, sliding her a glance. Shiloh looked like she was part of this cabin. Part of Wyoming. As if she'd always lived here. Her hair was tangled, eyes warm with happiness. Most of all, her mouth was gently curved upward and it sent an ache directly to his lower body. She was relaxed. "Looks like you've been working," he observed, pointing the fork toward her knees, which had some dust on them.

Laughing, she said, "I guess I should have changed before I came out here. I woke up at nine and ate a ton of pancakes and it was my turn to clean the house this week, so I did it. I wanted to do something to thank you for your thoughtfulness and we didn't have any dessert planned for tonight." Shrugging, Shiloh said, "I made an apple pie. I went over to Maud's home and she had some cellar apples from last year left over and she gave me a bunch so I could make it for us."

"Nice of Maud to do that," Roan agreed. He was starving. And it didn't take him long to finish off the thick slice of warm pie. Getting up, he took the plastic box to his pickup and pulled out a sack that contained his lunch he'd made this morning. Walking back, he sat down and opened it up. "Have you eaten yet?"

"No," Shiloh responded, and then she rolled her eyes. "I

was on a mission to get the house clean and that pie baked in time for your lunch."

Roan had three turkey sandwiches in his bag. He pulled one out, handing it to her. "Eat this."

Man of few words. Shiloh grinned and took it. "Thanks." She looked up, appreciating the east side of the porch now sporting the new railing. "Looks great, Roan. Did you have any trouble with it this morning?"

"I missed you." Roan scowled. And then he said more carefully, "I missed having a partner to help me lay that railing." He'd seen the sudden surprise in Shiloh's face over his first blurted admission. Scrambling, Roan didn't want to put pressure on Shiloh and quickly adjusted his words. He DID miss her, dammit. Coming out to the cabin this morning in first light, it felt damned lonely without her.

"I was torn," Shiloh admitted, enjoying the sandwich because she was equally starved. "I thought about you out here by yourself and that you'd need a second pair of hands."

"I got it done," he murmured, finishing off the first sandwich and reaching into the sack for the second one. "You need to give your palms a day off with those blisters on them. No sense in working today and then tearing them open. They'll heal faster if the blisters don't pop."

"Always a man of reality," Shiloh teased, brushing her hands off on the sides of her jeans. "But I'm going to stay, Roan. I don't want to hammer today, but I want to spend the rest of the day helping you to put up the rest of the railing."

Roan felt his heart lurch with sudden happiness. His mouth thinned as he regarded her. There was a stubborn look in Shiloh's eyes, the way she set her mouth, as if preparing for an argument from him. A grin leaked out of one corner of his mouth. "I don't suppose if I told you no, you'd listen to me?"

"Got that right, cowboy." She stood up, dusted off her

britches, and said, "I brought my gloves and I got my hat. I'm ready to be a gofer today and help you where and when you need a second pair of hands."

Roan sized her up, appreciating every inch of her lean, graceful body. "I'll bet you were a handful as a kid growing up." He saw her lips turn into a winsome smile.

"How did you guess?"

Chapter Twelve

Shiloh dawdled over her apple pie after dinner. At her elbow, Roan was making good progress in demolishing his portion. He'd dropped three huge scoops of vanilla ice cream onto it. She'd taken one scoop. Burning with curiosity, she asked, "Do you get home very often to visit your parents in Montana?"

Roan could sense her feelers out and aimed in his direction. "About once a year. I usually go up for the fall roundup, help my dad out with collecting about three thousand head of cattle that's wandered around their fifty-thousand-acre ranch."

"Wow," she murmured. "That sounds like a big ranch."

"It is." He savored sharing his meals with Shiloh. Roan couldn't imagine what life was like without her. She completed him in ways no woman ever had before. Just the way her brows moved around, he could see her mind flying along at Mach 3 with her hair on fire. What was she after? Roan could feel her stalking him. It wasn't a bad thing, just kind of amusing to him. She was a writer. Curiosity was high in Shiloh's world and he sensed she wanted to know a whole helluva lot more about him than she did presently.

She pushed the melting ice cream around on her half-eaten pie, thinking.

"Was your dad always a rancher? I thought he was in the Army at one time?"

"He was in for thirty years before he retired, came home, and took over my grandparents' ranch."

"Oh," she murmured, tilting her head, studying him. "Then . . . you're a military and ranching family?"

Nodding, Roan picked up his mug of coffee and took a sip. "The Triangle Ranch has been in my family for over a hundred years."

"Wow," Shiloh murmured. "That's amazing!"

He grinned. "Why is it amazing?" Roan couldn't help but tweak her, see where her plotting and planning to get info out of him was going.

"Well," she said, pushing the pie away, "I'm just trying to construct a story about who you are."

"Ah, truth at last."

She blushed. "Oh, come on, Roan! I'll have you know, you're the most closemouthed man I've ever met. If you can get away with stringing only one or two words together to answer me, you do."

"I call that succinct communications," he parried, his grin remaining. He saw her brows draw down into a scowl. Shiloh was a wordsmith and Roan knew she valued communication more that he did.

"I call it stunted conversation at best."

He chuckled and spooned in a forkful of pie.

"It's not funny," Shiloh grumped good-naturedly. "It's tough to hold a meaningful conversation with you, Roan."

"Don't I always give you answers when you ask?"

"Well . . . yes, but they're so short. There's no details. Just 'yes' and 'no.'"

"I see." He could feel her bridling over this idea of limited conversation with him. Looking for a way to get more than two or three words out of him. "I just gave you a long sentence about my family's ranch, didn't I?" he pointed out, enjoying teasing her far too much.

"And I loved it. I want more long complex sentences like that, Roan."

He shook his head and gave her a rueful look. "I'll bet when you were a little girl you just weaseled anything you wanted out of your mom and dad. Didn't you?"

She rolled her eyes. "There you go again, Roan. Changing the direction of the conversation. This isn't about me. I want it to be about YOU."

"Yeah," he murmured, finishing off the last of the pie, "I get it."

Shiloh sat back, pouting and staring at him. "Do you not want to talk with me? Is that it?"

Roan held her unsure gaze. His heart contracted because he could see she was stymied and hurt by his gruff shortness. "No, I like talking with you, Shiloh." A whole helluva lot more than he should. Roan saw some of her hurt go away, but the confusion remained in her gaze. "All my life, I've lived and worked around men. Not women. Men have a different language than women."

"Yes, it's called short, terse sentences. The fewer words, the better," she muttered unhappily, wrapping her arms around her chest. "And you're laughing at me. I can see it in the way your mouth is set."

Roan reached out without thinking, brushing a tendril away from her cheek and gently easing it aside. "Let's get one thing clear between us, Shiloh. I would *never* laugh at you. I might tease the dickens out of you, but I would never, ever make fun of you. That's not who I am. I don't believe in humiliating another person. It's not in my DNA."

Her lips compressed and Shiloh weighed his gruff words. "I know I'm a woman. I know I talk a lot. I guess maybe it's culture shock for both of us. I'm used to being around my friends who love to communicate. I enjoy it. And you live out here"—she gestured widely around the room—"by yourself."

"I do talk," Roan assured her, trying to curb his smile. Picking up his coffee, he added, "I talk to Maud. She's a woman."

"More than two words?"

"Yes, many more than two words." Again, confusion came to her face. Shiloh was one of those people who liked to figure out how a person worked, who they were and what made them tick. It was her writer's mind at work. Roan couldn't fault her on that.

"Well, then," she said defiantly, "why can't we hold more than a one- or two-word conversation, then?"

He raised a brow as he sipped the coffee. "I was trying to give you room, Shiloh."

"What do you mean?"

"Maud told me you were stressed out because of this stalker. You were coming into a strange house with a strange man in it." Shrugging, Roan said, "I didn't want to put extra pressure or stress on you. I wanted to be a shadow in your life until you settled in here, the stress left you and then I'd become more chatty, I guess."

Snorting, she muttered, "You're chatty?"

Wrong word. Roan quirked his mouth. "I'm not a writer, Shiloh. Maybe 'chatty' was the wrong word. I meant to open up a bit more to you once you were happy in here."

"Is that how you see me? As chatty?"

Oh, this was going sideways and Roan didn't want it to go there. He sat up and pushed his plate aside, folding his hands, holding her mutinous stare. She looked lush when her lower lip drew into a pout. He wanted to kiss it, run his tongue across it, feel Shiloh respond, feel her start melting into his embrace. "You're a highly intelligent woman with a very keen intellect. I don't know how you could say you've been chatty with me. We've barely spoken a paragraph to each other at any given time. Right?" he asked, and drilled a look into her widening eyes. Some of her pout and mutinous look dissolved.

"Oh. Well, you're right about that. We don't speak much to each other. Like two ships passing in the night, if you ask me."

What a little hellion. Roan swallowed his grin and remained serious for her sake. If he did grin she'd probably think he was laughing at her and he wanted to avoid that at all costs. "I don't have a problem speaking more than a paragraph to you, Shiloh. But I need you to give me the signal. Only you know when you're settled in around here, feeling safe. Comfortable." And more than anything, Roan's protectiveness was always there where Shiloh was concerned. "I guess we've reached that point?"

"Yes," she said, the frustration leaving her voice. "I don't want to have to pick and pry away at you all the time, Roan."

A corner of his mouth drew upward. "Pry and pick?" He saw a hesitant smile burgeoning across her lips. "I must be a nightmare to the writer in you, then? Being a man of few words and all?"

"That's putting it mildly."

The hellion was back and Roan saw the glint in her eyes, as if he were the target and she had him in her gunsight. His grin grew. "Why don't you tell me how you really feel, Shiloh?"

She blushed and then laughed. "Touché."

Roan laughed with her, feeling his heart swell in his chest. Shiloh was part pert teen, sometimes a willful, pouting child, but always a woman in his heart. Roan wished he could be more like her, but he had one speed and that was serious and responsible. Not that she wasn't, Shiloh was, but her ability to be utterly herself mesmerized him. She made him laugh. Made him feel lighter. Hell, even happy, if he'd admit it to himself.

She opened her hands. "Truce?"

"Sure, I don't mind surrendering over to you." That was a loaded statement with layers upon layers on it, but Roan saw her take it at face value.

"More than a yes or no?"

He stood and picked up the dishes and flatware, taking them to the sink. "What do you want to talk about?"

Shiloh stood and went to the sink and grabbed the dishcloth. "You. Your family. How you grew up. Why you went into black ops."

"I might have known you'd have a list," he said drily, watching her wipe the table off.

"I'm a writer."

"I'll bet you hide behind that label a whole lot, gal."

She grinned and washed the cloth out beneath the sink faucet. "It serves a purpose."

He grunted. "Maybe too much so." Giving her a glance as he placed the rinsed dishes into the dishwasher, Roan said, "I'd like to get to know the woman behind the writer label." Roan saw it hit Shiloh directly, her eyes widening a bit, her pupils growing black and large in response to his growling words.

She hung the cloth between the two sinks and pulled a towel off the rack and dried her hands. "Because?"

He pushed the door shut on the dishwasher and straightened, a few feet separating them. "Because you interest me. Isn't that good enough reason to pry and pick at you?" Her lips twitched. Shiloh tried not to smile, but failed. Roan decided it was fun sparring with her. Despite everything, the stresses still on her, Shiloh was able to be free and spontaneous. He found himself wondering how he'd lived in this big house alone for so long, without her vital presence, her sunshine smile, her quick intelligence that kept pace with his. Roan didn't want to see Shiloh leave. And he knew she was here for only two months.

"That's a good enough reason," she said mildly, hands on her hips. "And you won't have to pick and pry at me, either."

"You're an open book?" he guessed.

"You've got a rapier mind, Taggart."

He saw the gleam in her eyes dance. "It's my rapier wit that's saved my ass out on many black ops assignments, believe me."

"I like a man who thinks on his feet."

"And I like a woman who speaks her mind."

"Then we must be in communication heaven and not know it?" Shiloh teased.

Shrugging, Roan wanted to reach out and slip his hand into hers, but resisted. "Let's find out, Darlin'. I'm pouring myself a fresh cup of coffee and going to sit in the living room. Want to join me?"

"Are you throwing down the gauntlet?" Shiloh wondered warily.

"No, handing it over to you," he offered, pouring coffee into his mug. "Want a cup?"

"Please."

"Go pick out a spot for us?" Roan gestured lazily toward the living room. He wanted Shiloh to decide where he should sit. If he had his way, he'd sit in the corner of the couch, tuck her in beneath his arm, and never let her go. They could sit there and talk all night that way. But he knew he was fooling himself and was accepting of whatever made Shiloh comfortable. There was no way he was going to pressure her. As he poured her a cup of coffee, Roan tried to rein in the joy thrumming through his chest. He liked Shiloh's spunk. Her feistiness. Almost smiling, Roan knew she'd bring all of that to his bed. She was going to be a fearless lover and his body and heart ached for her.

Sauntering through the living room he saw Shiloh pull an overstuffed chair near one corner of the couch. Handing her the cup, he settled down on the couch, leaning back, his long legs crossed out in front of him, sitting opposite her. Shiloh had initiated that surprising kiss. Roan felt he knew her well enough to know she'd one day boldly walk right into his arms and tell him she wanted to go to bed with him. Such a fearless, beautiful creature. Keeping it all to himself, he settled back, his gaze holding hers.

"Would you tell me about your growing-up years?" she asked, looking at Roan over the cup.

"My dad, Al, was stationed at Fort Bragg, North Carolina, because he was with the Third Special Forces Group headquartered there. That's where I was born. Shortly afterward, my mother, Grace, went home to our family ranch. I grew up on my grandparents' ranch and when my dad got to come stateside for a year or more, then we'd move to where he was stationed."

"You had your grandparents to help you grow up even though your dad was gone?"

"Right."

"Are they still alive?"

"No." Roan's mouth quirked. "I miss the hell out of both of them. They were tough Depression-era stock, believed in work that paid off, didn't ask for handouts and didn't see themselves as victims."

"Do you carry photos of them?" Shiloh wondered. She heard an emotional catch in Roan's deep voice, saw a softening in his normally hard, glinting eyes.

"Afraid not. My mom has all the family photos at their ranch in Montana. I was in the U.S. Army from eighteen to age thirty-two. And because I was black ops, we never carried anything on us that could identify us or anyone else."

Shiloh felt sad for Roan. It was clear he was tied strongly to his family. "But you're out now."

His mouth moved into a cutting line. "Old habits die hard, Shiloh."

"I understand." She held the cup between her hands in her lap. There was such a comfortable feeling between them; as if they were old friends sitting down to catch up on each other's lives. Shiloh tried not to gaze at Roan's well-shaped mouth because it sent a skitter of heat and longing through her.

He frowned. "I'm trying to put myself in your place, Shiloh."

"Oh?"

"Both your parents are gone. I know how much I've always relied on my mom and dad. Being able to pick up the cell phone and talk to them. Send an e-mail. And you seem very family-oriented. The loss must be like a hole in your heart that never heals."

"You're right," she murmured, looking down at the coffee in her hands. "The hole in the heart is exactly right." His observations cut through her and Shiloh felt tears gather at the back of her eyes. She swallowed a couple of times, forcing them away. The expression on Roan's face made her want to cry, though. That hard mask he wore dissolved. And in its place, she saw a sensitive man who was very aware and in touch with those around him, in so many rich and wonderful ways. Shiloh swore she could feel his invisible embrace around her shoulders as he spoke quietly to her, his tone reflective. She detected sadness in his eyes— for her. It had been such a long, long time since she'd talked about her parents. Her heart twisted with grief.

"I'm sorry, Shiloh. You're a good person. I think your parents were a powerful support for you. When they got ripped away, it's tough to suddenly be standing alone and having to always be strong with no support."

"There's no one to lean on," Shiloh agreed softly, closing her eyes, feeling the tears creeping back. Tonight, she did not want to break down and cry. This was the first time Roan had opened up to her and she didn't want to lose that opportunity with him. Opening her eyes, she said mirthfully, "If I could have had a pair of cosmic crutches for a couple of years after that, it would have helped. At least I got to live with my aunt and uncle. And that was so much better than being put into the state system and sent to a foster home."

"You turned out beautiful, intelligent, kind, and incredibly creative," Roan said. "You've got a strong spirit, Shiloh. A helluva backbone."

She perked up. "What? You saw my backbone the other day when I was nailing that Trex down your cabin porch? Is that when you stopped seeing me as a New York City cream puff?" She saw delight burn in his eyes, that wonderfully strong mouth of his curving recklessly upward.

Snorting, Roan put the cup on the lamp stand and sat up, elbows on his knees, hands clasped between them. "I never thought of you as a cream puff."

"What then?"

"A city slicker."

"And while I may be that, I have other qualities and skills that move beyond that label."

"Indeed you do," Roan agreed. "I just wonder where you got that fearlessness of yours. From your mom? Your dad?"

She touched her red hair. "I got this, my green eyes and risk-taking personality, from my mom."

"What was she like?" Roan wondered.

"My mother was an artist. She studied at the Sorbonne, in Paris. She loved Europe and had many adventures over there in her early twenties." Shiloh grinned. "My mother ran with the bulls in Spain, right along beside the men."

Brows rising, Roan said, "That's really something. She didn't get hurt, did she?"

"No," Shiloh said, fondly remembering the story. "And I have photos of her with her Spanish boyfriend before, during, and after the run." Giving Roan a warm look, she added, "You'd have loved my mom. She was an absolute free spirit. She lived out of her heart. She did everything on emotional whim. She had such faith in the unknown. She never had a lot of money but it would always turn up when she needed it. To help pay for her art training in Paris, she worked as a cabaret dancer at a club in downtown Paris."

"I thought you might have some dancing genes in you."

"How could you know that?" Shiloh asked, amazed at his perception.

"Just watching you," Roan murmured. "You do everything with gracefulness whether it's pulling a plate out of the cupboard or laying Trex on my cabin porch. I thought you might have taken ballet lessons when you were younger."

Heat flashed up her neck and into her face. "I did." Staring at Roan, she whispered, "Do you read minds, too? Is this some special gift you created because you were in black ops?" She saw him grin and ruefully shake his head. It wasn't lost on Shiloh that Roan missed nothing. The man was more than just a casual observer of the human condition. He watched her and intuitively knew her without any background information about her younger life. That made her breathless and stunned, but not afraid of him. There was a quiet steadiness to Roan, a man of honor. A man of his word. And she felt so incredibly safe and protected when she was around him.

"I don't know where it came from," Roan admitted. "The male line of our family were all born with a caul over them. I was too."

"Ohhhh," Shiloh said, eyes widening. "If you're born

with a caul over you at birth, it means you're a seer. A visionary. Very psychic."

Holding up his hands, Roan chuckled. "Darlin', don't look at me like I'm some kind of fortune-teller because I'm not."

"But," Shiloh said excitedly, setting her cup aside, "you see."

"I think a better word would be 'perceive,' Shiloh. I'm good at assessing people. It's easy for me to read a face, a voice, and interpret a person's body language. It did come in damn handy when my team and I were in areas that were always dangerous and bad things could happen in a heartbeat. I'd like to think my gut hunches, my ability to observe, saved us more than a few times out on patrols."

"Did your team know you have this skill?"

"I didn't tell them I was born with a caul," Roan told her drily. "It wouldn't have gone over well with the guys. It's tough for military people to believe or trust something like I had. But over time, I proved my hunches so often they just accepted it and, later, were all very glad I had that skill in place."

"They just didn't call it what it was: You're psychic."

"No," Roan said wryly, "they'd have called it 'woo-woo.'"

She laughed. And so did he. "And so," she went on, her mind racing with connections, "I'll bet you're really good with wild horses that need to be tamed?"

"I've gentled a few," Roan admitted. "You have to work with animals from your heart, not your hand. I don't think it takes any special psychic abilities, just love."

"That's a wonderful way to look at training animals." Shiloh swore she felt his hand on her, stroking her, gentling her. The sensation was so physical that she felt dampness between her thighs. The man's voice was a low, vibrating growl. Roan's eyes were almost soft with feelings as he talked about the horses. Would he ever look at her like that, with that male tenderness? If she hadn't been here to see it, she would have never said that Roan Taggart possessed an ounce of tenderness. But now, she knew he did. Her longing to have Roan open up to her fully, to trust her, made her feel deep ache in her heart.

Roan rose and said, "I need to finish up the kitchen and then I'm hitting the sack. Dawn comes early tomorrow."

Lamenting their time was up, Shiloh slowly rose and brushed out the wrinkles in her white capri pants. "I'll take the cups over," she volunteered. "I'll help you clean up the kitchen."

Nodding, Roan walked with his long, easy gait to the kitchen while Shiloh cleaned up in the living room. Her heart was beating with renewed urgency. Right now, all she wanted to do was kiss this man and have him unveil his heart to her even more. There was something in Roan's eyes, deep, almost hidden, that told her he longed to be that man for her.

Fear from the past, though, drenched Shiloh as she placed the cups in the dishwasher. If she kissed Roan, where would it lead? To the bedroom? To wild, hungry love? And then what? The dawn of a new day always brought back reality, not romanticism. She would be leaving to go back to New York City. Roan would never leave Wyoming. Or the beautiful cabin he was building near Pine Hills.

Feeling pulled one way and then another, Shiloh let the urge to kiss Roan, to take him by the hand and lead him into her bedroom, reluctantly dissolve. Her last relationship had taught her she'd better have one eye fixed on reality. Unfortunately, she was exactly like her idealistic mother: a romantic at heart. An idealist, not a realist. And like her mother, Shiloh wanted to give her heart to the right man. And up until meeting Roan, she knew she hadn't met him yet.

Licking her lower lip, she turned and whispered, "Good night, Roan," and quickly left the kitchen. Shiloh knew if she stayed, she'd do something she'd be very sorry for come dawn tomorrow.

Chapter Thirteen

The morning was cold but refreshing. Shiloh was eager to take a ride with Roan out to the buffalo area of the ranch. Maud kept a herd of twenty cows, calves, and one bull mostly for the tourists who were dying to see what one looked like.

A week had passed since kissing Roan. As she used the hoof pick to clean out Charley's hooves, her mind and heart were never far from Roan. Oh, he'd been circumspect and, as promised, made no move to become intimate with her since that blazing, sky-opening kiss they'd shared on the porch of his cabin.

Shiloh was glad that she'd not only worn jeans, cowboy boots, and a long-sleeved orange tee, but also had added a heavy sheep's wool vest and her green nylon coat on top of that. Her fingers were near freezing by the time she was done with her gelding's hooves. Looking up, she saw Roan outside with his big black quarter horse gelding, Diamond, checking the cinch before he mounted up. Her heart swelled with so many happy emotions. Hurrying around Charley, she unhooked the panic snaps and let the cross ties fall against the walls. Patting his black-and-white paint neck, she ruffled his thick mane. Charley's ears flicked back and forth. He might be fifteen years old, but the cold morning made even him friskier than usual.

"Come on, Charley," she clucked, pulling at the reins, leading him out to where Roan sat slouched comfortably in the saddle. His gray Stetson pulled low over his eyes, his profile rugged. Diamond was pawing the earth, raising dust, wanting to go. Her gaze just naturally fell to that wonderfully strong, well-shaped mouth of Roan's. Shiloh saw him turn, his gaze meeting hers. She felt herself go hot with longing, her body clenching. The man could make her melt with just that calm stare of his.

"Ready?" Roan asked.

"Yep," Shiloh said, quickly mounting up. Laughing to herself, she'd become relaxed around horses and riding. A few weeks ago, she'd been paralyzed over the idea of riding. She had on a red baseball cap that Maud had given her and drew the bill down, trying to shade her eyes from the bright sunlight flooding the valley. Giving him a quick smile, Shiloh pulled on her leather gloves, wanting to get her fingers warm. "Lead the way."

Nodding, Roan barely touched the barrel of his gelding and the horse walked eagerly toward the pastures in the distance.

"Ever been around buffalo before?" he asked her as they rode side by side.

Shaking her head, Shiloh saw that they were going to ride between two huge pastures. "No. Why?"

Roan, who had just shaved and nicked himself earlier, carefully rubbed his jaw. "We'll be going to drive them into another pasture. It's June and the mother's are calving. The bulls aren't with them, but the mothers can be very protective of their young calf."

"Okay. What does that mean to a city slicker like me?" she asked, and flashed him a grin. Roan's mouth barely lifted. The lush greenness of the pastures infused Shiloh.

Overhead, she saw a red-tailed hawk flying in higher and higher circles in the sky. There were bluebirds everywhere, many of them sitting on fence posts. When they took off, that flash of brilliant blue always made her gasp with delight; it was almost an unearthly gorgeous color.

"Don't get Charley between a calf and its mother," Roan warned her. "Buffalo are a twitchy lot by temperament anyway. And cows are very protective of their young in a situation they consider threatening."

Worried, Shiloh said, "Maybe I shouldn't even be in there. I'm not that great a rider."

"Just stay behind me or on the outside of me and you should be all right," he assured her. "A couple of other wranglers are going to be meeting us and the three of us will do the herding. I thought you might enjoy seeing buffalo, being that you're a city slicker and all," he said, and one corner of his mouth hooked slightly as he gazed over at Shiloh.

Shiloh chewed on her lower lip, not so sure. She saw the gleam of confidence in Roan's eyes. He believed she could do it. "I'm a poor rider."

"Charley is old and wise. Just let him take care of you. Hold on to the saddle horn if it makes you feel better."

She had been trying not to do that because she wanted to appear able to ride without clinging like a greenhorn. "He would know what to do?"

Roan nodded. "Yes. Before Maud put him in the dude ranch as a child's horse, he was a damn good wrangling gelding the first twelve years of his life. He knows buffalo and cattle. You'll be safe on board him."

"Okay," she murmured, not sounding very sure of herself even to her own ears.

"You can stay outside the gate if you want." Roan saw the anxiety coming to Shiloh's eyes as they approached the pasture. He pulled Diamond to a halt at the gate and dismounted.

Shiloh was looking at all the brown humped buffalo cows and their frolicking calves. It looked bucolic. But the animals were huge! She saw about half a mile away, on the opposite side of the pasture, two wranglers opening up a large gate to allow the mothers and calves access to the area. Roan picked up his radio and talked to the other wranglers. Seesawing between staying outside the gate and following Roan in, she saw him finish off his chat with the wranglers.

Stuffing the radio into his saddlebags, Roan looked up at Shiloh. "Well?"

"I'm waffling."

He grinned. "Yes, you are."

Making a face, Shiloh admitted, "I don't want you to think I'm a weenie."

Chuckling, Roan lifted his hat and moved his gloved fingers through his hair. "I would never think that, Shiloh." He came over and rested his hand against the rear of her saddle, looking up into her indecisive features. "I'll respect you no matter what you decide. Okay?"

Grimacing, she muttered, "I'm going in with you." Looking around, anger tinging her voice, she added, "I'm tired of being scared all the time. If I was back in New York City, I'd be sitting imprisoned in my apartment, feeling like a convict behind bars because somewhere out there, a man wants to hurt me and I don't know who it is."

His heart wrenched. Roan eased his hand down her arm and caught her gloved fingers. "You don't have to prove anything to me. All right?"

She tucked her lower lip between her teeth, squeezing his hand in return. "I'm just tired of being scared, Roan."

"I know, Darlin'. But if you decide to come in, do it for yourself. Okay?"

Roan was right, she realized. "Yes," she muttered, releasing his hand even though she didn't want to. Just the intimacy Roan had automatically established with her calmed her, helped her gain perspective. "They're big, is all."

Roan patted her knee and nodded. "Yes, they are. But we're taller than they are when we're on horseback. Look at it that way," he said, and he ambled over to Diamond who was eagerly eating the lush grass.

Brows rising, Shiloh considered his words. He was right. She enjoyed watching him mount Diamond, his male grace. Wanting him. All of him. Why was life so damned complicated?

As Roan rode through and turned Diamond to catch the gate to close it, he saw Charley trotting in, a stubborn look on Shiloh's face. He grinned and said nothing. Keeping one ear keyed to the herd of twenty cows and their calves nearby, Roan got the gate closed and turned his horse toward where Charley was standing.

"Ready?"

Shiloh nodded, her gaze pinned on the big, lumpy brown herd of buffalo that stood looking at them. Their short, curved horns gleamed in the sunlight, wet with dew as the buffalo ate the grass. "Yes."

Roan reached out, briefly touching her chin. He saw Shiloh's eyes change, grow warm, and he saw desire flare in them. For him. He could feel it. Taste it. Every night he came back to the house after wrangling all day, he was tested again to keep his hands off Shiloh. To give her the room, the space she needed. Diamond was eager to mix it up with the herd, trotting sideways as Roan aimed him at the end of the wary bunch.

Before Shiloh could cluck to Charley, the spunky pinto drifted into a long trot, remaining on the outside of Diamond. She was amazed the horse knew what to do and tried her gawky best to ride at the trot.

Roan had pulled his lariat off a leather strap from around the horn and held it in his leather glove, the long, stiff loops slapping against his lower leg and boot. The way he rode, his familiarity with his horse's movements, the way he held those thick coils of rope, impacted her powerfully. Shiloh found herself wishing she had some of Roan's natural confidence. Charley picked up his trot and broke into a nice, easy lope, right at Diamond's rump, keeping pace with the tall, muscular quarter horse.

It was much easier riding at a lope, something Shiloh loved, that cradle-like motion. It reminded her of sitting in a rocking chair. She watched as the matriarch of the herd, an old cow who didn't have a calf at her side, whirled around, snorting jets of vapor out of her flaring nostrils as she stood her ground.

Roan slowed Diamond to a trot, his gaze on the matriarch. If he could convince her to move, the rest of the cows would follow. But he knew this old gal. They called her Maddy, as in "mad cow" because she was a testy ole buffalo with a history of pushing her thousand-plus pounds around with wranglers. He called over his shoulder, "Pull Charley back and get about a hundred feet away from me. Maddy can be a handful at times."

"Maddy?" Shiloh called, pulling Charley to a walk.

"Yeah," Roan said, "Maddy is bossy. And depending upon her mood on any given day, she's not afraid to take any of us on. But you never know which day that might be."

Great.

Shiloh quickly clucked to Charley and headed off toward the fence line, following Roan's instructions. She pulled her paint to a stop, resting her hands on the horn, watching Roan approach the snorting cow. She was digging her front, cloven hooves into the ground, clumps of mud and grass flying up into the air beneath her belly. Her head was down and she was shaking it. Fear for Roan rose in her, but he seemed relaxed and unconcerned as he pulled Diamond down into a walk. The rest of the herd was jumpy and quickly scampered behind Maddy, who was still standing her ground, her small wary eyes blazing.

Her heart moved up in beat as Roan slowed and made a wide circle to get behind Maddy.

The cow snorted and whirled around in a split second, facing Roan once more.

Gasping, Shiloh didn't realize how FAST a buffalo could move! It was amazing! Diamond's ears were flicking forward and back, his eyes riveted on the cow who continued to shake her head and paw her hoof into the mud and grass. Shiloh saw two other wranglers approaching at a fast gallop to get there to help Roan.

The herd suddenly broke behind Maddy, racing between the cowboys.

Maddy bellowed and launched herself at Roan and Diamond.

A scream lodged in Shiloh's throat, her hand flying to it, her mouth dropping open. Diamond deftly stepped aside, almost like a bullfighter making a ballet move at the charging buffalo. Only this cow was angry and she was aiming to plow into the dancing black horse. Roan leaned over as the horse whirled around and avoided the hooking horns of the buffalo, the rope slapping down on her wet, sensitive nose.

Maddy bawled and jerked to a halt, her nose stinging with pain. She turned, her thin tail twisting angrily, trying to avoid another warning slap of that lariat, digging her hind feet into the muddy pasture. She moved swiftly, barreling through the group of scattering cows and calves, aiming straight for the open gate at the far end of the pasture.

Shiloh watched as Roan pulled his horse to a stop, the animal breathing hard, its flanks bellowing in and out. He ran his hand down the gelding's sweaty neck, talking soothingly to him. The horse calmed instantly, settling down, nostrils flared wide. Shiloh clucked to Charley and he took off at a sedate trot.

As Shiloh pulled up, she saw the other two wranglers flanking the herd from behind, making sure they all funneled through the gate into the new pasture. She smiled a little at Roan as he placed the lariat back into the leather strap, allowing it to hang on the right side of the saddle.

"That was really something. Did you know Maddy was going to charge you?"

Roan lifted his hat and used his forearm to wipe his brow. "Yes, she always charges somebody. We've learned to give her a target and that her nose is the most sensitive spot on her body. Hate having to hit her, but she doesn't take no for an answer," Roan said, and settled the hat on his head. "Maddy's a good matriarch and there's been times when the Snake River wolf pack has come sniffing around, and she's chased them off." He smiled a little. "She's a good leader. Just doesn't like wranglers, is all."

Shiloh watched as the two cowboys dismounted and shut the gate to the other pasture. She returned her attention to Roan. He seemed unaffected by the whole event. "Aren't you shook up over Maddy charging you?"

Roan lifted his leg, hooking his knee around the horn of the saddle. He loosened Diamond's reins so the horse could relax. "No. Why?" he asked, squinting toward her, the sun directly in his eyes.

"My heart was pounding."

He shrugged. "Maybe knowing Maddy's routine helped."

She smiled a little. "Or is it your black ops background? Are you guys trained not to get excited or distracted during a firefight? Or something dangerous going on around you?"

Roan smiled a little. "Could be," he drawled, "but honestly I don't get rattled by much, either way."

"Your family genes?"

"Most likely. My mom's a cool cucumber. My father is laid-back and easygoing. Not much riles him, either."

"Well, I was impressed." She patted her heart. "I was scared for you. Okay?"

Roan met her eyes and nodded. "It's nice to be worried over."

Heat flowed out of Shiloh's heart, making her chest feel as if it were expanding. She saw kindness in Roan's look as he held her gaze. "I guess you're right," she muttered ruefully, "I am a bona fide worrywart."

Roan stretched slowly, arms over his head and then he lowered them. He unhooked his knee from around the horn and settled his boot into the stirrup. "I like you just the way you are, Shiloh. Come on, we'll meet up with the other two wranglers. We need to double-check and ride the entire fence line on that new pasture. A wrangler took a check ride around the fence line last week, but we can't afford these buffalo escaping and wandering around. That would cause all kinds of hell." He looked at his watch. "You'll be in the saddle a good three hours. Are you up for it?"

"I am, but I'll betcha my butt is gonna be sore when it's all over with."

"I like your sense of humor. Ready for a little canter?"

Was she ever. "You bet!"

Anton Leath sat on a wooden bench in the main square of Wind River on a warm late-June morning. It was ten A.M. And all the small shops around it were opening up, the restaurants busy with tourists who were driving through this town on Highway 89 with a population of fifteen hundred. He was dressed like a tourist, in a pair of jeans, hiking boots, and a casual dark blue T-shirt. Actually, he relished blending in because he liked camouflage. As a hunter in upstate New York, during deer season, he put on his camo gear and blended into the woodlands to kill a nice four- or five-point buck. Now, he sat on one of the many wooden benches placed around the square, a newspaper draped over his crossed legs, looking like a tourist simply enjoying the morning, with no particular place to go.

He pulled his cell phone out of his pocket and turned it on. Stupid Shiloh Gallagher had a fan page on the social media site. And every day she posted a photo and a paragraph about Wyoming. He should thank his lucky stars the girl was an idiot. She'd escaped him undetected by suddenly leaving her New York apartment. But then to think that he wouldn't trail her through social media sites? His full mouth pulled into a grin.

As he thumbed through the newspaper he was looking for ads for a gun shop. And also, any local news on the Wind River Ranch where she was staying. He felt a thrill move through him. Instead of hunting a buck, he was going to start hunting Shiloh. He should have taken his African skinning knife he killed her mother with and turned it on her and slit her throat as well. Shrugging, Anton couldn't change the past. But he was sure as hell going to change Shiloh's life once and for all. The bitch had put him in prison with her testimony. A sweet sensation of revenge drifted through Anton as his eyes narrowed on an ad from a local gun shop.

As a convicted felon, Anton couldn't own a firearm. So he'd found a druggie digging through a Dumpster at one end of the town by the name of Jerry Carpenter. For a small amount of money, the druggie, who had no criminal record yet, had agreed to buy whatever firearms he needed.

There was a small gun shop in town and Anton drove him over there. Carpenter worked as a server at a local restaurant and bunked in with four other druggies in a nearby small apartment. He made money to go drift off into marijuana la-la land. Fine by Anton. As long as the twenty-one-year-old scrawny kid could legally acquire the weapons he wanted, he didn't care what he did with his life. There would be a waiting period, of course, after Carpenter bought the weapons he'd put down on a list, but Anton wasn't in any hurry.

Next, he decided to go back to his hotel room and dye his blond hair dark brown. He was growing a beard and he'd dye it, too. He spotted a small article in the local paper about the new wildlife drive on the Wind River Ranch. Visitors to the area could drive onto the ranch and pay to go see the animals. Smiling a little, Anton decided it would be a wise move. He was fairly sure Shiloh would not recognize him. He'd wear dark glasses and a hat, and play tourist. Anton had no idea where Shiloh was at on the ranch. But he'd try to find out as he drove that loop road where different animals were kept in different pastures.

Time was going too fast as far as Shiloh was concerned. Another week had passed and she found herself happy. Every day, she woke up to Roan in the house. They shared breakfast and dinner together. He always packed a lunch and threw it in his saddlebags on his horse because he was out working somewhere on the ranch at lunchtime. She'd found her writing ability had come back. After breakfast Shiloh would clean up the kitchen and then go write in her bedroom on that beautiful hundred-year-old rolltop desk.

Getting up every twenty minutes or so, she'd walk across the road to the office and see if Maud or Steve needed her help.

Sometimes, Maud would ask her to do a little office paperwork and Shiloh was glad to fill in. She would divide her time between the office and the employee house where her book chapters were coming together, much to her relief.

She was sitting out front, giving John Harper, the office manager, a break from office duties when Maud wandered in. Her silver and black hair was tucked beneath her red baseball cap. She smiled at Shiloh and wandered over as she pulled off her dirt-stained gloves.

"You holding down the fort?"

Grinning, Shiloh nodded. "Yes. John needed to run an errand. I told him I'd sit and answer the phone for him."

Maud nodded and leaned against the wooden counter. "You know you've been here a month already?"

Glumly, Shiloh nodded. "I was just realizing that this morning after Roan left for the day."

"You seem happy here."

"I am." Shiloh looked around. "I really love Wyoming, Maud. I love the wildness of it. The beauty."

Wrinkling her nose, Maud said, "Winters are long and hard. We get three months of summer and that's about it, if we're lucky. You're here at the best time."

"But I love snow," Shiloh protested. She saw Maud's eyes twinkle.

"Maybe you should think of something more permanent here, then? You seem to be writing up a storm. You're happy. What else is there?"

"I know," Shiloh admitted softly. "I can't keep leaning on you for a place to stay. I was thinking of maybe renting an apartment in town and staying until September." Shiloh opened her hands. "I can write anywhere."

"Do you miss New York City?"

Shrugging, Shiloh said, "With that stalker back there, no. Out here, I'm free and it feels so wonderful, Maud. I've finally relaxed. I just don't want to go back home. At least, not yet . . ."

"Anything else tugging at you to stay around here?" she asked, raising her brows, giving her a pointed look.

Shiloh felt heat rushing up from her neck and into her face. Maud knew. "Well . . . uh . . . Roan is a very nice man."

Snorting, Maud pulled off her cap and threw it on the counter, running her fingers through her short strands. "I've never seen that man as happy as he is now. And I've known him for two years. Roan actually smiles every once in a while."

Rubbing her heated cheek, Shiloh avoided Maud's gaze. "I do like him but . . ."

"But what? You aren't in a relationship currently, Shiloh. What's there not to like about that cowboy?"

Sighing, she stared up at Maud. "He plays for keeps. He's not like a lot of guys I've been with before. Roan wouldn't walk away."

"So? What's the matter with THAT? There's a lot of women who would die to have a man who is true blue and loyal to his woman."

"I . . . just . . . well, I guess I'm commitment-phobic, Maud. I get scared about getting serious about a man."

"But you like Roan? Right?"

"Very much."

Maud shook her head. "I swear, Shiloh. What on EARTH is stopping you from having a good, solid relationship?"

Wincing internally, Shiloh said softly, "I don't know, Maud . . . I get scared. It's silly, really, but it's real and it's there, haunting me."

Maud studied her for a moment. "Maybe this reaction is based on losing your father at such a young age? I know your mama was terribly in love with him. And he got ripped away from her and you saw it. You were so young and children, God love 'em, are so impressionable at that age. It may have wounded you, Shiloh, sent you a message that if you really do love a man, he'll be ripped away from you, too."

Feeling bad, Shiloh whispered, "Yes, I think losing my dad suddenly like that really impacted me. I don't think I'm over it to this day. I loved him so much. And I saw my mother die emotionally after Dad had the heart attack. It was horrible. She cried all the time. I couldn't comfort her. I couldn't fix it and she was hurting so badly. . . ."

Reaching over the counter, Maud patted Shiloh's shoulder. "Nothing can fix a broken heart except love. Love always repairs those fractures we get in our heart."

"I guess I'm afraid to let love in." Shiloh gave the rancher a sad look. "And Roan . . . he's so patient with me. He respects me. He treats me as his equal. I know it's me. And the past. It's always the past. . . ."

"Well," Maud drawled, giving her an amused look, "I can think of a thousand women who would stand in line to find a man like Roan. And here, we're dragging you kicking and screaming toward him." She said soothingly, "Sometimes, you just have to jump into the water and have faith you're gonna swim and not sink."

Chapter Fourteen

Anton Leath felt smug as he trundled up the red brick walkway to the Wind River Ranch. With fifteen other tourists, he'd patiently stood in line outside the office at nine A.M., paying his money and getting his ticket to drive the wildlife loop road on the property. He stood on the sidewalk dressed in his tourist gear, looking like everyone else. His only concession was he wore a tan floppy hat and his sunglasses.

The morning was chilly and he stuck his hands into his dark green nylon jacket pockets. The nonstop talking around him always irritated him. Why couldn't people just be quiet? This was wide-open country and pristine. People had to ruin it by constant chattering. He wanted to hear the sounds of nature instead.

He'd seen a large house across the road from the office. It was connected by the same red sidewalk that led in a forked direction to the loop road. As his gaze ranged slowly, Anton wanted to absorb and remember what he saw. On their side of the road, there was a smaller unnamed office beyond the main ranch office.

Anton lifted his chin, stepping a little out of the slow-moving line toward the open office door. He saw a huge three-story red barn. And on the other side of it were square pipe holding pens with wranglers busy with Hereford cattle. It looked like they were vaccinating them but he couldn't be sure at this distance. He had a small pair of binoculars in his coat pocket and they could make the difference. Anton didn't want to pull them out and draw attention to himself. He wanted to blend in.

Where was Shiloh Gallagher? He saw her nowhere. Although, there was a small café between the major office area and those big red barns. And it was nine A.M. He itched to get out of line and wander down toward that area. Maybe she was eating in the café? A sense of contained rage ate at his gut. Automatically, his fingers curled into fists deep in the pockets of his jacket.

He saw activity over at the wildlife road entrance. A woman was opening the large wooden gate that would take tourists down to the loop. Anton calmed himself. Once he got inside the small, cramped office to pay his fee, he'd take any brochures the ranch offered. Perhaps there was another way to hang around the ranch without looking out of place after he finished the drive. This morning was a reconnoitering mission as far as he was concerned.

Later, as Anton followed the group of people down to the loop entrance where there were huge areas fenced off to keep cattle in nearby pastures off the wide, smooth road, he saw nothing to indicate that Shiloh was at the ranch. There were many places she could be.

In his pocket were several brochures. Among them, the ranch offered tourists one-, two-, or three-hour horseback rides on trails. There was a major dirt road leading opposite the loop drive and heading out between two huge, flat, grassy pastures. On the map he held, it read "Pine Grove."

As the group moved slowly to get their entrance ticket, Anton figured it would be a good way to get the layout of the ranch, provided he could prove Gallagher was here. Where the hell was she?

An hour later, done with the wildlife drive, Anton parked his car in the office parking lot. He was now going to begin his further exploration of the ranch. Anton was ambling up the red brick sidewalk, one of the last people to leave, and he spotted Shiloh. His heart beat swiftly in his chest as he saw her entering the main office of the ranch. She was in a pair of jeans and cowboy boots, wearing a dark blue nylon jacket, her hair loose and shining across her shoulders. He forced himself to keep shuffling up the sloping brick walk. He couldn't help but feel a rush of excitement. The asphalt lot where he'd parked his car was to the right of that office, along with everyone else's vehicles. He didn't want to be seen by her, although he doubted she'd recognize him.

As Anton crossed the street toward the parking lot, he saw Shiloh pop out of the office, take the steps, papers in hand. She moved quickly next door to the medical office and disappeared inside it. Smiling, he wondered where she was living.

Once seated in his rented car, a silver SUV, Anton waited, hoping to see Shiloh again. The windows were darkly tinted and he knew no one could identify him. He removed his jacket and sat watching the office area. Dividing his attention between that and the brochures he placed up on the dashboard, Anton felt low-key excitement. This was exactly like stalking a buck. A number of wranglers on horseback rode by, lariats in their gloved hands. There was no question this was a busy, working ranch. The largest in the valley.

Twenty minutes later, Shiloh left the first aid office, taking the wooden steps to the red brick sidewalk. Anton remained quiet, watching her. She quickly climbed the steps to the main office, disappearing inside. But she wasn't carrying the papers she had in her hand before. Was she working in the office? If so, WHERE was she staying on the ranch? He'd noticed a KEEP OUT sign as he'd walked with the group down the red brick sidewalk. A sign read: EMPLOYEE HOUSING. And it had a large white picket fence around the entire area, along with the big red KEEP OUT sign. He had also seen six large wood cabins beyond the main ranch building area. It appeared that tourists stayed in them.

Picking up the brochure, he read that the Wind River Ranch offered six cabins to tourists who wanted to stay on the ranch. The prices were in line with what a motel might charge. In another brochure was an illustrated map of the hundred-thousand-acre ranch. There were plenty of roads in and around the main area. He saw Pine Grove and the wide, flat dirt road that led between and around it. Anton wondered if Shiloh ever rode out in the area of Pine Grove. He could set up a hide, like a sniper, and lie in wait for her to appear. Of course, getting onto the ranch property wouldn't be easy, but not impossible. Anton saw another dirt road a mile from the main road into the area that led around and to the pine grove area, as well.

He saw most of the vehicles were gone, and decided he'd best be leaving too. He didn't want to draw any interest as to why he was sitting in the parking lot alone. Reluctantly, Anton slowly drove out of the lot and onto the main asphalt two-lane road that would lead to the entrance of the ranch. Smiling to himself, he felt his chest swell with pride. He'd hit pay dirt.

"I had the weirdest feeling this morning," Shiloh confided to Roan after dinner. They sat at the dinner table after finishing their dessert. She frowned and rubbed the nape of her neck.

Roan frowned. He saw anxiety in Shiloh's green eyes. It had been a while since he'd seen her like this. "Did something spook you?" he wondered.

Shrugging, Shiloh muttered, "I have no idea what happened. I was walking from the accounting office back to the main office when this horrible feeling came over me."

His mouth thinned as he heard the worry in her tone. "What triggered it?"

Frustrated, Shiloh said, "That's the problem. I don't know." She looked around the quiet house, the slats of the western sun flooding the living room area. "It really caught me off guard because I felt this same way when my stalker was standing outside my apartment door and waiting. . . ." Setting the coffee cup aside, Shiloh gave Roan a distressed look. "I am so happy here. . . . I've finally settled in and I'm relaxed. I don't worry about my stalker."

"And then this overwhelming feeling of threat hit you this morning?"

"Yes." Rubbing her brow, she shook her head. "It was stupid."

"Did you look around? See who was in the vicinity?"

"Yes, a quick glance. There were a couple of cars in the parking lot, some cowboys riding past on their horses, but nothing else. I mean, nothing out of the ordinary. That's what has me so flummoxed, Roan."

"Did you have a nightmare last night? Maybe that triggered the reaction this morning?"

"No . . . no, I slept really, really well. I woke up happy and looking forward to the day. To writing another chapter on my book that's due." She moved her fingers across the gold and red cedar table. "I don't know. It was crazy. Out of sync."

Roan moved the coffee cup slowly around between his

large hands. "Did you get this feeling of threat all the time back at your apartment in New York City?" He saw the stress and worry amp up in Shiloh's eyes. He wanted to hold her. He had sworn not to make any move in that direction with Shiloh. He would respect her boundaries although, God knew, it was the last thing he wanted to do. Roan KNEW he could calm her. Help her. Make her feel safe and protected. But Shiloh's fear of getting too deep into a relationship was scaring her away from him and Roan had no answer or way to get her to change her mind. She was worrying her lower lip; something she'd done often when she first came to the ranch. The last three weeks, he'd seen her relax. Until just now.

"I got that very same threat feeling at different times," she admitted quietly. "I'd be out jogging in Central Park and it would hit me. But not all the time. Just sometimes."

"Did you ever see a man watching you?" he wondered.

"There's so many men and women in the park, Roan, I couldn't honestly tell if one of the men was looking in my direction or watching me from the bushes."

"What other times did this feeling come over you?"

"In my apartment." She wrapped her arms around herself, closing her eyes, trying to push away the terror that she always felt when it happened. "I'd be at my desk writing, or watching TV, and it would hit me. And then, I could hear movement on the other side of my apartment door. Like . . . like he was rubbing sandpaper against the door. I could hear it. It scared the hell out of me."

He felt his gut tighten. "Did your door have a peephole?"

Nodding, Shiloh said, "Sometimes, when I heard that noise, I knew he was out there." She gave him an apologetic look. "But I was too scared to go check. To see who it was. I was afraid if I approached the door, he'd bust it down and grab me." She tapped her head. "Writer's imagination firing on all cylinders, believe me."

"So you stood or sat there listening to it?" Roan was getting a firsthand taste of how she was being stalked. The bastard knew exactly what he was doing.

"Y-yes. I'm ashamed of myself, Roan. I should have gone to the door. If I knew what his face looked like, I could have helped the police. But I was too damned scared. And I gig myself now that I didn't force myself to look out that peephole and prove there was a man out there trying to get into my apartment."

"Besides that sanding sound, were there any other indicators someone was out there?" he asked gently, seeing the fear drench her green eyes.

"Yes." Shiloh shivered and looked away, her voice strained. "He slowly started turning the doorknob. First one way, and then the other. It—it was horrible, Roan. I was so afraid he had a key to my apartment. That—that he'd open it up and come in after me."

To hell with it.

Roan set his cup aside and reached out, his large hand scooping up her smaller one. He saw small beads of perspiration on her upper lip, saw the scattered, wild look of a hunted animal that was trapped in her gaze. "You're here, with me," he growled. His fingers curved firmly around her damp ones. "No one is going to hurt you while you're here with me, Shiloh." Roan saw some of the fear dissolve, her mouth, tight and compressed, relaxing a bit. He was deeply touched that he had that kind of positive impact on her. But he'd known that from the day he'd met her at the airport. There was something magical that drew them to each other. They were good for each other too. Roan wished for the hundredth time that Shiloh understood their connection was solid.

"My head knows that," she whispered, giving him a

brief look, feeling shame. "But my emotions are shredded by six months of this terror, Roan."

He gently turned her hand around between his, holding her troubled gaze. "If this EVER happens again while you're here?"

"Yes?"

"Call me. I'll come from wherever I'm working and get to you as soon as I can."

"What will that accomplish?"

"I'm trained to see the enemy, Shiloh. And I'm good at looking at a lot of people and picking out a predator." He watched her gnaw on her lower lip, feeling the fine tension in her hand and arm. "You don't know what this guy looks like. Maybe his body language or the way he's looking at you would give him away to me."

"God, Roan . . . how did he find me out here?"

"You're assuming he did."

"The only time I get this horrible feeling is with this stalker."

Nodding, he asked, "Did you tell anyone where you were going?"

"No, only my editor knew. And she has no reason to tell anyone. She wants me to hand my next book in on time."

"Okay," Roan murmured, absorbing the soft touch of her fingers between his hands. "You're a famous author. You must have a blog? A Facebook page?"

"I do, but my webmistress, Chloe, handles that stuff."

"Did she know you were out here?" He saw Shiloh give him a sudden, stricken look.

"Oh, God," she muttered, touching her brow. "I've been sending Chloe photos and text with them. But I didn't tell her NOT to post them! What was I thinking?" and she scrunched her eyes closed, her hand pressed to her face, completely embarrassed.

"You were distracted," Roan soothed. "It's all right. You

can get ahold of her by e-mail tonight and tell her to stop posting them, but just to hold them until you get home." Roan didn't want Shiloh to go home. No way. But he knew she would.

"Y-yes, that's a good idea." She stared anxiously at him. "Do you think my stalker read those entries on my FB page?"

Shrugging, Roan said, "I don't know. But the reaction you had this morning says that he might be out here starting to stalk you again. What you need to do is check with Chloe to see if she did put that info up on your FB page to verify it."

"Yes, I'll do that, but I'm SURE Chloe put them up."

Roan hated to scare her, but he wasn't going to lie to Shiloh. He squeezed her hand gently between his, getting her attention. "Look, I'm here. We can tell Maud and Steve about this. They'll inform all the employees to be on the lookout for a man who might be asking a lot of questions, mentioning your name or asking where you're at. This can all be handled tomorrow morning, Shiloh. Unlike New York City cops who wouldn't believe you, we will." His voice dropped to a growl. "And we'll find the bastard. Stalkers usually hide in groups and they try not to stand out and be noticed" He could feel a fine tremor go through Shiloh.

Releasing her hand, Roan stood up and walked around to where she sat. He pulled the chair out and then pulled her into his arms, embracing her. Shiloh's arms went around his waist, her face pressed into his chest, as if to hide. He bit back a groan as she fully leaned against him, as if seeking sanctuary. Her red hair was loose and grazed his chin and jaw. Inhaling her special scent, Roan filled his lungs with it, feeling himself responding. It was the last thing Shiloh needed. She came into his arms because she trusted him. Not because she wanted sex with him. Getting a steel grip on himself, Roan willed away his reaction. He lifted his hand, lightly threading his fingers through that red, silky mass of her hair. Shiloh quivered and he wasn't sure if it was from the fear she felt or if the stroking motions were translating into something more heated between them.

Gritting his teeth, he stood quietly, holding her, but not crushing her against him. Shiloh had to know she was free to step out of his embrace anytime she wanted. And God knew, he wanted to stay in her arms. He pushed away the fantasy he had every night when he lay down in his bed, of her being in his arms, being there at his side, of them loving each other.

Sternly, Roan told himself his role right now was to make Shiloh feel protected. The more he slid his hand across her tangled hair, the more she responded by thrusting herself fully into his arms. Roan felt no more quivering. Aware of her breasts pressed against his chest, he felt their warmth, their curved softness. His fingers itched to cup them, taste them, have Shiloh come apart in his arms.

Cursing silently, Roan willed himself to do or say nothing. Just the simple act of slowly smoothing her hair with his hand seemed to tame this wild filly of his. And that's how Roan saw her: a wild, willful, independent filly, full of life, curiosity, and spontaneity. And he wanted to capture that, share that fiery spirit of hers. A slight smile cut across his mouth as he felt Shiloh languish in the gathering silence of the kitchen as he held her. No question, Shiloh WAS willful. But he liked that about her. In some ways, she was fearless. In other ways, fear controlled her life.

Roan knew as he felt her curves against his body that he could set Shiloh free from the fear. He felt his heart swell with a fierceness because he knew she would flourish beneath his hands, his experience and wisdom. But so would he because Shiloh would teach him about being more spontaneous, more in the moment. They were a good match for each other, no question. There was a natural balance they shared and, so far, Roan could see they worked off each other's strengths, not their weaknesses. And he knew from his parents' marriage, which had lasted so long, that they did the same thing.

He placed a light kiss on the top of her head. If he didn't ease her out of his arms, he was going to have an obvious erection. That wouldn't go over well right now.

"Better?" he asked gruffly, pulling her away just enough to look into her half-closed green eyes. Damned if he didn't see arousal in them. A deep ache began within his heart. He knew what love was. And he knew what love was not. Just the way her lips parted, he wanted to lean down, brush her mouth with his, an invitation. A promise of so many good things to come if she'd only trust him fully with herself.

Roan saw confusion come to her eyes and then Shiloh pulled away, moving his hand against her hair, pushing it away from her face. Yeah, he was confused too. Did arousal show in his gaze too? Most likely. If Roan could see it in her face, she was experienced enough to see he wanted her. He wasn't made of stone. He was a flesh-and-blood man. And it felt as if the heated air was vibrating between them, filled with possibility. With whispered promises.

Swallowing hard, Roan forced himself to take a step back from Shiloh. His erection was pressing painfully against the zipper of his Levi's. He needed to move it to ease his discomfort.

"I'll clean up tonight. Why don't you take a long soak in the bathtub?" His gruff words came out almost guttural because Roan wanted her so damn bad he could taste it. He saw Shiloh nod, frowning, the arousal doused in her wide, green eyes.

"Yes," she said, her voice almost wispy sounding, "that's a good idea. . . ."

Roan watched her turn and pad down the hall. Just the way her hips swayed, he felt the ache intensify his erection. Damn, but the woman was hot. Running his fingers through his short hair in an aggravated motion, Roan got busy cleaning up the kitchen.

As he worked, he didn't try to fantasize about Shiloh stripping out of her clothes, or sliding into the welcoming warm water, her skin glistening like diamonds. Taking the bar of soap, lathering up his hands and washing her. Every last, square inch of her. By the time he'd gotten the dishes into the dishwasher, wiped the table and counter down, Roan decided to get the hell out of the house. If he didn't, he was going to open that bathroom door.

Stepping out the front door, he saw the sun had set. There were high clouds above the valley, swirling like pink cotton candy across the sky. Roan sat down on one of the two rockers, the wood creaking beneath his weight. Across the street, everything was quiet. The tourists were all eating at the café. The other wranglers had called it quits for the day, heading home to the town of Wind River. He was sure Maud, Steve, and their family were dining at their ranch house right now. The lowing of the cattle soothed some of Roan's fractious energy. He moved slowly, arms on the rocker. The creak was pleasant and calming.

What the HELL had caused this reaction in him? Roan scowled and stared out toward the wildlife loop road, the gate locked, pink clouds drifting silently above the valley. Shiloh had been genuinely scared as she talked about her stalker. His mind moved like lightning across possibilities. He didn't doubt Shiloh. He believed her because he'd lived with her for a month and gotten to know her fairly well. She wasn't the type of woman to become dramatic or blow things out of proportion.

Rubbing his bristly jaw, Roan gazed around the quiet ranch that was settling in for night to fall shortly. He knew something had happened to Shiloh today. There was no way to pretend that level of fear. He could see it in the depth of her guileless eyes.

He decided to go see Steve Whitcomb tomorrow after breakfast, and check the logbook on the tourists who had visited the ranch for the loop drive at the time she'd felt her stalker. That was a first step because each tourist had to put down their name, phone number, and where they lived. He could hand the list to Shiloh and see if she recognized any of the names, addresses, or phone numbers. It was a start. But that was all. Roan wished mightily that if this ever happened again, Shiloh would get on her cell phone and head for the safety of the main office. If her stalker was here, he could kidnap her. Kill her.

Roan's mouth thinned, his dark brows drawing downward. His heart contracted with worry for Shiloh. Whether he liked it or not, he knew he was falling for her. He didn't want to go as far as admitting it was love. She was gun-shy and he knew she couldn't know how he really felt toward her. And yet, when she needed safety, she ran to him. And he swore he saw arousal deep in her eyes. So it wasn't all about protection between them either.

There really was something beautiful, something hopeful, growing between them, regardless of their situation. But would Shiloh ever step out of the fear that held her, to walk into his arms?

Chapter Fifteen

Roan had just gotten his shower, the towel wrapped low around his waist, and padded barefoot down to his bedroom when there was a soft knock on his door. Brows dipping, he turned, wiping water that was still dripping off his short hair. He'd remained outside a good two hours after night had fallen, allowing the crickets, frogs, and lowing of nearby cattle to help him ratchet down from his gnawing state of needing Shiloh.

He walked to the door in his bare feet and opened it. Shiloh stood uncertainly, dressed in a soft ivory sleeveless pajama top and a pair of boxer shorts of the same fabric and color. His heart bounded once to underscore how beautiful, how innocent she looked standing there, hands clasped nervously in front of her. It was the shyness, the yearning and anxiety in her green eyes that made him groan internally.

"What's wrong?" he asked, his voice low and rough-sounding.

"I-I just had a nightmare." Shiloh took a breath. And then she shook her head. "No . . . that's not the whole story. . . ." she said, lifting her head, meeting his narrowing eyes. It felt like he was looking inside her. He was intensely male, the dark hair sprinkled across his broad chest, the flexing of his muscles as he stood in the doorway wrapped in nothing more than the towel hanging off his narrow hips. His flesh glistened with water. A sense of protectiveness radiated off him toward her, infusing her, steadying the fear running rampant through her, turning it into something else. Longing for Roan.

Shiloh saw him hesitate, as if torn, the expression reaching his eyes. Wrapping her arms around herself, Shiloh held Roan's darkening gray gaze. His mouth thinned. She felt his unsureness about her standing at his bedroom door. "I'm not going to blame my nightmare as the reason I'm standing here," she said quietly. "For the longest time, I've wanted to . . . well . . . be intimate with you. It has nothing to do with my nightmare."

She saw surprise flare in his eyes. A muscle leaped in his jaw. It didn't take any guesswork as to the bulge of a growing erection she saw beneath the white towel. "This could all be one-way, Roan. You need to tell me now because if it is, I promise I'll never do this again." Shiloh gulped, feeling her heart beating like a rabbit in her chest. There was a thaw in his eyes, a lessening of tension around his mouth. She could smell the sage soap, and hungrily inhaled the scent into her lungs.

"We need to talk, then" was all he said, moving aside to allow her into his bedroom.

Her heart squeezed with need of him. Shiloh stepped into his room, wildly aware Roan was so close, almost naked, excruciatingly masculine, and calling to her in every way. She hesitated mid-room, turned, and looked toward him. Roan closed the door, facing her. Shiloh wasn't sure what she saw in his expression.

"Sit over there?" He pointed to the couch in one corner of the room.

Nodding, Shiloh sat down. She saw him coming her way, his lean, masculine grace taking her breath away. She took one end of the couch, curling her legs up beneath her. Roan took the other end, a few feet in between them.

"Are you mostly here because of the nightmare, Shiloh?"

She held his gaze. "No. I mean"—she gave him a weak shrug—"it woke me up, but I've had them before and I never came across the hall to see you." She saw him absorb her words, felt him wrestling with something known only to him.

"Why tonight?"

"You held me earlier. It felt so good, Roan. So right, but I wasn't sure you felt the same way."

"Shiloh, you've told me you're afraid of commitment. I'm not built the same way. Do I want you? Hell yes. But I'm not the kind of man who wants one night in the sack. Sex is great, Shiloh, and if that's all you want, then I'm not the one you're looking for. I'd be lying to you and myself if I didn't admit that I wanted you. And I think sex between us would be incredible. But for the right reasons."

She nodded, wrapping her arms around herself, studying him in the low light provided by a stained glass lamp on top of the dresser. "You play for keeps."

"I don't mess with the heart, Shiloh. It's too risky a proposition. My woman has to want a relationship with me in and out of bed. I like having that kind of connection with her."

"I guess I've always known that about you, Roan."

"It's a curse," he said, giving her a rueful glance. "If I'm going to risk my heart, I want to know it's for all the right reasons. I'm entering into something with a woman who is as sincere as I am. You've admitted to having commitment issues."

She held his gray gaze, feeling how much Roan wanted her. She felt as if she would die if she couldn't have this man tonight, to feel his arms around her, loving her, taking her, making her his. "That's why I came to your door tonight, Roan."

"What do you mean?"

"I guess . . ." she began, looked away for a moment, and then reestablished her gaze with Roan's. "I guess today impacted me differently. After I woke up from the nightmare, I wondered why I've been living half a life. Fear controls me. I've been afraid because I saw how my mother died inside after my father's heart attack. It scared me. I thought that anyone I loved fully would die on me, leaving me suffering like my mother did."

"It scarred you deeply," Roan agreed, sympathetic, searching her expression.

"There's something good between us," Shiloh whispered. "I've always felt it, Roan. And I have a month left here, and I don't know what to do. I want to explore whatever it is that we have. If you do. And I don't know what's going to happen. I feel like I'm strung between the past and the present. I don't want to go home to New York City. I want to stay here. I never expected to meet a man like you. I was running to get away from my stalker." With a grimace, she added sourly, "And now, he might be here. I keep trying to tell myself I made up my reaction earlier, but I know I didn't. I've always been sensitive to threat. I have a radar."

"Probably because you saw your mother murdered," Roan said, his voice sad.

"Yes . . . exactly. Since then, it's like I'm on constant alert and I can't stop it or turn it off."

"It's PTSD," Roan said simply. "Trauma affects every human, more or less."

Frustrated, Shiloh said, "So I've learned." She saw his expression relax, felt the tension dissolve in him. "Roan, I don't know where we're going with each other. If I leave in a month, what will happen to us?"

"I'm not asking you for what will eventually happen to us, Shiloh. No one can know that. What I do want is a full hundred percent commitment from you. I want your heart without strings attached. I don't know if our relationship will last or not, but I don't want to enter into something with you and feel you're going to bail because you're afraid to fully commit to me at some point down the road if it works out in that direction for both of us."

She tucked her lower lip between her teeth for a moment. "I've never had a conversation like this with a man before. I've met guys and they didn't seem concerned about commitment."

"Maybe all they wanted from you was sex?"

"I've thought that, too. They weren't into a heavy-duty relationship," she admitted. "And I made it clear up front that I wasn't interested in getting tied down, that I wanted to be free to be with whomever I wanted. They were okay with that. They wanted the same thing." She saw his mouth curve faintly.

"But you're more mature now. You may want something different at this point in your life."

Warmth flooded Shiloh as she thought about Roan's cabin, the labor of love that it was for him. The man worked hard and consistently toward his dream. He was willing to put his heart and soul into it. "Maybe I've just never met a man who demanded a serious, honest commitment to him."

Shrugging, Roan murmured, "Only you can answer that, Shiloh."

"Doesn't it bother you that I'm leaving in a month? It bothers the hell out of me."

"Sure it does, but I don't see it as the end of anything. It's just distance," he said. "There are airplanes. You could come out here for a visit."

"Or you could fly in and visit me?" She saw him grimace, understanding he didn't like big cities.

"I would," he said, holding her gaze.

She felt his words in her heart, which was opening widely to him. "I believe you. I can't promise you where this will go, Roan."

"I'm not asking that of you. All I need to know is that you're not going to let fear stop you from exploring me, finding out who I am. Discovering what we may have together."

Giving him a wry look, Shiloh said, "I think you're forcing me to look at myself, what I want, who I am."

"Good relationships always do that for both people, Darlin'. It's just a natural progression between them. It can bring out our self-awareness. It's not easy. But it's rewarding. None of us were born to live alone or be alone. It's natural to evolve into relationships, whether it's in business, friendship, or on a more intimate and personal level."

Shiloh stood up. "Then," she said in a low voice, holding his eyes, "I want to know you, Roan. All of you."

He stood and held her softened gaze. Slipping his hand into hers, he dug into her wide green eyes. "And I've been wanting to know you ever since I laid eyes on you for the first time at the airport, Shiloh."

She wondered why she'd fought so long and hard not to know this man who was the salt of the earth, who was blunt, straightforward, and brutally honest with himself and with her. Roan drew her into his arms, his mouth barely skimming hers, inviting her. A soft sigh escaped Shiloh as she moved into his arms, pressing her breasts against the wall of his chest.

"Are you protected?" Roan asked, his voice thick with arousal.

Sliding her arms around his broad shoulders, feeling the muscles tighten as she skimmed them with her fingers, she whispered against his mouth, "Yes . . ."

Roan eased her back just enough to hold her gaze. "I

don't have condoms here, Shiloh." His smile was crooked. "I wasn't expecting to ever use them here on the ranch."

Amusement tinged her voice and she smiled up at him. "It's all right. I'm clean and healthy."

"So am I."

"Then," she whispered, leaning up on her toes, her lips meeting his, "I want to love you. . . ."

His mouth cherished hers, in no hurry to explore the shape and softness of her. There was an exquisite heat that flowed through Shiloh and she languished in the strength of his arms. Roan kissed her gently, as if introducing himself to her. She was wildly aware of his hand ranging slowly downward, as if memorizing her.

"Tell me what you want?" he asked, leaving her wet mouth.

Blinking, Shiloh stilled in his arms, dampness settling between her thighs. Her channel felt as if on fire, cramping and wanting Roan. "W-what?" She saw him smile a little and he eased his fingers through her tangled red hair.

"What pleases you, Shiloh? What do you need from me? We're a team. I want to know what will make you fly apart in my arms."

The man shook her to her foundation. His eyes were hooded, flecks of silver in his narrowing gaze. Shiloh felt as if he were drinking her into his hard, male body and he'd barely touched her. Barely kissed her. "No man has ever asked me before," she said, giving him a bemused look. She saw his expression grow thoughtful.

"Then, Darlin', as we start loving each other, you let me know in your own way if it feels good to you or not. If you want more. Or less. Or for me to stop."

Her mind was already shorting out by sexual hunger and need of Roan. "Y-yes . . ." She sounded like a neophyte; someone who knew nothing. His chiseled mouth curved a little and he nodded.

Roan slid his ams beneath her, lifting Shiloh against him, carrying her to his bed, which had yet to be turned down for the night. She trusted him completely, slipping her arms around his neck, her brow resting against his jaw. He deposited her and turned, shutting off the light. Only faint moonlight peeked around the edges of the heavy drapes at the other end of the room.

Shiloh saw him pull the towel away from his body, her breath catching. He was fully erect and a keen yearning flowed sweet and hot through her lower body. As he placed his knee on the bed, the mattress sank beneath his weight. He sat facing her. The silence ebbed and her heart pounded with anticipation. The look on his deeply shadowed face was intense.

She sat up, pulled her top off, revealing her breasts beneath. And before she could wriggle out of her boxer shorts, Roan's fingers eased beneath the waistband, helping her to remove them. Shiloh wasn't one to lie helpless and let the man orchestrate their mating. She wanted to be an equal, enthusiastic partner in this beautiful dance that she was eager to consummate with him.

She knelt before Roan, her hands flowing around his hard jaw, watching his eyes shutter nearly closed as she leaned into him, taking his mouth eagerly, not wanting to wait any longer. His mouth was equally hungry, deepening her kiss, his breath hot and ragged against her cheek. As his large, callused hands slid around her rib cage, cupping her breasts, Shiloh moaned. He took that low sound into him, drawing her closer until her breasts were cupped fully in his hands. Her skin was on fire, the calluses on his palms causing skittering flames to pucker her nipples until she was desperate for Roan to touch them, tease them.

His mouth branding hers with a fierce passion, she felt his thumbs move languidly across her nipples as if reading her mind. Tearing her mouth from his, eyes tightly shut,

Shiloh cried out his name, the sensation so scalding and making the gnawing ache between her legs intensify. She arched against him, his hands cupping her, his mouth drifting down the slender length of her neck, setting her skin on fire. Gripping his taut, bunched shoulders with her fingers, all she could do was enjoy what he was sharing with her.

Roan lifted Shiloh, easing her onto her back to lavish her breasts even more, his hand drifting firmly down her body, sliding across her right hip, his long fingers opening and caressing the length of her thigh as he suckled her. Shiloh couldn't lie still beneath him, his hand wreaking a burning magic that was making her mew with anticipation. She couldn't catch her breath and she found herself as if in a tornado of pleasure as he began his sweet assault down the centerline of her body toward her restless hips and legs. She had wanted to please him, too, but the man had a plan and she was helpless beneath his onslaught, wanting to give him mindless pleasure, too.

As his mouth drifted to her rounded abdomen, kissing it, licking her belly button, her hips rose, her cry breathless with anticipation, her fingers digging frantically into his shoulders. Her breath was ragged and the expectancy of his mouth upon her sent her into a primal wildness. Roan eased her thighs apart, his fingers moving slowly inside her curved flesh, testing her, moving slickly into the dampness near her entrance. Her whole world burst into scorching fire as he traced his finger around her gateway.

An uncontrollable shudder worked through Shiloh as she arched against his exploring finger teasing that tight pearl near her entrance, sending her into a spinning universe. He captured one of her nipples, gently biting it and simultaneously placed a second finger within her. She cried out, her back arching, her hands frantic against his shoulders. Within moments, her body convulsed, a seismic shock wave of rupturing pleasure from an orgasm that saturated her lower body and flooded her with keen pleasure. And Roan didn't stop there. He knew how to get her body to give him everything she had. Shiloh felt a second orgasm shatter through her, her lower body throbbing with such scalding pleasure she felt faint as she suddenly collapsed against the bed.

Only vaguely aware that Roan had moved, feeling his strong male body cover hers, Shiloh slowly opened her eyes. Her breath was rasping, her heart pounding in her chest. She saw him plant his elbows near her upper arms, his expression tender as he looked into her dazed eyes. It was as if he were waiting and again, Shiloh was left knowing this man was a master of timing. After two major, rocking orgasms, her body was tender and needed time before she was ready for more. The smile he gave her flooded her with joy, his gray eyes clear, intense, and focused on her. Without a word, Roan leaned down, capturing her lips beneath his, the kiss gentle, unlike the raw throbbing sensations flooding her right now.

Drowning in his strong mouth that cherished hers, Shiloh made a soft sound in her throat, his hands framing her face, holding her. His tongue moved from one corner of her parting lips to the other. His breath was warm and it was an effort to lift her lids, so blown by the orgasms that still owned her body and soul. She had never met a man who could be this tender; as if he intuitively knew that she needed to rest between rounds. The glittering intelligence in his eyes told her Roan was completely in tune with her body, her heart. She felt as if her chest might explode with the pure, unadulterated happiness that Roan stroked and roused to life within her. She continued to drown in his mouth, feeling his strength as a man, feeling his tongue invite hers to dance with him.

The moment their tongues slickly met, a whole new ribbon of boiling sensations coursed through her. He emulated copulation and it triggered a primal knowing in her body and her hips just naturally lifted to meet his. A low cry lodged in her throat as he eased forward into her, testing her, allowing her time to accommodate him. The sensation was luxurious, expanding her, opening her, and she arched more deeply toward his tense hips as he held himself in check. Roan held her captive, slowly sliding in and out of her, her moans low and vibrating as the sensations stroked through her and intensified. He tore his mouth from hers, groaning deeply as he thrust fully into her.

A gasp of satisfaction escaped her as she clung to his tense, damp shoulders, feeling the surge of his maleness within her, taking her, driving her over another boiling edge of pleasure, to a place she'd never been before. With each thrust, she gave a little cry, but it was raw satisfaction, not from discomfort. Roan tunneled his fingers through her hair, his teeth clenched, eyes tightly closed and she felt him pump deep into her one last time before their worlds flew apart on them.

The explosiveness of her orgasm shattered through her at the same moment Roan climaxed within her. The sensations were so keen, hungry, and fulfilling that all Shiloh could do was sob with pleasure, her head buried against his damp shoulder as he gripped the long strands of her hair, his breath ragged. The strength of his body coupled with hers, the way her curves surrendered to his angles, the power of him as a man absorbed by her softness all conspired to make Shiloh faint and heady at the same time.

Gradually, Shiloh felt Roan's fingers begin to relax within her tangled hair as he caressed her temple and cheek, his body suddenly sagging against hers. She willingly took all his weight, absorbing his power and luxuriating in his warmth. Satiation flowed so strongly through her that she felt mindless, floating, and embraced with his heat and masculinity. Shiloh utterly relaxed beneath Roan, his male scent filling her, flooding her lungs like an aphrodisiac. Her lips lifted faintly into a smile of utter contentment. This man knew how to love a woman, no question. Her body was throbbing with pleasure and utter satisfaction.

Shiloh had no idea of how long they lay together like that. But it felt good. Intimate. Even more important to her, making love had never been so right. She weakly slid her arms around his broad, damp back, feeling his skin react to her touch. Kissing his shoulder, his face buried next to hers, his breathing harsh and short, Shiloh nuzzled against his sandpapery jaw, savoring everything about Roan. And despite his climax, she could feel him growing inside her once again. The man was like a stallion and she smiled, not sorry about that one bit.

And as Shiloh felt herself coming back down to earth, aware of Roan's weight, the lean muscling against her softer flesh, she greedily absorbed every physical sensation of him within her. Her hands ranged downward toward his narrow hips, fingers splaying out, and she sensuously moved her hips against his, a silent invitation. Instantly, he growled her name, automatically thrusting deep into her. Shiloh gave a moan of gratification, smiling, eyes closed, feeling the renewed pleasure of him growing thick and hard within her once again. Roan was hungry. So was she. It had been a year without an orgasm. And he knew how to play her body like a finely tuned instrument.

Roan lifted his head, smiling down at her, removing some strands of red hair away from her brow. "You feel so damn good to me," he growled, and he plundered her mouth, arching deep and hard into her.

The combination made Shiloh naturally arch to open herself as much as possible to his renewed strokes within her. She wanted Roan again. She wanted everything he could gift her with from his body to his generous heart. As his mouth left hers, he savored each of her nipples, bringing her to an edgy need once again. And as he settled on his knees, his hands spanning her hips, he drew her up against him until their hips locked, melting fire between them. Her mind instantly checked out as he thrust repeatedly into her, massaging the knot of nerves near her entrance, breathless as the powerful stroking movement drove her right over that cliff once again.

Shiloh felt her entire lower body explode and wavelets of pleasure rippled through her until she could barely cry out. The feverish intensity and throbbing orgasm unfurled within her. The strain of his body against hers, his grate of satisfaction reverberating through her, his fists curling into the bedcovers on either side of her head told her of the joy, the thirst of their mutual need and celebration for each other. Spun into light and oblivion, Shiloh smiled and clung to Roan's shoulders, feeling him take her, claim and brand her as his woman, once and for all.

Hot, liquefying sensations throbbed throughout her. Perspiration was running freely off her body. She could smell their sex, the scent like a perfume to her flaring nostrils as she slowly moved her fingers languidly against Roan's now relaxed shoulders. He lay heavily against her, his head next to hers, stroking her hair, holding her, words useless. Closing her eyes, Shiloh absorbed each of his ministrations, feeling herself sink a little more deeply into the flooding happiness swirling throughout her. Roan made her feel good about herself. Made her feel good to be his partner. There was sharing and a caring. And tenderness as he lifted his head, met her drowsy eyes, smiled into them, satisfaction burning deep in his gray ones.

This time, Roan eased out of her. He moved onto his side, bringing Shiloh against his long, hard body, holding her close, kissing her temple, her cheek, and finally, caressing her lips with such adoration that it brought tears to her eyes. Was this what it was like for her mother and father?

That their love was so deep, so all-consuming, that they fearlessly loved each other with all their heart? And this was how it felt? Nothing in her life had ever matched being in Roan's arms right now.

It must be, Shiloh thought, returning Roan's kiss, relishing his mouth upon hers. There were no more barriers. Just fused, joyous oneness. She could feel his heart beating in time with hers. Their breath mingled, moist and uneven. They were sweaty, weak, and satisfied. Roan tucked her head into the crook of his shoulder and laid his head on the pillow, his fingers tangling gently through her silken hair. His other arm went around her shoulders, supporting the small of her back, holding her fully against him. Fused. One.

Chapter Sixteen

Nothing had ever felt so right to Shiloh as these moments. There was such a sense of fierce protection surrounding her as Roan held her in his arms. The moonlight streamers grew bolder, the room became a softer gray. Sliding her fingers across Roan's chest, she felt his arms tighten briefly around her, responding to her caress. His jaw rested against the top of her head. Beneath her palm, she could feel the slow beat of his magnificent heart. Sensing the power that was a part of him, even when at rest, told Shiloh he was a warrior in repose, not really, fully relaxed. Maybe because of his many years as a Special Forces operator? There was so little she knew about him. And Shiloh wanted to know everything.

Sighing softly, she closed her eyes, content to be cradled in Roan's arms, his strength like a warm cocoon surrounding her. She could feel he was awake, not asleep. What was he thinking? Just feeling his lean, hard body against hers, she smiled, absorbing the potency of Roan into herself. Once again, Shiloh wondered if this was how her mother felt about her father. There was such a fierce need to connect with Roan at heart level. She felt Roan lift his hand, threading his fingers through her tousled hair. Her scalp tingled with delight, the skittering sensations making Shiloh almost purr, the sound vibrating in her throat.

"You are so easy to please," he growled.

Smiling, Shiloh remained in his arms. "Maybe you just know how to please me."

"We're good together." He pressed a kiss to her hair. "But I knew we would be."

"What else do you know about us?" Shiloh tipped her head back against his muscular, ropy upper arm, catching his darkened gaze, the moonlight making his gray eyes look softened in the refracted light. Roan looked satisfied. Thoughtful. Happy. She saw that beautiful male mouth of his curve slightly, his fingers stilling in her hair, caressing the back of her head.

"It's a sensing, not a knowing."

"Okay, what do you sense?" She saw his smile grow more. The man was such a Chinese puzzle! He never gave anything up willingly. And if she didn't ask just the right question, it wasn't answered. Was that his black ops training? Or just him? Shiloh didn't know, but determined in time to find out.

"I see a beautiful, wild filly that is happiest when she has the run of the range. She's free. . . ."

"You're calling me a horse?" Shiloh grinned up at him.

"That was a compliment, Darlin'."

Shiloh considered. "I guess you might see women as horses. You grew up on a cattle ranch in Montana."

"I don't see all women as horses."

Lifting her brows, she asked archly, "What does THAT mean?" She heard Roan chuckle. She got the sense he felt like he was dealing with a recalcitrant child who was asking too many questions. *Too bad*.

Roan leaned down, taking her mouth, moving his lips across hers, sending a longing through Shiloh once more.

The man knew how to kiss! Gradually, he left her lips, their noses almost touching.

"Is this what I'm in for? Twenty questions?"

Seeing the teasing, the amusement in his expression, Shiloh said pointedly, "You know I'm a writer. Writers are curious people. How could you think I wasn't going to ask you questions, Roan Taggart?" She warmed as she saw laughter gleam in his eyes.

"Which is why I see you as a frisky, risk-taking two-year-old filly. You're full of yourself. You're exuberant. You're fearless. You just move from your heart on a whim and follow whatever interests you."

Shiloh considered his larger explanation. "Why couldn't you have said all that in one paragraph earlier, Roan? See? I'm having to drag everything out of you again."

"You didn't have to drag me kicking and screaming into your arms."

Snorting, Shiloh said, "That's true." She saw him give her a know-it-all look, as if he knew her inside and out. "Okay," she muttered defiantly, "what else?"

He slid his hand down her long, supple spine, caressing her hips. "There's another question."

"And is this because you're steeped in black ops stuff? That you're closemouthed because you had to be? You know, you aren't black ops now. It's okay to open your mouth and speak more than one or two sentences to me. I'm not deaf. I love to hear what you think and feel."

Roan laughed outright, released Shiloh, stuffed a couple of pillows behind his back, and sat up. Resting against the headboard, he gathered her into his arms, hauling her across his lap, settling her comfortably against him. "I feel like I've opened up some floodgates," he said, and he kissed her nose, holding her petulant gaze.

"You know," Shiloh murmured, running her fingers

through the silky dark hair across his chest, "I see us as a mismatch. One person, me, relies completely on communication. You, on the other hand, are trained in black ops to say nothing of note to anyone. We really ARE opposites, Roan." She lifted her gaze up to his, very serious about it. "Doesn't that bother you?"

"No," he teased, sliding his fingers across her cheek, "because you're like a cattle prod, sticking me to make me cough up something of note."

They both laughed.

Shiloh nuzzled her brow against his jaw, never wanting this night to end, his arms warm and strong around her. "Okay, let's get serious now." She felt an instant shift around Roan. It was the oddest sensation; as if she had some kind of invisible link to him. Shiloh had never felt this with another man. Her fingers stilled on his chest and she closed her eyes, languishing within his embrace, wanting nothing more.

"What do you want to get serious about?" Roan asked, his palm against her cheek.

"My parents," she murmured, opening her eyes, staring across the silent room filled with grayish moonlight. "As I was loving you a little while ago, I wondered if this is how they felt about each other. How they felt as they made love with each other. A love so deep . . . so . . . incredibly magical and word-defying. And that's why my mother fell apart after my dad died. That she loved him with every breath she took. That she couldn't imagine life without him being a part of her life. Almost . . . well . . . symbiotic. They were actually one person. Maybe two halves of a whole who loved each other so completely that neither of them could ever survive without the other?"

Roan caressed her hair, his hand coming to rest on her

small shoulder. "My parents have a similar love. Did I tell you that?"

"No," she mumbled, scowling up at him. "Remember? I have to pull teeth to get anything out of you?"

"Guilty," Roan agreed, giving her a patient smile. "I think that since we were both raised with parents who honestly loved each other, we were very, very fortunate. I don't think a lot of marriages ever hit that pinnacle of love. At least, I haven't seen it. People stay together for a lot of reasons and it's not always because they love each other."

"I didn't know about your parents . . . that's wonderful, Roan." And Shiloh meant it.

"So you see?" he murmured, placing his finger beneath her chin, holding her gaze, "you don't always lose the person you love, Darlin'. My parents are proof of that. I'm sorry you lost your parents, but maybe now you can release that fear."

His insight was startling. Warm. Full of hope for Shiloh. She took his finger and placed a small kiss on the end of it. "You're just full of surprises, Taggart." She saw him give her a very pleased male smile.

"Stick around, Darlin', there's more to me than meets your eyes."

"Should I be afraid?" She gave him an impish look.

"I hope not. Maybe"—he caressed the length of her arm—"look forward to every night from now on sharing my bed?"

Shiloh tangled her fingers between his. Roan had such large hands, long fingers, sun-darkened flesh compared to hers. "You're serious?"

"I am," he said, and he held her gaze. "That's what I want for us, Shiloh. What do you want?"

Her lips twisted and she looked down at their joined hands. "I don't know why I always have the same reaction to that question. I start to sense fear."

"It's the past, Shiloh. You need to continue to work through it and let it go. Give US a chance?" He leaned over, catching her lowered gaze. "I'm the present, Darlin'."

Roan was right and she knew it. "The present is like a dream to me. A wonderful one. I'm trying, Roan. I really am."

"I'm no dream, Darlin'. I'm flesh and blood. This is reality and you're here with me." He smiled faintly. "And you were the one who initiated it, so I think you're more than ready to put your past to rest. Put your worries aside that anyone you might fall in love with is going to be ripped out of your life. I'm going nowhere."

Nodding, she felt her heart swell with more hope than fear. Roan's voice was low and vibrating with feeling for her. He was making no bones about wanting her, wanting a real relationship. Shiloh wanted the same thing. The past was so forbidding. "I think . . . I feel," she qualified in a whisper, "that part of my hesitation is the stalker, Roan. I'm terrified that someone is out to get me. It's probably silly and not logical, but I run on my emotions." She looked up at him, loosening her fingers from his, caressing his stubbly jaw, holding his dark, glittering gaze. "I'm sorry I'm not whole. I don't feel confident about the future because it scares me. I wish I knew who was doing this to me."

He gave her an understanding look. "We'll find out, Shiloh. I'm here for you. I hope you know that. You're worth caring about," he said, and he moved a few strands of hair off her cheek, his fingers sliding down her shoulder. "Let's take this one day at a time. If you want to share my bed, show up at my door like you did tonight. And if you don't, that's fine too. The last thing I want to do is make you feel pressured. What we have is good. And it's up to you as to what you want to do about it."

Some relief trickled through her. "Thanks for giving me that leeway, Roan. Until this stalker issue is closed, I just can't focus. I'm scared. Yesterday, I felt like I was back in my apartment. I felt trapped. Terrorized. And I don't know who this guy is. That's the worst of it."

Roan tucked her head beneath his jaw, holding her tightly. "I'm on this, Shiloh. I'm not going to let you be hurt by this bastard. I've not gotten black ops training for nothing. Tomorrow, when I drive into town, I'm going to see Sheriff Sarah Carter. She's in charge of the Lincoln County sheriff's department. I'm going to talk to her, get ideas, maybe some intel." He kissed her hair. "But you and I need to have a plan."

She roused, feeling safe for the first time since the stalker had entered her life. "A plan?"

"Yes. We each carry a cell phone on us at all times. I want you, if you EVER get that threatening warning again, to call me immediately. But as you call me, go to John's office. And he'll call the sheriff. We need to catch this guy. If you get that warning, it means he's nearby and most likely on ranch property. After John makes that call, he'll take you to their house and you'll remain out of sight and safe until a deputy arrives."

Shutting her eyes, Shiloh felt a quiver of fear. "He's really here. God . . ."

"It's different this time around, Darlin'. I'm with you. You have every employee on Wind River Ranch who will be told what's going on and we'll have a lot of people watching this situation. More eyes, more chances to nail this son of a bitch." Roan pulled her back enough to look at her. "That's the plan. Does it sound good to you? Anything to add to it?"

A chill worked through her even though Roan was holding her. No place was safe from her stalker. "It works," she agreed quietly, resting her head against his shoulder, wanting the world to go away as it had before in Roan's arms. "What am I supposed to do in the meantime, Roan?

Am I prisoner in this house? Do I go over and spend most of my time in John's office, instead?"

He slid his hand down her arm. "No. Continue what you've been doing, Shiloh. Just be more aware. Know the situational area and who is in it. That's all. The rest will take care of itself."

"Sometimes you're miles away, Roan. You'd never get back to the main ranch in time."

"That's why it's important to go to the main office as soon as you can," he said. "It's the safest place. John always keeps a firearm in his desk drawer. He's licensed to carry a concealed weapon and he sure as hell knows how to use it if things got out of hand. Most stalkers aren't that brazen, Shiloh. They sneak. They hide in the shadows. And most likely, this one isn't going to be bold, either."

"Okay, that sounds doable. I just don't want to become a prisoner like I was in my apartment, Roan," she said, and she looked up at him, pleading with him because she hated those six terrible months where she felt like a convict.

Roan kissed her brow. "I'll always be nearby, Shiloh. I'll talk to Maud and request that she utilize me closer to the headquarters area for now. I won't be that far away. I think she'll agree to the plan without a problem." He searched her face. "Does that make you feel a little better?"

She moistened her lips. "Yes, a lot better." And then she blurted, "But what if he kills you?"

Roan smiled a little and squeezed her tightly for a moment. "If he's a black ops dude, I'd be concerned, but I'm sure he's not. That doesn't mean I'll underestimate him, Shiloh. But there's damn few men who can get a drop on an operator. It would really have to be a special set of circumstances. And I am on guard, Darlin'. I have your back."

"That makes me feel good," she admitted. Just being in Roan's arms, against his powerful, warm, hard body, gave her a sense of safety she'd never felt. Shiloh had never felt happier.

He eased her out of his arms. Adjusting the pillows, Roan lay down. He brought her on top of him, settling her thighs against either side of his hips. "Come here," he growled, folding her against his length. "Your turn to be my blanket."

She smiled warmly, eagerly stretching out, her breasts lightly grazing the hair across his chest. "Mmmm, I like this." As she settled her core against his growing erection, her smile increased and she drowned in the glittering gray in his eyes. "You know what? I think you're a consummate strategy-and-tactics kind of guy. There's more than one reason for you wanting me as a warm blanket across you." She saw a feral look cross his shadowed features and she gloried in the sensation of his thickening erection against her moist core. Already, heated signals were racing up through her.

"I told you: surprises." He tangled his fingers through her hair, nudging it across her shoulders. It barely crossed Shiloh's mind that Roan knew she was a worrier and that by distracting her with his delicious male body, it would focus her on something else. Something positive. And oh, so good.

Roan drew in a deep, ragged breath as she moved like a sinuous cat against his hips, engaging his erection, feeling her wetness claiming him already and he wasn't even inside her. "You're a worrywart, Darlin'. We've talked about the situation. We've come up with a plan. You need to let it go." He slid his hands down her sides, feeling how warm and velvety her flesh was beneath his fingertips.

Shiloh gave him an amused look. "You do know that men's and women's brains are created differently? That we think differently?"

He shrugged, hands settling on her hips, anchoring and

firmly bringing her down upon him. "What? You gals have a worrywart brain?" he teased, chuckling.

She grinned, moving slowly up and down his growing length, watching the reaction in his face, the way he drew in a sharp breath, desire for her burning in his narrowing eyes. "Very funny, black ops guy." Her eyes closed as Roan arched, reaching, stroking her entrance. A sweet quiver moved through her. "Ohhh," she whispered, a purr slipping from her lips. "You feel so good in me. . . ." and her mind melted as he thrust fully into her slick depths. Her back arched and he gripped her, holding her as he began a slow, deep campaign to have her focus only on the burning, building pressure between them.

He expanded her, filling her, the sensations intense and making her exhale as scalding heat throbbed pleasurably throughout her lower body. Roan had barely touched her; merely teased her and she was so wet. So ready. Her body was aching for relief. That was amazing to Shiloh because it had never happened before. Maybe Roan was right: He held a lot of surprises and he was going to share each and every one of them with her. A low, guttural cry erupted from her as he stroked, teased, and triggered an orgasm within her. She stiffened, paralyzed with the radiating heat pushing outward in wavelets throughout her lower body, hurling her off that delicious cliff called pleasure.

She felt herself collapsing against Roan as the orgasm dissolved into continuing fiery undulations moving outward within her. His hands moved slowly, memorizing her, cupping her cheeks, thrusting deep into her. Roan gripped her, holding her against him, not done with her or her vibrant, throbbing body. She began to heat up once again with those short, sharp thrusts against that knot of nerves near her entrance.

A low sound caught in her throat as he captured her completely with his strength, guiding her body, milking it, drawing out a second orgasm that surprised Shiloh as it flowed sweetly through her. Roan understood female anatomy, no question, and she lay gasping against him, her fingers dug into his thick shoulders, eyes tightly shut, hurled into a bright universe of stars, suns, and moons. She heard him growl her name, felt him lift his hips, fusing with her, taking her hard and quick. There was no time to catch her breath, her flexing body so much living putty between his hands, hips, and body. Within moments, he grunted, stiffening, hands strong against her hips, arching into her, frozen with pleasure as he climaxed deep within her.

Shiloh had no idea where time went. Only that she lay on top of Roan with him buried within her quivering body. The sweat between them made their flesh slippery against each other. His hands roamed her body, soothing it, drying it, caressing it and making her feel lazy and indolent against him. Their combined sex scent filled her nostrils and it was a dessert of another kind to Shiloh. She weakly smoothed her hand across his damp shoulder, smiling softly, unable to speak; she could only feel and absorb him as a man. A very special man. No one was like Roan. No one.

Roan slowly eased out of Shiloh and then brought her to his side, tucking her in and pulling up a sheet to their waists. The tips of her hair were damp and curled from the perspiration between them. Her lips were slightly swollen from the hungry, branding kiss he'd shared with her earlier. Best of all, there was that *Mona Lisa*–like smile on her beautiful lips that told him everything. He'd satisfied her completely. Nothing made Roan feel better than pleasing his woman. It was everything. The sharing had been spontaneous, intense and hot.

Shiloh made a little sound of contentment as he leaned down, moving her hair aside, placing a slow, wet kiss against the nape of her neck. Automatically, she surged against his body, like a cat rubbing herself against him, the act sensual, teasing, and intimate. His kisses were provocative, her skin reacting wildly to his tongue, the small nips of her flesh, and then the kiss following the sensations. Shiloh had never felt so loved, so attended to, as if she were a priceless, fragile, sacred being who was being worshipped by a man who truly did love her.

Roan knew how to please her in large and small ways. The last thing Shiloh remembered thinking before she drifted off to sleep, exhausted and happy in Roan's arms, was why did she wait so long to walk into his life? He'd offered it to her before, but she'd been too afraid to take that step. And how much in the last two weeks had she missed by not being a risk taker with this man who was incredible in every way to her?

Chapter Seventeen

Roan quietly studied Shiloh as she slept. He had eased away, long before sunrise, to get ready for another day of work. The beginnings of dawn, that grayness between night and day, filtered silently around the drapes, allowing him to see the light softly caress her peaceful sleeping features. Her red hair was a tangled mass, but it only made her look that much more desirable. She was made for him. And he was made for her. Only, he knew that and Shiloh didn't. At least, not yet. A thick strand had dipped across her smooth brow and he gently lifted it away, allowing it to slip across her smooth, white shoulder.

She was petite against him. A slight smile pulled at one corner of Roan's mouth as he sat there, absorbing the shallow rise and fall of her breasts. Once again, he felt himself stir. Even now, as he inhaled deeply, he could smell her fragrant scent. The blanket and sheet had gathered and bunched around her waist and hip, the soft slope of her spine, that curve of her back calling to him. She was so slender against him. And yet, pound for pound, Shiloh was a fearless scrapper and that made Roan's mouth flex into a tender line. Reaching out, not wanting to disturb her sleep, because they hadn't gotten much last night, he lightly touched her shoulder, caressing her upper arm.

Roan desperately wanted to remain with Shiloh. Sleep at her side until she woke him up, those drowsy green eyes of hers filled with such shining love for him. And Roan knew she loved him. He'd seen it last night a number of times, almost as if the words were on her sweet lips to whisper to him, but she didn't.

He was content with the progress they'd made with each other, despite the hurdles that still stood between them. He eased the sheet and blanket up across her shoulders to keep her warm. Shiloh stirred, frowned slightly, and then burrowed her face more deeply into the pillow.

Another day, Roan promised himself. He rose without a sound, picked up his clothes, and opened the door. He'd get showered, shaved, and dressed in the bathroom, allowing her to sleep as long as she needed. His heart felt soft and tender within his chest, happiness thrumming through him as he padded down the hall.

Throughout the shower and shaving, Roan's mind leaped over the many issues Shiloh faced. If the stalker weren't standing between them, always a distracting and dangerous threat to her, he knew he could woo Shiloh into staying here in Wyoming. Even more important, living with him at his cabin. It was almost finished and in another two months, it would be ready to live in. He visualized Shiloh in the granite counter kitchen, looking out one of those large windows at the sink, taking in the beauty of the valley spreading out before the cabin. Or in the office he'd created, working on her next novel, happy and content.

His lower body remembered her ability to love him fiercely, freely, like that wild filly he thought of her as. Never had he met a woman so uninhibited, so fully confident of herself, her sexuality, as Shiloh. Whatever her wounds, they weren't in that direction. What they'd shared last night was beyond anything he'd ever experienced with another woman. He wondered if it was the same for her.

By the time Roan walked down the hall and to the kitchen, his mind was kicking forward into reality and what had to be accomplished this morning. As he made enough coffee for both of them, he decided he was going to eat over at the dining hall and then pull Steve and Maud aside, explaining the stalker issue in detail with them.

"Roan?"

Turning, he saw Shiloh rubbing her face, her thick red hair tangled around her shoulders, standing in her lavender bathrobe.

"Hey," he murmured, walking through the living room, sliding his arms around her waist, drawing her into his arms. "I thought you were asleep."

Shiloh nuzzled her face against his neck and jaw, her arms sliding around his waist. "I woke up and you weren't there," she mumbled sleepily. "I missed you. . . ."

Her drowsy, whispered words sliced right through Roan's heart and he pulled her close, inhaling her scent, her hair tickling his nose and cheek. "I didn't want to get up this morning and leave," he admitted gruffly, taming some of her hair away from her features, smoothing it across and down her small, capable shoulders. "You smell so damn good that I want to lift you into my arms, carry you back to the bedroom, and stay in there with you for the rest of the day." He felt Shiloh's arms tighten around his waist, a wordless agreement. Felt her lips brush his jaw as she looked up at him through sleep-ridden eyes.

"Would Maud get angry if you took the day off?"

Roan smiled a little. "She'd figure it out pretty quickly. She wouldn't get angry, but it would leave the crew short-handed and that wouldn't be fair to the team." He heard Shiloh make a muffled sound of protest, pressing her face into his chest, her hands sliding across his shoulders, his flesh tightening. Wanting her.

"We've just found each other. . . ."

More like he was waiting for her to discover them, but this wasn't the time to bring it up. "Darlin', I've got a lot on my plate today. As much as I want to stay with you, tie you to that bed so you can't leave it, it isn't going to happen."

Lifting her chin, Shiloh smiled drowsily into his darkened, narrowed eyes. "Then some other time? Maybe at your cabin? You almost have the bedroom and the kitchen finished."

He chuckled and dropped a quick kiss to her smiling lips. Because if he really, honestly kissed Shiloh deeply and hungrily like he wanted, there would be no turning back. Roan would take her to bed and pay the consequences for his selfish decision with Steve and Maud. "Sounds like a plan to me, wild filly."

She laughed, content to be held, burrowing into his chest. "My new nickname, no doubt."

"No doubt. You earned it last night," Roan promised, his voice thick with emotion. Shiloh was so damn warm, pliant, and curvy beneath that flimsy, silky robe she wore. His hands itched to pull it off her shoulders and allow it to fall to her feet, so he could hungrily stare at her beautiful, proud body. And then run his hands all over her in exploration, missing nothing. *Nothing.* Already, his erection was painful, pressing against the fabric of his jeans. "Would you like some coffee? It's about ready."

Nodding, Shiloh reluctantly allowed Roan to ease away. "That sounds good," she said, wiping her eyes, yawning.

Roan gave her a tender smile. Shiloh looked hauntingly fragile when waking up. How Roan ached for the time that Shiloh would be beside him in the mornings, and he could watch her pull from the arms of sleep and open her eyes to see him.

Getting a hold of himself, Roan led her over to the table and pulled out a chair for her to sit upon. He had a lot of things on his mind, chief among them to talk to Maud and Steve this morning.

Maud sat in her office chair, Steve perched on the corner of her desk, listening to Roan. The morning was young and they'd just opened up the office when he stepped in to ask them for their help.

"That's it," Roan said, standing, hands on his hips, the door closed behind him so no one could accidentally come in and hear them discussing the stalker issue and Shiloh.

Maud scowled and sat up. She twirled her baseball cap around on her desk, lips puckered in thought. "Okay, no problem getting that list of people who came for the Wildlife Drive from yesterday. If Shiloh recognizes a name, that's easy enough to show to Sarah Carter over at the sheriff's department."

Steve grimaced. He looked over at Maud. "Is Shiloh given to drama? Is she the kind of gal who makes up things?"

Maud considered his question. "No. Remember? I'd known Shiloh's mother, Isabella, for many years before she was murdered. I traveled back and stayed with them at their New York apartment. And I watched Shiloh grow up. She was always a quiet child, intense, but responsible. She wasn't one of these flighty little girls who was over-emotional, crying or begging to be the center of attention." Shaking her head, Maud muttered, "No, I'm inclined to agree with Roan that when Shiloh had that threat reaction yesterday, her stalker was here among us. A wolf in sheep's clothing."

Steve nodded. "Okay. I have to rely on you because I

don't know her that well." He rubbed his hand down his Levi's, scowling. Looking up, he asked Roan, "What if she doesn't recognize any of the names? That group was the only outsiders on the ranch yesterday. We have another group coming in"—he looked at his watch—"in two hours."

"With your permission, I'll ask Sarah about it. Explain what happened. Get her take on it. Her suggestions."

"That's good," Maud said, sitting up, folding her hands on her desk. "I darn well don't like the idea of a stalker here on the Wind River Ranch. That potentially puts everyone, all our overnight guests and our employees, at risk. What if he's carrying a rifle? Hiding a pistol? Starts shooting at everyone?"

Steve stood up. "That was my thought." He glanced at Roan. "Take the list over to Shiloh and let's get this ball rolling. And if she doesn't recognize any of the names, I think BOTH of you should go see Sarah at the sheriff's department. Shiloh needs to be kept in the circle on this too."

"Agreed," Roan said. He looked at Maud.

"How is Shiloh holding up?" Maud asked.

"Scared," Roan admitted. "Upset because her web-mistress accidentally put her photos and captions on her Facebook page."

Maud stood up. "I'd be scared spitless, too. That poor woman was a virtual prisoner for six months in her apartment before she got out here, Roan."

"I know. She told me about it."

Maud glanced over at her husband. "Steve, you in agreement that from here on out, until Sarah can nab this stalker, that we need to take Roan off the wrangling team? He needs to be nearby, keeping an eye on Shiloh. A kind of bodyguard."

"Sure, it's only wise. We don't know who this man is. You okay with that, Roan?"

Shrugging, Roan said, "Sure. I can be useful in the main ranch area. I can still work and do things that need to be done. If Shiloh calls me on her cell, I can be wherever she's at in a minute or less. The employee house isn't that far from the barn and corral areas."

"Right," Steve said, his face showing his tension and concern. "Okay, so we'll shift some wranglers around this morning. I'll have John redo the weekly schedule. Roan, you talk to Jake, the foreman, and he'll get you working in this main ranch area, per my request. Also, fill him in. We'll get everyone gathered in one of the barns later, after you've seen Sarah about this situation. The more info we can give everyone, the safer Shiloh will be here on the ranch."

Roan nodded. Jake Murdoch was the ranch foreman, an ex-Marine, and he got along well with his gruff boss. "Will do."

"Shiloh usually stays at the house writing," Maud told them. "And when she breaks from the writing, she comes over here and usually helps me or John at the office. Roan, do you think she should do that? Or should she remain out of sight. Hidden?"

Grimacing, Roan said, "Shiloh hates being cooped up. She's restless by nature."

"How about this?" Steve said. "This outside group is coming in two hours from now for a one-hour loop tour. They are the only strangers to come and go on our ranch property today. Maybe Shiloh could remain in the employee house for that hour? Do you think she'd go along with it, Maud?"

Maud nodded and set her cap on her black hair streaked with silver. "Let me go over and talk with Shiloh. Sometimes women just need to sit down and gab. She'll get it." Glancing at Roan, she said, "I'll take that list over to her too. And when I'm done, I'll bring it back here. In the meantime, Roan, get on the phone to Sarah and tell her what's going on. Tell her you need an appointment for yourself and Shiloh ASAP. I'll drop in and see her later this afternoon and add anything you two didn't. Hopefully, she'll have time to see you this afternoon. And keep us updated as things happen."

Shiloh was surprised when she answered the front door and saw Maud standing there with a piece of paper in her hand.

"Maud! What a nice surprise. Come in."

Maud stepped in. "I see you just showered and got dressed. Have you had breakfast yet?"

Smiling, Shiloh shut the door and led her into the kitchen. "I had breakfast with Roan earlier." She touched the damp ends of her hair. "And you're right: I just showered and dressed." She gestured toward the counter. "I was going to have my third cup of coffee. Would you like some?"

"That would be ideal. Can we sit at the table and chat for a moment?" Maud waved the paper in her hand. "This is the list of people who was on that wildlife loop yesterday. While we have coffee, can you go over the list? See if you recognize any name or address?"

"Ugh, that. Sure. Go sit down. I'll bring us the coffee."

Shiloh sat opposite Maud. She took the paper, her brows scrunched, slowly moving through the information on the page. Her other hand was wrapped around her coffee cup. Finally, she looked up. "I don't recognize anyone here, Maud. I'm sorry."

"No problem," she murmured, sipping her coffee.

Shiloh gave her a concerned look. "Do you think I made up that reaction yesterday?"

"Roan believes you. So do Steve and I. We're taking this very seriously, Shiloh." Maud took the paper and folded it up near her cup. "We talked earlier over in the office and we have a plan that I want to share with you."

Shiloh listened attentively. It felt like her world was once again crumbling beneath her feet. She felt the pressure of the stalker closing in on her. When Maud was finished, she said, "I'll stay here in the house and write that hour while the tourists are visiting. And I'll drive in with Roan if he gets that appointment with Sarah." Shiloh rubbed her brow. "I'm hoping I made it up. You know I have a very active imagination."

"Yes, you do, Shiloh, but you're not given to making up something like this."

She felt a little better that no one was blaming her for what had happened. "Maybe I should leave, Maud. I'm putting everyone here in danger."

"No," Maud said gruffly. "You belong here, Shiloh." She jabbed her finger down at the table. "There's nowhere safer than here. And you have friends and people who can support and protect you. That isn't true in New York City. So, no, you're staying right where you are, young lady."

Relief fled through Shiloh, although she still worried that others could be harmed by her stalker. "Thanks . . . I really do want to stay, Maud, but I don't want to have anyone else put at risk. My God, with all the crazy people going into an office, a campus or theater, murdering people, I worry it could happen here. To me . . . to all of you." Swallowing hard, Shiloh's voice quavered, tears burning in her eyes as she held Maud's stubborn blue gaze. "I could NEVER live with myself if I drew the stalker here and he murdered you . . . the wranglers . . ."

"Tut, tut," Maud said, reaching out, gripping her hand for a moment. "Now you ARE going wild with your imagination. This is Wyoming. We're Westerners. We know how to protect our own. You couldn't be at a better place for this to happen, so stop ratcheting up your worry. Okay?" Maud said, digging deep into her gaze.

Sniffing, Shiloh pushed away the tears from her cheeks. "Okay . . . but I still worry, Maud. I love all of you so much. You're like my new family and I—I just couldn't stand it if anything happened to you. . . ."

Maud rose, throwing her cap on. "Hush, Shiloh. We'll take this one day at a time." Walking around the table, she slid her arm around Shiloh's shoulders and hugged her fiercely, kissing her brow. "Now, let US do our work. Roan is at the tip of this spear and he knows what he's doing. He'll always be nearby in case you need him and you also have John right across the street from the house, as well. And I carry a weapon in my truck when I'm out on the ranch. We're armed here. You aren't alone in this gunfight."

Shiloh sat at the table after Maud left, her gut in a knot that refused to ease. She clung to the warm cup with both her hands. The morning sun's rays were bright through the windows, making everything glow. Last night had made her feel radiant, wonderful, and euphoric. This morning was a jarring fall back into harsh reality. *Roan.* Her mind and heart settled on him, as always. Just thinking his name calmed her fractious anxiety. Chewing on her lower lip, Shiloh sat in the quiet of the house, feeling raw and vulnerable.

WHO was after her? Why? Why her? Her mind clipped along at the speed of light. It made sense to her that whoever this man was, he was serious about getting to her. He'd made the trip from New York to Wyoming. And he'd found her. Swallowing against a tightening throat, Shiloh felt as if she were slowly suffocating beneath the situation. It was closing in on her. There was no safe place. Her fingers tightened momentarily around the cup. Her gaze swept through the living room. There were sets of windows, two side by side on both walls. Someone could open one of them and sneak into the place. They could walk soundlessly, checking rooms, finding her . . . Finding Roan as they slept.

Oh, God.

Making a frustrated sound, Shiloh pushed away from the table and stood up. The sensation of being trapped overwhelmed her. She needed to get out of here. Go for a ride. Clear her head. Riding always made her feel so free and wild. It sloughed off all her worries. Her anxieties. Already in a pair of Levi's and cowboy boots, Shiloh hurried to her room and snagged her nylon jacket, her baseball cap, gloves, and cell phone. She would go for an early-morning ride and be gone when the tourists came onto the ranch. She'd remain in the Pine Grove area, maybe even ride over to Roan's cabin, just be alone and feel safe.

Pushing out the door and making sure it was locked when she left, Shiloh hurried over to the office. She'd tell John what she was going to do and where she was going to ride. That way, everyone would know she hadn't been kidnapped by her stalker.

Roan picked up his cell phone. It was a call from John. He was out by the ranch corral, saddling the horses for the tourist trail ride for five families who would be coming down shortly after their hearty breakfast at the café. He listened intently, his chin lifting and spotting Shiloh walking with grim determination toward the barn above the corral where he stood. She was going to get Charley out, groom him, saddle him, and then ride to the Pine Grove area. He ended the call and tucked his cell away in his rear pocket, going to intercept Shiloh.

As he drew near he saw she'd captured her red hair into a ponytail at the back of her head, her green baseball cap low over her eyes. The set of her mouth told him she was upset. He took a dirt path from the corral up to the barn area. Shiloh looked up, surprised to see him.

"Hey," Roan called, falling in at her side as she walked into the barn, "John just told me you're going for a ride."

"Yes." Shiloh entered the barn and walked down the airy passageway. She picked up the lead rope off the hook on the front of Charley's box stall. "I have to ride, Roan."

He stepped aside as she slid open the box stall door. "Because the walls are closing in on you?"

"Sometimes," she muttered, bringing Charley out of the stall and leading him down the passageway, "my emotions and imagination mix too well, Roan. I imagine the worst possible case scenario and I can't stop thinking about it. And I want to break that energy. When I was in New York City, I'd jog in Central Park. Now, riding is going to do that for me, instead."

"I see." He ambled down to where the cross ties were located and then snapped them into place on either side of Charley's halter. Picking up a grooming box, he brought it over, handing her a currycomb. "It's a good idea." Roan watched her briskly begin to curry Charley, who stood there with his eyes half closed, enjoying Shiloh's attention.

"I thought," she said, straightening, looking at Roan across Charley's back, "that I'd go to Pine Grove, ride between them, and then have lunch at your cabin. If you don't mind?" She gave him a pleading look.

Roan placed his gloved hands on Charley's withers and rump. "Sure. Would you like a lunch partner? I could drive or ride out there and meet you." Roan didn't want Shiloh riding around alone. He could see her until she rode Charley down the road in the middle of Pine Grove. And then she'd be out of sight. He didn't like the possibility of her unseen by anyone at the ranch, but said nothing. Shiloh was clearly upset. But at his suggestion of lunch, her expression brightened instantly.

"Really? Could you? I know Maud said you'd be working just around the main ranch area from now on."

Roan gave her a lazy smile. "Sure. I'll saddle up Diamond and meet you there at noon. How about if I bring us each a sack lunch?" He liked the idea of sitting with Shiloh on the porch swing he'd installed last week. They could rock on the porch, eat, and talk. Roan knew he could calm her by just his presence. And he knew she had to talk it out because women felt better when they could communicate whatever they were feeling. He was a good listener. And he loved her. He wanted to remove the terror he saw deep in her green eyes that she would not admit to. At least, not yet.

"Oh," Shiloh whispered, suddenly emotional, "I'd love that!"

Roan covered her hand resting on Charley's back and squeezed her gloved fingers. "Good. Then it's a date."

"That sounds wonderful. It's really something nice to look forward to."

Roan tried not to be influenced by the quaver in her tone. But he was. He ached inwardly for the suffering that Shiloh was experiencing because of the damned stalker. Right now, he wanted to find that bastard and get his hands around him. He'd never stalk another woman again.

Roan saddled Charley for her, led the horse out of the barn, and helped Shiloh mount. He wasn't going to show how he felt toward her in public. At least, not yet. He settled the toe of her boot into the stirrup. Patting her lower leg, he said, "I'll see you at noon. Enjoy the ride. Everything is going to work out okay."

"Thanks," Shiloh whispered, leaning down, touching his shoulder briefly, smiling softly into his eyes.

Roan wanted to drag her off that horse, carry her inside the house, and make love to her. He knew how to distract Shiloh, to switch that imaginative mind off anything negative and focus it on something very positive and pleasurable. And already, his words, his calm demeanor, were having a deep effect on Shiloh because the fear and anxiety were no longer in her eyes. Every protective gene in his body was on guard and alert. And Roan would give his life to save hers if she was ever caught and attacked by that sneaky little bastard who had no name and no face.

Chapter Eighteen

Shiloh took the steps up to Roan's cabin. He'd given her the key to the front door. He'd been over here two weekends in a row and she hadn't. The porch was complete, the railing up and it was painted a dark evergreen color to match the lush green pastures that surrounded the cabin. Best of all, she noticed a varnished cedar swing he'd installed at one end of the porch. She'd sat in it, looking around, enjoying the peace. If only she could honestly feel this way again. Her gaze fell to Charley who was tied at the hitching post. His eyes were half closed, head hanging and one rear leg cocked up. How she wished she could relax like her sweet horse did. Rocking slightly, hands in her lap, she closed her eyes, feeling the welcoming heat of the sun's rays against her jacket. Mornings were always cool but thankfully, by early July they were no longer freezing like June could be.

Leaning back, she tipped her head against the cedar and sighed. Her body burned brightly with the memory of last night in Roan's arms. She'd never had a man make love with her like he had. Even now, she felt a new, gnawing warmth in her lower body coming to life. Just thinking about Roan, his hands upon her, his mouth wreaking scalding heat out of her body, made her clench and grow needy once more. Since the stalker, her sex drive had plummeted to nothing. But last night, it came back fiercely, hungrily, and a soft smile crossed Shiloh's lips as she replayed their night together.

Shiloh had no idea how long she gently rocked in the swing, but when she opened her eyes and looked at her watch, she realized a half hour had passed. And it would be another half hour before Roan would arrive on Diamond. Her heart expanded with joy. Out here, she could steal a kiss from him and not worry about anyone seeing them. She'd agreed with Roan last night that what they felt for each other shouldn't be common knowledge on the ranch. At least, not yet.

Shoving to her feet, she opened the gold and red cedar door, noticing that there was a new small window so a person could look out to see who was standing there. Pushing the door open, she stepped inside and gasped. The living room and kitchen were not only completed, but filled with furniture! Her gaze flew to the kitchen to her left. It was finished! Amazed, Shiloh left the door ajar, placed the keys on the foyer table, and took off her jacket and baseball cap. It was warm in the cabin and her boots thunked across the shining, highly polished floor. Everything was so bright, so hopeful-looking. Running her fingers across the black granite that sparkled with gold veins within it, she liked the huge island. There were now tall bar stool chairs with black leather seats placed on one side of it. The kitchen drew her like a magnet because she loved to cook, loved herbs and the wonderful fragrances that always emanated from them. The last time she'd seen the kitchen, it was a shell. She recalled Roan had shown her that he'd built two large windows in front of the double sink area so that while he was there, he could look out across the rolling beauty of the land.

Even better, he'd installed another window, a smaller one, on one side of the massive commercial stove and venting system. That was a thoughtful touch that told her Roan wanted the outdoors, as much as possible, to be inside his cabin. The Wolf stove had six gas-fed burners. The aluminum vent above was brushed and muted, allowing the gorgeous gold, red, and tan glass tile work on the backsplash to blend with the granite. Everything was understated, like Roan, as she leaned over and touched the long, rectangular glass tiles. They pulled in the color of the cedar floor. It was a thoughtful plan and Shiloh smiled, admiring Roan's gifts and skills for putting the tile in place. He was a man of many, many talents.

She turned, her gaze turning to the living room. Roan had put up a cedar railing to demarcate the kitchen from the other room. To her surprise, she saw a huge black, white, gray, and red Navajo rug that spread in the center of the floor.

He now had a dark brown leather couch and several overstuffed rust-colored chairs around it. Everything, she realized, was connected with that gorgeous hue of gold and crimson found in the cedar flooring. Her smile increased as she saw a red afghan folded across the back of the couch, the same color of the red of the cedar. Roan's eye for detail was surprising. Shiloh didn't think many men had this sense of color and design. Her mother, Isabella, had always been the fashion designer of their apartment. A warmth flowed through Shiloh as she remembered as a child that her father had problems matching colors and often her mother chose his clothing for him. And her father had been eternally grateful.

The cabin had been a shell ready to be painted the last time Shiloh had seen it. Now, it was a home. It clearly reflected

Roan's quiet strength and masculinity. But it wasn't a harsh male sort of design. Shiloh liked the warmth of the wood, the golden radiance of the sun sliding silently across the polished floor, creating reflective light everywhere. The brown of the leather sofa was actually toward the red end of the spectrum. The cedar coffee table in front of it looked hand hewn and designed. Shiloh would bet that Roan had designed it. The legs were curved and feminine-looking, with ball feet. As her gaze took in the tables at each end of the couch, she saw they were the same design. Almost as if Roan had introduced the curves to counter the angles elsewhere. A balance. She liked that, appreciating the beauty of the hand-carved cedar furniture.

There was a central light above the living room. So many people, she'd discovered, put antlers together with lights and used them as decorative Western features, but not here. Instead, as she turned and studied the huge central chandelier, her curiosity turned to wonder. Roan had used the same curving cedar design and they were like eight arms flowing sinuously from the center, outward. As she stepped closer, truly absorbing the sculpture, the art of it, her amazement grew.

Roan had twined two different types of wood around the main center post of the chandelier. One wood was reddish colored. The other, a deeper gold color, even more so than the cedar wood itself. They twined like vines, perhaps, four of them around each arm, to the end of it, so that there was a red and gold color on every other arm. And within the twined pieces of wood were highly faceted colored glass in blue, crystal clear, and green colors placed tastefully here and there. As the sunlight shot through the area, the crystals sparkled, creating a breathtaking collage of color.

At the end of each arm of the chandelier was a light hanging down from it. And surrounding the top of the light was a tentlike wooden roof with the twine of the colorful wood flowing around it.

She pressed her hands against her heart as she absorbed all that Roan had done to create this piece of incredible art that was fully functional. How long had it taken him to carve and make it? The details were so intricate and delicate. So feminine, as if honoring the beauty of women. Shiloh was sure he didn't consciously realize that, but as she looked around, there was decided balance between the hard angles of the masculine and the curves of the feminine. Her mother had taught her to look at everything in those terms.

"You found my surprise for you."

Whirling around, her eyes widening, Shiloh gasped. She saw Roan standing in the doorway, saddlebags draped loosely in one of his gloved hands. He was smiling, his eyes warm with what Shiloh recognized as love for her. And it really was. Her heart swelled.

"You scared me," she whispered, her heart pounding beneath her hand.

"Sorry. I didn't want to disturb you." Roan gestured toward the chandelier. "You seemed caught up in it." He walked in, taking off his gray Stetson and hanging it on a peg near the doorway.

"You're early," she murmured, going to the kitchen table where he set the saddlebags.

"No, I'm right on time," he teased. "It's noon. Were you off somewhere in your imagination? Did time fly by?"

She grinned and watched him pull his gloves off and stuff them in his back pocket. Those large hands, those long, callused fingers, had made her body sing like a harp last night. Already, her breasts were tightening and she could feel the nipples brushing against the silk camisole she wore beneath her blouse. "I guess it did," she answered, and glanced down at her watch. Sure enough, it was noon. "It's your fault, you know," she said, coming over to Roan, sliding her arms around his shoulders, reaching up on tiptoe to kiss him. "Your cabin is like an art gallery of the finest kind," she whispered against his smiling mouth. The predatory look in his gray eyes made her entire lower body clench with need. She felt his arms come around her, hauling her up against him.

Closing her eyes, Shiloh felt his mouth hungrily take hers. She wasn't sure who was more starved for the other, languishing in the heat and strength of his mouth as he cherished her lips. He crushed her to him, allowing her to feel his erection. Suddenly, she was far more hungry for him than her growling stomach was for food. And as he eased his mouth from her, she felt like the most beloved woman in the world. She saw his love for her reflected in the stormy gray of his eyes. It was so tough not to say anything. Shiloh couldn't. Not yet. There were so many unknowns between them with the stalker on the loose.

"I've missed you," he growled.

"No more than I have," she whispered, her voice breathy.

Roan reluctantly released her. "Come on. You must be hungry." He pulled out the chair from the cedar dining room table.

Shiloh gave him a wicked look as she sat down. "I'm starving for you. Again."

Roan gave her a heated glance and opened up the saddlebags, drawing out several containers and sandwiches. "Makes two of us, Darlin'. Open the containers? I'll get us some silverware and some plates."

She hadn't even thought to open drawers in the kitchen and as Roan walked into it with that casual stride of his, Shiloh smiled. Pulling over the first container she said, "You've been awful busy. Last time I was here, this was a shell."

"I've had two weekends to finish the drywalling and

painting," he said, bringing the silverware to the table. He set a bright red ceramic plate in front of her and himself. Sitting down at her elbow, he added, "And getting the furniture installed didn't take hardly any time at all."

"It's beautiful, Roan," she whispered, meeting and holding his gray gaze.

"Like it?" He opened another container and slid it between them.

"Like it?" Shiloh shook her head. "It's gorgeous. Did you make the coffee and end tables?"

"Yes. I had them out in the garage. Didn't you see them?"

Shaking her head, she whispered, "You're a woodworker, too?"

"I like working with my hands." And then he gave her a significant look.

Grinning, Shiloh said, "And I'm the lucky recipient of your hands, too."

"You're a beautiful carving, Shiloh. Someone I want to run my hands over, explore, and know."

Her whole body went hot over his low, gruff words, her hands frozen midair with the container. The man could turn her on like a light switch. "With you, my body feels like that chandelier you made," she said. "Molded, decorated— you made me feel so beautiful." She saw Roan's expression grow warm, a tenderness come to his eyes as he regarded her.

"That's nice to know." He opened the last plastic container. "You're a work of art to me, Shiloh. You always will be."

Every cell in her body quivered over his low timbre. Right now, she was starved but it sure as hell wasn't for food. Shiloh felt like jumping him here and now, but the idea of a hard floor to make love on wasn't exactly a turn-on for her. "Thank you. It's lovely to be thought of as a work of art." She spooned the potato salad, the three-bean salad onto her plate. Roan had brought thinly sliced beef sandwiches with horseradish mayonnaise, lettuce, and tomato on them for their main course.

"Do you like the chandelier?"

"Oh, I love it! I was so taken with your kitchen that I didn't notice it right away."

"You like to cook. Why wouldn't you go to the kitchen first?" he said, grinning.

Shiloh absorbed Roan into herself. He wore a blue-and-white plaid cowboy shirt with pearl snap buttons. The collar area was open, a dark blue kerchief around his thick neck. The man definitely had some sense of art and color combinations. "Guilty," she admitted. "That Wolf stove is to die for, Roan. And I loved the glass tile backsplash. You've been so thoughtful about the color scheme. It's not too masculine and its counterpart is the feminine."

Raising his brows, he smiled a little. "I hadn't really thought about it in those exact terms."

Smiling, Shiloh said, "I didn't think you would. But my mom saw everything through her artist's eyes like that. Whether it was angles or curves." She gestured to the chandelier. "How long did it take you to make that?"

"Oh," he drawled, "that's a project that's taken every stitch of my patience for nearly a year. I'd bring it out and work on it and the wood I'd wet to shape and curve it would snap and break. I can't tell you how many times I had to start over." And he shook his head, giving her a rueful grin.

"It's breathtaking," Shiloh said, so much passion behind her words. "And those faceted glass beads are the perfect addition to it. What made you put them on? What was your idea about it?"

Roan gazed up at the chandelier and then back at her. "I wanted the green to represent how lush this valley is with trees and grass." He gestured upward toward it. "The blue is to represent the sky. The transparent crystals are the stars I see in the Wyoming night sky."

She was mesmerized and deeply touched by his sensitivity, his ability to observe and then create such an incredible work of art. "Did you have a pattern? Or did you buy it?"

Shaking his head, he said, "There were many, many times when I wished I did, Shiloh. No, it was in my head. I made drawings on graph paper to figure out the dimensions, the length and width of each arm. Carving out the cedar template was easy compared to finding the right color of natural wood and then trying to get it to bend and curve."

"And you said it took you a year to do this?" *Talk about a labor of love*, Shiloh thought.

"Actually," Roan said, "when Maud gifted me with this five acres as part of my package as a wrangler working for the ranch, the design just popped into my head. After getting the cabin shell up, which took a year, beginning the second year, I started the design. I saw the chandelier as defining everything I wanted the cabin to represent."

"Wow," she murmured, awestruck, "you have such an amazing and artistic way of seeing the world."

He grinned. "Not bad for a black ops guy like me. Right?"

She saw some color come to his cheeks, realizing he was blushing over her heartfelt compliment. "No . . . not bad at all. There must be some connection between your career as an operator and your skills in carving and building."

"I don't see any."

She chuckled. "You wouldn't. It's my writer's curiosity to understand the connections of how a person sees their reality. That's how I create really great characters who have depth and breadth." Tilting her head, she asked, "Is your mother an artist, I wonder?"

"She sure is," Roan murmured, finishing off his lunch.

He wiped his hands on a paper napkin and pushed the emptied plate aside. "But her art is in quilting. She likes crocheting and knitting, too." He pointed toward the red afghan draped over the couch. "That's her work. I don't know if you went over to look at it, but it's pretty intricately knitted. She's great at detail work."

"That makes me feel good that your mom is here with you in that way."

Roan frowned. "Do you have things your mother gave you?"

"Yes," Shiloh said quietly. "When my parents died, I was in the will and I got everything. My mother worked on several paintings at once. She loved landscapes. Maud has two of them in her house. If you feel like it, you might go over and take a look at them."

"So you have some of her paintings?"

"I have four. And every one is priceless to me. She was working on a season theme before she was murdered by Leath. She'd gotten her art degree from the Sorbonne in Paris and she'd spent four years there. My mom loved nature. And she was always torn between the liveliness of the city and wanting to go live in the West. She made many trips out here. And she took a lot of photos. The season paintings were like a culmination of her trips to the West. I was only seven, but I remember walking into her art studio where she painted and feeling like I'd walked into a magical realm."

Roan frowned. "How do you mean that?"

"Her paintings," Shiloh said, finishing up her lunch. "These are big paintings, Roan. They are about four feet high and two feet wide. I remember when she was painting winter, that I came up and just felt like I'd walked into it, that I was a part of it."

"Because she painted so realistically?" he asked.

Nodding, Shiloh smiled. "Yes. It WAS like a photo, but it wasn't. But I felt it was so real, that it was like looking at it, it surrounded you and you were pulled into it."

"I'm definitely going to have to pay Maud a visit and ask to see your mother's artwork. It sounds incredible."

"Like your chandelier. It touched me in the same way. I could feel how alive the wood was. The twining of the other wood felt like it was living and growing before my eyes. I thought the blue, green, and transparent crystals represented how it breathed."

Roan smiled a little. "I like the way you view the world, Shiloh, seeing the beauty of it."

"I try to do that in my writing, too. I want my characters to leap off the page and breathe for my readers. I want them so alive that my readers believe they truly are real."

"Your mother had art with paints and you have art with words." Roan stood, taking their plates and flatware to the kitchen sink.

Shiloh stood and put the lids on all the emptied containers. "I like to think I got the best from both my parents," she murmured, her heart heavy because she missed them so much. Roan walked over to her. As she straightened, his arm went around her waist and drew her against him. The gesture meant so much to her, as if he felt her grief.

"Come on," he urged, "there's more for you to see. . . ."

As Roan guided her beneath his arm, he directed her to the wide, well-lit hall. He halted in front of one door halfway down on the left. "Go on in. Tell me what you think."

She met his gray gaze, saw warmth and need in them for her. "Another surprise?" She saw his male mouth curve.

"Darlin', didn't I promise you surprises last night?"

Chuckling, Shiloh put her hand on the brass doorknob and twisted it. "Indeed you did and you've been a man of your word." He released her and stepped aside as she pushed the door open.

Shiloh gasped as she stood in the entrance. She recognized the room because it was the master bedroom that Roan had shown her previously. Only, it wasn't a hollow shell anymore. She wasn't sure where to look first.

The drapes were pulled aside to reveal the huge window where light flooded the large bedroom. There was a mahogany sleigh bed against the far wall, covered with a colorful patchwork quilt. Shiloh automatically thought that Roan's mother had made the quilt for this bed. There were mahogany bed stands carved exactly like the ones out in the living room on each side of the king-size bed. As if to counter the dark wood, near the door to her right was an antique blond oak dresser. And on the other side of the door, another one of the same design and size. There was a settee in one corner, covered with a gold-colored fabric similar to what she'd seen in the chandelier hanging in the living room. And nearby a stool with the same fabric color and a rocking chair. Shiloh could picture herself curling up on that feminine-looking settee and reading one of her books on her iPad.

She was thrilled to see that the drapes were exactly like the quilt bedspread. They were heavy and hung to the cedar floor. No one lived in Wyoming without seriously heavy drapes across windows during the winter. It absorbed the cold air at the window. She saw a straight-backed chair in another corner where a person could sit down and take off his boots for the day. Everything had been thought out, was practical and yet beautiful.

"This—" she gasped, "is so incredibly gorgeous, Roan!" Shiloh turned to him, seeing the pride in his eyes over the work he'd done to bring this room together.

"Like it?"

"Love it." She shook her head. "Your poor mom must have gone to a LOT of work to not only create the bedspread, but the drapes. It's a stunning design idea."

"My mom had a year to make them," he reassured her. "And she wanted to do it. If I'd tried to refuse one of her quilts, she'd likely have killed me," Roan chuckled.

Shiloh grinned. "Your mom sounds so wonderful."

"Well," Roan said lightly, placing his hand in the center of her back, guiding her toward the master bathroom, "maybe one of these days you'll get to meet her."

She didn't have time to answer as Roan ushered her into the bathroom. She halted, feeling as if transported to another time and era. Roan had already laid down the ivory porcelain tile throughout it. The floor was heated so it would be warm in the winter. The huge area was decorated with a slipper tub with brass claw feet and Shiloh, who knew quite a bit about antiques, figured it was probably a bathtub from the late 1800s that Roan had somehow scored. There was a large oval quilt rug of the same patchwork colors as out in the bedroom. The windows were large, allowing southern light to flood the whole area. There were patchwork quilt drapes that did not go to the floor, tied back, to allow the light in.

"Ohhhh," she whispered, moving into the tiled area, "a spa!"

"Thought that might appeal to you," Roan said.

The spa was circular, the inside a pale blue and Roan had put dark blue tiles around the outside of it. There were three small steps up and into the lovely spa. Roan had tiled the outside of it with the same blue ceramic tile. To her right was the bathroom, the door open. It was large and roomy.

Shiloh moved to the other side of the room and stood, mesmerized. The shower was large enough to easily fit two people. There were two round raindrop showerheads on opposite sides of it. The tile was light blue on the floor. Along the first three feet of it, the tiles were made of that rectangular glass she loved so much. This time, the glass tiles matched the variety of colors in the patchwork quilt drapes and rug. The rest of the one side where there was no glass was of the same ivory-colored tile as the floor.

She ran her fingers lightly across the thick glass at the front of the shower. It was frosted glass and it had an old-time pattern sandblasted into it, reminding her of a design from the era of the antique bathtub. "I just love this, Roan. All of it." She turned, smiling up at him. "You've been really busy."

Shrugging, he said, "Idle hands and all that."

Shiloh could tell he was pleased with her reaction. "So when are you moving in?"

Lifting his hand, he brushed her cheek, holding her earnest gaze. "I was hoping you'd want to move in with me next week."

Chapter Nineteen

Shiloh heard the sincerity, the hope, in Roan's voice as he held her gaze. Her emotions were a mass of indecision within her. "I need time to feel my way through this, Roan."

"I understand," he murmured, slipping his hand beneath her elbow. "It's a lot to digest." Roan led her out of the master bedroom.

"What about the stalker?" she asked, her heart expanding with yearning for him. At the same time, the fear of the stalker never left her. It just went up and down in volume.

He pulled out a chair for her. "Just before I left the main ranch, I called Sheriff Sarah Carter over at the sheriff's department," he told her, sitting at her elbow. "We've got an appointment to see her at two P.M. today."

Relief sizzled through Shiloh. "Thank God."

"She will need you to tell her everything, Shiloh. From the moment this stalker started shadowing you."

"Oh, she'll get everything," she promised him, raw emotion in her voice. She reached out, touching his arm, feeling the muscles tense where she slid her fingertips across the dark hair scattered on his lower arm. "Thank you for coming with me."

"Wild horses couldn't drag me away from protecting you."

It was true. She saw it in the glint of his gray eyes. Heard the steel behind the words as he spoke them. "Well," she said, trying to smile and failing, "I'm grateful. At least out here"—she fondly looked around the quiet cabin—"I have people who believe me."

Roan picked up her hand, squeezing it gently. "And you have people who have your back, Shiloh. Steve, Maud, and all the rest of the employees, man or woman, are going to be watching out for you too. The more educated, aware eyes we have on this situation, the better protected you are."

"I hate what he's done to me, Roan." She rubbed the nape of her neck, giving him an apologetic look. "Every shadow became him waiting for me."

"That's a normal reaction, Shiloh," he soothed.

"But you would have handled it differently."

"There's a gulf between you and me in that regard," he told her. "I'm trained for close quarters combat. I know what I can do to defend myself. You've never been trained, Shiloh. Maybe what I should do is show you some moves that could render your attacker useless. I think if I show you those moves, you'll feel better. Much of your fear is based on the fact you don't have a way to defend yourself. Or am I wrong?"

Shiloh thought about it, her brows dropping. She glanced up at him. "You're always the quiet voice of reason, Roan. You're right. I don't know how to defend myself. I've never had a reason to learn."

"Let me show you the room at the rear of the cabin. Remember the big room that had a lot of windows and you wondered what I'd do with it?"

"Yes." She smiled a little as he slowly unwound from the chair. There was no question that Roan had a lethality to him. Just now, she became more aware of his warrior side. It wasn't something he had shown her before, but she suspected because of the topic, he was allowing her to see a part of him he kept well hidden. "Sure. Has every room in the cabin got stuff in it?"

"Well," Roan hedged, pulling her chair back for her, "most . . . but there's two rooms I've more or less left like an empty canvas to be painted on."

"I love your analogy." Shiloh rose and smoothed her jeans down her thighs. She followed Roan across the living room and down to the end of the hall. When he'd taken her through the rooms weeks ago, they had all been empty canvases. Now, they were thoughtfully and beautifully appointed.

Roan stepped aside and gestured to the brass doorknob. "Open it and go in. See what you think?"

Shiloh felt a little bit like a kid at Christmas, barely able to wait to tear off the wrapping on the packages. She pushed the heavy cedar door open. As she moved into the large, rectangular room, with a panel of windows on its southern wall, she halted. She felt Roan come to her side, his hands coming to rest on his hips. "Wow, this is a REAL workout room." There was a small gym next to the dining room at the ranch headquarters and Shiloh knew Roan was over there every morning, working out. But here, she saw not only weight-lifting equipment, but also half of the room was empty with only a dark blue mat covering the floor.

"I think you might be more interested in this half of the room," he said, leading her toward the mat.

Shiloh stood near the edge of it. "What's this for?"

"I was thinking that you really didn't know any defense moves so I decided to purchase a work mat and I might show you how to protect yourself once you went home."

She heard a tinge of sadness in Roan's voice. It wasn't anything obvious, but as she got to know him, she could sense a slight change of tone, or a look in his eyes or facial expression. "This is wonderful. And thoughtful," she said, and she gazed up at him, lifting her hand, touching his hard upper arm beneath the chambray shirt he wore. Shiloh saw that warmth in his eyes for her again and heat sheeted first to her heart, which expanded with a rush of joy, and then straight down to her lower body. She ached to love this man again.

"Well, if you want, we can always drive out here for an hour and do some practice moves. You just let me know."

Turning, Shiloh followed him out. There were two doors on her left and she halted at the one next to the gym. "What's in there? Have you decorated them, too?" Her curiosity was eating her alive. Everything else in Roan's home was inspiring to her. The surprise was he knew color and design. She looked up at Roan halted. He seemed undecided.

"Sure, go ahead."

Hesitating, Shiloh opened the door. It was an empty room, the large windows allowing in northern light. What caught her attention was the room was painted a soft, light lavender color. It was her favorite color. Roan came to her side and she looked up at him. Had he done this with her in mind? Her intuition told her yes. She wasn't going there. At least, not yet. "It's pretty," she said. "Nice and roomy."

"It's one of the two rooms that are the blank canvas," he said, giving her a slight smile. "The one next door is the same."

"As I recall, it was going to be a second bedroom?"

"Yes, still will be. This is the office."

Her heart beat a little faster. Roan had already invited her to come and live with him. It was such a huge step, the implications major in her life. And she waffled, feeling terrible because every particle of her being wanted to be with Roan. If only the stalker could be identified and found . . .

Shiloh could barely contain herself as Sarah Carter, commander of the Lincoln County sheriff's department, invited them to sit down. She had a glass-enclosed office, a huge maple desk, and there were two comfortable chairs out in front of where she was sitting. The midafternoon sun was muted because her office was on the north side of the massive three-story red brick building.

Shiloh liked the woman's red hair tamed into a bun at the base of her neck. Dressed in the khaki uniform, she was near Shiloh's own height of five foot nine and had light green eyes, the color of spring leaves, her face heart-shaped and beautiful. She thought Sarah might be in her late twenties, although she looked more college-age to her. There was an intensity to the sheriff's large eyes. Shiloh thought she missed little and that made her feel good. She introduced herself and shook Sarah's long hand. There was nothing weak about the woman but she didn't come off as tough and hard, either. That made her breathe easier.

"Roan was telling me earlier you have a story to tell me, Shiloh?"

She felt her palms grow damp and clasped them in her lap. "I do." She handed her the list of people who had been at Wind River the morning she felt threatened. Sarah thanked her and set it next to her computer.

Sarah opened up her laptop. "Fire away. I'm all ears. Let's see if we can help you."

Shiloh felt relief because Sarah was open and warm. The woman was totally unlike the New York City policemen and the detective who had come to her apartment, and the forensics team who had dusted her door for fingerprints of her stalker. There was doubt from the very beginning and the detective, especially, seemed to question her sanity. Taking a deep breath, Shiloh launched into the story.

She felt shaky and unnerved by the time she finished, an hour later. Sarah was dutifully typing everything into the computer. And sometimes, she'd asked questions.

Glancing over at Roan, who had gone and gotten them some fresh coffee, she took the cup from him, grateful he was there with her. She felt his blanket of protection as surely as he'd wrapped a real blanket around her shoulders.

Sarah scowled. She went to her notes in the desktop computer. "Okay, so let's look at Leath."

"But, he's in prison," Shiloh protested. "He's got five years before he can get out." She sipped the coffee.

"Well . . . let me just take a look and make sure," Sarah coaxed. "It'll take a moment of my time to double-check. I like getting a factual base to work from."

Shiloh couldn't see what was on the huge screen facing the sheriff but she saw her arched red brows draw into a scowl, her eyes suddenly narrowing.

"What?" she demanded, her heartbeat starting to take off. "What's wrong, Sheriff Carter?" Shiloh sat up, suddenly tense, gripping the paper cup in her hands.

Sarah looked over at her. "Anton Leath was given parole ten months ago. He was given five years off his original sentence for good behavior. He's now on probation. Didn't you know that?"

Gasping, Shiloh shot out of the chair, the coffee slopping over her and the floor. "No!" She flinched, hearing the cry of terror in her voice. It sounded like a wild animal that was trapped, screaming, knowing it was cornered and going to die. The scalding hot coffee burned her hand and lower arm, and she felt Roan's hand on her shoulders to steady her. He took the half-emptied cup out of her hands, setting it on the desk.

Gasping, Shiloh cried brokenly, "No! No! That can't be!

They'd have told me! They were supposed to call me when they were going to release him!"

Sarah stood and went over to a file drawer and opened it. She pulled out a small towel and walked over, handing it to her so she could wipe the coffee off herself. "I'm sorry, but it appears from what I can see, you were *not* notified, Shiloh. I'm sorry."

Tears burned hotly in her eyes and, blindly, Shiloh used the towel to dry herself off. Roan led her back to the chair, asking her to sit down. She barely heard him. Barely heard anything, a buzzing going on inside her head, her mind spinning and making connections. She sat and pressed her hands against her tear-splattered face, trying to get a hold of her wild, panicked emotions.

Roan sat down, sliding his arm around her shoulders. "Try to take some deep breaths, Shiloh. It will help settle the adrenaline surging through you."

Roan's low, quiet voice cut through her anxiety and terror. She felt the warm strength of his hand gently smoothing the fabric of her blouse against her hunched, tensed shoulders. Closing her eyes, hands gripped in her lap, she did as he asked, listening to him, his voice melting away a little of her terror. Finally, Shiloh lifted her head. She rubbed the tears from her cheeks and looked at Sarah.

"He's my stalker, then." The words came out hard and flat. Filled with palpable dread.

Sarah nodded. "Could well be. Hold on . . . let me get to his probation officer's record on Leath's whereabouts. . . ." she said, and she typed in some commands.

Shiloh looked over at Roan, so glad his hand remained on her shoulders. She saw he was upset, worried for her. Giving him a misery-laden look, she whispered, "I-I'm sorry. I didn't mean to lose it."

Roan shook his head. "It's okay, Shiloh. Did you burn

yourself?" he asked, and he slid his hand beneath her tense fingers.

She looked down, her skin reddened here and there where the coffee had splashed upon her. "N-no, I'm okay. It stings a little is all. It's nothing. I'll be all right. . . ." But she felt so far from all right, she wanted to run. Shiloh wanted to run directly into Roan's arms. She saw the glint in the recesses of his eyes, the hardness and determination and protection he wanted to give her. "God," she whispered, "I don't *dare* go back to Manhattan! That's his hometown, too."

Sarah looked over at them. "Okay, here's something that's probably going to prove that Leath is here in Wyoming, right now." She tapped the screen with her index finger. "His probation officer has noted that in the last month, Leath has failed to show up for three of his weekly sessions."

"That's got to be a violation," Roan growled.

"Yes, it is. They have a warrant out for his arrest," Sarah added. She held up her hand. "Hold on while I try to get his probation officer on the phone. Maybe he can give me more intel."

Shiloh felt as if the world had just collapsed in on her. Anton Leath was after her. She licked her lower lip and whispered unsteadily to Roan, "He promised to come after me."

Roan scowled. "What do you mean?"

"I was sitting behind him in the courtroom and after the jury sentenced him, he turned around and said when he got out, he'd come after me and finish it off." She saw Roan's eyes become shards of ice.

"You need to tell that to Sarah," he murmured, rubbing her shoulders gently.

"I will. . . ." she said, and she sniffed, feeling tears burning in her eyes again. Valiantly, Shiloh fought them away.

"You're upset," Roan said, giving her a small smile of encouragement, holding her shattered gaze. "There's no way you're going to remember everything the first time around. I'm sure Sarah will be asking you more questions as soon as she gets off the phone. Okay?"

Just his reassurance gave Shiloh purchase. "Y-yes." Her gaze went to Sarah as she made connection with the probation officer. She sat quietly, listening to Sarah's end of the conversation. When Sarah asked the officer to send her photos and the file on Leath, Shiloh started feeling a little relief. Sarah believed her. The sheriff's department would help her.

Sarah hung up the phone, her face grim. She held Shiloh's broken gaze. "You heard what I asked for. What we'll do is distribute Leath's photo to every deputy here in Lincoln County, as well as other law enforcement agencies in the surrounding counties, including the state of Idaho, which is less than fifty miles away from Jackson Hole." She frowned and rustled her slender fingers through a pile of papers, studying a schedule. "And I'm assigning a detective to this investigation, Shiloh. He will go undercover. I'm going to instruct him to be nosing around Wind River, and several other smaller towns along Highway 89 that run through the center of the valley. Our man will be dressed as a tourist so Leath won't be able to spot him that easily. I'll get this detective, who is coming on for the next shift, and give him the intel and his orders."

"That sounds wonderful," Shiloh whispered. She grimaced. "Sarah? Why didn't the New York City police find this out? Why didn't they check to see if Leath was already released?"

She shrugged. "I don't know. Sometimes departments get overwhelmed and steps are missed or thought to be low importance at the station. I'm sure when you told the police and the detective that Leath was in federal prison, they didn't bother to check your statement. They should have, but they didn't." She opened her hands. "They're human too, Shiloh. It doesn't excuse this mistake, however."

"It sounds like they put Shiloh's issue at the bottom rung of a lot of other investigations that were probably considered more high priority," Roan said.

"Exactly." Sarah nodded. "What ELSE can you tell me about Leath? Anything you can give me will help us to find him. Even if you don't think it's important, tell me anyway."

Shiloh nodded and closed her eyes, going back to the time when her mother started dating Leath, and slowly moved forward from that time until he stabbed her to death. It took another hour and by the time she was finished, Shiloh felt gutted and emotionally exhausted. It was five P.M.

"This is very helpful," Sarah congratulated her, giving her a look of sympathy. "All of this is valuable intel, Shiloh. I'm sorry we had to put you through it again."

"I'd rather do it because you at least believe me."

Roan pointed to the paper that Shiloh had given him earlier. "That's the list of people who were on the Wind River the morning that Shiloh had that threat reaction. She didn't know any of the people, but Leath could have put down a fake name, too."

Sarah picked it up, rapidly perusing it. "I wouldn't put anything past him, but I'll have one of my deputies run these names through our system, see if we get a hit. If we don't, then I'll assign someone to call every B and B, motel, and hotel here in our county, as well as in Teton County where Jackson Hole is located, to see if he's around and under the assumed name. If we get anything, I'll let you know right away, Shiloh."

"Good . . . thank you. But knowing Leath like I do, he's very sneaky and manipulative."

"All passive-aggressive behavior," Sarah agreed. She set

the paper aside and gave her an understanding look. "Right now, you need to go home and rest." She glanced over at Roan. "Are you staying at one of the employee's house? I'd talked to Maud about a week ago and she was telling me Shiloh was there taking a writing sabbatical."

"Yes, she's been at the employee house with me since she arrived," Roan said.

Shiloh compressed her lips. "Sarah? Am I safe there in that house? What should I do? Maybe I should leave the ranch? Keep everyone there safe from Leath? Go somewhere else?"

"Well," Sarah said, "given your warning reaction you had a couple of days ago, the law officer in me says it's possible Leath was on Wind River Ranch property looking for you."

A terrible, icy feeling dove down Shiloh's spine. "And if he really was?"

"Then none of us know, for sure, whether he saw you or not. Or if he realizes you're at the employee house. He could have asked someone. We just don't know. And as for you leaving the Wind River Ranch? No way. You have a passel of folks who are looking out for you. They are extra sets of eyes on this problem. Any one of them could spot this guy after they've seen his photo."

Shiloh glanced over at Roan and then focused on Sarah. "I don't want anyone hurt because of me."

"Frankly? If Leath is out here? He's picked the wrong place to be. The state of Wyoming is traditional old West, Shiloh. We carry guns out here and we aren't afraid to use them to defend ourselves if we're attacked. Steve will know what to do to keep you and everyone who works on his ranch safe."

Shiloh squirmed inwardly, not convinced. She felt a horrible guilt threading through her, knowing Leath wouldn't think twice about killing anyone who got in his way. "So?

I'm not safe there at the employee house? Right?" She glanced over at Roan, looking at the hard set of his face, his gray eyes alive with a hunter-like look. Right now, she felt him in his warrior mode. It was nothing obvious. He hadn't tensed up. His hands were relaxed on the arms of the chair. But she felt it around him.

"Is there anywhere else you can go on the property? Someplace you can't be so easily spotted?"

"Yes," Roan said. "She can stay at my cabin. I'm just about finished with the construction. It's located half a mile north of Pine Grove. There's a dirt road to it, but it's out in the open for a half a mile in every direction so we can see someone coming. There's no way to sneak up on my cabin."

Sarah looked at Shiloh. "Would you be willing to move into his cabin until we can get a handle on Leath? I know the area and it's a great hideout."

"Yes, I can do that. But does it mean I have to stay hidden? That I couldn't drive into town here and pick up my groceries?"

"For now," Sarah said, lowering her voice with apology, "it would be best if you went to ground. That you remained out of the public's sight."

"That's what I thought," Shiloh whispered, agreeing with Sarah. She gave Roan a distressed look. "I guess you're stuck with me."

Roan grinned a little. "There's worse things, Shiloh. We'll manage. All right?" he asked, and he touched her cheek momentarily, as if to calm her concerns, whatever they might be.

The touch of his fingers across her cheek sent a badly needed signal to Shiloh. She hadn't told Roan she would move in with him. He'd asked. She hadn't answered. Now it looked like she had no choice. Roan had to be feeling confused about where they stood with each other. And as soon she could, despite feeling exhausted, Shiloh silently promised him that she'd clear it up with him.

Sarah stood. "You have my phone number, Shiloh?" And she handed her a business card. "Put this in your cell phone address book. Also"—she looked at Roan—"Maud and Steve Whitcomb need to know what's going down. Tell them I'll fax them over a copy of Leath's photo and other pertinent info. That way, they can inform their employees and everyone will be on the same page. If Leath had the balls to go to the ranch once, he'll do it again. Especially if he saw Shiloh."

A new shiver of terror worked down through Shiloh. She knew more than anyone else what Leath was capable of doing.

"Got it," Roan said. He glanced at Shiloh. "And I'll be her big, bad guard dog."

"Good," Sarah said, relieved. "No one better than you, Roan. I know your black ops background." She moved her gaze to Shiloh. "You won't get any better bodyguard than Roan, so Shiloh, get some rest. And don't worry, we're going to find this dirtbag. We'll be in touch."

"God, I hope you can catch him before he hurts me . . . or someone else. . . ."

Shiloh almost felt like a convicted felon as she moved at Roan's side as they walked into the grocery store in Wind River. He needed to get food for the cabin and wanted her input on what to choose since she was going to be living there until Leath was apprehended. She stayed close to him in the busy grocery store. It gave her a sense of safety when there was none left for her.

The sun was behind the huge Wilson Range paralleling the sprawling ranch from the west as Roan drove them back to the Wind River Ranch. On the way there, Shiloh had been silent, her mind running a million miles an hour. Only Roan's quiet, calm presence allowed her some respite from the dread inside her. She felt a little relief as Roan drove them onto ranch property. He parked at the employee house, having agreed that they needed to move all her luggage and other items to the cabin.

As tired as she was, Shiloh regretted leaving the employee house. She liked it. But in a way, she was more looking forward to the warmth and intimacy of Roan's cabin. There was peace and tranquility there. And it made Shiloh feel as if she were living within his embrace whether he knew it or not. Roan would probably laugh at her, but she believed homes had energy and expression. Each had its own unique personality. And there was no question Shiloh looked forward to living beneath Roan's roof. And being with him every night, if he'd have her.

Chapter Twenty

Roan watched the exhaustion in Shiloh's face after they reached his cabin by truck.

"Listen," he told her, walking to where she was putting vegetables away in the refrigerator, "why don't you go take a hot bath? That always relaxes you." He slid his hand beneath her elbow, easing her away from the fridge and shutting the door. "I'll take care of the groceries," he said, searching her darkened green eyes. Roan could see she was on overload. Who wouldn't be? He was sure Shiloh was replaying the day Leath stabbed her mother to death. That one moment was branded into her memory for the rest of her life. The line of her mouth was tight and Roan sensed she was holding on with everything she had not to cry. Not to lose it.

"Yes," she murmured wearily, pushing strands of hair away from her brow, "that's a good idea. I'll do it. Thanks, Roan."

Roan released her, watching her walk, almost weave, across the living room and down the hall to the bathroom. She'd forgotten to take her clothes so he picked up her luggage, carrying it to his bedroom. Opening it on his bed, he pulled out what he thought she might need, including a large bag that had her toiletry items in it.

Knocking lightly on the door, Roan called her name. "I thought you might like these things," he said through the door. How badly Roan wanted to just walk in, gather Shiloh in his arms, and give her a sense of safety. He knew he could do that for her, even if it was just temporary.

Shiloh opened the door, dressed in her silk camisole and panties. "Oh . . . gosh, I'm not thinking." She reached out for the items, giving him a grateful look. "Thanks, Roan."

"Take a long soak," he advised. Roan was learning that Shiloh put on a mask of sorts around him. It wasn't done on purpose, it was just her reaction to a threat. He knew she needed to cry and he could see the tears banked in her eyes. She was still fighting them. Aching to help her, not knowing how, he stepped away and turned, heading toward the kitchen.

As soon as he had the groceries put away, he closed the drapes in the living room and bedroom. Night was coming on quickly. In the kitchen, he pulled the curtains closed across the windows. He didn't think Leath was on the property, but Roan didn't want anyone to be able to look into the cabin from the outside. Especially at night. The landline phone he had installed in the kitchen rang. Walking over, he picked it up and answered it.

"It's Sarah," she said. "We've got a hit from that list you provided us earlier. One of my deputies went over to a local B and B, showing Leath's photo to the owners. The owners said a man that looked similar to him had left three days ago. And the name on the Wind River list is the same one he used at the B and B."

Scowling, Roan asked, "What do you mean looked similar?"

"The owners said he did not have blond hair. He had

longish dark brown hair and a beard. Same color of eyes, same face shape, mouth and nose, however. And same height and build. I've got my deputy going over that room with our forensics team to see if we can lift some finger-prints. That would confirm whether or not it was Leath."

"Are you going to update the photo?"

"Yes. I've asked the woman, who had the most face time with Leath, to come down here tomorrow morning and work with our artist. Once she has something we can use, we'll e-mail out the updated one on Leath. We still can't be sure until and if we find fingerprints to prove it."

"I understand," Roan said. "Where did he go?"

"The owners said he was quiet and didn't say much and that he had a black nylon gym bag with him. Leath went over to the Barton Gym on Sixth Street like clockwork every morning for an hour and a half. I guess Leath is in top physical shape. And I've got another deputy going over to talk with Mike Barton, the owner of the gym, to see if he can identify Leath with the present photo. So, we have a lot going on."

"A lot of possibilities," Roan agreed. "So where is Leath now?"

"Good question. He didn't tell the B and B owners where he was going."

"What about a vehicle?"

"He had a rental car from the Jackson Hole Airport. We're chasing that lead down too."

Some relief flowed through Roan. "I'm going to call Maud and Steve and fill them in shortly."

"Good. If anything else breaks this evening, I'll be calling you, Roan."

"That will help."

"How's Shiloh doing?"

Roan looked over his shoulder, making sure she wasn't

in the living room or could hear his reply. "Rugged. Needs to cry and get it out of her system. She's scared."

"Understandable. This is enough pressure to kill a horse. I'm sure she's replaying her mother being murdered by this bastard, thinking she's next."

Grimly, Roan said, "It's not going to happen. Not while I'm around."

"You got any security system installed in your cabin?"

"Not yet, but I will."

"Okay, I've got another call coming in from my forensics team. I'll be in touch."

Roan hung up the phone. He could hear water running in the bathroom, Shiloh filling up that deep tub. Maybe a long, hot soak would help her relax. It wasn't going to take away her worry or the threat of Leath being around, but it would be comforting.

He'd fixed a couple of pork chops, steamed some Brussels sprouts, and made a salad by the time Shiloh emerged from the bathroom. Hearing the door open, Roan looked up from setting the table in the dining room. Shiloh had chosen her white capris, a simple green tee with long sleeves, and was barefoot. Her hair was loose and free around her shoulders, the ends curled from the steam.

"Hey, you feel like eating a little something?" he asked.

Wrinkling her nose, Shiloh came over to him. "Not really, but I know I need to eat whether I feel like it or not."

Roan could smell the light scent of oranges on her soft, moist-looking skin. He knew she loved citrus fragrance and had a body lotion she used regularly after taking a bath or shower. "I made a salad."

"I think I could stomach that," Shiloh said. She looked toward the kitchen. "It feels like a home now."

"What does?" he wondered, walking with her to the kitchen.

"The smell of the different foods in the air. Like someone is living here full time," she said, giving him a strained smile. "Sort of like bread baking in the oven and the odor permeates the house with that great smell."

"Would you like something to drink?" Roan had in mind a stiff belt of whiskey but he doubted whether she'd go for that. Shiloh wasn't a hard liquor drinker.

"No. I'm wigged out enough over everything," she muttered. Opening the fridge, she said, "I think I'll just have some tomato juice. How about you?"

Roan lifted the meat out of the skillet and placed them on a platter. "Sounds good. I'll take a glass too." He didn't like the pallor in Shiloh's face. The skin across her cheekbones was stretched and tight. Roan could feel the anxiety riffling around her, feeling damned helpless.

When she poured the tomato juice into the glasses, he saw a fine tremble of her fingers. Shiloh was trying to keep it together. What other choice did she have? As he put the food on the table and gave her a salad, Roan wondered if this was how she was those six months in her apartment. Most likely. It was a terrible way to live. To know you were being hunted daily.

"This is wonderful," Shiloh told him as he seated her at the table, gesturing to the colorful salad. She forced a smile as he walked over and sat down at her right elbow. "Our first meal in your cabin."

Roan pulled the dark blue linen napkin across his lap. "It is. I hadn't thought of it like that." How like Shiloh to note such things. They were emotional landmarks, he supposed, not something he was tied into. Maybe it was a woman's prerogative? Roan tried to be circumspect about watching how much Shiloh ate. She picked at the salad, not really hungry. He decided to tell her about Sarah's call. When he finished with the information, she looked a tad better. Probably because things were moving and people were actively involved in trying to prove Leath was around the town.

"When do you think Sarah will know about the fingerprints?"

Roan opened his mouth to speak when the phone rang. He excused himself and walked into the kitchen to answer it.

"This is Sarah."

"Yes?"

"My forensics team ran the prints they found in that B and B room. It's confirmed that it's Anton Leath."

Roan turned, seeing tension on Shiloh's face as she listened to the call. She had wrapped her arms around her waist, tense. "That's good. At least we know now, for sure." He knew Shiloh would feel the full weight of the information, and wanted to try to protect her from it. There was no way around telling her. "What now?"

"We ran the information on the rental Leath picked up from the Jackson Hole Airport. He used the same alias there as he did at the B and B and later, at the Wind River Ranch. We've e-mailed a copy of Leath with blond hair to every motel, hotel, and B and B in the area. We've added that he's dyed his hair brown and now he has a beard."

"So, if he's around, you'll find him."

"That's what I'm hoping. I just got done having a long, involved talk with his probation officer. Leath isn't without funds. He has an offshore bank account in the Bahamas. Before this guy murdered Isabella Gallagher, he was a multimillionaire construction corporation owner. The officer said that according to court testimony, as Shiloh told us, Leath threatened her with death after being sentenced. He told her she was going to die like her mother did. And this gets worse, Roan. Leath has been a big-time African game hunter. He has hundreds of trophies over the years. He also owned a weapons arsenal."

"So, the man knows how to shoot." A cold chill went through Roan.

"According to the officer, at one time Leath was on the Olympic shooting team, rifle competition. He's a sniper, Roan. Pure and simple."

Gut clenching, Roan knew exactly what that meant. "That big black gym bag that the B and B owner saw?"

"Yes."

"It could have been his weapons bag," Roan said in a lower tone. He knew Shiloh was listening. He wished mightily she wasn't within earshot.

"I hadn't thought of that, but you're an operator and you've carried your weapons around with you on deployment."

"Right. Could you get someone to ask her roughly the size of it? It would be helpful to me."

"I can. Also, Leath, because he's a criminal, he cannot legally buy weapons."

Snorting, Roan muttered, "And that stops no one who really wants to get them. Leath could have a shill buy whatever he wants. Have you thought of checking the gun stores in Jackson Hole? The one here in Wind River? Faxing all of them Leath's photo?"

"Already done. We're also going to get a list of weapons from each store that have been bought in the last three weeks. The officer figures Leath probably headed west about that time. He's missed three check-in dates."

Roan nodded, sensing Shiloh's building anxiety. "Okay, sounds good. Let's stay in touch." There was so much more he wanted to discuss with Sarah, but not in front of Shiloh. He knew by now she was a major worrier and for her to hear what he wanted to say to the deputy would probably do nothing but terrorize her further. Leath was a sniper. That's all Roan needed to know. It put everything into perspective. Leath was truly a stalker; he'd hunted big game in Africa. The man knew how to move quietly, in the shadows, come upon the wild game, fire his big rifle, and take the animal down.

This time, Roan understood the full picture. Leath was out to stalk, wait for the right opportunity, to place unsuspecting Shiloh in his sights and kill her. And he could do it from a long distance. Even as far as a mile away since he was really a sniper-quality shooter. And since Leath had been on the Olympic team, Roan had no question that he could be a mile from his intended quarry and hit his target. Worse, Leath could use armor-piercing rounds. They could go through a window, a door . . . And he shut it all down as he turned and saw the terror in Shiloh's eyes.

"It's him, isn't it?"

"Yes. Let's go to the couch and sit down. I'll fill you in." He pulled her chair back, held out his hand, and Shiloh placed her damp one into his warm, dry palm.

Shiloh tried to hold on to her escaping emotions as she sat down next to Roan on the couch, her knee resting lightly against his thigh as she turned, facing him.

"What did Sarah say?"

Roan told her almost everything. "Were you aware he was an African big game hunter?"

"Yes." Shiloh shivered. "My mother hated that part about him. When they got married, Anton wanted to hang the heads of the dead animals he'd killed all over her apartment. She wouldn't let him. It upset her so much. They got into a lot of heated arguments about it. Mom hated guns and violence." Shiloh shook her head. "And look what happened to her. She died violently."

Roan reached out, his large hand covering her two hands

clasped tightly in her lap. "Did Leath keep weapons at the apartment?"

"Yes, much to my mother's chagrin. He was always cleaning them on my mom's beautiful bird's-eye maple table. It was a hundred-and-fifty-year-old table that had been handed down through our family. Anton laid down a cloth over it when he cleaned his stuff, but she hated even seeing the weapons around. It really upset her. The place would smell like gun oil afterward for days. I hated it too."

"Did your real father ever have any weapons in the apartment?" Roan wondered.

"No. He was in the military, but when he got out, he left it all behind. There were never any weapons in our house until Mom married that monster."

"I don't mean to push you here, Shiloh, but do you remember the types of weapons he had in the apartment?"

Frowning, she shrugged. "I don't really know. There were huge, long ones. Rifles, I think. And he had several small handguns, but I don't know what kind they were. I couldn't tell one from another."

"Did he keep up his shooting skills after he married your mother?"

"Yes. He had a membership to several shooting ranges outside of the city. He always invited us to go along, but neither of us ever wanted to."

"If I showed you some of those long, big rifles he had from images on the Internet, do you think you could identify them?"

Rolling her eyes, Shiloh said, "Yes. Because they were so big, ugly, and powerful-looking."

"Okay, we'll do that tomorrow morning, sometime." Identifying the weapons would help Sarah check with the gun shops in the area. And if a rifle was purchased, it could be the one Leath wanted to use to kill Shiloh.

Shiloh searched Roan's face. His voice was low and

unruffled, but the line of questioning was unhinging her. "Why are you asking me all these questions about his guns? Did Sarah say something to you about them?"

"No. But Leath's probation officer gave Sarah the background on him. None of us knew he'd been on the Olympic rifle team."

"What does that mean? I don't understand."

Roan hesitated. "It's just a piece of information for Sarah. The guy is used to using guns. He knows how to handle them."

She sensed there was a lot more to his remark, searching his dark gray eyes, wishing she could read Roan's mind. "I don't know one end of a gun from another." She frowned. "Do you have weapons here, Roan?" It would make sense that he did because he'd been black ops. Those men were all trained heavily in the use of all kinds weaponry. They had to be.

Nodding, Roan gestured toward the room that would become a second bedroom. "I have a gun cabinet in there. You might have seen it. It's under lock and key."

The news made Shiloh feel better. As much as she hated weapons, if Leath was sneaking around, stalking her, he'd have a weapon on him, no question. "I don't know how to use one."

"I'll show you the basics tomorrow." Roan studied her. "Are you open to that, Shiloh? I know you don't like guns."

"What's my choice? If I don't arm myself, how am I going to protect myself if he comes around here? He'll shoot to kill me." Her stomach rolled over at the thought.

Roan squeezed her hands and released them. "If you feel like it, why don't I show you some combat moves in the gym tomorrow. Then, I can take you to the indoor shooting range in town in a day or two. Show you how a pistol works, how you shoot it so you won't be afraid of handling it."

"I like the idea of working out in the gym with you."

"And going to the shooting range?"

"I'll do it." Even she heard the resolve in her voice. Shiloh had grown up in a household where peace and diplomacy ruled, not guns and violence.

Roan lightly caressed her hair, moving some of the thick, silky strands off her tense shoulder. "I'm going to go clean up, do a little work on my laptop here in the kitchen, and then take a shower. You have a choice. I can either stay and sleep out here on the couch and give you my bedroom or you and I can sleep together. Which do you want it to be?"

Cold reality washed through her. She could die tomorrow. The thought eviscerated Shiloh. "I want to be with you, Roan." She saw tenderness come to his gray eyes and it muted some of the reality that this could be her last night on earth. And if it was, she was going to spend it with Roan.

Roan slipped into bed with Shiloh. They were both naked. He had stayed up until eleven P.M., researching the Internet on sniper hunting rifles as well as the type used by Olympic shooters. If Shiloh would look at the images tomorrow morning and be able to identify what Leath had in the apartment, he could then send the intel to Sarah. In turn, the deputies could look at the list of guns sold the last three weeks and see if the exact same rifle or its equivalent had been purchased. And by whom. He kept all those thoughts to himself as her warm, velvet body slid up alongside his. Shiloh snuggled into his arms, her leg over his, her breasts against the wall of his chest.

"Could you just hold me?" she asked softly, sliding her fingers across his chest, coming to rest on his shoulder.

"Sure," he murmured, pressing a kiss to her mussed hair.

"I don't exactly have sex on the mind tonight," she admitted in apology.

"Darlin', it's all right. I don't expect we'll be making love every night. Do you?"

She nuzzled against his thick neck, inhaling his scent, the sage soap, his maleness that always made her yearn for more from Roan. "I can't shut my mind off. I can't focus, Roan. I'm sorry. I'll probably be so restless tonight I'll keep you awake half the night."

"Hush," he rasped, sliding his arm around her shoulders, drawing her against him. "It's all right. I'd rather have you in my bed than not. Okay?"

"Even if I keep you awake?" she muffled against the column of his neck. How she needed Roan's arm around her, holding her tightly. He felt so strong, like a rock where she presently felt like Jello-O. As he stroked her cheek, Shiloh closed her eyes, feeling some of the tension bleed out of her.

"I want you here, with me, no matter what, Shiloh."

"I tend to talk when I'm nervous."

He chuckled, the rumble moving through his chest. "I can tell."

"What do men do? You don't seem to worry like a woman does."

"Just put it into a box," he said. "SEALs call it a kill box, but I prefer to call it something more benign."

"You can honestly stuff your emotions into a box within yourself?"

"Yes. Our focus is on the bad guy. Not how we're feeling. If we did let our emotions run wild, we'd never be able to focus on the enemy and kill him."

"Humph, that's a pretty slick arrangement you guys have in your brain. It's not how a woman's brain works. We're all about connections. It sounds like you guys have files and whatever file you pull out, that's your focus. And none of the other files open up to bother or distract you."

"Brain Science 101?" he teased, skimming his fingers slowly up and down her arm.

She laughed a little, relaxing more. "I guess. I've always been curious about how a man's brain works versus a woman's brain. It helps me create dialogue for my male characters, since I'm not a man."

"That, you aren't," Roan agreed. "Thank God."

Shiloh smiled a little, more of her tension dissolving. "Leath hated Mom talking all the time."

"What do you mean?"

"He didn't like us talking a lot. I don't know why. He said we were like two chattering squirrels. That we never knew when to shut up."

"You were a child. Children talk nonstop. They're learning."

"My mother didn't take that lying down, believe me. She told Anton if he didn't like hearing us talk, to move out."

"When did this happen?"

Sighing, Shiloh whispered, "About six months before he murdered her."

"It sounds like your mother was tired of being controlled and manipulated by him."

"I think so, but she never said that to me directly."

"Because you were a child. She wasn't going to put that on you. She protected you as much as she could."

"Yes, she did. But I saw and heard a lot. It was a small apartment. When Anton would chide my mother, try to humiliate or embarrass her, she'd get angry and get into his face. She was never one to hold back how she felt."

"Maybe an artist's temperament?"

"My mother was very confident in herself. She was independent. I still don't know to this day why she married that bastard. He was the exact opposite of my father. What did she see in him?"

"Maybe she was lonely, Shiloh."

"Yes . . . that's what I eventually thought, too. My mother was still so young, so beautiful and vibrant. She was such an extrovert. She loved going to parties, to galleries that held openings for her paintings. She loved interacting with people."

Shiloh sighed, beginning to feel the exhaustion claim her mind, her worrying thoughts starting to slow down and dissolve. "She'd painted a beautiful zebra and her foal on the Serengeti Plain of Africa. Leath had bought it."

"He hunted there."

"Yes. I loved the painting because the baby zebra was dancing around his mother. It was such a beautiful painting. So real. As if you could reach out and touch that little baby. My mom was an amazing artist."

"Do you have it?"

A rush of pain flowed through Shiloh. "No. About six months before Leath murdered my mom, they got into a screaming and yelling argument. He tore the painting off the wall in the den where he had his office, brought it out, and took it into her studio. He had a skinning knife in his hand and he shredded it in front of her." Shiloh's mouth compressed. "He did it to hurt her because he knew it was one of her favorite paintings."

"Jesus. Were you there when it happened?"

"It happened on a weekend. My mom had set up my little easel next to hers. She was teaching me how to paint when Anton came yelling into her studio. I was so scared. I saw murder in his eyes and I screamed as he charged toward my mom with the painting in his upraised hand. I ran to the corner and cowered, hiding my face, so afraid. That knife he had"—Shiloh shivered—"it was the same one he later used to kill my mother."

He caressed her tense back. "I'm sorry you had to witness that, Shiloh. What happened next?"

"They started shouting at each other. My mom was

furious because he'd scared the hell out of me. She stood up to him, and shoved him back, trying to push him out of her studio. He pushed back. My mom almost fell but caught herself. And then he held up the painting, stabbing and slashing through the canvas until it hung in shreds. It was horrible. I couldn't stop crying."

Roan scowled. It was a sign of things to come from Leath. And he was out there, somewhere, right now. But where?

Chapter Twenty-One

Anton moved his thumb lightly down the curve of his SOG SEAL Team Elite seven-inch blade. He sat in his hide on the largest of the two Pine Grove halves. It was the closest, distance-wise, to that cedar cabin sitting out half a mile away on the valley floor. And his target, Shiloh Gallagher, was in that cedar cabin.

The chill of the morning was deep as the sun just began to climb over the horizon. He'd been in his newly created hide, halfway up the hill, surrounded by Douglas fir, for two days. Getting lucky on his stakeout, lying prone in a pasture of deep grass on the ranch, he'd seen her ride up to the hills and disappear.

Anton had waited until night, left his sniper post in the pasture, and walked the mile to Pine Grove as marked on the topo map he carried. What surprised him was the cabin hidden on the other side of the tallest hill. And it was there that he'd seen not only Shiloh, but a cowboy. He'd lain perfectly still until they'd both ridden away. Clearly, there was a relationship between them and it only made him feel even happier that he could destroy both of them.

Moving his thumb down the titanium nitride–coated

blade, he visualized how he was going to use it on that bratty Shiloh. He'd stalked her for six months in Manhattan. And he found he enjoyed this stalking out here in Wyoming even more. Leath liked nature. He liked the challenge. He was the hunter. Shiloh was his quarry and, now, he was in active stalk mode with her whether she knew it or not.

The SOG SEAL knife was used by the black ops teams. It was a special knife created for special needs. His full lips pulled upward slightly as he closed his eyes, visualizing exactly what he was going to do with her once he captured her. He was waiting for that cowboy to drive off sometime this morning without her. He was hoping Shiloh would be left alone. Alone and unable to defend herself against him.

First, he would silently enter the cabin. He'd already checked it out at night, using his infrared rifle scope. It had two entrances. One on the east side and one on the west side. He'd looked into the windows when there was no one around. Laid out the room design in his mind. There was one working bedroom, so he knew where she'd be sleeping. Two rooms were empty except for what he thought might be a large gun cabinet in one of them. He knew of Shiloh's hatred of weapons, figuring the cowboy was the shooter, not her.

He had a police scanner radio on him and knew the Lincoln sheriff's department was actively trying to locate him. They would never find him. He'd spent time hunting in Africa in all kinds of challenging situations and changing conditions. Anton knew how to hide. None of these law enforcement idiots would ever think about looking for him here. He was sure they were tearing up Wind River Valley all the way to Jackson Hole from one end to another, trying to locate him. He'd left no trace of where he was or where he'd gone. Knowing how to stalk, how to become a shadow, using the night as his friend and cover, Leath smiled a little more.

The SEAL seven-inch blade was coated with a matte black finish of titanium, making it invisible in the night. There was no flash or reflection off it. The AUS-8 steel it was created from contained vanadium in it, making the blade incapable of breaking even when encountering the thickest bone in the human body, the femur. And he had been envisioning how he was going to use this knife on her.

He was pleased that the blade had serrated teeth all the way across the top, which meant he could jerk it upward, tearing open her flesh. The knife also had a staggered serration beneath it, as well as on the first third of the blade. Serrations were like tiny sharpened teeth that could surgically cut through soft skin and sink down, ripping and shredding fibrous muscle, ligaments, and tendons beneath it. The serrations were so sharp, it could move through skin and muscle to the vulnerable organs like a hot knife through butter with absolutely no resistance.

It was there that Anton could feel the blade sinking into Shiloh's soft, rounded abdomen, wreaking havoc, slicing her open, gutting her. He'd open her up so that she suffered in agony for days before she'd die. Gut wounds were always the worst. It was a slow, painful, and grisly death. He would keep Shiloh alive, tape her mouth shut so she couldn't scream, tie her hands up above her head, then watch her writhe in nonstop agony. Yes, he was going to enjoy every minute he spent with Shiloh, watching her slowly die over a three-day period. She'd die of peritonitis, septic poison finally reaching her circulatory system and going to her heart. Once it did, she'd die of cardiac arrest.

Anton was going to enjoy this so much, and he smiled more deeply, appreciating the serrated teeth on this specially made knife. He'd dreamed of this for years. There wasn't a day that went by when he wasn't creating a strategy to find her, stalk her, and then gut her. She'd put him away. He wished that she would live more than three days but under the circumstances, it wouldn't happen.

As he sat there, listening to the birds sing around him, his hide covered with green netting so that it was impossible to see, he thought about other scenarios. It would be easy to get her out of the cabin and back to his hide. He'd spent one full night with his small military shovel, digging out a rectangular hide. It was two feet vertically and six feet wide. Last night, he'd dug it deeper, five feet deep. Anton was waffling between gutting Shiloh right away or waiting and cutting her here and there, making her suffer like he'd suffered for so many years. She'd slowly bleed to death and he could control how long she remained alive. Maybe he needed to take another look at his plans. Anton knew when she disappeared, there would be a manhunt. But he'd take her in such a way that no one would be able to track him back to his hide. He knew how to do it from past experience.

He would have to make sure Shiloh was kept silent. She would have to remain in the hide with him, undetected. He'd have to feed her, give her water because he wanted her alive and alert. There were a lot of other considerations to change in his plans, but Anton would give his right hand if he could extend her suffering. He'd lived too long for this one moment in his life.

Sliding the SOG into the black nylon sheath, he set it aside. He'd brought plenty of MREs and there was a creek nearby. Luckily, he had purification tablets on him.

Anton knew a grizzly lived around the area, and Pine Grove was her territory. When he finally allowed Shiloh to die, he'd dump her body near where he had seen bear scat and leave it there. The grizzly would be getting one hell of a meal eating her up. Bears ate bones as well, so there would be very little of Shiloh left when it was all said and done. One day, someone might stumble upon a few bone fragments up on this hill, but that could be years from now and he would be long gone. Out of this country. Back to Africa, his first love. He would live like a king there.

So, what should he cut on her first? Anton didn't want her bleeding out. She'd die too quickly that way. No . . . it had to be something that would terrorize her, but not kill her. Something that would cause her agony. His mind ranged over numerous ways. He was used to skinning and gutting his African animals he'd taken down with his gun. Skinning. Hmmmm, that had possibilities. Skinning Shiloh alive. How perfect. It would cause her horrific pain. It might even make her faint from the pain, but he'd stop the procedure and wait until she became conscious. And then, he'd continue the job.

Shiloh's hands trembled as she rinsed off her lunch dishes to put them into the dishwasher. Her mind was going wild, leaping from here to there. She'd been able to identify the two guns for Roan that Leath had in their apartment when her mother was alive. Roan was pleased and sent the JPEG images directly to Sarah at the sheriff's office. Then, he'd told her to get workout gear and meet him in the gym. There, he'd shown her some Special Forces close quarters combat moves that could incapacitate someone who was charging her, trying to grab and capture her. She'd worked an hour getting accustomed to the moves until Roan was satisfied. Her muscles were tight afterward. Inwardly, she felt trapped once again.

And now, Roan had gone into town because Sarah had asked to see him. She'd seen him hesitate at the request because she knew he didn't want to leave her alone. At the same time, Roan didn't want her seen out in public, so she couldn't ride into town with him. Shiloh had persuaded him she'd be all right, feeling that Anton would never know she was here. How could he? Roan wasn't fully convinced of her argument, but reluctantly left, promising to remain in cell phone touch with her once an hour to make sure she was all right. Shiloh felt he was overreacting. This cabin was hidden from everyone. Very few people even knew it existed.

Looking out the window, she saw the noontime sunlight overhead, making the green pastures around the cabin look emerald. There were no trees in the pastures and no cattle right now. The five acres the cabin sat on were bracketed to the north and west of it. Straight ahead, to the east was open ranch land without fences. In the distance, Shiloh could see the mountain peaks of the Salt River Range. To the south of the cabin, a half a mile away, sat Pine Grove. Earlier, Roan had told her that no one could sneak up on the cabin and explained why. It had made her feel better. More settled.

She knew she wouldn't be able to write today, she was too upset over the situation with Anton Leath. Roan had made sure that the deadbolt locks on the front and back doors worked and had asked her to keep them locked when he was gone. Further, he'd checked all the windows and made sure they were locked as well. Shiloh felt trapped, Hunted, just as she'd felt in her small apartment.

She had to do SOMETHING. Anything to get her mind off what was going on around her. What would Roan find out from Sarah? Did they know where the monster who was stalking her was at? Had they located Leath? Roan had promised to call her and Shiloh waited on tenterhooks, her iPhone in her pocket, never to leave her side.

Unable to remain quiet, far too restless and nervous, Shiloh decided to deep-clean the cabin. Not that it needed it. It was brand-new, never been lived in before she stepped into it with Roan. But she couldn't remain sitting. She felt like a target, her gaze darting from one window to another. Shiloh hated the idea of pulling the drapes and curtains across all the windows. She loved the light that flooded the cabin, making it so alive and beautiful with color and radiance. For her to close the curtains would be admitting she was scared out of her mind. So, she kept looking at the windows from time to time as she dusted, frightened if she saw Leath's big, heavy face, his heavy-lidded eyes staring back at her.

She was coming apart at the seams. Shiloh's imagination was going wild and she could barely control it as her hands shook as she took the dustcloth over the coffee table.

The phone rang.

Jerking, a gasp escaping her, Shiloh dropped the cloth. She jammed her hand into her pocket, frantic to pick up the iPhone.

"Roan?" she asked, her voice low and strained.

"Yes, it's me. How are you doing?"

Shiloh grimaced. "Not well. My damned imagination is scaring the hell out of me. Did you find out anything about Leath?"

"A couple of things. No one has seen him. With the rifles you identified and the pictures I sent to Sarah, there's one gun shop here who sold a .300 Winchester Magnum, to a man. It wasn't Leath. Sarah thinks he was a shill who was sent to buy it and they've got the man in custody and are talking to him right now. He did identify Leath's picture. The sheriff's artist put out an updated drawing of him with the brown beard and hair. The man said he was the one who gave him money to go buy the weapons."

Her hand crept against her neck. Throat tight, Shiloh asked, "How many guns did he buy?"

"He's got a pistol and the .300 Win Mag. The man in custody said he also bought a SOG."

"What's a SOG?"

"It's a black ops knife that a lot of operators prefer when they're hunting tangos. It's a short blade, maybe seven inches long, but very easy to maneuver in tight quarters."

Shiloh's stomach clenched. "Oh, God, Roan."

"What?"

"Anton had an arsenal of knives when he lived with us."

"You'd mentioned that to me earlier. Does that SOG ring a bell?"

Tightly shutting her eyes, her voice tight and low, she said, "Yes. It was his favorite knife. He called it a gutting knife. He used to try to tell me about how he gutted his kills over in Africa. My mother would walk in and hear him telling me this horrible stuff, get angry, and tell him to shut up, that it was upsetting me."

"What a sick bastard. Your mother was right to stop him."

"Yes, well, believe me, I had nightmares for months after that because he described it in such awful, bloody detail."

"So, he had a SOG knife?"

"Yes."

"What kind? Do you remember?"

"I-I don't . . ."

"If I sent a JPEG of the knife to your phone, could you look at it and see?"

"Yes."

"Hold on . . ."

Shiloh saw the color photo of the knife pop up on her screen. "Yes, that's it."

"It's a SOG SEAL knife," Roan said.

She heard the grimness in his tone and it sent chills scattering through her spine. "What does it mean?"

"It means nothing at this point, Shiloh."

"Did they find Leath's rental car?"

"Yes. It was abandoned alongside the highway at a rest

stop about two miles from the town of Wind River. It was dusted for prints and they are his prints."

Frowning, she said, "Then where did he go?"

"Might have hitchhiked. Thumbed a ride from a passing car. Or an eighteen-wheeler. No one knows. Sarah has distributed the updated picture of Leath to the Forest Service at the Salt Range and Grand Tetons headquarters. Ray Paulson, the supervisor, is sending it out by e-mail to all his rangers. The rangers are going into the camping sites and asking campers if they've seen him. There's a huge net starting to be created, Shiloh. Sooner or later, someone will have seen Leath. It's just a question of when and where."

She wasn't sure if that was good or bad news. Rubbing her neck, she muttered, "I can feel him around, Roan. I swear . . . I can. Sometimes, I think it's my imagination gone wild. Other times, I know he's nearby."

"I don't disbelieve you," he said heavily. "Remember? The cabin sits out in a flat area. You can see someone coming from a long ways away."

Swallowing against her tight throat, Shiloh nodded, warily gazing around, looking at each window to see if she saw anyone standing there looking in on her. "Yes, I remember."

"The car rental company manager identified Leath from the original color photo of him. At that time, he had his blond hair. Sarah said he later dyed it brown after arriving here."

"That's good to know. To me, it means he intends to stick around. He's trying to camouflage himself so he can't be identified."

"Right."

She chewed on her lower lip. "When are you coming home?"

"Soon. Can I get you anything from town?"

Shiloh thought of a lot of smart rejoinders but said, "No, just you. I feel better when you're here with me."

"So do I, Darlin'. I'll call you when I'm on my way out of town. I'll be there shortly. I like coming home to you."

HOME.

Shiloh ended the call and slipped the iPhone into her pocket. *Home.* She gazed around the radiant cabin, absorbing the reddish-gold color of the main logs above her head. Roan had made this cabin with his own hands, his own sweat, following a dream. And he'd manifested that dream into this incredible cabin. And it was a home with them in it, she realized. It felt right to Shiloh. And good.

If only Leath would be caught.

Shiloh sensed Anton Leath around. She didn't know where, but she could feel his dark presence as she continued to clean the cabin. Her mind was whirling with all kinds of dreaded scenarios. Most of all, Shiloh couldn't get the vivid murder of her mother out of her mind. In the background, she heard the rumbling of a thunderstorm. It wasn't unusual, Roan had told her. They were created by the jagged-toothed Wilson Range mountains and then would roll furiously across the valley, pouring inches of rain over the lush, grassy area.

Hesitating, she went to the window and saw a huge, dark mass of roiling clouds blowing over the Western mountain range, coming directly her way. She loved thunderstorms and loved to run up to the top of the building, stand beneath an overhang, and watch one march across the city. Lightning didn't scare her and she loved to feel rain against her face. It always made her feel so alive. There was a massive, wide curtain of dark rain beneath the thunderhead as it rushed toward the cabin. A little excitement replaced her worry and anxiety.

When it got closer, Shiloh was going to sneak out the back

door, stand on the rear porch, and watch it just as she watched them in Manhattan. Judging from the speed of the storm, it would be here very shortly, sweeping across the Idaho border, heading east toward them. She was sure the town of Wind River was taking a beating of wind and rain, lightning often striking the area.

Her iPhone rang again.

"Hello?"

"Shiloh? It's Roan. I'm going to be late. We just got hit by a big thunderstorm and it looks like it's headed directly for the Wind River Ranch. The streets are flooded and there's all kinds of traffic snarl. There's also two accidents just outside of town on Highway 89 north. I'm stuck here on the highway while they get the ambulance to get people out of those two cars. I'm sorry."

She smiled a little, going to the back door, looking out the small window in the massive door at the storm. "Funny, I heard the rumble of thunder and I went out back to look and saw it over the town. I figured Wind River was getting slammed by the weather."

Roan laughed a little. "Yeah, this is one of those spring storms that plays hell on everything and everybody. You haven't seen them in action. Looks like it's heading directly toward our cabin from what I can see."

"Yes, it is. Fast, too."

"There's going to be a lot of local flooding," Roan warned her. "That cabin sits out on a flat valley floor and this is a downpour. It's going to turn grass into mud so don't go outside. Okay?"

"I thought I might go out the back door, stand under the porch roof, and watch it. I love storms. You okay with that?"

"Sure. So you're a storm lover? Something I didn't know about you."

Her heart warmed and swelled with love for Roan. "As

a kid, I'd always beg my parents to take me for a walk out in the rain when there was a storm in the city. I've always loved the wind, rain, thunder, and lightning. I was never afraid of it."

"Well, the thunderstorms over the Rockies can be brutal and dangerous, Darlin'. Just don't go out walking in it. Okay? We get a number of tourists killed every year because they're caught out in the Salt Range mountains and lightning strikes them."

"No worries. I'll just stick to the porch."

"Good. I'll give you a call when I can get out of this tangled mess on the highway. It's probably going to take an hour."

She laughed a little. "Turn around and go back to Kassie's Café and get some lunch. Might as well make good use of your time there."

Roan chuckled. "That's a good idea. I'll be in touch. . . ."

She pressed off the phone call, feeling warmth replace her anxiety. Shiloh didn't want to spook Roan by confiding in him that she felt Anton nearby. There was nothing he could do about it, anyway. She pushed the phone down into her jean pocket and went back to work dusting the living room. Wanting to tell Roan while on the phone that she had fallen in love him, Shiloh wished she were more bold about it. He was a good man and he cared for her. She could remember when her father was going to be delayed on a flight or caught up in city traffic, that he would always call her mother so she wouldn't worry. Yes, Roan did love her.

Some of her anxiety bled off as she busied herself. The rumble of the thunder was rapidly drawing near. She luxuriated in the growling, rolling noise. This would be her first Wyoming thunderstorm. And although they got some powerful storms in New York City, she sensed this one was different in every way. Perhaps, untamed. Wild. Unpredictable. Just like the West. There was nothing sedate, orderly, or controlled about the West compared to the East. Her mind ranged over the differences between Easterners and Westerners. The East was tamed first by people coming from Europe. It had over a hundred years of settlement before pioneers started pushing West.

Finished with the dusting, Shiloh washed her hands and put the cloth away in the pantry. The thunder was so close that she could feel the fine vibration of the sound rippling through the cabin. She loved that sensation, glorying in it. Going to the kitchen sink to wash her hands, she saw how suddenly dark the sky had become. The sunlight had been snuffed out, and roiling gray, black, and gunmetal-colored clouds were ominously forming over the valley, above the cabin. She was mesmerized at how fast the clouds were moving. Quickly drying her hands, Shiloh went to the closet, pulled out her Levi's jacket, and shrugged it on. She had her hiking boots on and between the two she'd be protected against any rain that might be swirling round, pushed by the wind.

Walking excitedly down the hall, she peeked out the window, making sure no one was out there on the large back porch. The lush grass was whipping around like living hair on the skin of the earth, driven by the approaching storm. It was almost black as the center of the storm was nearly upon the cabin. Thrilled, Shiloh stepped out onto the porch, closing the door behind her.

Chapter Twenty-Two

The wind gusted sharply, lifting Shiloh's hair, which was pulled back into a ponytail, as she turned around. Excited, absorbing the massive gray cloud that was nearly upon the cabin, she knew it meant a serious wall of wind would strike shortly. The breadth of the veil beneath the churning black and gray clouds that slowly seemed to rotate clockwise beneath the unseen cumulus far above reminded her of a tornado in the making. It scared but thrilled her. The scent of rain was heavy on the air. The lush grass, which always reminded her of a woman's long, flowing hair, was laid flat against the earth as the first powerful gust struck the cabin. It pushed her back against the door, the wind howling and fierce.

The entire area suddenly became dark. The wall cloud was thick, circular, and striking the area where the cabin sat. Trees to her left bent and groaned, the wind at least seventy to eighty miles an hour. The air was cold, cutting and howling around her, pummeling her body like invisible fists. She saw upper branches on the cottonwood trees snap, break, and sail off into the wind, carried across the yard. These weren't little branches. They were huge, massive limbs!

Her excitement mixed with awe and a little fear as she'd never experienced a storm of this mega proportion. Just as Shiloh turned to open the door to seek shelter, she caught a shadow out of the corner of her eye. A hand gripped her by the neck, fingers digging deep, hurling her off the porch, slamming her into the grass.

Gasping, Shiloh nearly lost consciousness, her head crashing into the hard earth. Eyes widening, she saw Anton Leath grinning savagely at her. He was in military camos, a knife in his gloved right hand. A strangled sound lurched out of her. Shiloh rolled, trying to get away from his hand snaking out to grab her.

"Bitch," Anton growled, gripping her by the shoulder, easily hauling her slight frame up into a standing position. He saw the terror in Shiloh's huge, shocked eyes. His lips twisted as he sank his fingers deep into her shoulder, watching pain flicker in her face. Thrusting the knife to her throat, the tip drawing blood just beneath her jawline, he snarled, "Fight me and I'll gut you right here. Now be a good girl and come with me."

Panic seized Shiloh. The wind roared around them, pummeling her. Rain suddenly unleashed from the dark, heavy skies. Pain serrated through her shoulder. "No!" she cried, trying to fight.

Leath snarled a curse, released her, and took the butt of the knife, striking her in the temple. He heard her shriek and collapse unconscious to the ground. Rain splattered him and he wiped his face, quickly looking around. The storm was perfect cover for him. Sliding the knife into a sheath on his right leg, he leaned down, picked up Shiloh, and lobbed her into a fireman's carry across his thick, broad shoulders. The rain was quickening, striking at his body like bullets being fired. He had half a mile to make it under the cover of this bastard of a thunderstorm. Even better, as he started off at a slow, unwieldy trot, his footprints would be washed out by the massive storm and no one would ever know he'd been here. Grinning, he hunkered and crouched, Shiloh's weight making him keep a slow, steady pace. He'd hit her hard enough, stunned her in the temple, that she wouldn't regain consciousness, he hoped, until he reached the hill where his hide was.

Roan was sitting at Kassie's Café having a cup of coffee when a terrible sensation rolled through him. Instantly, he recognized that familiar warning signal. *Shiloh.* Picking up his iPhone, he hit her number, and put the phone to his ear. The phone rang and rang and rang. Scowling, he ended the call. The storm was almost gone from the town of Wind River. Outside the main square, it was awash with flooding water rushing down the two main streets. Already, slats of sunlight were peeking through the ragged edges of the massive storm. There was even a rainbow forming in the wake of the storm. He remembered Shiloh was going to go out back and watch the storm's approach. If she was outside, she might not hear her phone ring, the wind, rain, and thunder erasing the sound of it.

Rubbing his neck, he didn't have a good feeling. Throwing some money on the counter, he eased off the stool and headed out the door, hurrying for his truck. The plaza was a mess. Water was running a foot deep, the storm drains unable to keep up with the flood. His truck would handle it. Chest tightening, Roan walked to the parking lot behind the café and climbed in. He knew there were two wrecks leading out of town. And he'd have to get the deputies who were stopping traffic to let him pass. Would they?

Something was wrong. He could taste it. And he'd had these warnings before as an operator in Afghanistan. It was a sign of the enemy nearby, an ambush. And he would get killed if he didn't listen to his powerful intuition. Was he overreacting? Worried that Shiloh was out back in that coming storm? She could have been struck by lightning. Or . . . and his mind didn't want to go there. Or, Anton Leath had either killed her or kidnapped her. His stomach churned with nausea. His mouth tightened and thinned, his fingers gripping the steering wheel as he drove slowly through the sloshing water covering the highway, heading for the hill still blotted out by falling rain from the end of the storm.

Shiloh felt nauseous. Felt being carried. Felt Anton's hands gripping her one ankle and her other wrist, holding her tight against his shoulders and neck. The rain was slashing down on her, her clothes soaked. Nausea and dizziness struck her again. She closed her eyes. He had captured her. And he was going to kill her. Just like he'd killed her mother. *Oh . . . God . . .*

Mind shorting out, barely able to think, Shiloh pretended to be unconscious, flopping around like a wet rag across Leath's massive shoulders. He was a powerful man. She'd always been afraid of him. His huge hands hurt her. Tightly shutting her eyes, her teeth jarring as he jogged heavily through the howling wind and rain, she tried to think. Where was he taking her? Opening her eyes, she recognized where she was through the pall of rain.

Hail began to fall, large, the size of marbles. It struck her in the head and she bit back a cry. The whole world became blotted out as the hail tunneled out of the sky, erasing everything around her.

Shiloh knew she didn't have the strength to fight Leath. Her mind spun between abject terror and thinking of somehow escaping. She tried to remember what Roan had taught her yesterday, the moves that could disable a man with her fists and feet. Where was he taking her? What was he going to do to her? Throat aching with dread, she felt him slowing and opened her eyes. The hail started to ease off and she saw the tall, dark shadows of trees just ahead of them. It had to be Pine Grove.

Water ran down her eyes and face, blinding her. Shiloh didn't dare move, didn't dare let Leath know she was conscious. *Play the rag doll. Play dead. Wait. Wait for a chance to escape from him. . . .*

Where was Roan? Despair flowed through her. He was still in town because of those car accidents. And even if he was trying to drive home now, the storm would stop him. Shiloh felt her whole world dissolving.

Leath slowed to a walk. She felt him grip her ankle and wrist more tightly. Pain reared up her arm and leg and she bit back a groan. He was now climbing. The sheets of twisting, bullet-like raindrops were somewhat softened by the thousands of trees that grew on the slight slope he was now climbing. She could hear Leath grunting and huffing, the hillside slippery and muddy. He fell forward, cursing.

Shiloh was almost torn off his shoulders as he slipped in the mud, going down hard. Leath recovered, one knee down on the earth, pushing himself upright, gripping her limbs hard, repositioning her across his shoulders. Breathing unsteadily, her nostrils flaring, she picked up his sour smell. It made her stomach turn. Oh, God, she was going to die!

Leath halted halfway up the slight incline. He was rasping for breath, chest heaving, hunched over with her lying across his shoulders. Opening her eyes, Shiloh saw a huge pit that reminded her of a hole that a coffin would be placed in. She saw green netting to one side. Part of the hole was filled with water, muddy and looking frightening to her. Leath cursed again.

Shiloh shut her eyes, pretending to be limp as he knelt down and eased her off his shoulders to the ground. Shiloh's heart was pumping wildly in her chest and she was afraid to open her eyes. What was Anton going to do? Was he going to stab her? She wanted so badly to open her eyes, paralyzed. And then, she heard him turn away. Heard his boots sucking in the mud, the sound moving away from her. She risked opening her eyes.

Leath's back was to her! He was leaning down, grabbing a shovel and he was ten feet away from her.

Now!

Shiloh slowly got to her hands and knees, her eyes never leaving Leath as he worked to shovel the water out of his hide, his back turned toward her. Her throat ached with tension as she stood. Dizziness assailed her and she violently shook her head, trying to get her balance. The trees would hide her if she could just make it silently into them.

The rain was coming down like an open faucet, the grayness making the hillside even darker. She dug her toes into the muddy earth and pine needles. Being careful, Shiloh stepped over a nearby branch, not wanting to make a sound. She slipped into the forest and, once there, began running toward the top of the low incline. She had to get help! And the only help was at the main headquarters of Wind River Ranch.

Her mind was wonky. She ran brokenly into the forest, the gloom covering her up. She knew Anton would discover her gone shortly. Could she run hard enough, fast enough, to get away? Shiloh knew she couldn't. Desperate, she kept looking as she dodged and ran around the thick brush here and there. Where could she hide? She knew he was a tracker. That he'd tracked big game in Africa for over a decade. She knew all his stories about tracking and killing those animals.

The hill was steep. Shiloh wasn't in good physical condition for this kind of rugged running and climbing. Black rocks stuck up and out of the pine needles, now soggy and slippery beneath her boots. She had no idea how long she'd run but she heard a howl behind her.

Leath discovered she was gone!

Oh, God . . .

Adrenaline poured into her bloodstream, giving her even more energy and strength as her legs pumped relentlessly toward the top of the slope. Shiloh remembered there was a sow grizzly bear with two cubs that lived on the other side of this area. Roan had told her about it earlier, to never hike on that side because it was the bear's domain. And that she had two cubs and would defend them quickly against anyone stepping onto her territory. Her breath came out in ragged spurts.

Thunder caromed overhead, shaking the entire hill. Rain slashed down into her eyes, blinding her. Shiloh tripped over a rock hidden by the pine needles. She went down, slamming belly-first into the floor, the breath whooshing out of her. Lying there, sobbing for breath, she anxiously jerked her head up, looking around.

Where was Leath?

She could feel him behind her. Tracking her. Stalking her.

Scrambling to her hands and knees, Shiloh pushed off, running hard for the very top of the hill. It was then that she remembered her iPhone in her pocket.

Thrusting her fingers into the wet denim, she frantically grabbed for the cell. Would it work out here? She knew during thunderstorms, cells often did not work, the invisible connectors destroyed by rain and lightning. If only it would work! The iPhone wasn't waterproof.

As she leaped and ran in and around larger rocks near the crown of the slope, she worried the rain had ruined the phone, and that she couldn't make a call for help. It was one mile down the dirt road from Pine Grove to the main ranch center. She had to run out in the middle of flat land where Leath would easily spot her.

Shiloh's breath was exploding from her. Lungs burning, she slowed, feeling her legs starting to cramp up from the exertion. She kept looking over her shoulder. Kept thinking she'd seen Leath's dark bulk appearing out of the gray pall of rain that surrounded her. Gripping the cell phone, her fingers shaking so badly she couldn't turn it on, Shiloh made a frustrated sound.

It wouldn't turn on!

Tears jammed into Shiloh's eyes. She shoved it back into her pocket, lunging for the top of the hill.

A shot rang out.

Bark flew a few feet from her face, the splinters striking the side of her face and neck.

Screaming, Shiloh winced, ducking and running over the crown.

He had a gun!

Sobbing for breath, stumbling, she hit a patch of wet pine needles, her feet jerking out from beneath her. Shiloh grunted, suddenly finding herself sliding down on her back and butt, heading straight down over a small cliff. She threw out her hands, a croak tearing out of her as she flew off into space.

Slamming into the rocks and pine needles twenty feet below, she landed with an "Oomph!"

Terrorized, she looked up the cliff. She saw Leath there, aiming his pistol right at her.

Screaming, she raced toward a huge fir tree.

The bark exploded near her head. And then several more bullets poured into the tree she scrambled behind, cowering, gripping the roots, trying to make herself small enough that he couldn't hit her.

A sudden bolt of light flashed above her. The whole area went blindingly light. Shiloh gasped, hands flying up to her eyes. She felt electricity tingling throughout her. The next thing she knew, she was being hurled through the air, tumbling end over end. The noxious odor of ozone stung and burned her nostrils. She landed hard, the wind knocked out of her lungs. She lay semiconscious on the ground, the rain pummeling her face, forcing her back to awareness.

Thunder followed.

As she lay there, partially stunned by the near miss of the bolt, the thunder shook the hill like it was Jello-O in a container. Her whole body vibrated with the fierce sounds rolling through the area.

Where is Leath?

Shiloh rolled to her side, forcing herself to her hands and knees. Dizziness assailed her. She heard herself gasping like a fish out of water.

Leath? Where?

Twisting her head, the pall of rain coming down even harder, making her feel like she was enclosed in a curtain she couldn't see through, Shiloh saw nothing but the torrent surrounding her. Beneath her hands water ran in violent rivulets down from the top of the grove. With a small cry, Shiloh launched herself to her feet, stumbling, running, wobbling down the other side of the slope. She couldn't see Leath. That meant nothing. He would find a way down that twenty-foot cliff and come after her. The rain was hiding her. She ran brokenly, her legs cramped, pain flaring up into her thighs. If she didn't run, she'd die.

Another zigzag of lightning sizzled overhead.

Shiloh screamed, throwing her hands over her head, ducking and falling.

The bolt hit somewhere nearby. The hill shook. The ozone filled the air and was rapidly dispensed by the curtain of heavy rain. Shiloh was blinded, unsure of her direction now as she slowly got to her feet. Her calves were cramping so bad that she could feel fist-sized knots in each of them. It hurt to take one step. Biting down on her lower lip, she forced herself to break into an awkward, stumbling trot, continuing down the hill.

The rain started to let up the farther downward she jogged, fell, got back up, and then jogged some more. The wind wasn't as fierce. Shiloh's hair was plastered around her. All her clothing was soaked, clinging to her body. She was chilled, her hands feeling numb from the coldness the storm had brought with it.

Suddenly, as she moved around a huge hole in the ground, she saw Leath.

He smiled at her, his pistol raised, no more than forty feet away from her, his back to the hole that had been dug out of the ground.

"STOP!" he yelled at her.

Shiloh jerked to a halt, staggering, facing him. Blinking away the water running into her eyes, her breath coming in gasps, she faced him. Leath's blue eyes were slits. The smile on his face sent icy terror through her. Her eyes were fixed on the pistol he held out in both his hands. His smile never wavered.

"You little bitch! You're dead!"

A huge dark brown shape hurtled out of the muddy hole in the ground.

Shiloh screamed.

The sow grizzly bear roared, attacking Leath.

Leath jerked around, his eyes growing huge. He fired his pistol five times into the angry eight-hundred-pound female grizzly before she leaped upon him.

Shiloh blinked, backing away, hearing Leath screaming, his arms flailing as the grizzly's five-inch fangs sank into his neck and shoulder. Blood was pouring out of the bruin's skull where he'd shot her, and she was furious, slinging Leath around like he was a rag doll between her massive jaws. Grunting, the bear took him to the ground, her huge front paws holding his body down so he couldn't escape.

Leath screamed weakly, raising his pistol, trying to fire it again at the angry bear.

Shiloh kept backing away, horrified. She stumbled over a rock, falling.

"I've got you. . . ."

Warm, strong hands caught her as she fell.

Roan!

She sobbed, jerking a look up at him as he hauled her against him, his pistol aimed directly at the distracted grizzly bear.

"Roan!" she croaked, her voice high, off pitch.

Roan pulled her around so she couldn't see what the bear was going to do to Leath. "Come on," he urged, tucking her beneath his arm, his arm around her waist, holding her close, holding her so she could remain upright. "He's dead already."

Everything became a blur. Roan was jogging down the flat, muddy road and she had wrapped her arm around his narrow waist. Her legs wouldn't work. The cramps were so painful she was crying out, unable to run with him. Roan stopped and had hauled her up into his arms, carrying her. The rain was slowing. It was no longer bullets hurled from the sky. Unable to cry, Shiloh could only feel relief as Roan approached his truck.

It as only when Shiloh saw three sheriff's deputy cruisers come racing up the muddy road, their flashers and sirens on, that she realized she was safe. Roan opened the passenger side of the truck and gently lifted her into the warm cab.

Shiloh stared in shock at his unreadable, wet face. He wore his black baseball cap, his face gleaming from rain, his eyes hard and narrowed. He was soaked, too. How did he know she was in trouble? Her mind was going into shock. She was safe. God, she was safe! And Leath had been killed by that grizzly bear! Roan was with her, talking to her, but she couldn't hear him. Everything felt disjointed.

Closing her eyes, Shiloh sank against the seat feeling Roan's hands around her hands. She was safe. Leath was either dead or badly injured. Shiloh hoped he was dead. How symbolic that the monster be killed by a wild animal. He'd taken so many wild animals' lives, made their heads trophies to remind him daily of his kills. She wiped her mouth with the back of her shaking hand.

Her hearing wasn't working. Even the police sirens seemed far, far away. She winced when a bolt of lightning danced across the sky, followed quickly by vibrating thunder. Her chest was heaving with exertion. The cold, wet clothing was seeping into her body, making her shake uncontrollably. Shiloh didn't feel she was any longer in control of her physical movements. Beyond exhaustion, her calves screaming with knots of unrelenting, cramping pain, she whimpered, trying to move her hand down her wet Levi's leg.

"Are you hurt, Shiloh?"

Roan's deep, low voice sank into her. She heard the anxiety in his tone. She opened her eyes, leaning over, pointing to her lower legs. It was impossible to talk, her brain was unable to put two coherent words together to make sense. All Shiloh could do was weakly collapse against the seat, her head tipping back on the top of the seat, eyes closed. She felt Roan pulling up her pant leg, rolling up the wet, stubborn material. And then, she felt his large, warm, wet hands find that horrible cramp. The moment he touched it, she cried out, jerking upright, her hand on his.

"No!" she sobbed. "It hurts!" and she looked deep into his dark gray eyes.

"Trust me, Shiloh. I'll ease the pain. Lean back?"

His voice soothed and calmed her as nothing else ever would. She barely nodded, weakness stealing even more into her limbs. There were sheriff's deputies moving past

Roan's pickup and scrambling up the hill where they'd just come from. One deputy remained behind, his rifle drawn, guarding them at the truck. The rain was lightening up, and there was no more wind. Shiloh could barely hear anyone speaking, but the voices were slowly turning up in volume. Had she been hit by lightning? Was that why her hearing was screwed? Shiloh didn't know and groaned softly as Roan's warm, long fingers slowly massaged the knot out of her right calf. The pain went away and she breathed raggedly, finally starting to relax a little. Roan rolled up her other pant leg, found the other knot, and did the same thing.

Closing her eyes, all Shiloh wanted was to be warm and safe. Roan was with her. Leath wasn't going to kill her. Oh, God, she'd come so close to dying! *So close.*

Warm tears burned in her closed eyes. They trickled down her muddy cheeks. She felt Roan's roughened thumbs removing them. A sob tore from her. Reaching out, opening her eyes, Shiloh threw herself into his strong arms. Just Roan's hands drawing her against him, the incredible warmth radiating from his powerful male body, made Shiloh cry even harder. Roan tucked her head against his shoulder and jaw, holding her gently, whispering words she couldn't hear, his breath moist and warm against her cold, wet flesh.

All Shiloh wanted right now was Roan. To be held. To feel safe. To be flooded with the fierce love he held for her. Never had she felt so protected as right now, in this man's arms. Roan had come for her. He couldn't have known she was in danger, yet he had. How? As she nuzzled into the wet nylon of the jacket he wore, Shiloh's mind began to shut down, the shock taking her, erasing all thoughts, everything. Except Roan's lean, hard body against hers. Holding her. Just holding her . . .

Chapter Twenty-Three

Moonlight sifted silently through the gossamer curtains into the bedroom. Shiloh was content to lie in Roan's arms, his body against hers. It was near dawn and she'd awakened, feeling his arms automatically tighten around her as they slept in his cabin. She felt Roan stir, realizing she'd accidentally awakened him. Three weeks had passed since Anton Leath's body, what was left of it, was carried off Pine Grove and to the medical examiner at the Lincoln County morgue. Shiloh had not watched, burying her head against Roan's chest, clinging to him, still not believing that it was really over. Finally. Once and for all.

"You okay?" Roan asked thickly, raising his head, his eyes half-open, studying her in the silence.

"Yes . . . Sorry, I just woke up out of the blue. I didn't mean to wake you up, too." She heard him grunt and then he propped himself up on one elbow. A few strands of dark brown hair fell over his broad brow. She reached up with her fingers, pushing them back into place, smiling into his drowsy features. "I should get up and let you sleep." She'd been waking up most nights with nightmares of the chase. With her almost dying.

"No way," Roan growled. He eased Shiloh on her back,

studying her darkened eyes, and realized she'd had another flashback. At least, with time, they were less potent and intense. Sliding his fingers across her jaw, he leaned over, capturing her mouth, feeling her open like a lush, warm blossom beneath him. Her world had been torn apart three weeks ago. Roan knew what it was like to get wounded and almost die. He knew the trek that Shiloh was undertaking to work through her own near-death experience.

Her mouth was sweet, opening eagerly to him. Her breath moist across his cheek and nose as he deepened his exploration of her. The happy sound in her throat told him she enjoyed it, her hands sliding across his shoulders, drawing him closer, her breasts pressing tantalizingly against his chest.

Finally, Roan eased his mouth from hers. Neither of them was breathing evenly at this point. Searching her eyes, he saw remnants of anxiety in them along with building arousal. Skimming his hand from her back down to her hips, he rasped, "Bad dream?"

"Yes, same one. I'm getting tired of them," she grumped, caressing his jaw.

"It's just another way to work out the trauma," Roan assured her, kissing her wrinkled brow. "You're getting fewer of them as time goes on. That's how it is."

Shiloh pouted for a moment. "It seems like a bad dream now, Roan."

"In time," he soothed, kissing her nose and cheek, "you won't have them anymore. It really will be in your past." Lifting his head, he smiled a little. "Besides, you have a lot to look forward to."

Her editor extended the deadline on her book because of the circumstances, much to Shiloh's relief. Roan had seen her in the newly decorated office in the cabin and she was going back to writing. She'd asked him to read the new chapter, trepidation in her expression. Roan had read it and thought it was good. The relief in Shiloh's eyes made him realize just how much she worried about being able to ever write again. The week after her escape from Leath, she had fallen completely apart. Roan had asked Maud for time off, stayed with her at the cabin, and helped her work through it. He didn't realize how much a person could cry, but was glad to be there for Shiloh, to hold her.

Roan finally realized that ever since Isabella's murder, Shiloh had sat on her grief, her shock and trauma. And it had all come due after her own near miss with death. Talking and crying had gotten her through the worst of it. And the last two weeks, Shiloh had found a new platform to live her life on. With him. She asked if she could live with him, to try out their relationship, to test it and see if it was going to stand the test of time. Roan knew it would, but she wasn't there. At least, not yet. But one day, he knew she would be. Every day, he was seeing her settle in, get back to what she loved, which was writing stories.

As he studied her clear expression, he traced her arched eyebrow. "Every morning when I wake up with you at my side, you're more beautiful than yesterday. Did you know that?" he asked, and he held her lustrous green eyes that widened over his words.

"No . . . I didn't know that."

"Well," he murmured, trailing his fingers down the slope of her cheek, "maybe I need to say it more often. Let you know that you hold my heart." He saw her lips part and soften, tears glimmering in her eyes. Shiloh was so easy to please. Roan was finding that if he told her what he was thinking, it made a huge impact on her. He was so used to working around men where a few words sufficed. But she was a woman and a writer. And words, he was finally grasping, were her lifeblood, the main highway into her heart and soul. And he was mindful of this because he loved her and he wanted Shiloh to finally be happy. He was going to learn to speak up or else. It wasn't easy for him, but she was worth his every effort.

"I like when you tell me what you're thinking," she whispered. "I'm not a mind reader."

A corner of his mouth hooked upward. "So you tell me but you keep finishing sentences I start. That's pretty impressive, Darlin'."

She searched his eyes, her hand coming to rest against his darkly haired chest. "Roan? I need to say something. Are you awake enough to talk? Or do you want to wait until after breakfast?"

He gave her an amused look because right now, his erection was pressing against her belly and he was wide awake. Roan couldn't kiss Shiloh without wanting her in every possible way. "Now's fine. What's on your mind?"

Taking a deep breath, Shiloh said in a low tone, "I've been thinking . . . about my apartment in New York City." She frowned. "I want to stay out here with you. I love Manhattan, but my soul is fed by being out here in the West."

That apartment was where Shiloh grew up, for the most part. She knew no home other than her aunt and uncle's home. He realized the importance of her decision. "Are you sure?"

Nodding, she closed her eyes and took a ragged breath. Reopening her eyes, she stared up at him. "It's been coming for a while now. Maud told me a long time ago, when she came back for my mother's funeral, that Manhattan owned my heart, but that my soul belonged in Wyoming. She was right."

His heart thudded with sudden joy, but he kept the reaction to himself because he could see how torn Shiloh was. "Maybe there's a compromise here?" he wondered out loud. "Your apartment is paid for. I know there are other fees to consider, but the mortgage is paid off. What if you leased it out? It would bring you in some income and it would still be yours. Be a part of your family history. A part of you."

Roan didn't think, at least right now, that Shiloh could sell it outright. That would be too much for her to emotionally bear. Maybe later. Maybe never. He would support whatever decision she made. He saw tears drift down the sides of her face and he gently smoothed them away with his fingers. He knew how much his family's ranch meant to him even though he didn't live there. It was still there. A part of his family's soul and history. A part of of him. He sensed how much the apartment meant to Shiloh. Every good memory she had of her mother and father were contained in it. And of course, the bad memories, too. But for the most part, that apartment had been her world growing up. It had more good than bad memories attached to it.

"I like that idea. I never thought in that direction." Shiloh gave him a tremulous smile.

"If you want, you could move your furniture out here. We could put some in the cabin here, and put the rest in storage until I can build on to the cabin." He grinned, seeing her rally, seeing hope flare in her eyes.

"You never said you were going to add on to the cabin."

Shrugging, he said, "The subject hadn't come up." Looking around, Roan added, "It's too small right now. We need a couple more bedrooms. Maybe a sunroom for you facing south because in the long winters around here, it's nice to sit in a bright, sunny room with green plants growing in it to remind you that winter isn't always going to stay."

Shiloh studied him in the gathering silence. "I have some family antique furniture that means the world to me, Roan. You wouldn't mind if I brought them out here?"

"Not at all." He gave her a small shake, smiling down at her. "This is your home too, Darlin'. Not just mine anymore."

He saw tears glimmering in her large, wide eyes. "I meant what I said three weeks ago, Shiloh. I love you."

More tears streaked down her cheeks. Sniffing, Shiloh whispered unsteadily, "You never gave up on me, did you?"

He gave her a grin. "I'm German. Remember? Stubborn as hell. When I saw you for the first time at the airport, I wanted you. I knew you were the one for me, Shiloh." Roan caressed her flushed cheek. "I never had any doubt about it. But convincing you to stay with me rather than go back to the East Coast was a challenge."

Shaking her head, she sniffed and smiled, sliding her hand around his thick, strong neck. "Funny. When I saw you, I knew you were the one, too."

His brows rose. "You did?"

Laughing softly, Shiloh said, "Yes. I fought it. I was distracted by the stalker, by not being able to write at the time."

"That chapter in your life is over now, Darlin'."

Becoming serious, Shiloh studied Roan. "Yes, thank God, it is."

"Do you want me to help you with the apartment?"

Nodding, Shiloh said, "I really prefer leasing it out. I-I can't sell it, Roan. It's like tearing out a piece of my heart and I would love for you to come back to it. See where I live."

"I understand. Just tell me how I can support you on this and we'll get it done."

Sighing, she leaned up, kissing him gently, her hand against his cheek. "You've *always* been there for me, Roan."

"And I'll always try to be."

"I love you, Roan . . ." Shiloh said, pressing against his erection.

Groaning, he laid her against the bed, capturing her jaw, angling it so that he could hungrily plunder her soft, parting lips. As he slid his mouth across hers, she twisted her hips, moving sinuously against his erection, letting him know just how much she wanted him. Shiloh wasn't shy about sex, enjoying it as a full partner. He gloried in her fearlessness and her hunger, which matched his own.

Their mouths clung to each other, sliding, deepening until he felt her hand come to his shoulder. She pushed strongly, silently asking him to lie on his back. He complied, breaking their heated kiss, seeing the glitter in Shiloh's eyes. She liked riding him. And he liked having her on top of him, sliding his hands around her waist, pulling her up and over him, placing her wet core against his taut erection.

As she settled down upon him, Roan clenched his teeth, drawing a swift breath of air between them. She was so heated, sliding against him, the ache building so fast that he groaned again, helpless beneath her onslaught. Her hips ground into his, her hands splaying out on his chest, arousal burning in her eyes, her lips parted, breath ragged as she pushed against him. Roan knew he wasn't going to last. And she didn't either because she leaned forward upon him, dragging her breasts suggestively across his chest as she lifted her hips just enough. Just enough for him to thrust deeply into her sweet, scalding confines.

Roan's fingers dug into her flared hips, being swallowed by her tight grip, tensing, his whole body going taut as she relentlessly continued her burning onslaught against him. He whispered her name as she sat up, taking him fully, smiling down at him, her hair tousled and framing her flushed features. It was the arousal, the lust in her eyes, that made him soar. This was the first time in the three weeks that he felt Shiloh fully here, with him. Present. Wanting him. Only him. The sensations amplified with each thrust of her hips sucking him more deeply into her. He groaned with each languid, teasing movement. She knew what she was doing. Knew what he could give her. And he wouldn't disappoint her.

Roan heard her sigh, head tipping back as he arched his hips powerfully against hers. Her lips opened. A sweet sound caught in her slender, exposed throat. Feeling her fingers begin to dig into his chest wall, feeling her body begin to contract around his, Roan knew she was close to coming. Sliding his large hands around her hips, he held her in place, thrusting upward, teasing that hard knot of swollen nerves near her entrance. He saw her suddenly tense, her back arching, felt her body contract violently around him, felt that sudden honeyed fluid flow powerfully around him as the orgasm exploded within her. Shiloh's crying out his name made him only want to please her more and he kept her angled, kept up the pressure upon that sweet spot in her body, watching her begin to melt and fly apart within his hands and body.

Just feeling Shiloh fused with him and seeing the satisfaction flow across her expression, the flush that rushed across her upper body and into her face, told Roan everything. He clenched his teeth, willing himself to wait as he teased every bit of that orgasm out of her trembling, damp body. She moaned, closed her eyes, and collapsed against him, her head nestled near his jaw and neck. Roan smiled, feeling the wild beat of her heart against his, felt her quivering with fulfillment, her small arms wrapping around his neck, holding him with her woman's strength. Her hair tickled his jaw and lips. Closing his eyes, he gentled his grip on her hips, allowing her to rest, to catch her second breath. Because Roan knew Shiloh enjoyed her orgasms and so did he. Sliding his hand down her spine, he felt how soft and pliant she'd become beneath his fingers. Her skin was warm, damp velvet. She was so alive, so sensitive and he felt his heart grow fierce with the love he held for her alone.

As he waited, Roan absorbed her weight against his taller, harder body. She was petite against him, but her spirit was huge, her heart even larger. Glorying in holding her, skimming her relaxed form against him, he had never felt happier. It didn't take long when he felt that invisible shift within Shiloh, felt her returning to her body from wherever that orgasm had taken her. She barely lifted her face, meeting his eyes.

"Your turn," she whispered, smiling down at him. And she twisted her hips, hearing him groan and stiffen.

Roan liked her ability to share, to want to please him as much as he pleased her. As she shifted, slowly sat up, pushing her hair away from her face, he smiled up at her. There was a glitter of arousal back in her eyes. She was ready for that second round, only this time, he hoped to coordinate it such that they would come together. There was a raw satisfaction gleaming in her eyes as she thrust and took him deeply into herself. Eyes closing, Roan rasped her name, his hands wrapping around her hips, feeling her plunge relentlessly against him, making his entire back arch off the bed as she brought him to a scalding explosion that tore his breath out of him. And as he felt the bolt of heat strike down through him, slamming him into another world where only light and explosions occurred, he felt her tense. Heard Shiloh cry out his name, her fingers dig frantically into his chest. There was never a better sensation—that coming together, their bodies taut, stiff, and paralyzed as the pleasure throbbed and moved through each of them.

Everything melted around Roan. It felt as if he were permanently fused to Shiloh's sweet, softer body accommodating him, felt a oneness that he'd never experienced before. In his mind, behind his tightly shut eyes, Roan knew it was their love for each other that was taking them to a whole new level of satisfying physical experiences. Savoring him, she rode him as if knowing how to prolong his climax and give him optimal pleasure. Her damp hips slid against his, her breath ragged with his, her strength matching his own as they clung to each other afterward.

It was the most freeing, the sweetest feeling in the world to Roan as Shiloh rested wearily against him, her breath moist against his neck. She was weak, her fingers barely skimming his other shoulder in silent thanks for being his partner. Yeah, he liked what they shared. Bed and sex had never been their issue. And as Roan moved his hand gently down her torso, feeling each of the slender ribs beneath her warm, soft flesh, he smiled, still caught up in that other universe where only visceral gratification spun around him. Shiloh knew how to please him, get the most out of him, and then come back to please him some more. It didn't get any better than this. Not ever.

Gradually, Roan recouped his strength. He eased Shiloh off him and gently tucked her in beside him. She gave him a drowsy smile, her eyes satiated with pleasure.

Closing his eyes, Roan wanted nothing more than this moment with Shiloh. He would always want this brave, beautiful woman. And silently, he swore he would protect her, give her room to grow and know herself in ways she'd never been given a chance to do. He would love and protect her. A new fierceness flowed through him as he held Shiloh close, felt her warmth against him. He wanted this woman to carry his children. She would be such a good mother. There was no question in Roan's mind, as he embraced her gently for a moment and then relaxed his arms a bit, that Shiloh was going to finally bloom here in Wyoming.

As sleep began to tug at his mind and emotions, Roan smiled, inhaling her scent. There was such hope for both of them. They had a future together. And this morning, making love with Shiloh, he could see the promise of things to come.

Kissing her tangled, silky hair, Roan felt Shiloh sigh contentedly against him. Her slender arm was draped across his waist, her leg tangled with one of his own. Their hips rested against each other, a reminder of what they'd just shared. "Go to sleep, Darlin'," he murmured against her hair. Because Roan knew every day from here on out was going to get better for both of them.

Shiloh's writing ability was back and Roan felt as if they'd turned a corner with each other. It was a part of her healing process, a trusting of him in her life, knowing that he really was there for her. As he relaxed and felt her begin to sag against him, telling him she had fallen asleep, Roan wondered about the love her parents had held for each other. They had been artlessly in love with each other. And that love had grown and bloomed between them. And Shiloh had been the rest of it.

Intuitively, Roan sensed that their relationship, and later, their marriage, would be just like that. His own parents had that deep, abiding love for each other. He'd grown up seeing it deepen and widen, become more enriched over time. And he knew Shiloh and he were capable of the same kind of love. What they had was so special. He had the right woman to take both of them to that heady height of lifelong love. Together. Forever.

Please turn the page for an exciting sneak peek at

WIND RIVER RANCHER

by
Lindsay McKenna.

Coming to your favorite bookstores and e-tailers
in January 2017.

Get to know all the wonderful people of
Wind River Valley!

Reese Lockhart's stomach was tight with hunger as he stood at the outskirts of a small Wyoming town called Wind River. The sign listed a population of two thousand. He'd gone a month without decent food. Six inches of snow stood on the sides of the road where he'd walked the last ten miles on 89A north. It headed toward Jackson Hole, where he was hoping he might find work.

The town, for a Monday afternoon, was pretty slow. A few pickup trucks came and went, fewer people along the sidewalks. He halted outside Becker's Hay and Feed Store, the aged red brick building standing two stories high. The red tin roof was steep and reflected sunlight off it, making Reese squint. Bright lights now hurt his eyes.

Taking a deep, steadying breath, feeling humiliated and fearful of rejection once again, he pushed the door open to the store. Would he get yelled at by the owner? Told to get out? It was early May but snow had fallen the night before, and the sleepy town of Wind River still had slush on its streets midday.

The place was quiet, and smelled of leather. He saw a man in his sixties, tall, lean with silver hair, sitting behind the counter. He was sitting on a wooden stool that was probably the same age as he was, an ancient-looking calculator between his work-worn hands as he methodically punched the buttons.

Girding himself, ignoring the fact he hadn't eaten in two days, Reese automatically swung his gaze around the huge establishment. A hay and feed store was something he was familiar with. Maybe the owner needed some part-time help? If so, he could make enough money to buy a decent meal. Shoving away the shame he felt over his situation, he saw the man lift his head, a set of wire-rim spectacles halfway down his large nose, blue eyes squinting as he watched Reese approach the long, wooden counter.

"Howdy, Stranger. Can I help you?" he asked.

"Maybe," Reese said. "I'm looking for some outdoor work. I saw you had several big barns out back and a granary. Do you have any openings?" Automatically, Reese tensed inwardly. He knew he looked rough with a month's worth of beard on his face and his clothes dirty and shabby. At one time, he'd been a Marine Corps captain commanding a company of 120 Marines. And he'd been damn good at it until—

"I'm Charlie Becker, the owner," he said, shifting and thrusting his hand across the desk toward him. "Welcome to Wind River. Who might you be?"

"Reese Lockhart," he said, and he gripped the man's thin, strong hand. He liked Charlie's large, watery eyes because he saw kindness in them. Reese was very good at assessing people. He'd kept his Marines safe and helped them through their professional and personal ups and downs during the years he commanded Mike Company in Afghanistan. Charlie was close to six feet tall, lean like a rail and wearing a white cowboy shirt and blue jeans. Reese sensed this older gentleman wouldn't throw him out.

The last place he'd gone into to try to find some work,

they'd called him a druggie and he was told to get the hell out. He smelled. Reese, when walking the last ten miles to Wind River, had stopped when he discovered a stream on the flat, snow-covered land and tried to clean up the best he could. The temperature was near freezing as he'd gone into the bush, away from the busy highway, and stripped to his waist. He'd taken handfuls of snow and scrubbed his body, shivering, but hell, that was a small price to pay to try to not smell so bad. He hadn't had a real shower in a month, either.

"You a vet by any chance?" Charlie asked, his eyes narrowing speculatively upon Reese.

"Yes, sir. Marine Corps." He said it with pride.

"Good to know, Son." Charlie looked toward a table at the rear of the store that held coffee, cookies, and other goodies that he offered his patrons. "Why don't you go help yourself to some hot coffee and food over there?" he said, and he gestured in that general direction. "My wife, Pixie, made 'em. Right good they are. I usually get a stampede of ranchers comin' in here when word gets 'round that Pixie has baked goodies," he said, and chuckled.

Reese wanted to run to that table, but he stood as relaxed as he could be, given the anxiety that was tunneling through him constantly. "I'd like that, sir. Thank you . . ."

"Don't call me sir," Charlie said. "Americans owe so much to ALL of you men and women who have sacrificed for us. Now, go help yourself. There's plenty more where that came from. Pixie usually drives in midafternoon with a new bunch of whatever she's been inspired to make in her kitchen that day."

Reese needed something worse than food right now, so he hesitated. "Do you have any work I might do around here, Mr. Becker?"

"Call me Charlie. And no, I don't need help, but I got a nearby rancher who is looking for a hardworking wrangler type to hire. You look like you've worked a little in your life," he said, and he grinned, standing, pointing to Reese's large, callused hands at his side. "I'll call over there while you grab yourself some grub," he added, and he waved his hand, urging him to go eat.

Nodding, Reese rasped a thank-you and felt his stomach growl loudly. He hoped like hell Charlie didn't hear it. But judging from the man's facial expression, he had heard it as he picked up the black, ancient-looking landline phone sitting on the counter to make a call to that ranch. As Reese halted at the long table against the back wall of the store, his mouth watered. He was chilled to the bone, his combat boots wet, his socks soaked, toes numb. The coffee smelled so damned good and he poured some into a white Styrofoam cup with shaking hands. He took a cautious sip, the heat feeling incredible as it slid down his throat and into his shrunken, knotted gut. God, it tasted so good!

Reese kept one ear cocked toward the phone call Charlie was making. *Let there be an opening for me.* He worried because even though he no longer stank, his clothes were dirty and long past a washing. He knew he looked like a burned-out druggie or a homeless person, his hair long, unkempt, his black beard thick and in dire need of a trim. Reese didn't have a pair of scissors on him to do the job. His scruffy dark green baseball cap was frayed and old, a holdover from two years ago when he was a Marine.

He eyed the box of colorfully frosted cupcakes and his mouth watered. He wanted to grab all of them, but his discipline and his sense of manners forced him to pick up just one. His fingers trembled again as he peeled the paper off the pink-frosted cupcake.

Swallowing the accumulated saliva, Reese bit into the concoction, groaning internally as the sweetness hit his tongue and coated the insides of his mouth. For a moment, he was dizzy from the sugar rush, his whole body lighting up with internal celebration as the food hit his gnawing stomach. Standing there, Reese forced himself to take slow sips of the coffee. It tasted heavenly. He heard Charlie finish the call and his footsteps came in his direction.

"Hey, Mr. Lockhart, good news," Charlie said. "The owner, Shay Crawford, is still in need of a wrangler. She's coming into town in about two hours, going to be dropping by here to pick up some dog food and such. Said she'd meet you at that time."

"That's good to hear," Reese said. "Thank you . . ."

Charlie nodded. "I have a bathroom with a big shower in back, over there," he said, and he jabbed his index finger toward the rear corner of the store. "It's got some shaving gear and such in there, as well. On your way there, pick out a pair of jeans, a work shirt, boots, and whatever else you need before she arrives."

"I don't have the money to pay you," Reese said, hating to admit it. But he understood what Charlie was really saying. The woman owner of the Bar C would probably NOT want to hire him the way he looked and smelled right now. The guy was trying to help him out.

Charlie gripped the arm of Reese's damp, dark olive green military jacket. "Come this way. Just consider my offer as grateful thanks from this nation of ours for your sacrifices, Mr. Lockhart. You pick up what you need. It's free to you. It's the least this nation can do for our vets." Charlie drilled a look into his eyes that told him he wasn't going to budge from his position or offer to him.

Reese was going to say no, but the man's face turned stubborn. He felt like he was in a dream instead of a nightmare. "Tell you what," Reese said, his voice suddenly thick with emotion. "If I get this job, I'll pay you back every cent. Fair enough?"

Charlie smiled a little. "Fair enough, Mr. Lockhart. Now, eat all you want and once you're filled up, choose your clothes, find a good Stetson, work gloves, and anything else you might need. Bring it to the counter and I'll write it up for you." Charlie studied his sorry-looking boots. "And get a pair of decent work boots to replace those guys." He gave Reese a grin. "They look like they need to be permanently retired."

One corner of Reese's mouth twitched. "Sort of like me," he admitted, more than grateful to the man. He felt like he was being treated like a king.

"Son, you're just having a bad streak of luck, is all. We all go through them at some point in our lives. You'll get through it too." Charlie released his arm and patted it. "I think your streak is gonna end right shortly. Miss Crawford is an angel come to earth. If you present yourself well, I'm sure she'll hire you. She's a good boss to work for. The people she hires stay and that says everything."

Reese watched Charlie walk back to the counter. Hot tears pricked the backs of his eyes. Reese swallowed hard several times, forcing them away. He ate four more cupcakes, and had three more cups of hot coffee, and felt damn near human in the next fifteen minutes. He found the jeans, work shirts, thick, heavy socks, a couple of pairs of boxer shorts, two white T-shirts, and carried them up to the counter.

Charlie scowled. "Where's your work gloves? You need a good, heavy Carhartt work jacket, too. Your Stetson? Get a pair of snow gloves. It stays winter until mid-June around here. And don't leave out getting a good, heavy knit sweater you can wear under that winter coat of yours," he said, and he pointed in another direction where a turnstile of men's sweaters hung with a spring for sale sign on top of it.

Chastened, Reese nodded, his throat locked up with shame.

"Oh, and serious work boots, Son." He shook his finger

in another direction where the footwear department was located. "Get a darned good pair. Don't skimp on quality because of price."

Reese wished he could turn Charlie's name into the White House and he be lauded as the hero he was to him. There should be recognition to civilians who helped out vets who were faltering or who had walked away from society. Charlie deserved a civilian medal of the highest order.

Once Reese located the rest of the gear, he brought it up to the counter.

"Grab your new duds and take a good, long, hot shower, Mr. Lockhart. There's razors, a pair of scissors in the medicine cabinet should you want to trim that beard and long hair of yours a bit."

Later, Charlie smiled from behind the counter as Reese approached it. In his hands, he held his old clothes. Reese smelled food. Real food. And then, he spotted two large Styrofoam boxes near Charlie's elbow.

"You clean up real good, Mr. Lockhart," Charlie said, rising and taking his clothes. "I'm assuming these are DOA?"

Reese nodded. "Yeah, pretty much. Thanks for your help here," he said, and he motioned to the clothes he now wore.

"Like I said," Charlie murmured, dumping the clothes into a huge wastebasket, "our country OWES YOU."

Charlie gave him the Styrofoam boxes, and told him the owner of Kassie's Coffee Shop had sent hamburgers over for Reese. Then Charlie showed him to a spot where he could eat the food. It was delicious.

As he bit into the burger, he closed his eyes, made a low sound of pleasure in the back of his throat, slumping against the metal chair. Reese knew if he gulped it down, he'd more than likely throw it up, so he tamped down on his animal desire. He chewed it slowly, savoring every last taste and bit of the lettuce, tomatoes, onion, cheddar cheese, and bacon on it. It took him thirty minutes to clean up everything. The apple pie was melt-in-your mouth, reminding him of his mother's own home-cooked pies.

An old ache centered in his heart. His parents wanted him home, but God, that had been a disaster. Reese wasn't going to make them pay for his PTSD and they didn't understand why he had to leave. He wasn't the best at expressing his shame over symptoms that he couldn't control. And he'd refused their money. His father, a hardworking mechanic, had saved all his life for their retirement and Reese wasn't about to let him give it to him. He had to stand on his own two feet, pull himself up by his bootstraps, and not accept handouts.

As he rose and placed the chair against the wall, he saw the door open. A young woman with light brown hair, slightly curly around her oval face, walked in. She was wearing a black baseball cap, a blue chambray shirt the same as he wore, a heavy Levi's jacket, and a pair of loose-fitting jeans that told him she had a lush figure hidden beneath them. His heart jolted as their eyes met briefly. She had sky blue eyes, just this side of turquoise, wide set, intelligent, and Reese sensed the same primal instinctiveness that he possessed. She was attractive, wearing no makeup, but her high cheekbones were flushed, as if she'd been running or working out hard.

His stomach clenched, and suddenly Reese worried that if she was the owner of the Bar C, she'd be afraid of him like so many other women who saw him were. In the Corps, wearing his uniform or utilities, women always gave him a pleasing look, scoping him out, their gazes telling him they'd like to know him a lot better. He almost laughed as he struggled to get his anxiety corralled. Since he'd fallen from grace, his scruffy, bearded homeless look scared the hell out of all females. Reese knew he wasn't a bad-looking man, but somehow, no woman could look beneath his present state of dishevelment and see the real him. He would NEVER hurt a woman or child. But the look in their eyes spoke of exactly that: that he was capable of violence against them. It was a bitter pill to swallow to be judged by what he wore instead of who he really was.

"Hey," Charlie called, twisting his head in Reese's direction, "Miss Shay is here. Come on up and meet her, Reese."

God, this was like a firing squad. All his life, he'd drawn straight As in school and in college. Always a winner. Always successful at whatever he tackled. He was first in everything he'd ever tried. And now, he was last. Dead last.

Squaring his shoulders, Reese walked toward the counter and watched as the young woman who was about a head shorter than him, maybe around five foot eight or nine inches tall, assessed him critically. Reese could feel the heat of her blue gaze stripping him from his uncovered head down to his boots as he rounded the corner of the counter.

"Shay, meet Reese Lockhart," Charlie said. "Reese, this is Shay Crawford, owner of the Bar C."

Reese saw a shadow flit across her eyes for just a moment, and then it was gone. Her mouth was full, lush just like her breasts and hips. A hum started low in his body, appreciating her purely as a woman. When she extended her slender hand, he engulfed it gently within his. Reese tried to keep the surprise out of his face as he felt the calluses along her palm and the roughness on her fingers, telling him she worked hard.

"Ma'am," he murmured, "nice to meet you. I asked Charlie if anyone needed a wrangler and he said you did." Reese released her hand, albeit reluctantly. To his surprise, she stood her ground even though he was a good six inches taller than she was. He didn't scare her and that made Reese sag inwardly with relief. Those fearless-looking blue eyes of hers were direct and he held her gaze, understanding she was feeling him out on an instinctual level. In the kind of black ops work he had done, instinct is what had saved his life so often. Reese sensed strongly she possessed the same powerful intuition herself.

"It's nice to meet you, Mr. Lockhart." She glanced over at Charlie. "He said you were a vet? That you were a Marine?"

"Yes, ma'am." Her lips twisted and she smiled a little. "Once a Marine, always a Marine."

Her lips pulled faintly at the corners. "You're right. You're still a Marine even if you're now a civilian. Call me Shay, Mr. Lockhart. I was in the service too. I'm fine with less protocol."

Reese nodded. "Manners are hard to erase," he noted, a slight, teasing note in his voice. "But I'll try."

She leaned against the counter with her hips, hands on the edge of the smooth oak. "What kind of work are you looking for?"

"Anything outdoors for the most part."

"You're a Marine, so you probably have some skill sets?"

"I ran a company, ma—I mean, Shay, of a hundred and twenty men and women."

Nodding, she assessed him more closely. "What was your rank?"

"Captain." Reese couldn't translate what he saw in her expression and whether it was good or bad news for him. He wondered if she was enlisted or an officer. Now was not the time to ask because this was an interview.

"I need a wrangler who's good at slinging a hammer and nails, Mr. Lockhart. I've got an outdoor arena I'm trying to get up with too few men to do it and it has to be covered before the first snow flies, which is usually mid-September around here." She gauged him for a moment, her voice husky. "I make a point of hiring military vets who are down on their luck. The Bar C is more than just a place to work. Much more."

"Okay," he murmured. "My skill sets are in the area of construction work. My father is a mechanic and I grew up learning how to fix anything that had an engine attached to it."

"That's good news," she murmured, brightening a little. Looking relieved.

"See?" Charlie gloated, preening. "I told you he was a man with a lot of talent."

Reese felt uncomfortable with such enthusiastic praise, but stood as relaxed as he could. Shay Crawford might be attractive as hell, but she was a woman with a helluva lot of confidence and she wore the mantle of leadership well. There was no wedding ring on her left hand, but that didn't mean anything. He was sure she was in a relationship. He didn't see her being snooty, bossy, or power-hungry because she was in control. Instead, she seemed pensive, studying him openly and without apology, searching his eyes, looking over his face and body. Reese thought he might as well be a horse she was considering buying. He was waiting for her to ask him to open his mouth she could look at his teeth.

"I'm dying of hunger," she told Reese. "Would you like to come over to Kassic's Café and have a cup of coffee with me, Mr. Lockhart? I can give you a lot more information about the Bar C there. If the place isn't too much for you to handle? I can always find somewhere that is quieter and has less distractions."

Reese gauged her and felt his heart stir. The honesty in this woman's eyes held him in thrall. He was shaken over her last comment. He frowned for a moment, processing it. Only someone with PTSD would ask THAT kind of question. He stared at her, trying to decipher more of who she really was. She stared back fearlessly at him, unafraid of his intense inspection. "Kassie's sounds fine. I can handle noise for a while," he said, nodding, settling the gray Stetson on his head. "Lead the way to the café."

Charlie put his purchases beneath the counter, saying he could come by later and pick them up. Reese thanked him and got to the door before Shay did. His stride was longer than hers. Opening the door for her, he saw her blush. Her cheeks stained red, her glance up at him, appreciative and something else. But what?

As Reese followed her to a dark blue Ford three-quarter-ton pickup, he watched the sway of her hips down those six wooden steps to the asphalt parking lot that held spots of melting snow.

He opened the door of the truck for Shay before she could reach for the handle.

Flustered, Shay turned and looked up at him. "Really, I'm not helpless, Mr. Lockhart. I'll open my own doors from now on."

He gave her an apologetic glance. "Manners die hard in me." And he smiled a little, seeing the warmth come to her eyes for a moment as she climbed in.

"Military men are like that," she admitted, a little breathless as she closed her own door.

Reese liked her backbone. She was a strong, confident woman. He opened the door and climbed in, his hopes rising. Shay Crawford would not have invited him to coffee if she wasn't going to hire him. His chest swelled with powerful feelings of relief. And as she backed the truck expertly out of the dirt parking spot, Reese buckled up, feeling that today was his lucky day.

Also available from Lindsay McKenna:

Her new military series,
Delos!

Nowhere to Hide

Tangled Pursuit

Forged in Fire

Broken Dreams

Secret Dream

Unbound Pursuit

All Delos titles available from your favorite e-tailer.

For more information,
please go to
www.LindsayMcKenna.com.

Connect with Us

Visit us online at
KensingtonBooks.com
to read more from your favorite authors, see books
by series, view reading group guides, and more.

for sneak peeks, chances to win books and prize packs,
and to share your thoughts with other readers.

facebook.com/kensingtonpublishing
twitter.com/kensingtonbooks

Tell us what you think!

To share your thoughts, submit a review,
or sign up for our eNewsletters, please visit:
KensingtonBooks.com/TellUs.

Books by Bestselling Author
Fern Michaels

__The Jury	0-8217-7878-1	$6.99US/$9.99CAN
__Sweet Revenge	0-8217-7879-X	$6.99US/$9.99CAN
__Lethal Justice	0-8217-7880-3	$6.99US/$9.99CAN
__Free Fall	0-8217-7881-1	$6.99US/$9.99CAN
__Fool Me Once	0-8217-8071-9	$7.99US/$10.99CAN
__Vegas Rich	0-8217-8112-X	$7.99US/$10.99CAN
__Hide and Seek	1-4201-0184-6	$6.99US/$9.99CAN
__Hokus Pokus	1-4201-0185-4	$6.99US/$9.99CAN
__Fast Track	1-4201-0186-2	$6.99US/$9.99CAN
__Collateral Damage	1-4201-0187-0	$6.99US/$9.99CAN
__Final Justice	1-4201-0188-9	$6.99US/$9.99CAN
__Up Close and Personal	0-8217-7956-7	$7.99US/$9.99CAN
__Under the Radar	1-4201-0683-X	$6.99US/$9.99CAN
__Razor Sharp	1-4201-0684-8	$7.99US/$10.99CAN
__Yesterday	1-4201-1494-8	$5.99US/$6.99CAN
__Vanishing Act	1-4201-0685-6	$7.99US/$10.99CAN
__Sara's Song	1-4201-1493-X	$5.99US/$6.99CAN
__Deadly Deals	1-4201-0686-4	$7.99US/$10.99CAN
__Game Over	1-4201-0687-2	$7.99US/$10.99CAN
__Sins of Omission	1-4201-1153-1	$7.99US/$10.99CAN
__Sins of the Flesh	1-4201-1154-X	$7.99US/$10.99CAN
__Cross Roads	1-4201-1192-2	$7.99US/$10.99CAN

Available Wherever Books Are Sold!
Check out our website at www.kensingtonbooks.com

More by Bestselling Author
Hannah Howell